*The new Zebra ... cover is a photo ... fashionable reg ... satin or velvet ... nosegay. Usually ... in design from the elegantly simple to the exquisitely ornate. The Zebra Regency Romance tuzzy-muzzy is made of alabaster with a silver filigree edging.*

## UNANTICIPATED DESIRE

"Francesca . . . may I call you Francesca?" Tolland asked in a low voice.

"Why?" she got out. "Everyone else calls me 'Frankie.'"

"But *I* am not 'everyone else,' my dear girl. Your name is Francesca, is it not? Has no one told you before that you are *much* more a Francesca than a Frankie? Frankie is too masculine a name for you."

He was almost whispering as he extended his hand to her and said, "It is something about your eyes, I think. Come, sit by me so that I may see them at closer range and better explain why I think of you as Francesca."

Languidly Frankie came and sat down beside him.

"That's better," he said as she turned toward him. He removed her spectacles and laid them aside. "And you must call me Drew; it's a name reserved for only my most *intimate* friends."

"Drew," she said as he turned to her and raised a hand to her cheek. His thumb caressed the side of her face as he gazed at her.

My God, Tolland thought, she really does have the most beautiful eyes in the world. Suddenly the game he was playing was abandoned and pure desire took over.

He felt heat rising in his body. "Francesca . . ."

His gaze shifted from her eyes to her lips, and framing her face with his hands, he slowly inclined his head until his lips met hers . . .

## ELEGANT LOVE STILL FLOURISHES —
### *Wrap yourself in a Zebra Regency Romance.*

**A MATCHMAKER'S MATCH**        (3783, $3.50/$4.50)
by Nina Porter

To save herself from a loveless marriage, Lady Psyche Veringham pretends to be a bluestocking. Resigned to spinsterhood at twenty-three, Psyche sets her keen mind to snaring a husband for her young charge, Amanda. She sets her cap for long-time bachelor, Justin St. James. This man of the world has had his fill of frothy-headed debutantes and turns the tables on Psyche. Can a bluestocking and a man about town find true love?

**FIRES IN THE SNOW**        (3809, $3.99/$4.99)
by Janis Laden

Because of an unhappy occurrence, Diana Ruskin knew that a secure marriage was not in her future. She was content to assist her physician father and follow in his footsteps . . . until now. After meeting Adam, Duke of Marchmaine, Diana's precise world is shattered. She would simply have to avoid the temptation of his gentle touch and stunning physique — and by doing so break her own heart!

**FIRST SEASON**        (3810, $3.50/$4.50)
by Anne Baldwin

When country heiress Laetitia Biddle arrives in London for the Season, she harbors dreams of triumph and applause. Instead, she becomes the laughingstock of drawing rooms and ballrooms, alike. This headstrong miss blames the rakish Lord Wakeford for her miserable debut, and she vows to rise above her many faux pas. Vowing to become an Original, Letty proves that she's more than a match for this eligible, seasoned Lord.

**AN UNCOMMON INTRIGUE**        (3701, $3.99/$4.99)
by Georgina Devon

Miss Mary Elizabeth Sinclair was rather startled when the British Home Office employed her as a spy. Posing as "Tasha," an exotic fortune-teller, she expected to encounter unforeseen dangers. However, nothing could have prepared her for Lord Eric Stewart, her dashing and infuriating partner. Giving her heart to this haughty rogue would be the most reckless hazard of all.

**A MADDENING MINX**        (3702, $3.50/$4.50)
by Mary Kingsley

After a curricle accident, Miss Sarah Chadwick is literally thrust into the arms of Philip Thornton. While other women shy away from Thornton's eyepatch and aloof exterior, Sarah finds herself drawn to discover why this man is physically and emotionally scarred.

*Available wherever paperbacks are sold, or order direct from the Publisher. Send cover price plus 50¢ per copy for mailing and handling to Zebra Books, Dept. 4140, 475 Park Avenue South, New York, N.Y. 10016. Residents of New York and Tennessee must include sales tax. DO NOT SEND CASH. For a free Zebra/ Pinnacle catalog please write to the above address.*

# A Perfect Match
## Meg-Lynn Roberts

**ZEBRA BOOKS**
**KENSINGTON PUBLISHING CORP.**

ZEBRA BOOKS

are published by

Kensington Publishing Corp.
475 Park Avenue South
New York, NY 10016

First Printing: April, 1993

Printed in the United States of America

# *Chapter One*

Leaning negligently against the doorjamb to her niece's room Frankie Verdant munched on an apple as she tried to read the book balanced precariously in her left hand. From time to time she glanced up and gazed at the scene of disorder before her bespectacled eyes. Her beloved sister Daphne, with the dubious help of two abigails, was trying to prepare her daughter Laurel for a large, gala ball at the home of Lord and Lady Chatterington, particular friends of the family. Laurel was making her come-out tonight with her friend, Sally Chatterington.

"Laurel, dear, do not fidget so," Daphne reproved mildly, putting her finger on her chin as she considered her daughter's hair.

"But this will never *do*, Mama." Laurel objected to the plain white bow.

"We must tie up your hair with one of these ribbons, my dear. It cannot be left to hang about your shoulders like a schoolgirl's, you know," Daphne gently admonished.

"Oh, but, Mama, a white bow *will* make me look like a schoolgirl. I think I should be allowed *some* color in my hair even though I am a debutante. My gown is white, isn't that enough? I do so want to look grown-up tonight."

"It will do you no good to fly up into the boughs, Laurel, my love. We have tried a multitude of colors and styles already with little success." Daphne gestured at the untidy room. "There must be *one* amongst all this lot that will satisfy you."

Laurel had tried every bow and furbelow in her possession as could be seen by the riot of fabric of every hue in the rainbow littering her room. Items of clothing were hanging from bureau drawers, covering the pretty little four-poster bed, protruding from the open wardrobe, and forming a tangle at the feet of the four persons crowding the room.

Frankie watched as a very pretty, and very harried, Lady Daphne Rose Whittgrove fussed round her lovely young daughter. Frankie thought idly that anyone could tell the two were related by the resemblance of their porcelainlike complexions, sea green eyes, golden blond heads, and petite stature. They both had light girlish voices, too, despite the fact that Daphne was a matron of some thirty-six summers.

The resemblance ended there, however, Frankie conceded with a grin, for Daphne, her hair askew, wispy tendrils framing her lovely face, and her voluminous draperies floating about her, was very much with child, while Laurel was quite slender and had all the bloom of maidenhood upon her delicate cheeks. For the occasion, Laurel was dressed in a deceptively simple gown of white muslin embroidered with white silk roses, while her golden hair, as yet undressed, was hanging down her back. The search for a ribbon to thread through her curls was causing a considerable amount of turmoil and for the moment had served to distract Frankie from her book.

"What folly!" Frankie shook her head over the proceedings. Who would have imagined there would be so much commotion just because Laurel was getting dressed up to go to a silly dance? She resumed her study of the volume she held, only to have her eyes drawn once more to the scene before her as Laurel's maid, Tizzy, sneezed violently. The inexperienced young abigail was suffering from a particularly vehement head cold. Frankie made a mental note to brew up a batch of her famous catarrh mixture with which to dose the girl later.

Her eighteen-year-old niece, preparing to make her bow to society, was experiencing a different sort of ailment. Frankie diagnosed it as a case of the fidgets. She smiled and shook her head slightly as she saw that Laurel was driving her mother and the two maids nearly mad with the way she kept changing her mind about what to wear for the forthcoming ball. She had been discarding shawls, gloves, reticules—silk, satin, and beaded—and a whole bandbox full of hair ribbons almost as soon as they were presented to her by one or the other of her three attendants for as long as Frankie had been standing in the doorway. Laurel's room now resembled a picked-over jumble sale at the local church bazaar.

Frankie wished Daphne would let her treat her niece with a tisane of camomile tea, as she knew it would calm the girl's nerves. Indeed, she thought perhaps Daph and the two abigails would benefit from a cup of the brew as well.

"Please, Mama, I'm never going to be ready at this rate," Laurel exclaimed anxiously, stamping her small foot in vexation. Frankie glanced at her usually vivacious and even-tempered niece and saw that tears stood in the girl's lovely green eyes while her lips positively trembled. Such a to-do this society business was! Frankie thought disgustedly.

"Now, Laurel my love, I know you are to make your first appearance amongst the *ton* in a very short while, but you must try to calm yourself. It will be such fun to

7

go to Sally's ball. She is your bosom bow, after all, and Lady Chatterington will ease your way." Daphne indulgently forgave her daughter the small outburst. She well remembered what it was to suffer from a debutante's butterflies.

Frankie could see that the abigails' *aid*, if such were the proper term for the poor assistance they had rendered thus far, only increased the confusion in the room. Tizzy, with her intermittent sneezes, was making them all jump, and Fennel, Daphne's own trusted dresser, was adding to the farcical show with the acerbic comments she directed toward the younger abigail, recommending that she put her head under a sack. Frankie grinned at the comical scene as she lifted one finger of the hand that held the half-eaten apple and pushed her spectacles higher up on her nose. She bit back a laugh when she saw Fennel, a paragon of the proper conduct befitting a lady's maid if she had ever seen one, sniff in a huffy way and cast a baleful glance Tizzy's way. The girl was in such an advanced state of alarm she resembled nothing so much as a bird caught under a cat's paw—albeit, a bird with watery eyes and a *very* red nose.

Daphne's own flustered sensibilities and high-pitched excitement caused her to exclaim, "Oh, plague take it! I shall lose my wits soon. Where is your aunt? Frankie, Frankie, where are you?" she called, raising her sweet voice.

"Here, sister mine." The answer came from the doorway, just a hint of amusement evident in the musical timbre of that low, melodious voice.

"Ah, there you are, my dear," Daphne cried as she whirled around, startled at her sister's voice coming from so close by. "Oh, Frankie, not with your nose in a book again!" Daphne lamented as she took in her sister's occupation. Frankie glanced down at the page she had been reading, and indeed her nose was almost touching

8

the rather large volume she balanced somewhat peri-lously along her left arm.

"One of the best places for a nose, Daph," Frankie said flippantly as she looked toward her sister.

"I declare, if you're not dealing with those pesky horses, it's your peculiar interest in brewing up all manner of foul-smelling concoctions that you must be forever reading about!"

"Yes, I'm just trying to nose out the latest herbal recipe . . . One never 'knows' when it will come in handy."

Daphne never appreciated her sister's humor, and at the present moment she could have readily crowned her.

"Why do you stand there in that careless fashion, Frankie my dear? Can't you see that we require your assistance to help Laurel dress?"

"My help? Don't be goosish, Daph—'twould be more of a hindrance. Besides, I doubt whether a fifth person could be crammed into this room much less be of any use. And you well know that my legs are such a length, were I to wade into this jumbled mess I might entangle myself in the garments lying about. Why, such an attempt might lead to one of my famous 'accidents,'" Frankie replied humorously.

"Pshaw, Frankie. If you took the least care what you were about and stepped along at a ladylike pace, there would be no accidents—and so I've told dear Alfie any number of times. You forget that you're not out in a paddock the whole time."

"Oh, Daph, you know I am not of much use at such frivolities as a young lady's toilette. I would far rather be outside working with my horses."

"Indeed, I know it all too well! But you are a lady of quality. You would be far better occupied if you took as much interest in your gowns as you do in those stupid horses of Papa's."

9

"Horses are not at all stupid. In fact, they are quite intelligent," Frankie protested, but seeing that Daphne had turned back to Laurel, she shrugged her shoulders and grinned; dear Daph could be such a ninny sometimes. In Frankie's opinion her sister had inherited a bit of the bird-wittedness that characterized their beloved, but always slightly muddled, mother, Myrtle.

"M'lady, what are we to do with Miss Laurel's hair, then?" Fennel interrupted, questioning her mistress.

Daphne, getting quite giddy from her constant whirling around, turned yet again and waved a small hand in perfect distraction at her abigail. "If you please, dear Fennel, comb out Miss Laurel's hair once more and see if you can pin it up in the simple style we tried earlier. We must make haste now, for I've already ordered the coach. Tizzy, do try to control your sneezes, and see whether you can locate the green ribbon I suggested from the first."

"Must you wear those dreadful spectacles, my dear?" Daphne asked in exasperation as she stepped through the piles of clothing toward Frankie and peered closely at her younger sister. It was a disconcerting habit she had, and Frankie gazed back somewhat impatiently at being subjected to such a close inspection.

"They are singularly unattractive, you know. They obstruct one's view of your eyes. And you have such lovely eyes, Frankie dear. So darkly fringed and such an unusual shade of blue—I've always said they were violet, like your middle name . . . Mama must have had a premonition, so uncanny to have called you Francesca Viola . . . How could she have known that the name would match the strange color of your eyes else?"

"'Tis another of your odd notions, Daph, this idea that my eyes are something out of the ordinary. It's only that they are rather strangely colored and of a near-sighted disposition," Frankie mocked in a self-deprecating manner.

"No, no, your eyes are quite gloriously beautiful, Frankie dear. They're not like Verdant eyes though, for the rest of us all have this changeable shade of green, and I must say, none of the rest of us is in the least nearsighted." Daphne screwed up her own eyes as she continued to peer up at her taller sister. "I believe you only fancy yourself so. Pshaw. It is an affectation only. You can easily dispense with those spectacles."

"No, indeed I cannot. If I expect to see two feet in front of myself, then I cannot 'easily dispense with them.' I should cause you all manner of embarrassments if I were to trip over my own feet at this 'do' to which you expect me to accompany Laurel." Frankie unconcernedly took another bite of her apple. She was used to Daphne's attempts to talk her out of wearing her spectacles. These little whims of her sister's to turn her into a lady of fashion soon passed, so she disregarded them.

"Dear me!" Daphne's gaze fell to the apple. "Why must you be eating an apple just before you are to attend a ball?" The delicate blond head shook in mild reproof. "With all manner of food before you—I make no doubt Clara will provide lobster patties and a large assortment of cold meats and cheeses, not to mention ices and frosted cakes—I should think you would want to save your appetite for the supper at the Chatteringtons."

"Oh, Daph, 'tis only an apple," Frankie said unrepentantly as she demolished the last bite and laid the core down on a convenient Sheraton side table. She had absentmindedly picked up the maligned fruit from a dish in the library and had begun to eat it on her way upstairs. Daphne, who believed it wise for ladies to partake lightly before a grand occasion, had given them only the most modest of dinners. Frankie supposed that she did not

11

have a fashionably dainty appetite. Being used to hearty country fare, she had been hungry.

"Is this the style you mean, m'lady?" Fennel begged for Daphne's attention.

Daphne walked back to Laurel, casting a critical eye over Fennel's handiwork as she stepped round her daughter and viewed the effect of the soft style from every angle. "Oh, yes. That will do nicely, thank you, Fennel. We just need the ribbon to hold it in place and add that bit of color. "Haven't you located it yet, Tizzy?"

"Ah-choo! No, ma'am—ah, no, your ladyship."

"It must be here somewhere. Continue to search, please."

Frankie kicked aside a garment that lay in her path and advanced with her long, easy stride into the room to stand at Daphne's elbow and peer at her niece, wondering what she could possibly do that would be of the least use. She had no comments or suggestions to offer on the girl's dress or hair style. What did she know about such things? Her whole life had been spent at Verdant Meadows Stables, working with her father's horses—now hers and her brother James's. Frankie bit back a laugh at the assortment of articles on Laurel's dressing table.

"Ah, what an arsenal of grooming implements. You must be planning to lay siege to the *ton*, niece, not just make an appearance among them!" Frankie turned and, limping slightly, began to make her way through the debris and out the door. "I shall leave you to armor yourself, then, with the help of your aides-de-camp."

"Oh! You are limping," Daphne exclaimed with concern as she noticed her sister's uneven gait. "What in the world have you been doing now? You haven't been out in the stables when you were to be preparing for tonight's ball, have you?" Delicate blond brows lowered in displeasure.

"No, indeed, Daph. I've only been in the library. By

12

the greatest good chance this fascinating book of Alfred's fell out of the bookshelf and clipped me slightly." She held up the volume and smiled. "Not to worry, though. I'm not much hurt. I shall shake it off in a moment. If I did not think so, I would brew a posset and apply it to my foot for some while."

Frankie felt it was unnecessary to explain that as she had entered Sir Alfred's library earlier in search of her misplaced reticule she had tripped on a rucked-up bit of carpet and catapulted forward. Catching the edge of one of the bookcases as she fell, she had caused several volumes to fall out.

"How lucky!" she had cried a moment later when she had adjusted her spectacles on her nose and read the title of the particularly large tome that had just hit her on the toe. *Recipes for Herbal Antidotes: Ancient and Modern* was just such a work that appealed to her, for it had long been her hobby to concoct various medicaments for those around her, both human and equine. She had thought the moldy, old volume looked particularly interesting, for it promised to demonstrate the desirability of using herbal remedies to treat everything from headaches to gout to childbirth to sprains and broken limbs.

Daphne squinted at the dusty volume clutched in her sister's hand, then noticed for the first time the state of Frankie's dress—or lack of it, for Frankie had not changed from her old afternoon dress into evening wear appropriate for chaperoning Laurel to the Chattering-tons.

"Frankie, Frankie. What am I to do with you? My dear, has it not occurred to you that it is time and past to change your gown?" Daphne gave a martyred sigh and blamed her distracted nerves for her not having taken in the enormity of her sister's sin of omission at first glance.

Frankie looked up in surprise and her spectacles slid down her nose. She pushed them up impatiently, then looked down at the old brown merino round gown she was wearing. "No need to make such a piece of work over it, Daph. It will not take me above a minute to change. Don't fuss so."

Laurel, who had been listening with half an ear to the conversation between her mother and aunt, began to giggle impishly. "Oh, Aunt Frankie, really . . . ! Mama has done nothing *but* fuss for the past fortnight . . . Still, surely you will want to make a good impression tonight and will wear your best dress for the ball?"

"Francesca Viola Verdant, you have come to town expressly to chaperon Laurel for me. You knew that you would be going to Clara Chatterington's ball tonight. You didn't forget, did you?" Daphne's brows rose in disbelief and quite disappeared under the frivolous fringe of curls artfully arranged over her forehead as she considered this distinct possibility. "Be pleased to make haste and change."

As Frankie was dispatched to her room to dress, Daphne turned back to her giggling daughter. "There *must* be a way to convince dearest Frankie to take more interest in her wardrobe . . . Why, oh why, is your father away at this particular time, my dearest Laurel? Just when I most require his assistance here. I do not see how dear Alfie's presence on the continent can aid Wellington in the least!"

"But you forget, Mama," Laurel said as she danced this way and that under Fennel's attempts to pin a spray of flowers to the waist of her gown. "Papa is providing advice to General Wellington about securing the best supplies for the least expense. He is a member of the government—is he not?—and his counsel is much heeded."

"Oh, Laurel, what has that to say to anything? Your dearest Papa deals in financial matters, not in soldiering. He has not the least notion of fighting, I'm sure. He could render the general his advice from London . . . Do stop fidgeting, dearest."

Amid a constant succession of peppery sneezes, and after an ineffectual search through the wardrobe and dresser drawers, Tizzy finally located the pale green ribbon edged with gold that had been suggested from the first. It lay on the floor, caught partway beneath a jean half boot that was lying in the corner where it had been rather casually flung by her young mistress. Tizzy produced it on a sneeze, and Laurel's golden tresses were at last bound up to everyone's satisfaction.

"Ohh, Mama! It does look well, doesn't it?" Laurel happily contemplated her image in the looking glass. Fennel and Lady Whittgrove breathed audible sighs of relief when Laurel pronounced herself happy with the results of their efforts.

"Oh, I say, m'lady, that patik'lar shade of green is just the thing for Miss Laurel. See 'ow it brings out the color in 'er eyes, m'lady," Fennel remarked, showing her mistress how the color of the ribbon complemented and emphasized the green of Miss Laurel's wide eyes, thereby bringing them to the attention of any interested observers.

Daphne, ever a doting mother, hoped her abigail was right. She raised her own eyes to the ceiling painted with smiling pink and white cherubs and devoutly hoped that any "interested observers" would be male, eligible, and plentiful.

"Miss Laurel will attract a parcel o' suitors this night, I'll be bound." Fennel, echoing her employer's prayers, was now in a mellow mood, abandoning her characteristic tartness for once.

"Tizzy, please find Miss Laurel's shawl," Daphne directed the hapless maid. Tizzy looked about at all the clutter, a somewhat helpless expression on her face. A loud sneeze issued from the girl. "And, Tizzy, do go to

15

bed after you have done so. You do seem to be suffering from the most dreadful head cold," her kindhearted mistress added.

"Fennel, would you fetch my pearls? I believe they are in my dressing table—somewhere in the muddle. You will find them, I'm sure, dear Fennel." Daphne stood back to admire her daughter. "I think they will add just the right touch, my love."

"Dearest Mama! Your pearls! Thank you . . . If only Holly and Ivy could see me now," breathed Laurel, twirling round as she gazed at herself in the looking glass, "how envious they would be."

"Yes, I wish we could have managed to bring your sisters up to town with us," sighed Daphne, "and dear little Teddy and Georgie, too."

Fennel pressed her lips together primly as she left the room to go on her errand. Whatever her affectionate mistress's sentiments on the subject, Fennel knew that the rest of the household were eternally thankful that the other Whittgrove offspring—all four high-spirited—had been safely left behind at Sir Alfred's country seat. Prickly Miss Holly and clinging Miss Ivy, horse-mad Master Edward and tear-away Master George—Lady Daphne had named her daughters after various bits of verdure and her sons after kings of England—were in the capable hands of their governess and nurse respectively, leaving the mistress free to supervise the come-out of the lively Miss Laurel and to await the birth of the newest Whittgrove without the multitude of distractions the presence of all of her children would have caused.

"'Tis the greatest pity I cannot accompany you this evening, my love." Daphne had made Laurel aware of the unwritten but stringent rule that prohibited those who were enceinte from appearing at any but the most modest of family parties.

"Oh, Mama, do you truly think Aunt Frankie will be a

*suitable* chaperon?" Laurel questioned anxiously for the twentieth time in two days. "She's been living at Verdant Meadows *forever*. And she talks of nothing but herbal medicines and horses and riding—and that odious breeding business Grandpapa left to her and Uncle James . . . Heavens, Mama! How ever am I to go on?"

"Well, my love, I have to entrust you to some older female and it had best be a relative. She *is* a darling, you know. Let us hope that she will soon learn the ropes. You mustn't worry—Sally's mama, Lady Chatterington, will help to oversee things tonight." Despite her reassurances to her daughter, Daphne much feared that Frankie had not the least notion of how to go on. However, she wisely kept this reflection to herself.

And then, too, Daphne had an ulterior motive in asking Frankie to chaperon Laurel, for heretofore she had been remiss in certain sisterly duties regarding Frankie's future. "I'm not such a hen-wit as dearest Alfie thinks me after all," she chuckled as she hatched her scheme.

Dearest Frankie, she thought, well, really Francesca. That was how she had been christened, but she had always been known affectionately in the family as "Frankie." We shall see about a suitable *parti* for you, too, little sister, Daphne told herself with secret satisfaction.

She was determined now to give Frankie a season as well as introduce her own daughter to the *ton*. Frankie was socially inexperienced, Daphne knew, as she had lived all her life at Verdant Meadows in Cambridgeshire and their parents had done very little socializing in the neighborhood. And when their brother James had taken himself off to join Wellington's staff two years ago, the task of overseeing the management of the estate and looking after the breeding stables built up by their father had fallen wholly to Frankie.

17

Daphne knew that her sister did an excellent job of it. But she thought it was unfair that her darling, albeit sometimes quite unaccountably outspoken, sister should have to slave away on the estate with no fun at all, conveniently forgetting that for Frankie working with horses was the greatest fun so that it had been almost impossible to drag her away.

Daphne sighed. Only when her own unexpected condition had become apparent had she succeeded in convincing Frankie to come to town as a special favor to her. She had argued persuasively that under the circumstances she needed a relative to accompany Laurel about during her come-out season and Frankie was just the one.

"I trust I am now suitably attired for this starched-up ball of yours," Frankie remarked casually as she reappeared in Laurel's bedchamber still holding the much-prized but very dusty volume in one hand and marking her place with one long, shapely finger.

"Achoo! Do take that dusty thing away or I shall be in the same state as poor Tizzy." Daphne sneezed into her lace-edged handkerchief, then peered closely at her sister's gown.

She put her small white hand up to her mouth to stifle a groan of astonishment as she took in the full horror of her sister's chosen costume for the forthcoming event.

"Suitably attired? . . . Oh, dear," Daphne uttered in failing accents.

Frankie was dressed in a severe, inky blue silk gown with just enough dark lace trim to qualify as evening wear, though it was sadly out of fashion. It had a flounce around the hem that caused it to sweep slightly along the floor as she walked, when the fashion was for shorter gowns that showed an inch or two of ankle; and it was

18

poorly cut so that it suited her just slightly more than her accustomed baggy morning attire.

"Heavens, your gown must be six years out of date at the least, Frankie dear, besides being a most bilious color that makes you look twice your age. 'Tis a pity you did not arrive in town earlier, else we should have had time to outfit you decently for Clara's ball. Have you nothing more . . . more *stylish* to wear than this old silk of yours, my dear?" Daphne had intended to commission several new gowns for her sister before the start of the season, but Frankie had arrived only two days previously. One of her mares had been late in foaling, and Frankie could not bring herself to leave for London until the new colt was standing safely at its mother's side.

"You know I cannot abide fuss. Besides, I have already spent the spare cash this quarter. I have just purchased a new filly—a roan. You should just see her, Daph; she will make an excellent breeder. I intend to match her with Red Devil. Why, her points alone—"

"Please, Frankie! We have no time to discuss the Verdant Meadows Stables. You are going to a *party*, for heaven's sake. Why you must always choose these dark colors, cut much too fully for your excellent figure, I fail to understand. They do not suit you, my dear, for you are quite slender, you know."

Frankie laughed, a deep, throaty laugh. Its subtle timbre held a very feminine, alluring quality. "You know I care not how I look. Why, I would much prefer to wear trousers day in and day out, as I do at the Stables. So much more comfortable, you know." From behind her spectacles Frankie's violet eyes twinkled down at her sister. Indeed, her preferred mode of dress at home was a pair of her brother's old trousers, which were well suited to her long legs and much more convenient than skirts when she was exercising her beloved horses or going about her duties on the estate. A high-nosed old dowager

19

neighbor of theirs had once remarked unkindly that Frankie Verdant's masculine appellation appeared to have had an effect on the way the girl dressed, but the remark never came Frankie's way. She remained blithely unaware of any criticism but Daphne's, which she always laughed off, and even if she had heard any expressed, she would have preferred to go on pleasing herself anyway.

"Well do I know your penchant for unconventional dress! You have the most unaccountable tastes. What a nuisance that you are so much taller than I. My gowns would not even come to your ankles!" Daphne shook her head sadly, a frown pulling down the corners of her pretty bow-shaped mouth. Though twelve years younger, Frankie towered over Daphne by half a foot.

"Yes, I'm almost as tall as James." Frankie mocked her own unfashionable inches.

"You're not! Why, he's well over six feet!" Daphne protested. "And you're not over five inches taller than I am, I'm sure."

Frankie roasted her sister. "Well, one of us had to take after Papa! Just because you and Mama and your daughters are all such squabs—"

"No such thing!" Daphne pulled herself up to her full five feet, two inches.

Frankie tried to soothe her ruffled feathers. "Oh, I'm sure it's much more fashionable to be a petite blonde than to be built like an Amazon as I am . . . and such a swarthy one too."

"An Amazon? Humdudgeon! You talk a deal of nonsense purposely to vex me, my girl. You're tall like Papa and James, whereas my girls and I are petite like Mama. Your dark coloring is like Papa's, too."

"Yes, and James is a mixture. He has Mama's coloring, but not her short stature."

"James? What does James have to say to anything? We're speaking of your dark hair—oh!" On the words

Daphne's attention turned to Frankie's hairstyle.

"Your hair is not even dressed!" Daphne saw that wisps were flying around Frankie's head. The strands had escaped from the tight, thick chignon of glossy chestnut curls that had been confined at the base of her neck.

"Your hair is such a deep, lustrous color. It would shine so if you would brush it forward and let it curl around your face and shoulders, not pull it back in that unattractive way."

"It matters not, Daph."

"Matters not! How can you say so? You look to be quite at your last prayers in that gown with your hair so . . . Do you not care that you reflect no good credit on *me* dressed as you are? Everyone shall think that Alfie has stinted me on the funds to present you properly. La, I shall be laughed to scorn by all the odious old cats."

"But, Daph, you're not 'presenting' me. I'm to be Laurel's chaperon—and you want me to appear as a suitable companion for your daughter, don't you? I am respectably dressed, I vow. Surely a chaperon should be a lady of a certain age who has given over thinking of modish gowns and the latest ways to style one's hair." Frankie laughed. She didn't give a tinker's fiddle for what the old cats thought, but she was sorry to distress her sister. The whole idea of social rules and regulations, acting according to some unwritten but widely accepted code of behavior, aping the latest modish styles and striving to keep oneself always in fashion, seemed something of a joke to her. She just could not take it seriously. There were so many other things that were much more important—which of her mares was due to be in season next, for instance . . .

"Respectably dressed? Oh, Frankie, Frankie, you look as though you are about to attend a funeral, not a ball! And if you think any of the ladies of the *ton*, no matter what their ages, have given over thinking of modish

21

gowns and the latest coiffures, then you are fair and far out, my girl! . . . Here, take my Norwich shawl. The creamy lace will give you some color. And, oh, I know, let me get my diamond necklet and earrings to give you some dash."

Frankie shrugged her shoulders and returned her attention to her book, fascinated to read about a cure for the megrims involving henna soaked in hot tea while Daphne went off to her own room in a swirl of draperies to fetch the jewelry.

"She looks a positive dowd!" Daphne muttered to herself. "Lord, help me, I shall go distracted. Dear, dear Alfie, why must you be away just when we all need you the most! Ah me, I suppose we shall scrape through somehow."

# *Chapter Two*

Not more than three streets away on this particular evening a rather tall and athletic gentleman was making his languid preparations for a formal entertainment he had deigned to attend. In contrast to the frenzied activity in the Whittgroves' elegant Georgian townhouse in Grosvenor Square, the gentleman's red-brick lodging in Bruton Place was a model of quiet, unhurried decorum.

"Another tedious ball for the debs," Tolland Hansohm, the owner of this modest establishment, murmured. He was quite calm as he made his preparations for the evening.

"What was that m'lord?" asked his long-time valet.

"Nothing, Worthy, nothing." Tolland smiled wryly. "Just talking to myself. Must be a sign of senility setting in."

"Your lordship is always funning," commented Worthy in his typically lugubrious fashion. He disapproved of any sign of self-deprecating humor in one of his lordship's breeding.

"Ah, you feel it bad form for a member of the aristocracy to indulge in such odd humors, do you, Worthy? I quite agree . . . but you've been attending me long enough to know my foibles."

"As you say, m'lord."

It seemed to Tolland that he had been attending such affairs as the upcoming social event for close to ten of his thirty winters. He went when he was in town because it would be impolite to refuse and because he really had no desire to hurt people's feelings, especially not those of one as good natured as this evening's hostess.

He was a gentleman who had the felicity of being accepted everywhere. Indeed, he was universally admired, and his sporting exploits were imitated eagerly by the younger scions of noble houses. Because Tolland was rather cool and formal in his social relationships, always striving for perfection of manner and form, it was sometimes whispered by the gossips that he was full of conceit, thinking himself so high and mighty.

The jealous and ill-natured longed to see him get his comeuppance, complaining, usually after being hit by a shaft from his unsheathed wit, that the man walked hither and thither with his nose in the air, too conscious of his own consequence. These exceptional few sourly hoped that the weight of that appendage would one day bring him down.

Despite his detractors, Tolland's standing was such that he was a welcome addition to any social or sporting gathering. He had a wide circle of acquaintanes and a few favored intimates. Young men admired his athletic abilities, in particular his expertise with horses. He was always well mounted on high-blooded animals, and his skill in driving a spirited team was without equal. Accounted to be well informed about current affairs and the arts for one who spent so much time in sporting pursuits, he was well received among the parents of his admirers, too, as he was always perfectly polite and his conversation was never boring. The possessor of so many envied abilities considered himself, if not the most modest, at least the most reasonable of fellows.

*     *     *

Tolland was in the small dressing room that gave off the large and imposing master bedchamber, making his final preparations for the occasion. Worthy stood beside him, holding an exquisitely cut black evening jacket as he watched his employer's movements with considerable interest. Tolland was engaged in the intricate task of tying his neckcloth.

"Ah, your lordship is going to attempt the Mathematical tonight. It's a delicate operation, sir . . . requires a steady hand, such as only a man with your lordship's iron nerve possesses," Worthy commented with approval. He often remarked to his fellow servants that his lordship did him proud.

"Yes, the Mathematical. Something subdued, I think, to match my mood," Tolland murmured as he began to wind the white linen cloth round his neck with long, slim hands whose appearance belied their latent strength.

Tolland had already donned the black knee-breeches that were *de rigueur* for a *ton* ball. Over his shirt of closely woven white lawn he had chosen to wear a watered satin waistcoat of palest silver grey. As he wound the cloth round his neck the material of his shirt tugged snugly across his broad shoulders. Tolland could not abide loose or ill-fitting clothes, everything had to be cut perfectly to fit just so, with not an inch of waste at shoulder, waist, hip, or knee. Just a touch of lace at the cuffs of his shirt served to temper the severity of his appearance. The new style of moderation in the male wardrobe, introduced by George Brummell, was one that he embraced whole-heartedly.

Tolland was interrupted in his task by the un-mistakable voice of his cousin, Sir Montagu Addle-cumber, who broke in upon him before Jenks, his butler, could inquire whether it was convenient for that young

25

gentleman to be received.

"Was you goin' to the Chatterin'tongue affair tonight, Tol?" the young exquisite asked in high-pitched tones of hope and admiration.

"Can you never wait to be announced, Monty?" Tolland sighed at ruining his neckcloth and indicated that Worthy should hand him another of the pristine white linen squares. "Must you always be such an impetuous young rattle?"

"By gad! Ain't you pleased to see me, coz?" Addle-cumber, known to his friends as Monty, strolled into the dressing room clad in an embroidered gold satin evening coat over satin knee-breeches of a dark mustard color. As his cutaway evening coat fell back the crowning glory of the brilliant ensemble was revealed—a waistcoat of striped red, green, and gold silk. Tolland winced painfully as he took in the splendor of this gaudy concoction, thinking Monty would have no need of a linkboy to light his way home tonight, the waistcoat would surely glow in the dark.

"My dear coz, you look to be a very Pink of the Ton!" Tolland did not give voice to the thought that Monty looked a regular quiz, loaded down as he was with rings, fobs, seals, and other male affectations. And his lank wheat-colored hair was pomaded with Oil of Macassar, too, Tolland noted with a grimace.

Monty preened himself, his thin chest swelling with, to his ears, his cousin's unwonted praise.

"And of course you are welcome, Monty, if only you would contrive to entertain yourself below for a brief time. As a consequence of your rashness, you find me in dishabille—I know I shock your sensibilities."

The gullible Monty gaped at his cousin, openmouthed. "Heh? Been dished by a bee? By gad, didn't know you was ill, coz. Should have asked Jenks to look in first. Accept m'condolations."

26

Monty stepped forward and looked closely at his relative, but could see no outward sign of illness. He scratched his yellow pate and nodded wisely, "Nasty thing to creep up on one, that ole dizzy bee. Guess you ain't goin' to the Chatterin'tongue ball then."

"Chatterington, Monty, Chatterington. And yes, I will look in for a time as I am expected. I would not want to disappoint the garrulous Clara—I would never hear the end of it. She has another of her reed-thin redheads to fire off this season."

"But you've got dizzy bee. Ain't it catchin'?"

Tolland rolled his eyes heavenward. "Dishabille, Monty, dishabille. It's a state of undress, not a disease."

"Oh." Addlecumber digested this. "Don't look undressed to me, by gad. Just need a jacket and neckcloth and you'll be right as a trivet. Sure you ain't dizzy still?"

Monty's sorely tried cousin ignored him. Long experience had taught Tolland that the best tack was to change the subject. "Don't tell me you're going to do the pretty, too. Didn't think you had time for the debs. Has Miss Chatterington caught your fancy already?"

Much discomposed, Monty gave a strangled cough. "Uhh . . . don't even know the Chatterin'tongue chit. Couldn't tell 'er from Adam."

Tolland raised a skeptical eyebrow. "Oh, you could tell her from *Adam*, surely," he remarked dryly.

A thought struck him, and he added with a knowing gleam in his eyes, "Ah, then what vessel of pulchritude takes you there? What fortunate Eve, what young goddess, what Aphrodite is to have the benefit of your undying devotion?"

"Eh? Don't think the Chatterin'tongues will allow the likes of *them* to cross their porthold," said the slow-witted Addlecumber, his brown eyes almost starting from their sockets as he mistook his cousin's playful remarks.

"Ah, forgive my pleasantry, coz." Tolland smiled

wryly. "I wish you joy of whichever creature you intend to pursue. May she be wounded by Cupid's arrow the moment she sights you."

"By gad, Tol, you may well infect not to know that Lady Amelia perchance will put in an apparition."

Tolland winced. "Ah, that barb of beauty, that merciless mercenary, that most insensible of women. So, she's back in town already." He sighed. He knew Monty had mooned after the lady since first laying eyes on her at the end of last season. *Her* interest, though, was clearly, and most unhappily, in himself. That interest, however, was in no way reciprocated.

"Bless me, Tol, you've hit 'er off as sure as mutton to cheese. Lady A.'s beatitude is known near and wide . . . 'er aroma's the effluence of m'existence. One glimpse at 'er appendages sends me into unspeakable altitudes. Damme, if she ain't the very pineapple of a woman!" Monty sniffed the nosegay fastened to his lapel and smiled inanely.

"Yes, her 'pinnacles' *are* noteworthy," Tolland agreed affably.

"There's some who'd cast dispersions on 'er composition. Glad you ain't one of 'em, coz."

"*I* cast *dis*persions on the lady! Heaven forfend! I advise you to give chase, keep on the scent, and run her to earth before she reaches cover."

"Hee-hee. She don't estimate me, coz." Addlecumber sighed dramatically. "'Tis you she has in 'er orb, Tol."

Tolland well knew that Lady Amelia Reynard, daughter of the Earl of Foxwell, had her yellowish-green orbs on him. Indeed, she had dogged his footsteps constantly since her come-out three years previously. Tall and auburn-haired with large cat-like eyes, the beautiful Lady Amelia was commonly termed "the Fox" among Tolland's set for her red curls and vixenish ways. He frowned as he recollected that the rumor she was on

28

the catch for him had been the subject of gossip and speculation in the gentlemen's clubs and the ladies' drawing rooms since the fatal night he had led her out at Almack's on her first attendance of those famous rooms.

Tolland considered it one of the few mistakes he had made in an otherwise flawless career of squiring eligible young ladies about with no danger to himself of being caught in parson's mousetrap. Yet he had provided grist for the gossips' mill by favoring Lady Amelia that one evening, and he regretted it. For he prided himself as much on his impeccable manners and faultless judgment as he did on his immaculate appearance. And those same impeccable manners had kept him disentangled from female skirts—at least respectable ones—for more than ten carefree years.

Lady Amelia was a thorn in the rose-strewn path of his existence. She was a pesky plague. The Fox was a sly creature, undeniably beautiful but too much like his domineering mama to endure. In fact, he was content to just drift through life with never a thought of permanent female companionship.

"Heard a rumor Aunt Aurelia's comin' up to town," Monty remarked suddenly.

Tolland gave a violent start and ruined his second neckcloth. "Where did you hear such a thing?"

"From Mama, don't y'know—sisters . . . my mama and Aunt Aurelia—your mama, y'know."

"Yes, yes, I am only too aware that Aurelia is my progenitrice."

"By gad! Is she though? . . . Damme, thought she was your mama." Monty scratched his head.

"Had you no Latin at all at school, Monty?" asked Tolland shaking his head as a humorous grin lit his face. "Thank God it's only our mothers who are related and our fathers were in no way connected! But when did you receive this communication from Aunt Augusta? I think

29

it highly unlikely that my mother would come to town at this time of year." Tolland was not keen to see his parent at this or any other time.

"Had a letter 'bout a fortnight ago." Monty scratched his pale pate again. "P'rhaps she ain't comin' to town. Might've got it muddled, don't y'know. Was deuced crossed, it was. Could swear she had some destitution, though. Why not here, by gad?"

With a heroic effort of concentration, Tolland successfully tied his third neckcloth despite Monty's chatter. The stoic Worthy, who strongly disapproved of Sir Monty's coats, was at last able to help Tolland on with his jacket.

"You may go, Worthy. I would not want the sight of Monty, here, in all his sartorial magnificence to make you bilious," Tolland commented dryly.

"Very good, sir." Worthy bowed himself out of the room, giving one disapproving sniff over his shoulder at Sir Montagu as he went.

"Ah, yes. Now I recall," Tolland said calmly as he straightened his cuffs. "My sister Lillian is breeding again. Undoubtedly my mother is going to visit her." He was glad to keep well out of the way of breeding females; he assumed they were invariably peevish and pulled down in looks.


Tolland considered himself fortunate that he rarely saw his female relations in town. His mother, who had a slight arthritic ailment, no longer frequented the metropolis, and his three sisters were married to country gentlemen and safely occupied with their young families.

As the youngest of four children and the only male, Tolland reckoned that he had suffered "a monstrous regimen of women" from his earliest days. In particular, his domineering mother, who, having finally produced the long-awaited heir, alternately coddled and tyrannized him in his childhood and young manhood, driving him to try to achieve perfection and independence by her constant comments on his supposed flaws and inability to do things for himself.

He had resolved to get away from her rule at the earliest opportunity, and when he had completed his undergraduate days at Cambridge, he nad gone up to town permanently. Once escaped from petticoat government, he determined to remain free and unfettered. He was content to let one of his nephews stand his heir.

In general he kept his distance from women of his own class, though he occasionally squired about one or the other of the acknowledged toasts for a week or two. He had a weakness for beauty of face and form, but had never formed a serious *tendre* for any woman. He vowed he would never go about with a besotted look on his face like some moonstruck young nodcock always dancing attendance on some feather-headed society chit. No, a little dalliance, some light flirtation, was the only sort of love game he planned to engaged in for the foreseeable future. The only passion in his life he would save for his horses . . . and the quality of the shine upon his Hessian boots!

# Chapter Three

"Well, niece, I suppose your mother's efforts were worth all the trouble—you certainly look like a princess. Are you ready to lay siege to the heart of any charming prince who happens by?" Frankie teased as she and Laurel settled themselves in the Whittgrove town carriage half an hour later than planned. It was an old-fashioned vehicle but large and comfortable. They both leaned against the soft, satiny squabs with simultaneous sighs of satisfaction.

"As the only prince who may 'happen by' would be Prinny—and his charms quite escape me, though Mama says he was quite handsome when he was younger and not so grossly fat—I suppose I shall just have to settle for some lesser gentleman." Laurel giggled from her corner. She had emerged from her bad humor like a butterfly from a chrysalis and now fluttered with excitement in her new-born confidence. Several peeps in her looking glass before they left, and her mama's raptures, had assured her that she looked just the thing.

Frankie laughed and eyed her niece a little uneasily. She was surprised to find herself somewhat perplexed. Expecting to be indifferent to the experience of venturing into the *haut ton*, she was surprised to feel a stirring in her blood. The idea that it could be nervousness she rejected, but a vague feeling of apprehension she would admit to. Now what was it Daph had said about how she was to conduct herself and watch over Laurel tonight?

"You must not allow Laurel to dance with the same partner more than twice." Daphne had rattled on. "Oh, and she must not waltz at all, you know. Try to see that she is introduced to all the eligible young men—Clara will help you there. Make sure she is never seen to be a wallflower—take her to the ladies' withdrawing room or among the potted plants, or *somewhere* if she is without a partner for a set." Daphne had paused for breath.

"And you must not forget to accompany her in to supper, you know. Laurel must not be without the company of her chaperon *then*, for she could be with some horrid young man who will take her off to a dark corner and try to flirt with her or, even worse, with one of those young clodpoles who know not how to procure anything for one to eat or drink or how to conduct themselves in the least."

But Frankie could not remember the half of it. She had made a comical face and teased her elder sister instead.

"Good heavens, Daph, it sounds as if you are planning a military campaign, not a simple evening at an insipid party. Alfred and James should have you with them in Spain."

That had put dear Daph in a huff, Frankie recollected with a smile. "You are fair and far out if you think anything about it is *simple*." Daphne had wagged a finger at her.

And, indeed, Frankie knew she should have questioned her sister as closely about her duties for this infernal ball as she did her groom at home when she consulted him about the condition of her horses. She supposed that it *was* quite an important occasion for Daphne and Laurel, however silly and tedious it seemed to her.

She was somewhat abstracted and put the knuckles of one gloved hand to her mouth as she pondered the difficulties ahead. The taste of glove was not pleasant. Frankie removed one offending item from her hand, then the other, and laid them on the seat beside her, intending to put the gloves on again when they arrived.

Laurel addressed her suddenly, causing Frankie to jump. In her surprise, she unthinkingly grasped the diamond necklet at her throat, and broke the clasp.

"Aunt Frankie?" Laurel peeped up at her aunt in a coy manner. "Do you have to wear your spectacles tonight? It would be so much better if you would leave them behind."

"Better for whom?" Frankie laughed as she put the broken necklet in her reticule, then reached up to remove the dangling diamond earbobs that irritated her beyond endurance. "Not for me, for I could not see where I was going, much less keep my eye on you, dear niece. And I think it would be much more embarrassing for you if I were to fall on my face or blunder into someone, as I would surely do, than merely be seen wearing my spectacles."

However, Daphne could have told her that she was quite wrong in thinking that her eyeglasses were protection against "accidents," for she was only a trifle myopic, and her occasional clumsiness was due more to absentminded distraction or absorption in some other subject than to actual ungainliness.

"Alfie says we are not to tease you, Frankie dear, about being clumsy" Daphne had once remarked. "He says it is no such thing, and I declare, he is in the right of it, for it's only when you are inside and hemmed in by Mama's

35

cumbersome furniture and cramped rooms that you blunder into things. And while I am about it, I shall take you to task about your habit of flopping onto the nearest seat. You must take care to seat yourself in a more ladylike fashion, dearest, instead of stretching your legs out before you as though you were a man," Daphne had lectured mildly.

"Indeed, Alfie says, and I have remarked upon it, that when you are outdoors, mounted on one of your horses or going about your duties on the estate, there is not a more graceful woman to be seen in the county." Sir Alfred had further noted that there was an unconscious athletic grace about Frankie's movements that drew the eye of a careful observer.

Laurel interrupted Frankie's recollections. "Aunt, have you really no wish for more fashionable clothes now that you are come to London?" she asked curiously. "Do you not wish to visit all the shops and see the splendid wares to be found here?"

"Seems a frivolous way to spend one's money," Frankie retorted. "Not to mention boring one to flinders. 'Tis a waste of time, if you ask me. Why, I could find a hundred-and-one things to buy for the stables with the cash I would have to expend to outfit myself as your dear mama seems to think necessary."

Laurel, used to the Aunt Frankie of Verdant Meadows, could not imagine why her aunt would choose to ignore all the marvelous, fashionable shops now she was come to London and would be moving amongst the denizens of high society.

"But Papa would stand the nonsense. And I declare, the shops in town seem like heaven when one has been used to the services of Mrs. Millsop, our local seamstress at home, you know. She used to make up all my gowns. But those were for a schoolgirl. Now for my come-out I

36

have a proper wardrobe. And Mama would see that you had all the most modish gowns, too, if only you would let her."

"What do you consider a 'proper wardrobe,' then?" Frankie inquired with amusement.

"Why, one must have morning robes and tea gowns, walking gowns and carriage dresses for day, and ball gowns for the evening, of course. Oh, and spencers and pelisses and shawls as well as hats, gloves, ribbons, shoes, slippers, and boots, of course." Laurel counted the items off on her gloved fingertips. "Why, I've even had a new riding costume made up. Have you seen it yet, Aunt Frankie?" Though she was an indifferent horsewoman, Laurel was pleased with the effect of the soft green velvet outfit.

"Aha, a new habit! I hope that means you have been practicing your riding since I saw you in the autumn, for your last performance at Verdant Meadows was sadly lacking. Has your father bought you a new hack? If not, I can send to the Stables for a sweet-going little mare which will suit you admirably."

Frankie's thoughts flew in one direction, Laurel's in another, according to the dictates of their interests. Unfortunately for aunt and niece, these rarely intersected.

"Surely you will wish to visit the shops and refurbish your wardrobe at your first opportunity, for you will be out with me every day these next weeks and you will be remarked if you are not in the first kick of fashion," Laurel persisted, not understanding why her country-bred aunt showed not the slightest interest in turning herself in to a fashionable lady of the *ton*. "You can be sure all the tabbies will comment else."

"Oh, Laurel, I pay no heed to high-born felines, and I expect they will pay no heed to me," Frankie answered, a

37

smile in her pleasant, throaty voice.

"But, if you don't give a snap for what the ladies think, what about the gentlemen? Have you not thought to catch a husband while you are here?" Laurel asked, much interested in her aunt's answer.

"Why, no, I am satisfied to go on as I am. I cannot abide the notion of hanging on some man's sleeve. And I dislike the phrase 'catching a husband' excessively. When we talk of 'catching' something, it begins to sound like contracting some disease or other," Frankie answered on a laugh, for truly in her four-and-twenty years she had not thought much about marriage. "No, you'll never catch me falling into some man's arms!"

Oh, she was aware that Daphne, in her typically haphazard fashion, had tried to bring suitors to her attention from time to time. But these few gentlemen were soon dismissed from her thoughts to be replaced by more immediate concerns, such as which fodder was likely to last through the winter without spoiling, what preparation she should apply to the injury to the dappled colt's left hock, or whether there should be an increase in charges for the Stable's stud services.

In Frankie's opinion the chosen town gentlemen had resembled nothing so much as hunted hares as they had scampered from her presence. She never took pains with her appearance, and her manner with them had always been businesslike as she had looked them squarely in the eye from behind her large spectacles.

Daphne had tried to tell her that the men she met were either somewhat frightened or were annoyed by her straightforward manners, deep voice, and formidable knowledge of both estate management and the breeding of horses. Her sister's complete lack of "feminine" charms, not to mention the odd sight she made in spectacles often sliding halfway down her nose, left

Daphne feeling exasperated and frustrated. The erstwhile suitors never had a chance to see the extremely attractive woman behind the competent manager and horsewoman.

When taken to task, Frankie had replied, with a twinkle in her eye, "I see no good purpose to be served by being coy or missish. I have no delicate feminine sensibilities, you know—don't know why I should pretend that I do."

"Do you not want a family of your own—your own establishment?" Laurel broke into her aunt's thoughts.

"But I have my own establishment. I have everything I want at Verdant Meadows," Frankie responded truthfully. She liked to live in the moment and had so much to interest her and to occupy her time that she truly never thought of the future.

"But Uncle James will marry someday, and you shall have to live elsewhere, will you not?"

"Why, I suppose so. I have not the time to think on such things. When and if that happens will be time enough."

"Oh, Aunt Frankie, you haven't got a romantic disposition. How disappointingly prosaic and dreary . . . Did Mama give you a list of the most eligible bachelors to be seen at Lady Chatterington's tonight?" Hardheaded but softhearted, Laurel was determined to make the most of her season. She knew far better than her aunt the practicalities involved in entering the marriage mart.

"Why, no. You will have to ask Lady Chatterington when we arrive. I expect she and your mama have had their heads together. She will know who keeps the best stables and who is the most clipping rider among them," Frankie said, straight-faced.

"Aunt Frankie!" Laurel giggled. "Mama would stare to

39

hear you talk so. She is more concerned with a gentleman's family and his funds than with his horses!"

"But only consider, dear niece, how a gentleman handles his cattle is a telling clue to the man himself. Depend upon it, he will be eligible if he knows and values good horseflesh. Be sure to accept invitations to ride or drive out with your suitors. You will be able to form a good idea of a man's skill and judgment that way." Frankie warmed to her subject. "And you could not do better than to inspect his stables—or his mews in town. Look into the mouths of his animals—that will tell you if he has a care for them, has a gentle or rough hand on the reins, if he is patient or inflexible, competent and skilled or incapable of proper control."

"Oh, Aunt, what an idea! As if I could bear to go poking around the teeth of such great beasts! I cannot judge an eligible *parti* by looking at his mount!"

"Nevertheless, a gentleman's judgment of horseflesh must be sound and his treatment of his cattle gentle. The horse's mouth will reveal the man, I always say. Remember, you will have to run in tandem with the fellow for the rest of your days."

"Oh, you're funning me!" Laurel giggled aloud at her aunt's absurd ideas. "You're the most complete hand, Aunt Frankie."

"Is it so important to meet an eligible bachelor this soon, anyway? Why not just enjoy your dancing partners as they come? There will be many more gentlemen to meet during the season."

"Well, one doesn't wish to form a *tendre* for an ineligible gentleman," Laurel answered practically.

"Yes, indeed. To be seen with a man whose mount is all show and no heart—or worse, a decided slug—does not bear thinking of, does it? Good heavens, niece, do not be thinking of forming a connection at your very first ball!

40

You cannot be sure that those with the best blood animals will seek you out right away."

"Perhaps, even if you are funning, you would judge a man eligible for yourself by looking at the horseflesh he keeps, but your absurd, teasing ideas of how to go on will not serve me at all. I want to meet a handsome, *young* man who will care for me—not some smelly, *old* gent fresh from the stables who thinks of nothing but horses."

"You are very young to be thinking of tying yourself up for life at any rate, are you not?"

"Why, I'm older now than Mama was when she married Papa! I am at an age when most girls make their matches, you know. And anyway, the cream of the crop will be at the ball tonight. Sally told me her mama had upwards of one-hundred and fifty acceptances—and most of those will surely attend."

"Good lord! Will there indeed be so many people at this affair. However shall I keep you in sight all evening?"

Laurel chattered on in a dreamy vein. "I wonder if Lord Harry Markham will be there? I forgot to ask Sally if he had accepted his invitation. He is really most heavenly!"

"Well, I don't know who this Lord Harry Markham might be, but I have yet to see a man who is 'heavenly,'" Frankie responded dryly. "He might ride a 'heavenly' horse, perhaps . . ."

"Well, I saw Lord Harry riding in the park when Mama and I were out in the barouche, and he was truly heavenly. He has such strange hair—almost white it seemed from that distance—and the sun made it shine as if he had a halo around his head, just like the pictures in church. And he sat his horse so well that I could not help but admire him. It was a magnificent horse, too, Mama said. You would have approved," Laurel added.

Frankie grinned. "Well, that shows you, then."

"Oh, Aunt Frankie, it would be of all things wonderful if Viscount Sterling puts in an appearance this evening." There was a wealth of awe and wonderment in Laurel's voice. "Lady Chatterington confided to Mama that he had accepted her invitation but she didn't rely on him to arrive until late . . . *And,*" Laurel intoned dramatically, "he does not disdain to dance with the debs—well, sometimes, Lady Chatterington said. How exciting it would be to have a dance with him!"

"And who might this Viscount Sterling be?" queried Frankie. "Another 'heavenly' young man?"

"You've never heard of the 'perfect' viscount everyone raves about? Oh, Aunt Frankie!"

"No, how should I know of him? He's not one of the Seven Wonders of the World, I don't suppose."

"Why, he's a top-of-the-trees Corinthian! I dare say one could call him a nonpareil. He must ride over twelve stone at the least, I should think. He would be well up to your weight, Aunt Frankie. But more importantly, his approval assures one of success. He knows how to go on in all situations, Sally says. He is always dressed to perfection, is as handsome as a god, and his address makes one want to swoon!"

"What! Have you been addressed by this Olympian already?" teased Frankie in mock astonishment.

Laurel blushed and said, "Why, no, Aunt, as I am just out I haven't actually *seen* him yet, but I've heard Sally Chatterington and her friends talk of him."

Frankie's curiosity got the better of her. "Does he indeed ride above twelve stone? I wonder what kind of cattle he keeps. Mayhap he would be interested in purchasing some of our new foals or using the services of our stud. Perhaps I should seek him out."

"No, no, Aunt Frankie," Laurel screeched, "you

mustn't! It would not be at all the thing."

Frankie considered it huge fun, and probably highly undeserved, that the unknown gentleman was accorded such high accolades and it amused her to encourage her niece to speak of this paragon. "Well, and what does such an angel of a man look like? Have you any idea, since you have not laid eyes on him yet?"

"Sally says his voice can charm the birds from the trees—at least that's what she heard her mama telling an acquaintance. And he's very tall and handsome with black hair and eyes, too . . . at least that's what Sally overheard."

"Aha! Quite the corsair, I perceive," Frankie remarked. She had read the poetry of the fascinating George Gordon, Lord Byron, and was quite fond of his swashbuckling heroes.

"Yes—very tall, quite dark, and ever so handsome." Laurel continued unabated. "Sally says his face is perfection with a form to match—such wide shoulders that other men envy and girls would love to be held against," the knowing Laurel enthused.

"Rather warm talk for young ladies not yet out," Frankie countered, then laughed. "With his coloring, he sounds to be more of a devil than an angel."

"But, Aunt Frankie"—Laurel repeated Lady Chatterington's encomium—"his appearance at a party means that the evening is a success, and I do so hope that Sally's come-out ball will be a success." Laurel sighed as she leaned her delicate cheek upon her white-gloved hand and contemplated the unnamed glories in store for her this evening.

"Rubbish," snorted her disbelieving aunt. "He sounds like a snob of the first water to me. A ballroom dandy. A caper merchant. What would such a diffident dandy do on the sporting field? Come a cropper at the first fence, most like."

"There you are wrong, Aunt, because he is a member of the FHC, the Four-in-Hand Club, you know, and Sally's brother Phillip says he is the best of the Corinthians. He is known for tooling his curricle at a high rate of speed round the most dangerous corners, and his horses are accounted to be the best in town. He is sometimes called 'My Lord Perfection' you know."

"So, he handles horses as well as young ladies. It will be amusing to see this Corinthian of yours . . . No, no, do not fret. I shall not approach him about the Verdant Meadows Stables . . . Is this pattern card of manly virtues married or single?"

"Oh, single, Aunt, to be sure."

"What! I'm surprised. He sounds a delightful confection—good enough to eat, in fact. I wonder he has not been gobbled up already if his seat is as wonderful as you say!"

"Oh, Aunt, what silly, teasing things you do say!"


The much praised and much maligned Andrew Tolland Hansohm, Viscount Lord Sterling, had at that moment completed his leisurely and slightly bored preparations for Lady Chatterington's ball.

"I say, Tol, you goin' to Chatterin'tongues or ain't you?" Monty asked plaintively as his elegant cousin sat, very much at his ease, in his book-lined study, slowly sipping a glass of sherry. Monty had tossed off his own glass at a gulp.

"Yes, yes. As I told you, I fully intend to look in for an hour or so, but it is not the thing to arrive too early at these little affairs. One does not like to appear too eager." Tolland smiled lazily at his cousin. "Let others anticipate our arrival," he advised Monty with supreme confidence

44

as he leisurely rose to his feet.

So it was with an untouched heart, secure in the knowledge of his unblemished reputation, that Viscount Sterling set off for Lady Chatterington's ball, with his cousin Monty Addlecumber in his wake. All was right with his world, and an unopened bottle of his best Madeira awaited him in his study upon his return from various evening excursions. Yes, it was indeed a comfortable, not to say luxurious, life, he thought as he left his house. Almost perfect, in fact.

# Chapter Four

Frankie and Laurel arrived at the imposing mansion of Lord and Lady Chatterington in Berkley Square feeling somewhat disheveled after a tedious delay. Their carriage had been caught up in a long line of vehicles waiting to disembark at the large Palladian-style house.

"I do hope the evening will not prove that much of a trial," Frankie sighed as she descended from the carriage. "Perhaps I shall spot one of our stable's customers." She brightened at the thought.

She followed Laurel up the staircase of the somewhat modestly decorated Chatterington House to greet her hostess. Daphne could have told her that Clara Chatterington was a famous nipcheese when it came to spending money, especially on something as frivolous and transient as party decorations. And with good reason, for Lord Chatterington, despite his exalted title, was not so well to grass as one might suppose. But Frankie didn't take much notice of her surroundings.

"Dearest Laurel, how pretty you look," the voluble Lady Clara declared as she warmly welcomed her guests. Laurel curtsied to her, then placed her small hand in Lady Chatterington's.

"How is your dear mama? Such a pity that she could

not attend. Sally has been on pins and needles all evening—she is awaiting you in the ballroom. I declare, I believe she has a thousand things to say to you." She turned to Frankie and was momentarily speechless at the sight of the tall, bespectacled woman in an exceedingly old-fashioned dress.

"How do you do, ma'am? I'm Frankie Verdant, Laurel's aunt, you know. My sister Daphne has often spoken of you. She much values your friendship."

Frankie's warm voice melted Lady Clara's frozen vocal cords.

"Miss Verdant, so you are dear Daphne's sister!" she said, making a bid to recover. "Welcome, my dear. You are not at all alike, are you? She's so . . . and you're so, so . . . Well, I *am* pleased to see you here this evening. 'Tis a great pity, girls, but I cannot abandon my post here yet awhile—there are still guests to come and be greeted. Tsk. I know not what has become of Lord Chatterington." The good-natured lady looked all about for her delinquent spouse.

"I shall have Philip take you in." In the absence of her lord, who had long since effaced himself, Lady Chatterington delegated her son to do the honors.

"Miss . . . Miss Whittgrove." Philip cleared his throat noisily and extended his arm to Laurel. The young man had such an awestruck look on his face that Frankie was hard put not to laugh. She could not know that he was used to thinking of her niece as a slightly untidy schoolroom friend of his sister, Sally. And now before his eyes, Laurel had been transformed into a diamond of the first water, albeit a diminutive one.

"Philip . . ." Lady Chatterington nudged her son with an elbow, reminding him that another lady was waiting to claim his other arm. Belatedly, and somewhat red-faced, he turned to Frankie, "Miss, ah, Verdant."

After Philip's rather abashed request for a dance with

48

Laurel was prettily granted, and after enduring the squeals and giggles attendant upon the reunion of her niece and Sally Chatterington, Frankie stood back as a rush of young men made their way to Laurel's side and requested the honor of leading her out for one or the other of the evening's scheduled sets.

The musicians had been tuning their instruments even as she and Laurel had entered the gaily festooned ballroom and now young Philip Chatterington was claiming Laurel's hand for the first dance and leading her out to the floor. Frankie pushed her slipping spectacles back up on her nose with her index finger and gazed about at the colorfully dressed throng, all bejeweled, starched, and perfumed, some impeccably and some garishly garbed. She was at somewhat of a loss. She felt a burning desire to go out and gossip with the stableboys in the Chatterington mews, but knew that Daph would be distraught if she let this particular filly out of her sight. She smiled and shook her head over the very idea of finding herself in such an unlikely place as a London ball at the start of the season.

The sense of rightness about his existence accompanied Tolland as he entered the crowded confines of Chatterington House. This was his world. He was one of its rulers, one of its arbiters of fine manners.

Monty, he noted, had already scampered up the staircase, anxious to discover if Lady Amelia were in attendance. So Tolland was all alone when he was pounced upon by his beaming hostess.

"Oh, Lord Sterling, how good of you to come. We had quite given up on you, you know. So late—but thankfully here at last! How kind in you to favor us—so, pleased, my lord." Clara Chatterington greeted him with unrestrained joy, as was her wont, leaving him in no doubt as to his welcome in her ballroom.

"But how else was I to secure a private moment with you, dear lady?" he bantered smoothly as he bowed over her hand.

"Go on with you, my lord! Such a tease." His hostess tittered like a schoolgirl and slapped him playfully on the wrist with her fan.

The good lady was as effusive in her greeting to the man himself as she was unstinting in her praise of him to her friends, enhancing his exalted reputation even more. She had good reason to think the world of the gentleman. He had been kind to her older daughter, Lettice, the year before when it looked like that somewhat gawky, carrot-headed young woman would not "take" during her first season. But when it was seen that Sterling did not deem her too farouche to lead out, others followed suit. And with the moderate social success she enjoyed after this momentous event, Letty Chatterington found herself engaged to a highly eligible, though equally gawky, young baronet in a matter of weeks.

So, in common with her sister hostesses in the *ton*, the lady welcomed the viscount with open arms. His appearance added the glow of success to their entertainments. He could be counted on to do his duty by the less popular debs as well as find favor with the acknowledged beauties.

The young ladies were flattered when he danced with them, and the older ones vied with one another to set up a flirtation with him—in which activity they were inevitably unsuccessful. The matchmakers had given up on him as an eligible *parti*. His title was respectable and his fortune adequate, but he was never serious about any of their charges and anxious mamas had abandoned attempts to entice him with their fledglings long since. It was said that my lord Sterling was not a marrying man.

Still, his very air of aloofness and inaccessibility,

together with his imposing physique, caused many a young woman to sigh over him anyway and to indulge in secret heart-burnings for a few days before giving him up as a lost cause and going on to favor more attainable, though less handsome, gentlemen than My Lord Perfection.

In reality, the gentleman was neither so dark nor so absolutely handsome as he was often reputed to be, although the matter of his height was not in dispute. He was tall enough to suit any maiden's fancy. However, his hair was dark brown, not black. He was not swarthy but lightly tanned. His mouth was not thin and cruel but full and generous and often curled up in a quirky smile.

There was nothing noteworthy about his brows—he did not arch them expressively or lower them ominously. As for the appendage that was said to be his downfall, his nose was neither so remarkable nor so uplifted, as some said, but merely a slightly aquiline addition to the center of his face.

Actually his features were saved from being commonplace by his one claim to manly beauty, his intriguing deep blue eyes. These he considered too much like his mama's wide orbs, and thus he kept them half closed much of the time, which gave him a rather cynical and knowing appearance and often deceived observers as to their true color.

So, rather than the handsomeness of his features, it was his air, his superior physique and athletic grace, his elegance and perfection in dress and manner that accounted for Viscount Sterling's reputation and gave him that indefinable something known as good *ton*.


Tolland finally escaped from the effusive grasp of his hostess and stopped to straighten the cuffs of his shirt as he glanced at himself in a large gilt-framed looking glass hanging on the wall just outside the ballroom. He pressed down a fold in his meticulously tied cravat just a tad with his long fingers and critically arched a brow at himself a moment before he turned to take a step through the large double doors that were thrown open upon the glittering scene of merriment. Just as he stepped into the room he felt himself collide with someone.

"Oof!" issued from two pairs of lips simultaneously as the viscount and a lady careened off one another.

"Your pardon, ma'am," Tolland said in a frigid tone. He noticed a pause in the conversation nearby as several heads turned in his direction. "I was not aware that there was a race in progress round the perimeter of the room, madam, or I should have taken more care."

The tall woman he had collided with said nothing, but stood staring at him belligerently. He automatically raised his quizzing glass to his eye and surveyed her from head to toe. What a singular creature, he thought, as he saw before him a woman dressed in an old blue silk gown, her face concealed behind a pair of large spectacles.

His apology made, he turned his back on the incongruous apparition and sauntered over to join a group of his cronies, Freddy Drake, Lucius Pendergast, and Harry Markham. He tried to put the odd encounter out of his mind though he was uncomfortably aware of his rudeness to the woman. She had taken him by surprise and caused him to feel awkward for a moment, he told himself by way of excuse, because he had felt himself observed when the attention of several guests had been drawn to his *faux pas*.

His friends were full of talk about a new beauty who was making her first appearance at a *ton* function that night.

"She is a lovely little diamond of the first water!" exclaimed Lord Harry Markham, fourth and youngest son of the Duke of Ampleforth. Harry was a young man of noble family but few prospects.

"She is so tiny and exquisite!" proclaimed another young man standing nearby.

"Ah, here you are, Tol, with Rattlepate in tow, I see." Markham greeted his friend and waved his hand in the direction of Addlecumber who was circumnavigating the ballroom at the time. "Have you seen the new beauty? But, no, how could you, you've only just arrived—late as usual."

Tolland again raised his quizzing glass and looked idly about. "A new beauty, you say?"

"Sir Alfred and Lady Whittgrove's eldest, I believe. The delicious little blonde dancing with young Chatterington at the moment," answered Harry.

Tolland deigned to turn his head and study the couple pointed out to him. He saw a young girl, very small but with a neat figure and a mass of blond hair twisted up attractively in a green and gold ribbon. In the movement of the dance he caught a glimpse of her exquisite features and smiled in appreciation.

He turned back to his friends. "But she's just a child! She cannot be above seventeen?"

Harry assured him that she was turned eighteen. "I dare say there's no space left on her dance card for you since you always choose to arrive fashionably late."

"I presume *you* have secured a dance from the way you are gloating."

"To be sure I did. The moment I was presented to her. I think she has captured my heart," Markham declared in melodramatic fashion.

"Ah, surely you jest, Harry. She's just a babe. You'll find little enough amusement there," Tolland remarked, not taking his friend seriously, though he did feel a niggling alarm. Markham was his closest friend among the Corinthian set, and he chafed at the thought that

Harry would thus easily desert the ranks of the unshackled.

"Well, but, Tol, just look at that perfection of face and form! Did you ever see a sweeter countenance!" Markham's face lit up as he watched the girl. Quite like a love-struck swain already, Tolland thought disgustedly.

"As you say, Harry, she should have a delightful year. Let me know if the chit's temperament is as sweet as her face."

"Ah, Tol, you are a cynic. Could a young lady who looks thus be of a sour disposition? No, no, it's against the laws of nature!"

"Well, we'll put it to the test, shall we? I shall engage to lead her out for one set and endeavour to ascertain the young lady's true colors."

"Oho, so you would cut me out, would you, you devil," Harry laughed. "I wager she would have me sooner than she would a great, tall tyrant like you. Why, she would be afraid to put a foot wrong in your company. With me, she will be comfortable." Harry smiled confidently.

"Am I so formidable, then?" Tolland questioned in a teasing vein.

"We all know that you are perfection itself. Never a word or action out of place. You're without the flaws of most of us mortals, Sterling. Only thing is, a young thing like that can't be at ease with you. Know what it is? You're *too* perfect—smooth as glass, you know, and others slip upon you. Can't have the ladies falling down, now can we?"

His friends could not have said why Lord Sterling held himself rather aloof. He had a natural reserve—his critics said he was "too high in the instep"—that made him seem cold. But, while always proper and sometimes rather lofty, he sometimes went out of his way to be kind—as in dancing with an unattractive young lady who

54

had been left to decorate the wall at an evening party—and sometimes cutting—as in administering a sharp setdown to a dashing matron who made a cruel remark about the same young lady within his hearing.

With his cronies, Tolland was used to the kind of give and take just meted out by Lord Harry. He knew his companions admired him and only twitted, as friends will do, in comradely fashion. He had no fear that he really could discompose the young lady. He watched her dance for a time, admired her grace and beauty and wondered idly where her mother was. He was not really acquainted with the Whittgroves. Sir Alfred was involved in government affairs, he knew, but he did not really remember meeting Lady Whittgrove in society.

He strolled over to where his cousin Addlecumber stood, looking like a lost puppy as he soulfully gazed about the scene. "What! You do not stand up with your true love, Monty?" Tolland asked playfully.

"She ain't here," Monty pouted.

"Lady Amelia didn't 'put in an apparition' after all, then?"

Monty shook his head sadly.

"No jewel to ornament your sleeve tonight, heh?" Tolland continued. "Despair not, coz. Just look at the sea of beauty before you. Surely one of these barques of virtue will do instead. Look, there is a young deb with hair the exact color of the Fo—er, Amelia's . . . Perhaps her disposition will be more agreeable. I dare say she will be more amenable to your charms. Go to it, man. Wade in amongst the nubility and carry off one of these vessels of loveliness."

"You funnin' again, Tol? . . . ain't you?" Addlecumber peered uncertainly at his cousin.

"Ah, coz, forgive my ill-conceived attempt at humor," Sterling said, clamping a hand to Monty's shoulder. "I was indeed 'only fooling.'"

After assuring Addlecumber that he had only been exercising a cousin's prerogative to tease unwary relations, Tolland meandered idly about the ballroom for some little while chatting amiably with friends.

When Philip Chatterington had led Laurel away for the quadrille, Frankie had pushed her spectacles more securely into place, had tucked up a few strands of hair that had come loose from her chignon, then had drifted near the door only to collide with a tall, well-dressed gentleman who had just entered the room. The top-lofty fellow had proceeded to give *her* a set-down in most glacial accents after the accident.

Had she tripped, Frankie asked herself, and backed into him? No, she hadn't tripped—she was sure she hadn't. The man's long stride had carried him directly into her. Yes, it had been entirely the fault of the dandified swell, she thought heatedly, and to imply that it had been her doing, as he clearly had, was the outside of enough!

Why, the man had looked at her as though she were as out of place as a donkey at a thoroughbred race. She had stood fuming after his mocking apology and had watched as he turned his broad shoulders on her and walked away, quite unconcerned for any hurt she might have taken.

She remembered the sight of his magnified eyeball staring at her through his quizzing glass. It had reminded her of an enormous and quite hideous cod's eye gazing vacantly at her from the fishmonger's window in the village near her home. She almost laughed aloud as she made the comparison. Except this man's eye had been frosty rather than vacant. A supercilious *ton* dandy was all he was, she assured herself. Not worth letting her unruly tongue loose on the rascal and making a scene—

Daph would definitely disapprove. She tried to suppress the memory that rose unbidden, of a pair of broad shoulders atop the tall, well-formed physique of a born athlete. Yes, undoubtedly he was a buck of the first water. For some unfathomable reason the thought made her all the more angry.

To calm her temper, Frankie strode over to the colonnaded hallway that bordered the ballroom on two sides. There she communed with a potted palm until she could rejoin Laurel. As she stood peering out at the couples whirling by her place behind the fronds she began to mull over her sister's objections to her attire and hair style. Maybe she did need a new gown or two, she thought as she looked out over the fashionables gathered in the Chatterington ballroom. She reached up to pull Daphne's elegant Norwich shawl more tightly over her gown to cover its faded, worn silk . . . only to find it was not there!

"Drat! What did I do with that shawl?" She realized that she must have let it slip from her shoulders in the carriage and had neglected to retrieve it.

Frankie touched her ears. Blast it! She remembered that she had removed those irritating earbobs, too . . . and the necklace had broken. "Well, I guess I *do* look rather like a scarecrow at this elegant *ton* 'do,'" she thought to herself, a half-smile pulling at her lips.

There was nothing else for it but to disentangle herself from her herbaceous retreat when the quadrille ended and make her way to where Laurel was standing. She saw that her niece and Sally had their heads together, chatting and giggling. They were surrounded by several enthusiastic and admiring young gentlemen.

The crowd parted and Frankie could see that a rather well-dressed man with gleaming hair was bowing over her niece's hand. Laurel turned and smiled radiantly in Frankie's direction as she took the arm of the gentleman who was leading her out for the next set. Frankie stared after them, assessing the gentleman, remembering that Daphne wanted a full report next morning.


Laurel blushingly regarded her partner. It was none other than the gentleman she had so much admired in the park—Lord Harry Markham—and her opinion of his visage was only confirmed by closer inspection. He really did have an almost choirboy aspect, with his white blond hair, pale hazel eyes, and slightly crooked lower teeth adding interest to his youthful face.

"I am the luckiest man in the room at the moment, Miss Whittgrove," he said, soulfully.

"What . . . ?" Laurel gave a start, so busy was she cataloguing his features that she had forgotten to initiate any conversation. "I am afraid I was not perfectly attending, my lord," she apologized, blushing an even deeper shade of pink as she did so. The deeper color only enhanced her lovely complexion in Harry's eyes.

"Ah, that's a blow. Here I was congratulating myself on my luck in securing a set with the most sought-after young lady at the dance and she does not 'perfectly attend' when I speak to her. You have wounded me, Miss Whittgrove, indeed you have."

"What can you mean, sir—I mean, my lord?" Laurel peered up at him suspiciously, at last seeing the teasing twinkle in his hazel eyes.

"I mean that I am with the most beautiful woman in the room."

"*Me?* What nonsense!" Laurel laughed outright. "La, my lord, I shall think you an accomplished flatterer."

"Ah, but you wrong me. I merely speak the truth, when there is such an exquisite object before my eyes. I greatly fear that all the other gentlemen present will be calling me out after this." Lord Harry continued to tease

58

her and gently flirt with her until Laurel relaxed and teased him back.

"Well, all the other ladies in the room will envy me my good fortune, for I overheard more than one of them remark on the desirability of securing a dance with you."

"Oh? I am intrigued. Tell me more, Miss Whittgrove."

"For your dancing skills, of course, my lord. Your expertise is held in high esteem. What else could you think I meant?" Her green eyes laughed up at him and Harry was captivated. He had admired her delicate beauty enormously the moment he was presented to her, but now he found her charming and unaffected. Had he been hit at last? he wondered. And so swiftly?

Tolland was making his way across the room when he saw his cousin Monty approach a young lady with brightly colored hair and bow over her hand. It appeared that his bumbling relative had indeed secured a red-haired partner for a set of dances.

However, the young lady's tresses could not be described as a true shade of auburn such as Lady Amelia boasted; no, they were definitely more carroty in hue. And her figure did not compare with the Fox's voluptuousness, either, he noted critically. The lady was rather tall and angular but there was a good-humored look upon her countenance that augured well for his cousin's happiness during the next half-hour. His lips formed themselves into a slightly lopsided curve—he had a job to prevent himself from grinning outright as he watched Monty lead their hostess's daughter into the dance. He stopped abruptly to enjoy the scene.

His careless halt sent him into a near collision with a lady—again! Only by swiftly swiveling his lean hips to one side did he avoid another embarrassing moment. He stopped to adjust the fall of lace over his hand in a seemingly negligent manner, giving himself a moment to regain his equilibrium.

"You!" Tolland heard the word uttered in low, feminine tones.

"Good God!" he muttered under his breath as he looked up from his task. He was completely taken aback to discover the same frightful quiz of a woman who had favored him with her carelessness earlier looking daggers at him from behind her gleaming spectacles.

Dumbstruck for a moment, he was finally able to collect himself enough to lift his quizzing glass—to hide his chagrin as much as anything—and to gaze at the audacious woman who seemed to be implying by her fixed stare that the near collision had been his fault. Surely it was just a perfectly harmless accident . . . Why, it could have happened to anyone. He stood uncertainly, unable to issue the apology he knew in the back of his mind was necessary whether or not the encounter had been his fault.

He was further discomposed by the woman's eyes, magnified through her spectacles and then reflected in his own glass, remarking *him* in as rude a fashion as he was staring at *her!* He stepped back to escape that unnerving gaze and wandered away in a state of distraction. Really, the strange woman was most remarkable. Had she wandered in off the street? he wondered. And to make him lose his composure—twice! Such a thing was unprecedented. He walked about the edge of the ballroom for a few minutes, brooding on his unaccountable fall from gracefulness. Why, he wasn't clumsy even when he was foxed! He clamped his lips together in annoyance, then took himself off to the refreshment room. Perhaps a glass of wine would help him recover his composure.

Sally Chatterington had been giggling with her friend

Laurel, who was excitedly relating the details of her dance with Lord Harry Markham, when they were approached by the garishly dressed but well-meaning Sir Montagu Addlecumber. He made them a flourishing bow before grinning down at them in a hopeful fashion.

One look at the gentleman's out-of-date and overly ornate costume nearly sent the two young ladies into whoops of laughter. Only by studiously avoiding looking at one another were they able to contain themselves as Sir Monty bowed over Sally's hand and requested the honor of a set with her.

Sally had been hoping against hope that Viscount Sterling would seek her out, as he had her sister Letty the previous season, and ask her for a dance. She was not a vain girl. She knew perfectly well that she would never number among the beauties as her friend Laurel undoubtedly would. But she was kindhearted and would never be so silly as to turn down a partner in any guise. More loath to sit out a set than to be seen with the slightly addled Sir Montagu, she swallowed her laughter, along with her disappointment at it not being his cousin requesting her company, and graciously accepted Addle-cumber's hand for the ensuing country dance, while Laurel went off with the darkly handsome and devilish-looking Mr. Lucius Pendergast.

"M'dear Miss Chatterin'tongue," Monty addressed her when a movement of the fast-paced dance brought them together briefly, "must say, your energy's devilish condemnable."

"Why, thank you, Sir Montagu . . . I think. If it comes to that, you are an energetic dancer yourself."

"Like to supplement you on your dainty pedicels." Breathing heavily, Monty nodded several times and smiled happily at her even as he wiped his brow from his exertions during the dance. "By gad, your dancing feats are prodigious."

61

His garbled compliment caused poor Sally to look down in utter confusion to see what was the matter with her rather slender feet. She wondered if her shoes were torn, and her toes poking through. She lost her step and blundered into Monty who gallantly took her elbow and set her to rights again.

"Whew. Roastin' work, this caper-merchant business. Beginnin' to feel like an overdone pigeon, don't y'know." This was the next bone thrown into the conversational graveyard.

Sally, at a loss to follow his meaning, bravely smiled up at him and said, "You are not an effete dancer, yourself, sir. Quite a feat to know when to turn and when to dip, is it not?" she teased.

"Heh? M'feet gone wrong . . . ?"

Sally laughed merrily. "You put a great deal of effort into your dancing, Sir Montagu. Is it a pastime you favor often?"

"Heh? Oh, aye. Does make the time pass, don't it, by gad? You young ladies like to shake a leg every night of the season. Must say, it's a wonder your limbs don't jellify from the aggravation."

Sally giggled, highly diverted by his singular mode of speaking—all topsy-turvy. "Oh, no, Sir Montagu. I enjoy dancing above all things. The season has just begun, but I'm sure my limbs will survive the exercise and still be intact when it's time to retire to Papa's country seat in June."

A movement of the dance separated them again as Sally began to think Sir Montagu's absurdities were quite amusing. He certainly seemed a *gentle* man, at any rate, she told herself, quite pleased with her choice of partner after all, even if he was a most malapropian knight. It was a relief that she didn't have to put on airs and graces or come all missish with him. She could simply be herself in his company and enjoy the occasion.

As the set came to its conclusion, Monty extended his elbow to escort Sally to a vacant chair under the colonnade, but she was breathless from the exercise and bade him take her over to an open window where they could enjoy some fresh air before claiming partners for the next set.

Sally was quite as hardheaded as her friend Laurel and knew her chances of making a brilliant match were quite remote. With little claim to beauty and a meager dower—despite her father's large house, the family coffers were bare—she was not about to let this simple but well-meaning knight escape her company before she made a push to engage his attention. He was Viscount Sterling's cousin, after all.

Accordingly, she batted her eyelashes at him and pursued his laborious but highly entertaining conversation until they both became aware of a commotion in the ballroom. A great crowd of people was rushing toward the refreshment room and chattering excitedly.

# Chapter Five

When Laurel had joined the next set on the arm of dashing young Mr. Pendergast, Frankie was resigned to the fact that she should seat herself among the chaperones. But one look at the purple-turbaned brigade filled her with such an urge to laugh that she walked off in quite the opposite direction. She had seen one old dragon actually raise a lorgnette in order to scrutinize her and heard the matron murmur "How extraordinary!" in tones of strong disapproval. A primitive urge to unwind the old biddy's headgear almost overtook her before she could retreat from the field.

Really, these old tabbies of Daph's had sharp claws. Frankie decided she had best look to her wardrobe after all if only to preserve the peace. Otherwise some of the old harridans were sure to provoke her into coming to cuffs with them before her tenure as Laurel's chaperon ran its course. She laughed to herself.

And, to be honest, as she saw the new mode of Grecian style gowns exhibited on *every* figure, whether full or slender, tall or short, she had to admit that Daph was right about her attire. The puffed sleeves and high waists banded under the bosom of the gowns were not unpleasant in style, she decided. The skirts falling in straight lines to the floor would leave plenty of room for her long legs; she could walk about quite freely. Yes, she definitely approved, and decided she would have one or two such frocks made up.

Frankie's purposeful stride took her to a rather dark, unoccupied room. "Ah, refreshments," she said happily. In the ill-lit room she could just see that food and drink were laid out on tables for the guests. The majority of candles had not yet been lit. Undoubtedly the servants were waiting for some sort of signal from Lady Chatterington, Frankie thought with her typical insouciance. She decided that she would just get something to slake her thirst and cool her temper before once more facing down the uncivil horde collected in the ballroom.

Frankie had just helped herself to a small glass of punch and turned to look out into the brightly lit, noisy ballroom when she suddenly felt a tugging at the hem of her gown.

A gentleman was beginning to say, "I *do* beg your pardon, madam . . . ," when she realized that her skirt was tearing. She turned quickly to look at the man who had trodden on the material. Unfortunately, at that moment the man, trying to step back, slipped slightly on the freshly polished wooden floor, his foot caught in the torn material of her gown.

At her swift movement and his slip, which thrust him forward, their foreheads collided with a cracking sound. Her spectacles went flying to the floor.

"Oh," Frankie exclaimed in astonishment as she was pushed backward by the force of the impact. The man reached out to catch her, but instead lost his balance and fell down with a bump, knocking over a nearby table set with extra glasses, a crystal bowl brimming full of punch, and an elaborate, cut-flower arrangement.

He took Frankie down with him.

Frankie found herself crushed against the broad chest of the rather tall gentleman. She felt slightly stunned for a moment and relaxed her full weight against the length of the well-muscled male body beneath her own. Despite her drenched clothing, a curious sensation of warmth flooded through her where they touched and the stiffness in her neck muscles eased for a moment so that her head nestled in the crook of his neck. She was vaguely aware of a mild but pleasant citrus aroma coming from the man's cheek, which did nothing to calm her already fast-beating heart.

She recovered her senses sooner than did the man who had cushioned her as he bore the brunt of the fall . . . and realized that her full lips lay against his cool cheek, while his breath tickled her ear.

Frankie tried to shift her weight and pull away. Her movements jolted the man back into his senses, and as he moved, trying to raise himself, his knees came up to grip Frankie's slim hips. She was thoroughly trapped for a moment in his semiconscious embrace.

She pushed hard against his chest and quickly got to her feet; punch, flowers, and debris dripped off her as she did so. She backed away from the man—and felt the flounce of her skirt rip off completely as she stepped back. The material was entangled around one of his evening pumps, she realized too late.

Searching round on the wet floor, she found her spectacles, thankfully unbroken, and replaced them on her nose. She looked down to see the tall, elegantly dressed gentleman looking quite dazed as he sprawled on the floor in the middle of the wreckage. Several damp, drooping flowers decorated his hair and chest while blood trickled from a slight gash in his forehead.

At the sight of his injury Frankie put off her embarrassment and started toward him, thoughts of what to do about his cut in her head. She took out her handkerchief and reached down to wipe away the blood. Her underlip caught between her teeth, she looked at the wounded man with compassion, then had to bite down hard to prevent her lips from curling up in a grin at the ludicrous look of consternation on the gentleman's face.

The stunned man was unspeakably embarrassed as he passed a hand over his wet face to clear his vision and found himself lying prone amidst the debris of broken glasses and damp flowers in Lady Chatterington's dimly lit refreshment room. He was too angry to be aware of a wrenching feeling in his left ankle.

"What a diabolical female," he thought to himself as he looked up at Frankie. Her damp hair had come loose from its tight chignon and was flying wildly about her face. He saw that her incredible spectacles were askew on her wet nose, and to his critical eye she looked as if she had dived into a stagnant pond fully clothed. "And I must appear no better," he thought a moment later as water dripped down his aristocratic nose when he lifted his slim fingers to remove bedraggled flowers from his hair.

He saw that the strange woman was bending down, extending a handkerchief toward his forehead. "*You* again!" he gasped, as he came fully to his senses and recognized his nemesis from the ballroom. "Don't come near me, madam! I don't need a ministering angel. You've caused enough havoc for one evening!" he heard himself say meanly.

"Don't be so childish! You've been cut by a piece of glass and your forehead is bleeding. Here, let me press this cloth against the wound to staunch the flow." As she bent to her task he growled deep in his throat and threw up a hand to ward her off.

"My God, the crowd will be in on us at any moment,"

he exclaimed in horror as he fully realized their situation. "I cannot be found this way."

He tried to raise himself on the foot he had landed on when he fell. "Oh, bloody hell! . . . I've twisted my ankle!" he exclaimed as he became aware that he was actually hurt in addition to being wet, sore, and, most of all, mortified.

Frankie reached down a hand to help him up, but he forcefully pushed her away as he again tried to raise himself. She lost her footing as he did so and slipped on the wet floor. Down she went, landing in his arms with her lips smack up against his! Both of them immediately broke the contact, each feeling unaccountably breathless from such an awkward and intimate physical encounter.

As they fought and slithered, trying desperately to move away from one another, they found themselves inadvertently grasping various bits of each other's clothing—and person—in their struggles.

He found himself clutching the bodice of the woman's dress and was disconcerted by the feel of firm, rounded flesh.

"Remove your hand at once, you despicable libertine!" Frankie cried in outrage seconds before she found her fingernail caught on one of the buttons of the man's evening breeches.

"Oof! Unhand me, madam!" he gasped, slightly breathless. Completely disconcerted, Frankie jerked her hand away quickly, part of her nail tearing off in the process.

Each was unable to stand upright unsupported on the slick surface. Frankie finally managed to brace herself against the wall and rise as her hapless partner in the accident uttered a stream of disjointed curses under his breath. She moved away from him, still breathing heavily from the effort and the awkwardness of her predicament, her wet hair now streaming down wildly over her shoulders.

The once elegant gentleman finally rose unsteadily to his feet, supporting himself on the wall panels as Frankie had done. Bits of broken glass and damp flowers fell off him as he leaned against the wall to catch his breath. His beautiful evening jacket and knee breeches were wet and disordered. A piece of Frankie's skirt was still wrapped around one of his evening pumps, and his dark hair, which had been perfectly combed, now sadly disheveled, was falling into his eyes—eyes that had taken on a murderous gleam as they stared across at the drenched apparition he beheld before him.

"Why, you, you . . ." Words strong enough to express his feelings failed him momentarily.

"Just what are you about, you clumsy woman?" he fairly shouted, his famous sangfroid completely deserting him. In his angry, dazed state he felt that she had deliberately tried to compromise him.

Frankie, who had been expecting a profuse apology, was outraged by this unfair attack. "*Me!* What was *I* doing!" she yelled back. She was too discomposed herself to consider that the man was so upset he didn't know what he was saying. "The whole incident was *your* fault, my fine popinjay. My only contribution to this debacle was my unfortunate presence in the room when you came stumbling about. Are you inebriated? Or was I simply the victim of your clumsiness?" she asked furiously. She felt almost exhilarated, so pure was her anger.

"I did not come in 'stumbling about' as you phrase it!" he shouted, a pulse pounding in his temple.

"You did too!"

"I most certainly did not!" He felt powerless to stop arguing with her and depart before they were discovered, she goaded him so.

"Don't be so blasted childish, you silly man. Can you not admit your fault?" Frankie stamped her foot in vexation. When her hackles were up, as they were now, she would wade into the midst of any shouting match, no matter how much bigger and louder her opponent.

He tried to gather the shreds of his shattered dignity about himself as he moved away from the wall, squared his broad shoulders and tried to look down his nose at the infuriating female. "You, madam, are a menace. Your presence creates a hazard. Every time I've turned around tonight, you've been there to trip me up. Was it deliberate? Or is it your normal way of carrying on? What did you think you were doing, anyway? Trying to compromise me? I assure you, such a trick won't work." He hoped his set-down had been sufficiently freezing to damp down her fiery retorts and cause her to drag herself away chastened for daring to cross swords with him.

"The question, sirrah, is what do you think *you* were doing? you bumbling oaf!" Frankie shot back, not cowed one iota by the tall, athletic man looming over her, and determined to give as good as she got. "You must be half-sprung indeed to run me down so! I imagine you always ram your horses and override your fences, too!"

"Half-sprung?" His shattered dignity, hanging by a thread, was immediately in tatters. "Ram my horses!" he sputtered, almost choking with rage at her insult to his horsemanship. "I wasn't the one who caused this debacle, madam. It was *you* blundering into *me* that caused this whole catastrophe! You are the one who must have imbibed too much!" he roared, completely out of control.

"I have never before encountered such a cow-handed whipster!" She continued to upbraid him, refusing to be intimidated by either his freezing set-downs or his burning anger, though aware that she was beginning to shake. "I'll have you know I was standing quite still,

71

enjoying a glass of punch when you stepped on my gown—ruining my only ball dress—and overset us both."

"I did not!"

"You did too!"

"Did not!"

"Indeed, sirrah, you did. You must have the gait of a mule to be so clumsy—and the disposition of one of those stubborn animals not to see that the whole incident was your fault!"

"How dare you speak to me this way! I shall not tolerate it! Do you know who I am, madam?"

"I know that whoever you are, you ill-bred fellow, you are no gentleman!" Frankie hissed, low-voiced . . . and saw the man's head snap back as if he had been struck.

His face went purple with rage as he ground his teeth in fury. Terrible oaths trembled on his lips. His vaunted iron nerves and cool control snapped under the unprecedented emotional upheaval. He was so angry he could not speak further, but stepped forward to grab his antagonist, ready to do her some violence.

He leaned forward, seized the woman by her surprisingly narrow waist, and prepared to shake her until her teeth rattled in her head when all at once the crowd was upon them. She shoved against the hard wall of his chest just as he let her go, and he fell back heavily on his injured foot with a sharp intake of breath to muffle the curse that rose in his throat.


Someone had spread the news of a contretemps in the refreshment room. There was a deafening cacophony as people gabbled and shouted, jostling one another as they crowded in, some losing their balance on the wet floor as they did so, exclaiming over the upturned table, broken glassware and flowers strewn about, asking one another

72

what had happened and who had been involved. Lady Chatterington's servants scurried among the crowd trying to right the table, mop the floor, and clean up the mess.

Their hostess alternately cried over the ruin of her table and exclaimed over her two guests who seemed to have had some sort of accident.

The one, she saw, was a bedraggled lady.

And the other . . . "Oh dear," she moaned faintly with a hand to her brow. The *other* was that most exquisite of Corinthians, that model of perfection and comportment, the incomparable Tolland Hansohm, Viscount Sterling!

"Oh, Lord save us," she groaned. "Sally's come-out will be ruined!"

Tolland and Frankie continued to glare at one another. Frankie's violet eyes were fairly shooting off sparks of animosity from behind the lenses of her steamed-over spectacles. Tolland had to clamp his lips together to keep from uttering the blood-curdling oaths that were on the tip of his tongue, ready to spill out and shock the crowd even further. A muscle twitched in his cheek, while a trickle of blood still coursed down the side of his face from his cut forehead.

They may as well have been the only two persons in the room for all the notice they took of the others milling around them, offering solicitous comments, brushing them off, trying to straighten their clothing.

Laurel ran up to Frankie and whispered, "Oh, Aunt, what happened? Are you hurt? Oh dear, come away, Aunt, do, and let me repair your gown." She pressed up to Frankie, whose heaving breast and tightly compressed lips attested to the effort she was making to control her temper.

Sally had joined her mother and tried to calm her, but

Lady Chatterington abruptly abandoned her palpitations and resumed her typical voluble fussiness. "I am quite recovered, my dear. I declare, 'tis my duty as hostess to see to my guests first," she said valiantly, trying not to worry about the shocking mess in the room and, more importantly, any social repercussions that would result from the incident.

The good lady turned to the poor bedraggled woman, who stood back in the shadows, glaring angrily at Lord Sterling.

"Oh, dear me, *no* . . . she *can't* be—but, oh dear, yes, she must be—dear Lady Whittgrove's sister!" Lady Chatterington muttered under her breath as she realized that the woman was indeed the relative of her dearest friend. She realized, too, that dear Lady Whittgrove's sister was standing with her petticoat exposed. This highly improper and most diverting sight galvanized the redoubtable woman into action.

"Oh, heavens above! Lord save us! Oh, goodness gracious me," Lady Chatterington cried as she sprang forward and bundled Frankie out of the room posthaste. Mercifully Laurel was shielding her aunt from view, and in the gloom and general confusion and disorder of the room, Frankie was whisked away before anyone could get a good look at her.

Lady Chatterington turned from seeing Frankie and Laurel out the door, and in a loud, distracted voice, began issuing orders. "That's right, Jeffers, you and Hurst right the table and clear away the debris," she directed the footmen. She was horrified when she saw that the greatest damage was to poor Viscount Sterling's evening clothes.

"Why, my dearest Lord Sterling, I am so sorry. Mercy upon us, I know not how such a thing could have happened. You must let me apologize. Do forgive me." His hostess addressed him in a loud, worried voice. She

74

flapped her hands helplessly about her as she turned to a scurrying footman. "Jeffers, bring a cloth quickly so that the viscount may dry himself off."

She went up to Sterling, and as she saw the cut on his forehead, lamented, "Oh dear, your poor head! Tsk. Fie upon it, I know not how that table came to be placed in your path, my lord."

Markham, overhearing the comment, laughed. It sounded for all the world as if Lady Chatterington believed the furniture had risen up and knocked his friend down! He went over to the viscount, put a hand on his arm, and attempted to lead him away.

"I say, old man, what happened in here? Lots of broken glass about. Did you try to take advantage of the lady? Or did she slip?" He laughed slightly at his own joke, but was quelled immediately when Tolland turned a murderous look on him and shook off his arm. Harry would have been shocked to learn that the disruption had been caused by his refined, smoothly controlled friend.

Sally began to fan her mama as Lady Chatterington went on in a perfectly demented fashion, apologizing profusely to the man who had actually wreaked the havoc! "I shall have Chatterington investigate the matter completely," she went on. "Oh, 'tis a pity your poor jacket is ruined, not to mention your breeches, too. Good gracious—I should not speak of them. I know you will be so good as to contrive to forget my remarks, my dear viscount . . . Lord save us, I shall go distracted."

Tolland was so preoccupied with his own anger and embarrassment that he did not have to contrive to forget his hostess's remarks for it was improbable that he heard them at all. With his carefully guarded dignity in tatters, all Tolland wanted to do at that moment was stride quickly from the room—but, strangely, he was frozen to the spot. He closed his eyes briefly. A sensation of unreality overtook him. He prayed that he was just in the midst of a very unpleasant dream—a nightmare, in fact—and that when he awoke all would be right with his perfect world.

"Do you go along with my son, Lord Sterling. Philip! Philip, where are you? Ah, here he is, my lord. Philip will take you to his dressing room and lend you a pair of dry breeches."

The incident enlivened a rather flat occasion for the guests and gave them something to gossip about and speculate on for the remainder of the evening.

"Imagine the proud, oh-so-correct Viscount Sterling involved in such a scene!" one sloe-eyed matron repeated to her neighbor behind her fan.

"Did My Lord Perfection indeed tear the dress half off that woman?" asked another, a barely suppressed grin on her gleeful face.

"Who is this mysterious woman?" several people wondered. In the crowded confusion of the ill-lit room no one had gotten a good look at her, and descriptions of the unknown female and of what had happened differed wildly from person to person. Events were quickly exaggerated so that some of the guests began to wonder maliciously if the woman had actually been compromised and to spitefully imagine what would happen if my lord Sterling were forced to offer for her.

Lady Chatterington need not have worried. Her ball was quite made—one of the most memorable events of the season. "What luck to be in attendance!" was the refrain heard on everyone's lips.

# *Chapter Six*

Unaware of the speculation that spread like wildfire among Lady Chatterington's guests, Laurel accompanied her fuming aunt to the ladies' withdrawing room. "Alas, your gown is past mending, Aunt Frankie . . . but 'tis just as well," she commented practically, as she fingered the worn material of the dress.

Frankie had no concern for her gown. "Oh, that abominable man! How dare that top-lofty, rag-mannered lout insult me so! Saying the whole incident was my fault, indeed! How dare he!" Frankie stormed, trying to keep her anger red-hot so that she wouldn't think of how her pulses had raced at her recent, embarrassingly intimate contact with the tall, well-built gentleman. She did not concede that mayhap he had as much reason to feel upset as she and had reacted out of character, hotly and without rational thought about what he was saying and doing to cover his own discomposure.

"Whom do you mean, Aunt?"

"Why, that ill-bred, starched-up dandy who stepped on my gown, galloped into me, and sent me flying to the floor before he proceeded to insult me in quite an ungentlemanly, childish fashion, that's who!" Frankie replied heatedly, keeping to herself what else he had done as his hands had inadvertently grasped various parts of her person. "'Tis his just deserts that he came a cropper and landed there himself."

Some of her ire dissipated as she remembered how ridiculous the man had looked with flowers decorating his hair and chest. She tried unsuccessfully to conceal her wide, engaging smile at the thought of such an impeccably dressed man looking so bedraggled. Why, the look of astonishment on his face had been hilariously incongruous.

Laurel stared incredulously at her grinning aunt and asked, "But do you not know who that was?"

"We were not formally introduced, if that is what you mean, before he proceeded to knock me down," Frankie answered dryly.

"B-b-but, Aunt Frankie, that was . . . was V-i-viscount Sterling! The . . . the Corinthian I told you about . . . on the way here." Laurel was giggling helplessly, feeling fearful and tickled at the same time. "Don't you remember?"

"Corinthian? The man's accounted a prime sportsman, you mean. How ridiculous! I wouldn't let that ungainly clod within twenty paces of a broken-down nag much less a prime bit of blood!" Letting someone who was inept handle a horse was sacrilege in Frankie's book. She arched a brow. "You must have confused the fellow with someone else. Perhaps he has a brother who has a reputation for superb horsemanship," Frankie joked, not without some mad hope that such was the case. For if such a superbly built man were to show to advantage in the sporting field, she felt she would have met her ideal— not if he were rude and coldly cutting in other situations, of course, she quickly amended, modifying her uncharacteristically fanciful thought.

"No, no, Aunt, I assure you. That was he, Lord Sterling. Sally pointed him out to me the moment he

78

entered the room, she was so excited. There could be no mistaking such a tall, handsome man—however wet." Laurel continued to giggle. She was amazed that she was not having hysterics over their probable social ruin, but the situation seemed too farcical to dwell on that.

"Do you mean to tell me that was the nonpareil you were praising to the skies on our way here?" Frankie exclaimed in mock astonishment.

"Oh, yes, indeed. 'The handsomest man at the ball,' Sally said."

"Handsome? Was he? I don't remember. I was too busy defending myself," Frankie replied evasively. She had remarked his height and superb build, but she had imperfectly observed the gentleman's features in the dim refreshment room, although she had been virtually nose to nose, toe to toe, and everything else in between with him. She had been too stunned at first, and then too furious, to see him clearly even at that close range but her overwhelming impression had been that he was a formidable, virile, and very attractive man. Such an impression she preferred to keep strictly to herself, however.

"And if that was your Corinthian, then either his reputation has been greatly exaggerated, or he was foxed and his brain so addled by drink he thought he was in the boxing ring by mistake, for he was so anxious to sport his canvas that he engaged *me* in a sparring match," she remarked in a lighter vein. It was useless; her anger was evaporating however much she tried to keep the fire of her resentment burning.

"Oh, Aunt, how you love to roast me! As if Viscount Sterling would do such a thing!"

"Well, I ask you? How else could one explain his actions?" Frankie laughed.

Lady Chatterington, accompanied by Sally, erupted into the room in full sail. "I am so sorry, my dear

79

Miss . . . umm . . . my dear."

"Miss Verdant, Mama," Sally hissed behind her fan.

"Ah, yes, Miss Verdant. My dear! I cannot *think* what could have occurred to cause such a shocking mishap." Frankie quirked a brow at the chattering woman.

"How such a dreadful thing could have befallen you will always remain a mystery to me. I hope you were not much hurt. I fear that it must have been a great shock to you, my dear Miss Verdant, as it was to me!" Lady Chatterington fanned herself vigorously.

"And to poor *dear* Lord Sterling! Why his breeches were quite soaked through! The poor man! A shocking sight! Why, it was a deal worse than some of the ladies who damp their petticoats, for being such a lean, well-muscled man—well, my stars!—everything was visible, you know.

"But let us not think of that," the garrulous matron continued. "We should not speak of it . . . though I know not how I shall contrive to forget it . . . Cannot your gown be mended, my dear?"

"As you see, ma'am," Frankie gestured at the ruined garment.

"No. Well, come along with me." She closed her fan with a snap of determination. "We shall have you put to rights in a trice. Letty, my elder gel, you know, left behind one or two gowns from her come-out last year. We shall see if my abigail can find something suitable for you, my dear." Inexorably Frankie and Laurel were swept along in Lady Chatterington's wake and led upstairs to her dressing room.

"You are tall, like my girls," Lady Chatterington said as she cast her eyes over Frankie's figure through her jeweled lorgnette. "Mayhap you are not quite so thin, though."

One of the gowns they found was deemed suitable, although it was cut much lower than Frankie was used to.

80

When she had slipped the gown of soft lilac muslin over her shoulders, Laurel exclaimed, "How well it looks on you, Aunt. 'Tis just such a color as you should wear."

"Yes, indeed. I declare the gown fits you amazingly well, my dear . . . although perhaps it *is* a bit tight in the bodice," Lady Chatterington commented when her abigail had finished buttoning the gown up the back.

"Come along, girls. We must return to the ballroom and staunch the gossip. Higgins will arrange your hair for you, Miss Verdant." Lady Chatterington rushed Laurel and Sally out of the room with as much energetic bustle as she had ushered them into it, leaving Frankie to the mercies of Higgins, her cheeky Cockney abigail.


"Miss, ye do 'ave remarkable thick 'air," Higgins commented as she combed out Frankie's locks, first to dry them, then to rearrange them. "'Ave ye h'ever taken a notion of 'avin' h'it cut just a bit . . . just 'ere, so's ye would 'ave some soft curls round yer pretty face. Leave h'it long 'ere at the back, see, and wear h'it up, or . . . 'angin' down h'over yer shoulder."

The abigail's deft fingers seemed to work magic with her tresses, Frankie thought, as Higgins pulled her hair back softly and pinned it up so that a long, glamorous curl fell forward over her left shoulder. Higgins then tied this with a deep lilac velvet ribbon to match the trimming on the gown.

"Can that be me?" Frankie exclaimed in disbelief as she peered at herself in the looking glass on the dressing table. "Why, I look quite amazingly different. I dare say I wouldn't recognize that woman if I passed her on the street." She laughed and shook her head in amazement.

"H'oh, h'indeed, miss. Ye look very pretty, h'indeed, jist as a young lady h'ought." Higgins beamed at the young woman transformed by her handiwork. She would have been amazed to learn that Miss Verdant had four-and-twenty years in her dish. Higgins had pegged her as not above nineteen or twenty.

"Miss 'as such loverly h'eyes. Do ye 'ave to 'ide 'em behind them h'eye-cheats?"

"Why, yes. I cannot see otherwise," Frankie replied with surprise. She was unused to compliments on her looks, despite Daph's frequent comments. She didn't believe she had "lovely" eyes; when she thought of them at all, which wasn't often, she regarded them only as short-sighted and rather commonplace, despite their strange color.

"H'oh, but, miss . . . at a ball, 'ow much do ye reelly 'ave to see?" Higgins persisted. She thought Miss Verdant was one of the most lovely young ladies—excepting the Misses Chatterington, of course—that she had ever "cast 'er peepers h'over" and it excited her to bring out the loveliness concealed behind unpromising clothes, badly arranged hair, and spectacles.

The kindly abigail saw before her a woman with a flawless complexion of exquisite ivory and eyes a mixture of violet and purplish-blue that she had never seen the like of before; besides which, they were framed by such arching black brows and fringed with such long black lashes that Miss Verdant resembled some exotic Eastern lady Higgins had seen illustrated in one of Lady Chatterington's picturebooks. And her rich chestnut hair was so thick, when brushed sufficiently, it shone with such gleaming highlights, that her remarkable complexion and eyes were set off to perfection, Higgins thought in an admiring assessment.

With the lady's lithe figure, small waist, well-curved bust, and long shapely legs, she should certainly be a hit with the gentlemen, Higgins reckoned with a knowing gleam in her eye, even though she *was* taller than the average.

82

Higgins found Miss Verdant totally unconscious of her charms, and this added to her determination to try to convince the lady to make the most of her assets. So unspoiled was the young lady's demeanor and such a frank, open manner she had, it was a pleasure to "do" for her, the abigail thought jovially.

"What h'I means h'is, miss, couldn't yet put them nasty things h'aside just for an evenin'."

"Well, I much fear I would run into something," Frankie replied with a smile. Then, remembering that she had been wearing her spectacles this evening and they certainly hadn't provided much protection, she took them off and absently put them in her reticule resting on the dressing table.

"H'oh, just take a gander at yerself, miss!" Higgins chortled, directing Frankie's eyes to the glass. "H'it 'minds me, Miss, m'lady Chatterington's 'ard of seein', too. M'lady wears 'er spectacles when lookin' over 'er h'accounts and such like. But, when she 'as 'er at 'omes or goes out of an evenin', she takes one of them glasses on a stick with 'er. Couldn't ye do as m'lady does, Miss?"

Frankie smiled at the abigail and said, "I will think on it. Thank you for your assistance this evening. You have been very kind."

"God bless ye, Miss, h'it's been a reel pleasure!" Higgins, holding the brush in her hand like a scepter and presiding over her kingdom with queenly authority, beamed with delight at Frankie's transformation. "Ye be a new lady, ye be." She chortled in glee, as she prepared to go down to her long-awaited tea and regale them all belowstairs with the tale of how she had changed an ugly duckling into a swan.

Frankie considered the abigail's words, echoing as they did some of the things Daph had been nagging her about earlier. She had never worried about dressing fashionably or looking attractive. She had thought it completely unimportant. She usually took no notice of such things, but tonight it had been impossible to ignore the churlish remarks and unkind stares of these so-called "polite" society people.

Now a niggling desire nipped at her to turn the tables on those who had made her evening so unpleasant. Several of the guests had stared at her in a most uncivil manner; once she had thought herself the object of pleasantry between two gentlemen, one of whom had nudged the other and gestured toward her before both had laughed. She would certainly like to show them! And those dowagers who had quizzed her so discourteously. And that rude gentleman of the refreshment room! Would it not be fun to give him a leveller! It would be an interesting experience to try such an experiment. If by aping their manners and fashions, she could set them down a trifle, then she would accept the challenge. She had never been known to shy at throwing her heart over a hedge, however unfamiliar the terrain on the other side.

In this rather abstracted state, Frankie stepped out of Lady Chatterington's dressing room and absently made her short-sighted way to the top of the stairs. She paused there for a few moments, lost in thought. Then she reached for the beaded reticule dangling at her wrist, meaning to take out her spectacles before she descended so that she could see her way to the ballroom, only to discover the bag missing.

"Oh, fie upon it! What did I do with that dratted reticule?" she asked herself, then realized that she must have left it on Lady Chatterington's dressing table and turned to retrace her steps. But in her abstraction she was not quite sure which was Lady Chatterington's room.

"Now was it the second door on the right, or on the left?" she wondered, unsure for a moment. Then she strode confidently forward.

She opened the second door on the right onto an ill-lit room—surely a dressing room from its size—and stepped in.

Philip Chatterington, at his mama's bidding, had indeed taken Viscount Sterling upstairs to his dressing room and loaned him a pair of dry breeches. Tolland, not feeling up to facing *anyone* at present, had declined Philip's offer to fetch his father's valet, as he did not have one of his own. The young man left Tolland to change in solitude. The laughter of Lady Chatterington's guests as he'd left the refreshment room still rang in Tolland's ears, and the avid curiosity upon their faces still tormented his brain. That such an accident could have happened to him was intolerable! It was beyond belief! Utterly impossible!

It was then that Tolland made a nasty discovery. Chatterington was a slender young sprig and unfortunately Philip's breeches were much too snug for his own muscular thighs. He found to his mounting frustration that he couldn't button them up. He cursed vociferously at this latest hobble. He seemed to have been plagued by a constant stream of catastrophes since he had stepped inside this accursed house! Some mocking god was making sport of him with these trials, he thought with brittle humor.

There seemed to be no bell pull in young Philip's room, and he knew of no other way to summon a servant short of bellowing down the hall. He could not put his own breeches on again for they lay in a soggy heap on the floor along with his ruined jacket, waistcoat, and the neckcloth he had spent so much time folding so precisely.

"Blast it all to hell and the devil!" he cursed violently. Standing in nothing but his shirt sleeves and the unbuttoned breeches, Tolland ground his teeth and beat his clenched fist against the dressing table at this fresh disaster. Was it only an hour ago that he had thought everything was perfect? he wondered, his lips twisting ironically. He glanced up and spied a full decanter of brandy on the dressing table. He reached for the bottle and the crystal snifter beside it, releasing another harsh curse and banging the bottle against the side of the glass in his haste to pour himself a strong drink.

"Devil take it! I'll be stuck here all night! ... Damnation to the season! And damnation to all women anyway!" Not the least of his grievances was the knowledge that he had clearly come off the worse from the encounter with the unknown female. He remembered the fury in the woman's stance when she had pronounced him no gentleman during their name-calling shouting match. He fingered his chin as though a blow had actually landed there—yes, he had richly deserved that facer for his unmannerly behavior, no matter how much she had provoked him. What in the name of heaven had possessed him to rip up at her so vehemently?

He rubbed his chin in a characteristic gesture as he recalled going to get a glass of punch. He had been staring out into the brightly lit ballroom a moment before turning into the relative darkness of the room where the refreshments were set out—Lady Chatterington must have been economizing for there certainly had been a sparsity of candles. Yes, he had been momentarily blinded, as he sometimes was of an evening when he had been looking into a lighter space and then tried to adjust his vision to a darker area. He'd sensed that there was someone there—a dark figure. Yes, her gown had been very dark.

His ankle had twisted in the material of the woman's gown, and reaching forward to steady himself he'd grabbed the woman and taken her to the floor with him—

virtually pulling her on top of himself. Tolland swallowed uneasily as he remembered the feel of the surprising curves under that unmodish gown pressed against his body. And her lips had been pressed to his face, too!

The woman had practically jumped to her feet and then had stepped back hastily as though contact with his person were distasteful! There had been a further sound of ripping, and his foot was suddenly free of the material. Damnation! a piece of her skirt must have been torn off entirely. And then, when he had been trying to fight off her unwanted help in rising, he had pulled her down on top of himself again instead!

And he remembered something else. "My God!" he thought, his lips had actually tasted hers, and they had not been at all nasty. Oh, no, indeed. Quite the reverse; they had been surprisingly soft and warm and yielding—for just those few seconds, of course. Well, he wouldn't stand for being made to look foolish of by some dowdy, undoubtedly mad, long-in-the-tooth spinster hoping to entrap him. Could she possibly have arranged the whole thing? He speculated for a moment only to disregard such a preposterous thought.

He poured himself another large measure of brandy.

"Higgins?" Frankie whispered in her low, musical voice as she entered the darkened dressing room, absently closing the door behind herself. The abigail must have extinguished most of the candles before she left, Frankie thought as she moved toward the dressing table to search for her missing reticule and spectacles.

The figure in the dim shadows turned unsteadily, sloshing brandy from a full snifter over the ruffled wristband of his shirt and hand as he did so.

"Who the devil are y—? . . . Ah!"

Tolland fell back as if he had been struck, so stunned

was he by the vision of a dark angel standing not ten feet away. Tall and shapely, with a cloud of dark hair framing her beautiful face, the lovely young woman seemed one more part of his confused dream—but a very pleasant part for the first time all evening.

"By all that's holy! You do teach the torches to burn bright, *mon ange*," he exclaimed in a fit of poetry as he gazed into eyes glinting brightly in the flickering candlelight.

"Good lord! I'm afraid I've mistaken the room. I *do* beg your pardon, sir . . ." Frankie said, not near enough to recognize her nemesis from the refreshment room.

"I may not be Higgins, whoever the lucky devil may be, but perhaps I'll do as well, *mon ange*." Tolland, who had been drinking brandy as though it were water to blot out the memory of his recent embarrassments, staggered toward Frankie only to stop suddenly and make a grab for his unbuttoned breeches. In his foggy state he had dropped the grip he had on the too-tight breeches and they had slipped slightly down his legs, revealing the linen smallclothes beneath.

"How dare you, sirrah! Clothe yourself at once!" Frankie's vision sharpened somewhat as she clearly saw the white of the gentleman's nethergarments in the dim light of the brace of candles on the dressing table. She began to back round the side of the room, unknowingly abandoning her position of comparative safety as she moved away from the door to the hallway, her only means of exit from the room.

Her throaty voice, as warm as the brandy he was drinking, sent a thrill down Tolland's spine, and in his muzzy state, he felt his legs begin to wobble.

Frankie continued to back away from him as he set down his drink and advanced toward her, still holding up his breeches with one hand.

"Well, my dear, a woman who comes into a

gentleman's dressing room must expect to see him in some state of undress," Tolland said as he pulled the breeches round his waist as tightly as he could manage, breathed in, and managed to close the two top buttons.

As he came nearer, Frankie recognized him now from their earlier encounters. She stopped moving for a moment and stood staring at the tall, muscular man before her, dressed in only his shirt sleeves and the too-tight breeches.

She realized her mistake in moving away from the exit to the hallway. "Don't come any nearer," she said huskily, as she quickly backed toward the door again.

Tolland took a hasty step forward, but just as he reached out to catch her by the shoulders and stop her from escaping, a loud, peremptory knock stopped him in his tracks. Before either of them could react further, someone pushed open the door, hitting Frankie a glancing blow in the back and causing her to catapult forward, straight into Tolland's arms.

He was only too ready to receive her and smiled down at her rather lopsidedly as he clutched her to his breast. "Angel," he whispered and without a moment's hesitation brought his lips down to cover hers in a swift kiss.

"I say!" Philip Chatterington entered the room only to be brought up short by the sight of a woman in Tolland's arms. "What's going on here, my lord?" Philip questioned as he stared at them, goggle-eyed. He didn't recognize the lovely lady in Tolland's embrace. Had such a charmer been at his mother's party? he wondered, mouth agape.

Tolland looked up from the mesmerizing eyes of the startled woman he held in his arms. "I think at this juncture it would be a good idea to take yourself off, young Philip."

"No, no—wait!" Frankie tried to say, but seeing that he was very much *de trop*, the red-faced Philip had already fled, hastily slamming the door behind him and drowning out Frankie's call.

"Let me go, you blackguard!" Frankie tried to struggle, but Tolland held her so tightly and his blazing blue eyes gazed down at her so hungrily that she was momentarily overwhelmed. A strange sensation coursed through her veins at the contact. Her heart was beating rapidly in her breast. She had never been held this closely by a man, and never, never had she felt so strong a physical reaction—why, her bones seemed to have turned to water. What in the world was happening to her? she wondered in some distant corner of her mind.

As the door closed behind Philip, Tolland tightened his hold on her.

"Such eyes, madam!" he said in a whisper as his eyes bored into hers from only inches away. "Such a *heavenly* body . . . Yes—you must indeed be an angel!" His gaze traveled down her body for a moment before coming back up to rest on her full, wide mouth. Frankie looked at him wide-eyed, feeling too stunned to move. She doubted that her legs could support her at that moment should she make the attempt.

"There's nothing else for it, my dear angel." Tolland knew that he must kiss her properly or regret it for the rest of his life. Slowly he brought his lips down to hers and began to kiss her softly, then more deeply. In the midst of his passionate kiss, he had the strange feeling that he had encountered her somewhere before—had even embraced her and tasted her soft lips.

Frankie's arms crept up round his neck, seemingly of their own accord, as she felt herself begin to melt into his kiss. Then, as she tasted the brandy on his lips, she regained control of her disordered senses and pushed him away. "Let me go! How dare you, you cad!," she said as she delivered a full-bodied, stinging blow to his cheek and turned quickly toward the door.

His cheek stinging madly, Tolland lunged for her, only to be brought up short by a loud, ripping sound. His too-tight breeches had split down the back!

"Damnation, what next?" he groaned, as Frankie groped for the door handle and made her escape.

# *Chapter Seven*

The recent commotion did not seem to have cast a damper on the evening as Lady Chatterington had feared, rather otherwise, for the ball had taken on an added gaiety and a new sparkle after the excitement of the accident. There was much speculation as to what had happened to the woman involved in the incident. The general conjecture was that she had left the house— voluntarily or otherwise.

Her lips still tingling, her breathing still shallow, Frankie flew down the stairs in a temper, forgetting to search for her reticule and spectacles, wondering what on earth had possessed her to let herself be embraced so ardently without putting up more of a fight.

"That blasted rake! Who does he think he is that he can maul me about so!" she fumed. It was the most unlucky mischance that she had chosen the wrong door the first time she had tried.

She traversed the ballroom, peering about, trying with some difficulty to locate Laurel. No one seemed to recognize her as the woman involved in the contretemps with Sterling as she made her way from one side of the room to the other. Indeed, two or three gentlemen turned to look at her with appreciative smiles on their faces. One gallant even made her a flourishing bow. Frankie didn't take much notice; she was still too caught up in reflecting on her recent encounter and had completely forgotten that she had been "transformed" into a glamorous lady. Nor did she have an inkling of a notion that her cheeks glowing with such high color and her eyes gleaming so brightly caused more than one male to turn and stare after her appreciatively.

Quite by good luck she came upon Laurel in conversation with two gentlemen near the floor-to-ceiling windows at the southern end of the room. Frankie hoped she might persuade her niece that it was time to take their leave. She wanted to put as much space as she could between herself and the mad monster getting himself thoroughly foxed abovestairs.

But a sparkling Laurel was happily enjoying her first ball, despite the interlude in the refreshment room, and was quite prepared to dance the rest of the night away.

"Oh, Aunt Frankie, there you are." She turned to Frankie, a bright smile lighting up her whole face as she took in her aunt's changed appearance. Not missing a beat, she made Frankie known to the two gentlemen at her side.

"May I present Lord Harry Markham and Mr. Freddy Drake . . . Lord Harry, Mr. Drake . . . my aunt, Miss Francesca Verdant."

Lord Harry took Frankie's hand, saying, "A very great pleasure, Miss Verdant." His hazel eyes twinkled down at her in such a knowing way that Frankie was immediately suspicious that she had been discovered after all. "I see that Miss Whittgrove does not have a monopoly on all the beauty in the family, as I had thought. It must be a family trait—well, amongst the ladies of the family, anyway, I trust." He laughed lightly at the small pleasantry.

Frankie was nonplussed at the compliment and looked with raised brows to her niece.

"Lord Harry is a very great tease, Aunt Frankie," Laurel whispered *sotto voce* behind her fan, glancing flirtatiously up at the gentleman as she did so. Then, bending closer to Frankie's ear, she whispered, "The new hair style definitely suits you, Aunt. And I'm so glad you've left off your spectacles."

Frankie blinked as Freddy Drake bowed over her hand, much more swiftly than had his friend, and uttered a garbled compliment.

"How do you do, Mr. Drake?"

"Don't let Freddy's manners offend you, Miss Verdant," Lord Harry said laughingly. "The poor fellow hasn't much use for social gatherings, I'm sorry to report. He's much more at home in the saddle than at a fashionable party."

"Then he should have much in common with Aunt Frankie for she has a great love for horses. She runs my grandfather's stables, you know."

Freddy's ears perked up at this piece of information, and he turned a beaming smile on Frankie.

"You don't say a lady like you runs a breeding stables?" Freddy asked.

"Oh, yes. Indeed, I have charge of all our horses at Verdant Meadows Stables." Frankie grinned widely at his look of amazement.

"By Jupiter! If that don't beat all! Why, those are the best breeding stables in Cambridgeshire!"

Seeing that she had a willing listener, Frankie fell into her businesslike manner usually reserved for the stable's customers, and began to satisfy his well-informed questions about the stock at Verdant Meadows. Nothing could have been guaranteed to afford her more pleasure and to more readily take her mind off her recent encounters with the arrogant viscount than Drake's enthusiastic interest.

Frankie continued to converse with the likable young man as Laurel danced off on Lord Harry's arm once again. She and Freddy sat and talked about nothing but horses and hunting until both lost track of the time. He was a member of the Corinthian set, a well-muscled young man of medium height and rather fair complexion. He did not seem at all dandified, and when he confessed that he rarely frequented balls and was an indifferent dancer, Frankie decided she liked him amazingly. Athletic and sporting mad, she thought; surely he would be a valuable customer for Verdant Meadows.

"You say your father bought Arabian mares to breed with an English-bred stallion?" Freddy asked with avid interest.

Frankie happily launched into a knowledgeable explanation of how her father had carefully built up the reputation of the stables, over the twenty years preceding his death, by the acquisition of superior blood stock, both Arabic and English. "He bred his mares to a succession of thoroughbred stallions culminating in the birth of our prize colt, Red Devil, eleven years ago. The Devil is a descendant of the Godolphin Arabian, you know."

"Good God! He was one of the greatest thoroughbreds ever known in this country!" Freddy was suitably impressed.

"Yes, indeed. You should come and meet the Devil someday, Mr. Drake. He has grown into a magnificent stallion. His services are much in demand, as you can imagine . . . He is the sire of my own horse, Black Demon, though Demon has not the Devil's color," Frankie explained.

"By Jove, Miss Verdant, he sounds first rate! I hope you'll allow me to see him."

96

"Why, certainly. I'll be happy to put Demon through his paces for you, sir."

"What say you we make up a riding party for tomorrow? . . . Perhaps Markham and Miss Whittgrove would care to join us?" Freddy was anxious to have a gander at this horse of Miss Verdant's.

"I'm afraid Demon has not yet arrived from Verdant Meadows. He should be here within the week, however."

"What a shame. Perhaps you would care to accept one of my mounts until your own horse can be brought up to town, ma'am?"

"Thank you, sir, that is most kind, but I have arranged to ride my sister's hack in the park until Demon arrives."

"Well, then, we could still make up our party, couldn't we?"

"Yes, of course, providing my niece has no other engagement. I should enjoy it." Frankie did not expect that Daph's animal would tax her skill, but as she hated to miss even one day in the saddle, she would ride anything until she had her own beloved gelding again. She was confident that she rode as well as any other lady in London, and suspected that even some gentlemen would have a hard time keeping up with her.

It was her hope that Demon would be noticed and inquiries about the ancestry of such a first-rate blood animal would follow. What better way to bring his sire, Red Devil, to the attention of the *ton?* She would not feel as though she had totally abandoned her duties if the Verdant Meadows Stables could be advertised in such a way.

Freddy was duly impressed by Frankie's knowledge of horseflesh, and although not known as a ladies' man, he admired her style of beauty, too. He took her into supper, where they joined Laurel and Markham and put the idea of a riding party to them. Both immediately accepted. Laurel did so despite the fact that riding was one of her

97

least favorite activities. She had another inducement to cause her to agree.

Much to Frankie's amazement, her hand was actually solicited for two sets of country dances after supper. Although she had not much experience at this particular diversion, she acquitted herself well. Only with her brother James, when he was learning the social graces and needed a partner, had she had any practice in standing up with a gentleman. But with her inborn athletic grace, and a heretofore unsuspected aptitude for dancing, and despite the fact that she was not wearing her spectacles, she got through the sets without once tripping up or disgracing her partners. Though she found most of those partners to be fashionable fribbles full of foolish, faddish chatter and empty, fulsome flattery that left her with no opportunity to mention the Verdant Meadows Stables. Just as well, she harrumphed to herself, such foppish gentlemen could not be competent sportsmen, she was sure.

As the ball wound down to its inevitable conclusion, Frankie stood chatting with Lord Harry. He was determined to make a good impression on Miss Whittgrove's chaperon. He had been given quite a leveller by that young lady. Why, he thought, his heart had turned over in his breast when he'd first gazed into her ever-changing green eyes and seen her smile up at him so winsomely. "The little darling!" he thought to himself.

Frankie couldn't help but like him. He was an easy companion, and no doubt about it, he knew horses as well as did his friend, Freddy Drake. This business of chaperoning Laurel about could afford her some pleasure, after all, she thought happily, temporarily putting the earlier incidents of the evening from her mind.

Unaware that Frankie had been the woman who had been involved in the accident with his friend, Markham began to recount the viscount's injuries.

"I fear my friend Sterling will long bear a reminder of this night's adventure. He took a nasty cut on his forehead. A wound like that could leave a permanent mark," he remarked conversationally. "And he'll be hobbled for some time with that turned ankle. Wouldn't like to have a taste of his temper when he's told he can't ride for a few days!"

"Was the gentleman much hurt, then? I did not realize . . ." she broke off. Despite her dealings with the infuriating man, Frankie's concern was aroused when she heard that his injuries might have serious consequences. In the dark shadows of the dressing room she had not remembered his head injury, nor had she realized that his ankle was hurt. She had not thought anything but his consequence had been bruised during the earlier episode.

"I hope there is no chance of permanent disfigurement, then, from this evening's accident. And I know that I should dislike it excessively if I had to forgo my daily rides," Frankie remarked, surprised that she should feel sympathy for the man after his insulting behavior. But she did. Her interest in alleviating physical ailments and injuries was aroused. She had a recipe for a mixture of olive oil and St.-John's-wort flowers, known as red oil, that she had used from time to time with some success on deep cuts to the horses' legs in an effort to promote healing and lessen scars. And she *did* know of a wondrous herbal preparation for twists and sprains. For a brief moment she had an overwhelming urge to send the viscount something for his wounds by way of Lord Harry, who seemed to be on intimate terms with him. But she checked the impulse before she could give in to it.

Why, the man had amorously assaulted her upstairs after earlier telling her quite unequivocally to get away from him, that he wanted none of her help. Clearly, he

99

did not realize who she was when he had made his improper advances. Nevertheless she would leave him alone to suffer the consequences of his clumsiness, as he so plainly wished.

Fie upon it, why should I care what becomes of him? she asked herself impatiently, annoyed that this discussion had caused her to remember him as he had looked sprawled on the floor with flowers covering his head and chest and a disoriented look in those blue, blue eyes gazing woozily up at her from under the shock of wet, dark hair falling into them . . . and as he had looked later when he had held her tightly and gazed down at her out of those same brilliantly colored eyes. Really, his behavior to her made any solicitousness on her part unthinkable, she reminded herself severely.

"Do not overly concern yourself, Miss Verdant," Markham said, breaking into her thoughts. "Tol can do with something to mar his perfection, you know. Might turn him into a human like the rest of us mortals." He laughed.

"I take it the viscount is a bad-tempered man?" Frankie inquired.

"No, no, Miss Verdant, you misunderstand. It's just that Tol has had a flawless career. He's never had an accident of any kind before, that anyone is aware of. I daresay he hasn't taken a tumble since he was in leading strings." There was good humor radiating from Lord Harry's eyes. "He's the best of good fellows, but sometimes he needs the starch taken out of him. He shall come about, never fear."

Laurel came up to them at that moment, and Frankie was standing near enough to see how Lord Harry's face lit up at her niece's approach. Laurel, too, was smiling at the young man with a look upon her countenance that her aunt could only describe as moonstruck. Though usually unperceptive, Frankie could almost feel the tug of attraction between the pair as they smiled at one another.

Oh lord, Frankie thought, Laurel has gone and formed a *tendre* at her very first ball! Well, I must say Lord Harry looks like a true sportsman, at any rate. We shall just have to see how he sits his mount and handles the reins, she mused.

"Well, niece, I believe 'tis time we took our leave," she said aloud.

"Oh, no, must we, Aunt Frankie?" Laurel breathed out the words soulfully, still gazing starry-eyed at young Markham who could not take his own eyes from her face. "Please, let us remain a while longer," she begged.

"I am much afraid that it has gone half past one already. Come, Laurel, we must go."

"Pray, allow me to escort you to your carriage, Miss Whittgrove . . . With your permission, of course, Miss Verdant," Lord Harry entreated, extending one arm to Laurel and the other, a bit belatedly, to Frankie.


An excited Laurel amused Frankie on the way home with incessant chatter about the people she had met and the events of the evening. At one point she brought a look of annoyance to Frankie's face by remarking that "Viscount Sterling looked devastatingly handsome even with his wet black hair falling over his face and into his eyes in the refreshment room." This was accompanied by a gusty sigh. As though the gentleman were some hero of a gothic romance by Mrs. Radcliffe! Frankie thought, disgustedly.

"I give not a fig for his looks!" Frankie insisted in some heat. But, contrary to her vehement exclamation, she could not forget anything about the man who had first assaulted and insulted her, then kissed her. The fellow must be mad as a hatter, she thought with a reluctant grin.

101

When she and Laurel reached Whittgrove House, Frankie was not sorry to hear Fennel's report that her ladyship had been unable to keep her eyes open, hard as she had tried to remain awake until they returned, and so had gone to bed. Frankie was glad that she could postpone her chat with Daph until the morrow, for her mind was still in a whirl after the evening's adventures. She tried to sort things out as she lay awake long after she had retired to her bedchamber.

Uppermost in her confused thoughts was why Sterling had kissed her and called her his angel when she had blundered into the wrong room. In all her uneventful four and twenty years such a thing was unprecedented. True, she had just come from Higgins and the looking glass had told her she looked quite unlike her usual self. And true also, she hadn't much experience of the *ton*, but she'd certainly been able to handle any of its many male denizens who'd come to Cambridgeshire to buy horses or to use the Stable's breeding services.

Why was it that she had responded to his kiss in such a way? She loathed the man, didn't she? Then why couldn't she get his kiss out of her mind? What in the world had happened to her, anyway? Why, her senses had been swimming and her knees had nearly buckled! Just to think of it now sent her pulses racing . . . His kiss had been soft and tender, quite unlike anything she had expected a kiss to be, and he had held her pressed so tightly to himself—but he had been dead drunk, of course.

She wondered how he would respond to her if he was sober, and a grin lit her face in the dark as she considered how he would react when he came face to face with her again when she had gotten her new wardrobe. She chuckled at the thought that it would be interesting to confront him again in her new guise as one of those fashionable, empty-headed females she so despised.

More soberly, she wondered if men always took advantage of women so? She didn't know, not being experienced in the wicked ways of the *ton*. Of a certainty she had been partly at fault by blundering into the wrong room. What a sight he had been, looking even more untidy and rumpled, if such a thing were possible, than he had looked in the refreshment room. On a sputter of laughter Frankie remembered how he had almost lost his breeches. How embarrassed he must be at this very moment!

And then, disgusted with herself for giving so much of her attention to such a fashionable fribble, Frankie turned her thoughts away from the viscount and focused once more on her horses and the Verdant Meadows Stables.

She couldn't help but wish that she knew what was going on there, however much she trusted her head groom Trot—Phineas Trotmore—to see to the everyday running of things. She and her brother had worked hard to maintain the standard set by their father; up with the sun, in the saddle half the day, and to bed late into the night after toiling over the estate books. But it was a labor of love and she sorely missed it. Now she would distract herself by making a May game of the gullible *ton* by disguising herself as a lady of fashion. She laughed to herself at the absurd notion of Frankie Verdant as a frivolous featherhead and promptly fell asleep.

After the lovely woman had run out of the room, Tolland cursed anew the disasters of the evening. He pulled on his own wet ruined breeches, limped down the stairs, called for his carriage, and managed to take himself off home. His brain was in a whirl from the brandy fumes and thoughts of not one, but two, unknown women he had met so disastrously that evening.

To be allowed to wallow alone in his misery was more than the viscount could have hoped for. With perfect timing, his cousin crossed the hallway just as Tolland descended the stairs. Monty immediately decided to give the viscount the honor of his company on the way back to Bruton Place. A dubious honor, Tolland considered it as he looked askance at Monty sitting opposite him in the carriage.

He thanked God Monty didn't know about the episode in young Chatterington's dressing room, Tolland sighed. He rested his throbbing head on his fisted hand and gazed glumly out the window, trying to forget the events that had led to the most disastrous evening of his life.

"In quite a tempest, you was. Ain't never seen you so up in the boughs, coz," Monty chattered on to his scowling relative.

"Up in the boughs! . . . Hell and the devil man, I had every right to be in a temper!" Tolland shouted, with a menacing frown marring his handsome features. *Every right . . . every right . . . every right to be in a temper,* kept reverberating through his aching head all the way home.

"How'd you come to be flailin' about so, Tol?" Monty asked, as he grasped the viscount's arm to help him from the carriage when it halted in Bruton Place. "Ain't like you at all."

Tolland descended from his carriage with difficulty, hampered by his sore ankle and by Monty hanging onto him. He attempted to shake his arm loose from his cousin's grasp as he limped up the steps to his front door and addressed his unwanted convoy, "I wish you would take youself off, Monty. I don't need you to escort me home."

"Don't want to put a damper on the evenin', but you're as wet as a herring, coz. Think you can limp into port on your drenched peg?"

Tolland just looked at him with pursed lips and lowered brow.

"Tell you what—you was dished by that deuced dizzy bee thing again, Tol."

"Dishabille, dishabille!" shouted Tolland, feeling more sorely tried than ever.

"Egad, no need to put yourself about," said the lanky knight, covering his ears. "Always have the *ton*'s attendance, coz; didn't know you'd want to make yourself the toast of the evenin', as well. Something wet, don't y'know! . . . Heard that dashed gabble-mongerin' Lady Chatterin'tongue eulogizin' to you, too, after you'd dearranged her furniture for her. Whew! Whole ramshackle lot in the place must've seen you sprawled. Hee-hee. Looked a real Adolphous with damp flowers in your hair, y'know," Monty continued in a high falsetto. "Damn me, I ain't ever glimmered so funny a sight." He guffawed loudly.

"Damn you, then! Why don't you go home?" asked Tolland, rudely. "Deuced jabbernoll," he muttered.

"Wouldn't think of disbandonin' a sinkin' ship, coz, when it's got a leak in its brow," he said, pointing to his own forehead. "Might tipple to starboard on your wounded pedestal, don't y'know." Here Sir Monty collapsed on the steps, overcome with mirth.

Jenks opened the door to his grimacing, disheveled employer. The astonished butler, used to the most civil of greetings from the viscount, received only a grunt in reply to his "Good evening, m'lord . . . Sir Montagu."

The correct retainer could only look with amazement from his usually impeccably groomed employer, who now looked as though he had pulled through a hedge backward, to the indecorous sight of m'lord's cousin doubled up with laughter on the front step.

Tolland stomped through to his study. Monty, recovering somewhat, picked himself up and trailed along, the sight of his wet and rumpled cousin still affording him much amusement. The viscount uncorked the bottle of Madeira sitting on his desk and poured himself a generous portion. His upset at the unwonted loss of control, both physical and emotional, he had exhibited that night was considerable. The final humiliation of ripping open the borrowed pair of breeches down the rear seam had sobered him up quite considerably, and despite the quantity of brandy he had drunk earlier, he felt the need for further consolation.

Addlecumber watched him down the wine in two gulps. "By gad, thought you was wet enough to damp down any amount of fire without pourin' more liquid down your gullet. Sure to sink now, coz."

"Your misguided remarks are out of place, Monty. I'm in no case to tolerate your execrable jokes tonight," Tolland said through gritted teeth, as he filled his glass again.

"Ain't you gonna offer me a glass, Tol? Both drown your doles, don't y'know—would've thought you'd want no more a-drownin' tonight, though," Addlecumber positively sputtered as he delivered himself up of yet another bit of ill-timed and muddled drollery.

Tolland saw nothing else for it. He took hold of his cousin's beautiful jacket near the neck and bundled him to the door, calling loudly to his butler, "Throw him out, Jenks. There's a good fellow."

"Here, I say, Tol. Take a damper." Nothing seemed to quell the unquenchable Monty. "No need to ruin m'coat, y'know. 'M goin', 'M goin'. Heave ho!" And with that Parthian shot Addlecumber took himself off, leaving his relative to his soggy reflections.


Tolland removed his wet, ruined jacket and limped to his favorite chair where he sat in his shirt sleeves in front of a low fire. He held the untouched glass of Madeira in his hand and touched his still tender forehead gingerly. He was thankful, at least, that the bleeding had long since stopped. The damn thing would likely leave a scar, he thought with a grimace. That was a trifle to mar his good looks, the permanent scar would be to his reputation.

He raised his injured foot to a footstool, picked up a Meissen vase from a nearby table and fingered its cool, rounded shape as he sat back to let his thoughts run where they would over the evening's disaster and to contemplate his next course of action.

Tolland ran his long, slender fingers through his disordered locks in an effort to come to grips with the calamity. In all honesty he had to conclude that the incident in the refreshment room had not been the woman's fault. But then, it had not exactly been his. It was just a most infelicitous accident.

Hell and the devil! He *never* had accidents! He was known for his athleticism; he had always been exceptionally well coordinated and balanced on his toes. He had *never* fallen from a horse, for instance. Even when he was mounted on a spirited, half-broke stallion or when he was jumping an impossible obstacle in the hunting field, he had always brought himself and his animals off safely.

True, he had been knocked down in the ring once or twice, but that was because his opponent was the great Gentleman Jackson himself. The former champion was able to pop one in over his guard now and then.

Would people stare and gossip and point him out as the clumsy oaf the woman had called him? He could not bear to be taken for an object of fun. He kicked at the fender with his right foot in frustration, forgetting he was wearing only evening pumps, thus sustaining a bruise to his hitherto uninjured foot. He cursed again, then sighed.

And he had been inexcusably rude to the poor, dowdy

107

woman afterward. Why had he lost his temper so thoroughly anyway? That she had put him in the wrong galled him unbearably. He had always considered himself an unemotional, even-tempered sort of person. Why, he dealt in icy set-downs, not choleric outbursts!

Who was she anyway? He supposed that he should find out and apologize . . . But no, it would be too distasteful to make any inquiries about the fiendish creature. Perhaps she *was* someone's lunatic aunt, and her relatives would take exception to the rudeness he had shown her and would be calling him out on the morrow.

Damn! He would find it difficult to ride tomorrow with a bad ankle, but he wasn't going to miss his favorite exercise. Blast! And damn, again!

Devil take it! He hated to be caught off guard in any situation. What was most unendurable was whether his social standing, his reputation for impeccable behavior, would be diminished in any way? He had spent ten years building up an impenetrable shield of invulnerability. But there was really nothing to concern himself with. The whole thing would be forgotten in a week, most like, he tried to assure himself. People would just assume that he was the innocent victim of a clumsy woman. After all, she wore spectacles; there must be something wrong with her eyesight.

He again recalled those grinning faces staring at him as he left the ballroom. God, but he had wanted to vanish into thin air. Many pairs of eyes, alight with glee at his fall from gracefulness, had turned his way, and much nudging and whispering had gone on as he had quickly made his way out of the ballroom, trying not to limp and not daring to hold a cloth to his bleeding head as he went up the stairs to change his wet clothes in young Chatterington's dressing room.

Chatterington's dressing room . . .

Would that he had gone straight out and ordered his

coach instead of going upstairs! But no! The memory of that face would haunt his dreams for many a night.

Tolland bit his lip as he laid his head back against the chair cushion and closed his eyes, letting his thoughts turn to the other unknown woman—the woman who had appeared suddenly in the dressing room to find him in dishabille.

My God, but she had been beautiful! Even in the light of the single pair of candles burning on the dressing table he had seen her loveliness well enough. Her bewitching eyes had sparkled even in that dim light, and her deep, musical voice had turned his bones to butter.

Hang it all! He couldn't help kissing her. The urge had been irresistible. She had felt so good in his arms—so right. They had been of a height, a perfect match, and the thought of her heavenly body held tightly against his sent his temperature soaring again. He had never known such an overwhelming physical response to a woman in all his life.

Why, drunk as he was, he would probably have been down on one knee making her an offer in another minute if his damn breeches hadn't ripped!

He closed his eyes again and fancied he could still detect the scent she wore, a delicate flowery perfume; he hadn't encountered its like before. He winced, pulling at the cut on his forehead. Devil take it, he thought, the permanent scar wouldn't be from the wound he had sustained to his body but the one to his heart—inflicted by his unknown dark angel. Now if she were the one to demand restitution, he would have a hard time refusing to comply. But—damn it all!—he didn't even know her name.

Fool! Idiot! What the blasted hell was wrong with him! Was he losing his mind? Or had he been knocked down so hard by the dowd that his senses had been disordered?

Thank God the solicitous Lady Amelia hadn't been

there to see his disgrace. The Fox would have been sure to use it in some way to entangle him in one of the schemes that he had successfully evaded for three years now. Probably would have insisted on accompanying him home and bandaging his foot, too. Blast the woman! Blast all women!

His lips twisted ironically; consigning half of humanity to perdition didn't make him feel any better. He reached for the decanter and poured himself another glass of the amber-colored wine. Perhaps these Bacchic rites would provide some temporary consolation at least. He sighed.

# *Chapter Eight*

Laurel and Frankie did not lie abed much past nine of the clock next morning despite their raking of the night before. An hour later saw them seated in the breakfast parlor, partaking of a light repast, when Daphne fluttered in and began to question them in an excited fashion.

"Well, my dears, tell me all about it," she said as she smiled at them expectantly. "I vow, I could not for the life of me keep my eyes open last night, try as I might."

"I believe you have cause for congratulation, Daph— your daughter is a raging success," Frankie said, looking over to Laurel who was smiling happily. "She did not sit out one dance. I don't know where she found the energy. I wish she would show as much in the saddle."

Daphne clapped her hands together like a girl and bubbled over with joy. "Were you much remarked, then? I had hoped you would be much sought after. Who were your partners, my love? Who took you in to supper? Did you truly enjoy your evening? Pray, tell me *everything*."

"Well, Mama, I danced with Sir Lucius Pendergast, Mr. Freddy Drake, Sally's brother, Philip, Mr. George Osbourne, Lord Harry Markham," Laurel colored faintly as she pronounced the last name and watched carefully

111

for her mother's reaction, "and three or four others whose names I cannot recall just at present. I have saved my dance card upstairs. Do you wish to see it?"

"Oh, above all things. What fun! Fancy you attracting all those young bucks!" Daphne was in high gig. "And who was your supper partner, my love?"

Laurel flushed and looked slightly confused as she replied, "We were with a large group of people at supper, including Lord Harry Markham and Mr. Drake. Of course, Aunt Frankie was there, too—that was after the mishap." Laurel immediately clapped a hand over her mouth, but it was too late.

"Mishap?" said her fond mama, delicate blond brows rising in anxious query as she looked at Frankie.

"Well, Daph, I was in the refreshment room when a gentleman trod on my skirt and tripped. He fell against a table and my skirt was torn. It was all a most unfortunate accident." Frankie decided that an abbreviated account of the scene and its aftermath was most politic.

"Oh, Mama, you'll never guess who the *gentleman* was," interrupted Laurel, greatly excited. "It was 'My Lord Perfection'!"

Daphne's rounded eyes were a mirror of her daughter's as she heard this news. "What! Surely not Viscount Sterling! Why Tolland Hansohm is accounted a great nonpareil! A high stickler, indeed. Why, 'tis too droll for words!"

"Oh, yes, it was indeed the Nonesuch," Laurel giggled. "Then Aunt Frankie had to change into a gown left behind by Letty Chatterington, for her own was rent beyond repair. Oh, Mama, Letty's gown suited her extremely and she left off her spectacles, too."

"Did you, my dear? How happy I am. 'Twas a great piece of good fortune, then, this mishap of yours." Daphne beamed at her sister.

"Yes, and everyone remarked how well she looked.

112

She will have to order some new clothes now," Laurel said on a giggle, while she almost bounced in her chair in satisfied glee.

After an admonition from her mother not to be such a harum-scarum girl, Laurel subsided and Daphne directed an inquiring glance at Frankie.

"Well, I plan to order two or three new gowns. And I shall certainly have a new habit made up directly, for my Demon should be here any day now," Frankie answered. In the clear light of morning, she considered that the money spent on clothes could well go toward the purchase of new breeding stock for Verdant Meadows instead of being thrown away on gowns, many of which she did not envision wearing above a time or two.

"Pish-tish. Don't talk such fustian," said Daphne firmly. "You need a whole new wardrobe to replace all those dismal rags you brought with you."

Frankie raised a hand in caution. "I have not decided how extensively I shall add to my wardrobe. There is a mare I wish to purchase from the squire, and I do not have all that much cash to spare."

"Oh, all you ever think about is horses!" Daphne exclaimed in exasperation. "Let the Stables go hang, for once. You shall not be such a goose as to go about not properly gowned—why, 'tis folly. The *ton* will think you ever so 'green' if you persist in dressing like a shag-bag. Now, shall I have a seamstress call here or will you use Madame Eugénie?"

"Well, we can't have the *ton* thinking me 'green,' now, can we," Frankie asserted, a light flashing in her eyes as the snubs she had received the evening before were brought freshly to mind.

Daphne clapped her hands happily as Frankie agreed to visit Madame Eugénie that morning. "What fun! Oh dear, I do wish I could go with you to help choose all you will need." And visions of shoes and bonnets, gloves and

113

shawls, ribbons and fans, flitted through her head. "Do let us have your hair cut into a more fashionable style, too. It will suit you amazingly, you'll see," Daphne chattered on enthusiastically.

An hour later saw Frankie on her way to Bond Street. If she was going to turn herself into a lady of fashion, then she was determined to waste no time about it. She grinned as she remembered Daph's ecstatic exclamations when she had announced her decision at the breakfast table.

The day had dawned fair but with a chill wind blowing. Those who ventured out stood in danger of being bowled over by its gusts. Frankie was on her way to her sister's favorite dressmaker, Madame Eugénie, a rather exclusive modiste, patronized not only by Lady Whittgrove but by a goodly portion of the *beau monde* as well.

She was accompanied by Laurel's maid, Tizzy, whose cold had abated somewhat but who was still capable of taking her unawares at odd moments with an explosive sneeze or two. The little maid insisted that she was "right as a rivet" after being cajoled into imbibing one of Frankie's herbal mixtures.

"Woods, wait here for me," Frankie said to the Whittgrove coachman as she got out of the carriage at one end of Bond Street. "Come along, Tizzy." She blithely set off on a brisk walk with the maid snuffling and sneezing at her heels. It was a lovely, invigorating morning in Frankie's opinion, despite the cold breeze, and there was a spring in her step as she took in the sights and sounds along the fashionable street, usually crowded with elegant shoppers and strollers.

Her spectacles glinted in the morning sun as she strode along. She intended to send Tizzy to purchase a lorgnette for her while she herself was busy at the modiste's. As she walked down the street she was amused several times by the sight of men chasing their tall, beaver hats as they

114

were blown off by the stiff wind. Few ladies had ventured out in the gale, she noticed.

She was wearing a serviceable old grey pelisse and an ugly poke bonnet that had the advantage of being tied tightly under her chin. Despite Daphne's protestations that the modiste should come to the house so that she would not chance being seen by any gossip-mongering old cats, Frankie had refused to fall in with her sister's wishes.

"There's little likelihood I'll embarrass you today, Daph. Who would recognize me?" she had argued. "Especially in such an unlikely place as Bond Street!" she had added, mocking her own heretofore lack of interest in such a modish place.

Today her first priority was to have a new habit made up as she had always intended. Her old brown worsted was just a tad shabby—it received such hard usage, it was no wonder. Daph had tried to get her to look at some of the illustrations in back copies of the *Ladies' Magazine*, but Frankie was not interested.

"Good lord, why else does one hire a modiste if not to select the color and material for one's costumes as well as supply a good cut in the garments. Anything will do for me."

Daph, of course, had been horrified and had written out instructions for Madame Eugénie for the riding costume, as well as a list of frocks that she wanted her sister to have made up. The slip of paper was safely tucked away in Frankie's pocket. Daphne had insisted that the new habit was to be made of velvet, a deep green shade if Madame Eugénie could procure such a color in the soft, luxurious cloth. It was to be trimmed with black frogging and topped by a black velvet hat with a green feather like the one she had seen illustrated so dashingly in her latest copy of *La Belle Assemblée*.

Frankie had grinned at her sister's enthusiasms and

promised to obey, for once. Now that she had given in to Daphne's wishes and was going to order a new wardrobe, the old dragons and a certain gentleman would just have to look out, she thought with a martial gleam in her eyes at the anticipation of some fun.

Her attention was caught by some political illustrations displayed in one of the shop windows along the fashionable street. She stopped to peer in the window and veered across the pathway to have a closer look at them. Ah, a satirical cartoon! A caricature of two dandies out on the town, Jerry Hawthorne and Corinthian Tom, no doubt. She had seen this sort of pictorial satire before in a periodical her father had subscribed to.

Tizzy gave a particularly violent sneeze, and a moment later Frankie felt someone stumble against her and fall over her feet. With a muttered oath a gentleman fell to his knees on the pavement.

Frankie put her hand on the window pane to steady herself and turned to see what had happened. "Not again!" she exclaimed.

For there on the pavement was Lord Sterling, looking as belligerent as he had in the Chatterington refreshment room, his somber good looks unexpectedly enhanced by his scowl. His hat had tumbled off and his wind-blown dark hair was falling over a white sticking plaster on his forehead. He was holding a cane in his left hand; the knuckles were bleeding and appeared to have been scraped in his fall.

He knelt forward on all fours to retrieve his curly brimmed beaver before the fierce wind could snatch it away. He grabbed the hat and then righted himself as quickly as he could on his injured foot.

"*You!* I might have guessed! Do you intend to make a career of tripping me up, madam?" he exclaimed.

He had such a cold look on his face as he pronounced these words that Frankie, momentarily robbed of speech

116

by his haughty stare, was checked in her move to help him up. He looked so utterly different from her last sight of him, as she had broken out of his embrace to the sound of ripping material the evening before, that Frankie found it hard to credit this was the same man.

Little Tizzy was grasping her arm in a painful manner, whispering, "Come away, miss, do," and trying to pull Frankie away even as she gave vent to a whole series of sneezes.

However, Frankie was not going to walk away from another set-to with the gentleman. No, indeed. "'Twas not *I* who tripped you up," she said. "'Tis your own propensity for not looking round about you and then tripping over your own two feet that is your downfall, my lord. After all, what can you expect if you insist on hobbling down a public street with an injured foot?"

"You, Madam Dowd, are a menace. Why do you not look where you are going instead of always stepping in front of people? You proceeded across the pavement with nary a glance through your eyeglasses to see if anyone was coming," the viscount fairly shouted.

Tizzy sneezed.

Tolland glared.

In expectation of some fun, several passers-by stopped to stare at the two persons angrily glaring at one another in the middle of the busy pathway, with a little maid holding onto her tall mistress for dear life.

This did not inhibit Frankie, who hardly noted the presence of the onlookers, from responding, "Here. I believe it's you who need these, my lord." She took off her spectacles and held them out to the viscount. "You seem not to have the advantage of your quizzing glass today. Perhaps 'tis *you* who cannot see where you are going."

There were cheers from the crowd of bystanders at these words. A remarkably tight-lipped Tolland looked at

117

the object held out to him as if at a viper, bowed slightly, and limped off in the opposite direction looking sadly the worse for wear. His usually shiny Hessians had been scuffed deplorably in his fall, his hat and trousers were dusty, and the cuff of his left sleeve was dirty and frayed.

Frankie found that she was shaking with fury, but collected herself, replaced her spectacles, straightened her hat, and walked on at a rapid pace to the modiste's with Tizzy almost running beside her to keep pace.

Really, he is a most infuriating man, she thought to herself, and if she could teach him a lesson in manners she would. Imagine! Blaming me for tripping him up. *He* walked straight into *me*, she fumed. Of course, to be fair, he was hampered by his sprained ankle and this wind pushing everyone about so.

Then she remembered the chagrin writ large across the viscount's handsome features and her anger abated. She felt heat rise in her cheeks—from temper, she assumed— as she remembered their other encounter. Had he really held her and kissed her so demandingly only a few hours before? She was determined to make him apologize for his rudeness and admit his fault, and if she could attract his interest in her new guise, then what better way to give him his comeuppance. If there was another reason for her actions, Frankie was not quite experienced enough with the vagaries of the heart to recognize it.


Tolland lurched off from his encounter with his disastrous dowd in a fog of anger. He had not looked up to see his antagonist without her glasses as she made that outrageously insulting gesture of holding out her spectacles to him, thus missing the sight of his angel in the devil's own temper with fiery sparks fairly shooting at him from her unmistakable violet eyes, and thereby missing the chance of recognizing her.

He cursed the decision that had taken him to Bond Street just at that particular time. It had been a mistake to try to disregard the pain he still felt in his injured ankle and keep to his regular routine. But he didn't want anyone to think he was hiding his head after last evening's disasters.

The finely drawn lines round his mouth tightened on the thought that fate seemed to be playing a most disagreeable game with him. He was so busy nursing his grievances against the infernal woman and his own ill luck at falling in her path once again that he passed by, without seeing them, several acquaintances who raised their hats to him.

Lady Amelia Reynard, with her chaperon Mademoiselle Menaçant beside her, hailed him from her passing carriage, leaning precariously and quite immodestly out of the open window to do so, but he neither saw nor responded to her greeting shouted in affected, and inaccurate, French. *"André, mon cher, bonjour, comment allez-vous?"* The words were garbled as the long feather from her elaborate hat blew in her mouth.

His cousin Monty, however, was not to be ignored when he came trotting up briskly from across the street. "Eh, Tol, saw the whole thing," he yelped. "Stap me, if that deuced bee ain't been chasing you again. Back you up. Vouch for you, too." There was no ignoring the jangling noise issuing from Monty's vocal cords. He had a painfully loud voice when he was excited.

Tolland recovered himself enough to answer, "Damn it. There's no need to screech so, old man. I haven't challenged her to a duel, you know."

"Aye, that's the ticket—just what you need. Challenge her to a duel, by gad. First one to fall over his own feet loses. Hee-hee." Thus the comfort offered by his cork-brained but ever-loyal relative.

Tolland climbed into his carriage, which had been

119

waiting for him at the end of the thoroughfare. He was thankful to conceal himself behind its leather panelled walls, and directed his coachman to take him home immediately. He was sure that what he needed to blow the cobwebs of this confounded lingering nightmare away was a good, long ride on his favorite mount. After he had fortified himself with a substantial dinner and several glasses of wine while he rested his aching ankle on a footstool, he determined to saddle his chestnut and spend the afternoon riding in Hyde Park.

Women! Tolland thought darkly as he dwelt on his recent contretemps. Yes, a good, long ride would be just the thing to restore his injured feelings and pump up his sagging spirits.


The viscount's unsympathetic relative Monty had "glimmered" his adored Lady Amelia as her carriage continued down Bond Street and turned off toward her father's house in Hatchard Street. His left hand fluttered to his heart for a moment as he smiled quite besottedly and immediately took himself off to pay a call on his lady love, with some idea of intercepting her carriage and handing her down when she arrived.

He stood about in front of her house, twirling his cane and peering down the street for a sign of her equipage for some moments before deciding that she must have returned before he had arrived. Finally he turned about, ambled up the steps to her father's townhouse, and banged on the door with the knob of his gold-tipped cane.

Sir Monty's knock was answered by one of those superior beings frequently employed by personages whose station in life is much above their ideas. Told coldly on her doorstep that the lady was not at home, Monty took the information at face value, for the knight knew not the knotted subterfuge that was a frequent component of the dealings among knavish high-society nobs. He employed none in his own social conduct.

He smiled inanely and, with the knob of his cane, saluted the fish-faced butler who conveyed the false information. "Right you are. Be back tomorrow, m'good man," he said as he flipped the servant a coin.

"I doubt, sir, that my lady will be at home then, either," fish-face said in tones of haughty dismissal. The dart glanced harmlessly off Monty's artless armor.

Not finding the object of his attentions at home, and not knowing just what to do with himself for the next hour, Monty walked where the wind blew him and was dumbfounded to find that his footsteps, or the playful zephyr, had landed him in front of Chatterington House.

"How the deuce did I get to Chatterin'tongues?" he asked himself foolishly as he took off his tall beaver hat and scratched his yellow head absentmindedly, his pale locks bowing about in the breeze.

Just at that moment Sally Chatterington, evidently about to engage in a shopping excursion, emerged from the house accompanied by her abigail. She stopped, suspended in the act of tying her bonnet more securely under her chin, and uttered an "Oh!" of astonishment on seeing Sir Montagu looking confounded as he stood at the bottom of the steps, waving his hat about in the swirling air.

"Why, good morning, Sir Montagu. Were you coming to call on me so early? How kind!" She smiled broadly as she beamed down at him.

"Must've been," muttered the confused Addlecumber who still had no idea how he had come to be in this spot.

"I am just on my way to Bond Street. You may accompany me, if you wish, sir," she said boldly. "Perhaps we can hold one another upright in this gale."

"Escort you there. Be pleased to."

Sally giggled as Monty continued to stand with hat

held up in the air, a ludicrous look of surprise writ large on his mobile face. "You must clamp your hat down tightly or else this wind will snatch it quite away, Sir Montagu."

He finally tipped his hat and replaced it on his head as the young lady tripped gaily down the steps to meet him. He smiled happily at her.

"This has fallen out well. We can entertain one another along the way," she said as she linked her arm through his and turned him about in the right direction.

So pleased were they with one another's company that, after a morning spent calling in the shops along Bond Street, they rewarded themselves with a trip to Gunter's Parlour for an ice. Here Sally laughed so hard at Monty's absurd chatter that she ended by dripping her ice down her chin and could only be thankful that none of her acquaintance was present to see her rapid descent to schoolroom behavior.


The gale of the morning had blown itself out, leaving a fresh scent in the spring air, and a sunny afternoon raised the spirits of the several parties who planned an outing in the park. Laurel and Frankie looked forward to their ride with equal anticipation but for entirely different reasons. Frankie, of course, always welcomed the opportunity to be outdoors to indulge her greatest passion. Laurel had a decided interest in seeing a certain gentleman again; she would even brave mounting a horse, her least preferred form of exercise, to be in his company. Shortly before four o'clock the two ladies repaired upstairs to change into their riding costumes, both anxious to be out of the house.

It was a short ride from Sir Alfred's residence in Grosvenor Square to Hyde Park. Frankie rode ahead with

Freddy Drake. She was wearing her old brown worsted, of course, for even such a miracle-worker as Madame Eugénie couldn't finish so fine a garment as a velvet habit in under six hours! Frankie, however, had not a care that she was not dressed in the height of fashion this afternoon, though. What possible difference could one more day make? she thought in her typical carefree manner.

She took not much note of her companion's turn-out, either. His olive green jacket over buckskin riding breeches was correct, if not very dashing, riding wear for a man about town. But she did look critically at Freddy's mount and was able to compliment him wholeheartedly on the large bay mare whose name, she learned, was Charity.

"And she is as sweet a goer as her name implies," he remarked fondly. Frankie suspected that she had encountered the true love of his life.

"Ma'am, you do have a remarkably fine seat," Freddy remarked gallantly after watching her maneuver through the London traffic. Even mounted on her sister's plodding mare and wearing a shockingly shabby habit, he could see that Miss Verdant was a true horsewoman.

"But that animal leaves much to be desired. Are you sure you will not accept one of my horses until your own mount arrives? I would consider it a privilege if you would consent to exercise one of my hacks while you are here." Freddy was admiring the way she sat her horse, but he was finding that his memory of the very attractive lady of the night before must have been at fault or had disappeared with the coming of day, for Miss Verdant was, sad to say, a bit dowdy with her mud-colored habit and her hair all tucked up under her large riding hat. Though she was extremely well informed about horses, of course, and greatly interested in his hunting stories, much to his delighted gratification.

123

"Thank you, sir, but as I mentioned last night, my own horse, Black Demon, will be arriving soon from home," Frankie said. "I must admit, this mare of Daph's has the gait of a mule. Still, she will suffice for now. I am thankful to have her, actually, for I need to blow the cobwebs from my brain this afternoon," she remarked as the *clip-clop* of the horses' shod hooves rang against the cobblestones of the street. She easily negotiated round a parked carriage, a barrow of fresh flowers, two children playing in the street, and sundry other obstacles blocking their way even though she was not wearing her spectacles. Usually it was only when she was peering into the distance that she had difficulty making out faces or objects.

"Not used to racketing about till all hours, ma'am?"

"No, indeed. Late nights are not what I am used to. I am usually up with the birds, for there are a multitude of chores to see to at the Meadows. I must be in the paddock by half past seven, at the latest."

"I take it from what you said last night that you exercise many of the horses at the stables yourself," remarked Freddy, ready to renew their previous conversation.

"Oh, indeed, yes. It is one of my greatest pleasures." And the pair energetically indulged themselves in a lively discussion of their mutual interests even as they enjoyed their present ride.

Drake and Frankie rode on ahead and entered the park gates. Markham could see that Laurel was an adequate but cautious horsewoman who was unused to London traffic. They proceeded more slowly as he kept a careful eye on her.

"How well you look this afternoon, Miss Whittgrove! One can hardly believe that you danced the night away only a few hours before," he said gallantly. And she was lovely in her pale green velvet habit, a froth of lace at her

124

throat, a saucy little bit of a hat perched on top of her blond curls.

"Thank you, my lord," Laurel replied on a catch of her breath. Lord Harry looked remarkably well himself this afternoon with the sunlight glinting off the strands of his white-blond hair as he bent his hazel eyes on her. A teasing twinkle lurked in their depths, she could see.

"And did you enjoy your first proper London ball, Miss Whitgrove?" Markham asked, admiring her glowing complexion. There seemed to be a light shining through this golden girl, so bright were her eyes on this fine spring afternoon.

"Oh, yes." She smiled at him, her whole face lighting up, and his heart turned over. "Poor Mama! She was so relieved. I was in quite a fidget before we left for Lady Chatterington's last night, you see. But everyone was most kind. I never expected to have so many partners," she confided naively.

Markham was charmed. She was obviously an unspoiled beauty. "Did you not, Miss Whittgrove? I did for you, the minute I saw you."

"La, my lord, are you flirting with me again?" she asked, twinkling up at him. "'Tis a most teasing habit you have."

"Who, I? Flirt? Why, it's unheard of!"

Laurel laughed as he intended she should. They were in the park now, riding some distance behind the other two in their party.

Frankie turned occasionally to try to keep her niece in view, but she found that Laurel and Markham were too far behind for her to make them out clearly, squint though she would. Since leaving her spectacles in Grosvenor Square, she had been wishing she had brought the lorgnette Tizzy had procured for her that morning. But then she recollected that the use of such a gadget would have been vastly impractical on horseback.

125

She smiled to herself as the thought crossed her mind that she should have a quizzing glass on a great long ribbon to clamp in her eye, like the one Viscount Sterling had used the night before. Was his vision disordered, too? she wondered. And was that why he had made such a spectacle of himself and her?

Well, she reasoned to herself as her thoughts turned to her chaperoning duties, Lord Harry seemed like a perfectly respectable young man. She did not think Laurel would come to any harm in his company.

The urge was strong in her to let her horse break into a canter, but she doubted that the mare was up to any kind of speed. She was moving at a fairly sedate pace with Drake beside her. She knew that Laurel could not bear to do much more than walk her horse cautiously along. So Frankie determined to have as much exercise as she could and then make her way back to her niece. She breathed in the fresh spring air and gave herself up to the enjoyment of her ride.


Lord Harry was leaning over toward Laurel to hear what she was saying when he was hailed.

"Harry. A very good afternoon to you," said the newcomer, who saw that Harry had wasted no time in making up to the girl who had charmed him the night before. It must be serious, then.

"What, Tol, you up and about today? I made sure you would be off the foot for a week!" Harry greeted the viscount.

Tolland frowned. "There's nothing the matter with me." He was confident that his injured forehead could not be seen; his hat was pushed well down and the cut was totally covered.

Markham looked down at his friend's booted foot as it rested in the stirrup. Tolland glanced down and steeled himself not to flex that limb. He had contrived a tight wrapping for the ankle himself, ignoring Worthy's admonitions to apply cold compresses and rest it for a day. He had to admit that he could feel a twinge, particularly after the further abuse the ankle had received from his fall of the morning, but it did not hurt enough to prevent him from taking his daily ride in the park. He would have to be three-quarters dead to forgo that most pleasurable part of his day.

"Miss Whittgrove, may I present Viscount Sterling? I don't believe you met last night." Markham made the viscount known to Laurel.

Indeed, Laurel remembered that she had not had a chance to meet the viscount formally the evening before, though he had been pointed out to her from a distance early on. My Lord Perfection, Sally had called him. He had disappeared, of course, when she had come back from escorting her aunt upstairs. She was also acutely aware that his set-to with Aunt Frankie last night had nearly been their social undoing.

"Miss Whittgrove," said Tolland, bowing slightly and touching his hand to his hat. Laurel blushed as she met his gaze and inclined her head. She had to look elsewhere and bite down hard on her lips to keep herself from giggling, so strong was her memory of the events of the night before and the way the stiff viscount had looked after the accident, dripping wet with a few straggling flowers in his hair.

"Who is the woman riding ahead with Freddy?" Tolland questioned. He had remarked her exceptionally fine seat as she put her horse through its sluggish paces. And, although the woman's habit was decidedly shabby, as always in matters of equestrian sport, his interest was stirred. There was a gasp and a repressed sputter of laughter from Laurel. Tolland looked at her curiously for a moment, then back at Lord Harry who was speaking to him.

"Why, it is Miss Whittgrove's aunt, on a rather plodding mare, though." Despite Frankie's suspicions that he had guessed her identity, Markham was not aware that Laurel's aunt, who in the attractive lilac gown had supped with them the evening before, was the same woman who had been involved in his friend's mishap earlier.

Tolland, too, had no idea that the woman at the ball was in any way connected with the Whittgroves.

"Oh, yes." Laurel recovered enough to speak up. "Aunt Frankie cannot abide job horses, but she would rather ride Mama's slug than not go out at all. She is a regular trooper, a 'goer' as my brothers say. She's a bruising rider, and of course she oversees all that stud . . . umm . . . horse breed—er, all the business matters at Verdant Meadows Stables. She hunts with the local pack, too, and I believe she loves no one so much as the local Master of Fox Hounds. Her own horse will be here soon. Then you will all see something." Laurel spoke with pride of her aunt's abilities in the saddle, though her heart was beating erratically with the fear that they were about to be discovered.

Tolland raised his eyebrows at the mention of Verdant Meadows for he had heard of the excellence of the stables there. With increased interest he glanced again at Freddy and his companion, and debated with himself whether it would be worth riding ahead and making the acquaintance of the woman. He was always interested in acquiring good horseflesh. There was a decided twinge in his ankle at that moment, so he decided that he could easily make her acquaintance at some other time. He bowed again to Markham and Miss Whittgrove, expertly wheeled his chestnut about, and rode away.

Tolland's timely exit saved him from the snares of

Lady Amelia Reynard, who was in the park tracking him down. Familiar with her quarry's habits, she knew he would likely be riding there at that hour. She had spotted Sterling's tall figure and unmistakable white-stockinged chestnut stallion and was urging her horse to a trot, trying to reach the viscount before he left the park. She was breathing hard with the effort of trying to get her plodding mare to move, jiggling the reins up and down with one hand and holding onto her hat with the other.

Her abysmally ineffectual efforts almost led her to ride straight into Frankie. But, as she waited for Freddy to come up, Frankie easily maneuvered her mare round Lady Amelia's horse, which moved first in one direction and then the other. The poor animal was trying to respond correctly to the confusing signals it was receiving through the pressure of the bit in its mouth.

"I say there, Amelia!" Drake hailed the woman. "Watch what you are about! And have a care for your horse. Don't saw at the reins so, or you'll ruin the creature's mouth."

Lady Amelia at last managed to bring the baffled animal to a halt. The reins nearly slipped from her grasp when she exclaimed, "Oh, how tiresome!" as she saw Sterling leave through the park gates.

"Well, Frédéric, you've made me miss André," she said petulantly, her emerald green eyes giving off sparks of frustration. It was her habit to presume a more intimate relationship with her male acquaintances by addressing them with Frenchified versions of their first names. In the viscount's case, she used Andrew, his unused first name.

Frankie was amused to see that the pouting woman wore a most remarkable equestrian costume. The habit was an elaborate gold and black affair, and the tall military-style shako perched on her gleaming red curls had a tendency to tilt to one side or the other. There was

129

no denying it was a *striking* costume. It struck Freddy's eye most painfully, Frankie thought as she saw him wince. Perhaps the woman hoped to make up in style what she lacked in skill, for Frankie could see that she was a most inept horsewoman.

Frankie sat relaxed in the saddle, holding her leather reins loosely, in perfect control of her mount. She regarded the rather ill-natured lady, an amused smile on her face, though she was relieved to hear that the viscount was riding out of the park. That he had been there without her being aware of his presence had given her a momentary jolt and had shaken her out of her customary calm.

"*I've* made you miss him! Don't be ridiculous, Amelia. And, a hint for you, Sterling don't care to be called by that silly Frenchie version of his name any more than I do. Tsk. If you knew what you were doing with that animal—and I don't know what you're doing on her, anyway; you certainly can't control her correctly—you wouldn't have nearly ridden down Miss Verdant, here," said Freddy, pointing to Frankie with his riding crop. "Thank God, *she* knows how to manage a horse and moved safely out of your way!"

"Who?" asked Amelia, glancing carelessly in Frankie's direction but not acknowledging her presence by so much as a nod. She spotted Markham approaching and said, "There's Harry. I must ask him what happened last night. It's all over town that André was assaulted by some strange woman in spectacles. Imagine! Some ghastly hussy thinking she could trap the Viscount Sterling by such a ridiculous stratagem! . . . How unfortunate that I was not able to attend the ball myself. I should have given the creature a piece of my mind! Everyone knows that Sterling favors *me*!"

She rode off at these waspish words—words that caused Frankie to clench her jaw in indignation. Well, of all the nerve! she thought, the tightening of her lips signalling danger for any opponent. Just who does that woman think she is? But it dawned on her that although her name was as yet unknown, she was one of the parties to the latest *on-dit* setting the *ton* on its ear. She glanced at Freddy, but he appeared not to have heard the woman's remarks. His head was turned toward the horse and rider continuing on down the next lane.

"Pity that poor beast has to carry the Fo—er, Amelia." He gave a tsk of annoyance. "That cow-handed female is incapable of properly controlling her mount."

"Showy creature," Frankie murmured ambiguously, keeping her temper in check with difficulty.

"Fairly jobbed at the poor beast's mouth, just now. Did you see? Shouldn't be allowed within a mile of horseflesh, good or bad, for a poorer rider I have yet to see." Freddy turned to Frankie, shaking his head over Lady Amelia's antics. "Did you happen to hear about the commotion at the Chatterington ball last night? Afraid poor Sterling had rather a dust-up . . . Didn't see you about until supper, did I?"

Frankie, determined to show no emotion, said off-handedly that she had been with the chaperons.

Markham and Laurel came up with them just then. Lord Harry laughed as he related how he had turned off that gossip, Lady Amelia, making light of last night's incident. "Sterling seems to have forgotten all about last night's contretemps. He doesn't seem to be suffering any adverse consequences from the encounter, even though he limped from the scene of chaos last night." He laughed. "He's shaken it off, most like."

The four riders turned their horses and made their slow way back to Grosvenor Square, each contemplating what had been learned during the ride: Laurel that Lord Harry was an easy companion as well as a most charming and handsome young man, and that she had already gone

131

and formed a *tendre* for him, regardless of her mama's veiled hint that morning at breakfast that he was an unsuitable *parti* since his papa, the duke, was thought to be a pauper despite his exalted title; Harry that he was definitely going to court the sparkling little Laurel Whittgrove; Freddy that he had never seen a finer horsewoman than Miss Verdant; and Frankie that Lady Amelia Reynard was a shrew, that she would have to be on her mettle if she encountered her again, and that Freddy Drake was a pleasant companion who was slap up to the mark, a true sporting gentleman who certainly knew his horseflesh. She could tell at a glance that Charity's mouth would reveal no cow-handedness about the man.

Tolland returned to Bruton Place not ill-pleased with the response of his ankle to the afternoon's lengthy ride. It had been uncomfortable but nowhere near as tender as he had expected after his fall earlier in the day. He would have been bad-tempered indeed if he had had to miss his daily exercise.

Sporting pursuits were the breath of life to the viscount. Ever since he was a boy he had taken solace from them. They provided an escape from the house where his overbearing mother held sway, so he had put all his passion into outdoor activities of a sporting nature.

Tolland was not precisely a cold man or an unkind one; rather, he was reserved and wanted to keep his distance. He hid behind a facade of manners so that few, if any, knew the man behind the comportment and the title. He fancied himself content with his busy life, filling his days with a constant stream of activities. He never sat home of an evening, or even an afternoon. He did not enjoy reflection. He relaxed after tiring himself out thoroughly.

132

And if all his efforts led to a kind of ennui or exhaustion of spirit, he was not consciously aware of it.

He was so preoccupied with the quest for excellence in his sporting life and elegance in his social life that there was no time left for romantic pursuits. He was not a man of passion. Indeed, one could have said he was unawakened in affairs of the heart. He was not averse to affairs of the body, however, and when he felt the need of more intimate female companionship, he had an occasional rather detached fling with an experienced courtesan.

He had never felt the emotion some called "love" for any female, nor was he in the confidence of any friend who had. Those of his circle who did marry either went on with their activities as they had before or dropped out of the set entirely, completely absorbed in their domestic arrangements. So, given his temperament and lack of experience in such things, the viscount had no reason to believe in romantic love. When occasionally he did see a man and woman who seemed perfectly in tune with one another, neither one nor the other seeking to dominate but living together in harmony, it fleetingly crossed his mind that it would be nice to have such a relationship, to finally relax. But the thought would be so fragmentary and transient it was forgotten in the next moment.

Tolland had been only ten when his father had expired—from a surfeit of managing females, the young man irreverently suspected. His mother then oversaw the estates with her man of business while he was kept hard at work with his tutor; any spare time he spent outdoors with his horses—riding, driving, and hunting —or in shooting and fishing. When he came up to town he found the hours he had whiled away in these pursuits at home stood him in good stead among the athletic young men of his set. He had a well-muscled physique, a natural coordination and lightness of foot, so he soon outshone them all with his skills. Even when he took up boxing and fencing with professional men in town, he excelled. He became the leader of the Corinthian set, and it was even whispered as he rode by on his magnificent white-stockinged chestnut, "There he is! I see him! It's the Nonesuch!"

A smile would tug at his lips at these words. After being told for years by his mother that he was imperfect in so many areas, he relished hearing those whispers of his perfection and thoroughly enjoyed his reputation as a nonpareil. He outshone others in Corinthian pursuits, and with his elegance of manner, he was an ornament to any drawing room. My Lord Perfection was a sobriquet he did not disdain to own.

# Chapter Nine

Demon snorted. He waited, saddled and restive, for his mistress, ready for a good hard ride in the brisk early morning air.

Frankie strode down the path to Sir Alfred's mews at the back of the house, humming cheerfully to herself. She had thrown on her old, tattered habit, completely forgetting her engagement to accompany Laurel to the Chatteringtons at mid-morning, and now greeted her horse happily, reaching up to stroke his velvet nose as he nudged her and danced about.

"Ready for a gallop, are you, my Demon? Well, you shall have one."

Without more ado, she set out for Hyde Park in tearing high spirits. Black Demon had arrived from the Meadows' stables the evening before, and she had not had the patience to resist taking him out at an unfashionably early hour. Demon, with his strong legs and good heart, was fresh and full of frolic after but a night's rest. She gave him his head, and they had dashed madly through the park for several minutes, luckily encountering nary a soul. Both rider and horse were breathing heavily at the end of their run; then Frankie, remembering that such a thing "was not done" looked around guiltily. Demon had appeared to glance around, too, with such an anxious look in his eye that Frankie gave a spurt of laughter. "Safe! No one to see us, Demon." She exhaled in relief. "Well, they've missed a treat, haven't they, boy?" she said proudly as she gave him a good hard pat.

When Daphne arose somewhat later she found that several boxes had been delivered for her sister from Madame Eugénie, among them the dashing new riding costume. She was miffed when she realized that Frankie hadn't waited to change into the new garment before her ride. She shook her head sadly, wondering if the task of changing her sister into a fashionable lady was an impossible one.

But when Frankie returned, revived and in good spirits after her ride, she gave in with good grace to Daphne's request to try on some of the new gowns.

"Well, Daph, will I be the belle of the ball, do you think?" she asked, smiling in a self-deprecating manner, as she tried on a deep green sarsenet evening gown with a half-skirt of pale silver overlace.

"Indeed, I *do* think you could be one of the belles of the ball, if only you would learn to conduct yourself with a little less . . . er, *exuberance*, Frankie dear. We shall have my coiffeur call tomorrow morning to style your hair, and Laurel's could do with a little trim, too," Daphne said happily. She derived much vicarious enjoyment from seeing her tall, little sister try on the new gowns and anticipated seeing to it that her hair was styled in a more becoming way.

"An old maid like myself would be ill advised to expect to be much noticed." Frankie laughed at Daph's raptures. But, determined to carry out her scheme, she nevertheless embarked wholeheartedly on the process of disguising herself as a modish lady, again thinking the idea a good joke.

136

*          *          *

When the butler opened the door to Lord Harry Markham in Berkley Square that morning, he was not astonished to see that yet another visitor had arrived on Lord Chatterington's doorstep. They seemed to have been appearing with a certain regularity for the past hour or more. Luggins had not been surprised to admit Miss Laurel Whittgrove accompanied by Tizzy, her little maid, earlier in the morning. Miss Whittgrove was a bosom bow of Miss Sally's and the young ladies often enjoyed a comfortable coze, he knew. Much giggling and an occasional squeal could be heard coming from the second-floor drawing room, even penetrating to the hall below where Luggins waited patiently in his chair by the door, trying to grapple with the morning's papers.

When there was yet another tattoo upon the knocker, Luggins rubbed his shiny bald pate wondering why her ladyship had forgotten to inform him that there was a party being given on the premises this morning. He wondered if Maise—Mrs. Bap the housekeeper, that was—had done some extra baking. There would be no bearing her if she hadn't been given sufficient notice to provide refreshments for the army of young men waiting on Miss Sally.

But when a loud banging a quarter of an hour later rang in his ears, followed by a demand for admittance by the son of the household who maintained lodgings elsewhere, and ten minutes after that a young gentleman Luggins could only describe as a fop in fancy dress landed on the doorstep, the old butler had had enough. After he had conducted Sir Montagu Addlecumber upstairs, Luggins called one of the underfootmen to take up the post by the door, while he took himself belowstairs for a cup of tea and a comfortable chat about the commotion in the house with Mrs. Bap.

*     *     *

Laurel looked up from her place on the blue- and gold-striped settee between Mr. Lucius Pendergast and Lord Roger Reynard, and blushed as Lord Harry Markham approached her and took her hand. She felt a definite lurch of her stomach as his warm lips briefly saluted her fingers. She could not deny that she was thrilled to see him again.

She and Sally had been entertaining a large group of young men since her arrival an hour or more ago. What had started as a chance for the two friends to exchange gossip and confidences had rapidly turned into a boisterous party.

Now Markham easily detached Laurel from her two admirers and invited her to take a turn about the room with him. "For I'm persuaded, ma'am, that sitting in one place for too long impairs the circulation," he said with a definite twinkle in his eye. Laurel readily allowed herself to be convinced. However, as they walked to a corner of the room, she was slightly discomposed by the sight of Sally's brother, Philip, propped against the wall staring at her moodily.

Sally had been enjoying herself, even knowing that she was not the object that had brought the suitors to her drawing room. Most of the young men had got wind that Laurel was with her that morning because they had called at Sir Alfred's residence first and been informed of Miss Whittgrove's whereabouts by her papa's accommodating butler, Hedge. The good-hearted Sally didn't mind, but she wished her brother didn't look so hangdog. Good God, she thought, it was plain as a pikestaff that Philip, who had never been in the petticoat line, had formed a *tendre* for Laurel. Wonders would never cease. She shook her head in amazement.

When Sir Montagu Addlecumber was ushered in,

Sally's face broke into a wide grin. She saw that Sir Montagu had the air of one bursting with the latest *on-dit* as he stared about at the occupied room.

"What! You here, Addlepate!" Lord Harry greeted him in his teasingly affectionate manner.

"Heh? By gad, known you forever, Harry." Sir Monty's eyes protruded a bit more than usual as he answered in a disconcerted fashion. "Thought you'd've stubbled to it by now—m'handle's Addlecumber, don't y'know."

Sally took pity on the discomposed knight. "Now, Sir Montagu, you come along with me and make yourself comfortable," she said as she went up to him, took his arm, and led him to a loveseat where she immediately bade him tell her how he had occupied himself that morning. Being presented with such a gaping opening, Monty proceeded to pour out into Sally's willing ears the amazing piece of news that Lady Amelia Reynard had just inclined her head to him when he had passed her near his cousin's house on Bruton Place, and then he proceeded to regale her with his garbled version of the latest gossip.

"My love, I own, I'm not at all sure 'tis a good notion to be seen exclusively with Lord Harry," Daphne declared that evening, as she once again put the finishing touches to Laurel's evening attire.

Laurel had that morning consented to allow Lord Harry to accompany her to the musicale planned for that night at the home of Lady Lavinia Wynchcombe, a woman who fancied herself a most discriminating devotee of Terpsichore and a connoisseur of mellifluent strains.

"It will give rise to gossip and expectations that I have no wish for you to be subjected to . . . I'm sure your papa would not approve," Daphne chided mildly when she heard who was to be her daughter's escort. "Lord Harry is quite a delightful young man . . . so handsome! So unfortunate that he is the fourth son—and one of ten children, you know—of the Duke of Ampleforth. His father is prolific—but unfortunately not wealthy. I'm afraid Lord Harry's prospects are decidedly limited, my love, as I've mentioned to you before. From all I can discover, his papa's estates are much encumbered."

Daphne put her finger to her chin and said consideringly, "Now Freddy Drake is a highly eligible young man, and most pleasant. You said you danced with him at Clara's. Could you not encourage him a bit? But, it is early days yet, and I dare say there are many pleasant and handsome gentlemen of good family who would consider it a great boon to accompany you about, dearest. Can you not allow them a chance to be in your company and converse with you, too?"

Laurel reluctantly agreed to encourage some other gentlemen, though in her heart she knew without a doubt that Lord Harry was the one for her.

Daphne had decided that Laurel could wear one of her more elaborate gowns after receiving advice from Lady Chatterington "to dress her almost as though for a court presentation, my dear Daphne. To be seen at Lady Wynchcombe's musicale—why, 'tis as good as making one's bow at the Queen's Drawing Room!" Lady Wynchcombe's "evenings" had the reputation of being more for show than for genuine enjoyment of the talent she presented. And Laurel had not been at all reluctant to abandon the demure muslins for once.

Unaware of her mother's strictures, Lord Harry duly arrived that evening to see a smiling Laurel awaiting him at the top of the staircase. As she descended, she almost took his breath away, so lovely did she look in her dress of white lace edged in palest primrose.

"Am I awake, or do I dream?" Lord Harry wondered as

he bowed low and then looked up with a twinkle in his eye. "Miss Whittgrove, behold me overcome. You are surely a vision from above come to delight all mere mortals who behold you from here below." He took her hand and raised it to his lips for a fervent salute.

"I believe you mock me, sir. Unless you mean that I have come from abovestairs, for indeed I have." Laurel giggled.

"As I live, Miss Whittgrove, you do me an injustice. You do *indeed* look enchanting this evening!" There was a gleam in the young man's eye as he gently teased her. But behind his flippant exterior, Lord Harry's heart was hammering at his ribs. Lord, he had never beheld such a delightfully natural beauty! He truly did believe that he was lost, completely lost. The victory was hers. She had rolled him up, horse, foot, and guns without even one minor skirmish, let alone a battle. He wanted to wave the white flag of surrender. He couldn't wait to surrender!

Laurel, too, was feeling decidedly short of air, for Lord Harry was quite spectacular himself. His gleaming locks of white gold had been brushed until they shone. He was attired in a dark blue satin coat over a lighter blue waistcoat and black pantaloons. His pristine white shirt and neckcloth were dazzling to behold and reflected a light onto his handsome face that would have made any young lady swoon with pleasure, she was sure. And the warm light in his hazel eyes as he looked at her was the gleam that sent Laurel's pulses racing.

Frankie followed the couple from the room, not minding that Lord Harry had neglected her. He was so enchanted with Laurel, he did not look closely at her companion or he would have realized that Miss Verdant was almost as attractive as her niece on this occasion.

"Oh, Lord Harry . . . " Daphne called, seeing that he had left Frankie behind.

"Never mind, Daph. You can not expect Laurel's

141

young men to consider her aged chaperon."

"Fie upon it! You look quite up to snuff tonight, Frankie dear." Daphne's campaign for Frankie's transformation had begun. She had agreed to wear the green sarsenet gown and her hair, though pulled back and fastened in a coronet at her nape, was more becomingly arranged.

"I wish we could have contrived something more à la mode with your hair." In Daphne's opinion Frankie's hair was still bound too tightly to her head to show to best advantage. "But the coiffeur will be here in the morning. He will know just how to cut and style your mane to best advantage."

"Well, one day more or less will not make much difference, will it?" Frankie said blithely.

At least Daphne was satisfied that her little sister would not look out of place at a fashionable gathering on this night. "Oh, Frankie, have you the lorgnette?" she asked.

"Do not be in a quake, Daph," Frankie answered. "'Tis right here." She patted her reticule. She had tucked in her spectacles as well. "For emergencies," she had told herself.


"Oh, Lord Harry, 'tis as good as Carlton House!" Laurel breathed out, her hand tightening on his arm as the three arrived at Lady Wynchcombe's amid a glittering throng of music lovers.

"Yes, Miss Whittgrove, Lady Wynchcombe does herself proud. You are right, 'tis spectacular," answered Markham, covering her little hand with his own strong one. This was no simple evening of music for a select few but an all-out squeeze of the first order.

"You will have to stay especially close to me, or I shall lose you in this crowd," Harry said flirtatiously, taking a firmer hold of her arm.

"I wouldn't *dream* of leaving your side, my lord," Laurel said coyly, a dimple showing in her cheek as she looked up at him.

Lord Harry found seats for them near the back of the large room set up for the entertainment. That it did not have the best acoustics was of not the slightest concern to Lady Wynchcombe, who was tone deaf. Not even the complaints of her temperamental star performers served to convince that redoubtable woman to change the venue. The musicians were, after all, only the bait to attract the denizens of high society to her entertainment. She had invited two hundred people, and the only place to seat them all was in her vast ballroom.

There was a terrific clamor in the room as Lady Wynchcombe tried to quieten the boisterous assemblage. Soon a modicum of order was restored and she signalled a pianist who was to perform a solo to begin. With so many persons in the room, it was not to be expected that there would be perfect silence, Frankie supposed. In addition to suffering the din, she found that she was having difficulty seeing past the crowd to the front of her room through her lorgnette. So, after a quick look round to be sure no one observed her, she surreptitiously reached for her spectacles and put them on her nose.

Laurel caught her at it. "What are you about, Aunt?" she hissed. "Must you use those specs? Mama would not approve."

"I'll only wear them for a moment so that I can see the musicians," Frankie whispered back. It was not often that she had a chance to hear good music played and sung, and she began to enjoy herself despite the extraneous noise. She was especially fascinated to hear Signora Pettrini, a famed Italian soprano, sing an aria from an Italian opera. The woman was so large that she shook like jelly when she trilled the high notes.

143

"Aunt Frankie, just look at that woman's outfit." Laurel giggled as she nudged her aunt in the side. The woman's costume was indeed most extraordinary. It seemed to consist of a brilliantly colored gold and silver tunic that fell from her shoulders in a straight, three-foot-wide length to the floor.

"'Tis her plume—or whatever those feathers are supposed to represent—that puzzles me. She's bound to tickle anyone who comes within ten feet of her," Frankie said to her niece, but she had already lost Laurel's attention to Lord Harry again. There were three preposterously tall peacock feathers protruding from the back of the *signora*'s head, fastened in her hair by a gold band that ran round her brow, while heavy gold earrings dangled and danced from her ears.

Frankie was so fascinated by the enormity of this sight that she forgot to remove her spectacles when an interval was announced at the end of Signora Pettrini's aria. Markham and Laurel, absorbed in one another, were not really aware of what was going forward in the gigantic "music" room. Lord Harry guided Laurel through the crowded chamber, and Frankie squeezed after them, still thinking about the amazing scene she had just witnessed. As she walked toward a table where a cold collation was set out, she heard a commotion behind her and turned to see Viscount Sterling in the arms of an elderly gentleman—with whom he seemed to be having heated words.

Tolland had come out of the music room feeling bored. Signora Pettrini had no power to astound such a sophisticated man about town; he had seen her like many times before. He raised his quizzing glass unhurriedly and gazed about the room in a leisurely fashion. Suddenly he spied the bespectacled dowd who had tripped him up twice now coming straight toward him. Blood rushed to his head at the memory of the disasters her presence had provoked. In an effort to move out of her path, he veered away too quickly on his still tender ankle, and without proper attention to his surroundings. His misstep caused him to blunder into Lord Haughtly, a high stickler if ever there was one. The elderly peer put his arms up to protect himself and steady the viscount.

"Egad, sir, look what you're about." Lord Haughtly tottered backward several steps, staggering under Tolland's weight. "You're a great tall fellow to be stumbling about here. If you can't hold your drink, stay at your club—don't come here amongst the ladies," the old man lectured severely.

Controlling his simmering temper with an effort, Tolland apologized, assuring the ancient lord that he was not intoxicated but had recently suffered an injury to his foot and was still not steady on his pins.

"In that case, sir, I suggest you take yourself home and rest the injured limb and do not go about where you are a danger to yourself and everyone else." With a great "Hrrmph" Lord Haughtly brushed down his jacket sleeves, straightened his clothing, and tottered off in high dudgeon.

Tolland clamped his jaw shut on an angry retort and limped from the room, pausing at the door to turn and direct a menacing glare straight at Frankie who was staring, with raised brows, at the proceedings. She had no idea that she had again precipitated his accident and was at a loss to understand his glare. She had not seen him before she turned and beheld his tall, elegant form collapsed against that rude and arrogant elderly gentleman. Yet before he'd left the room he'd looked as though he somehow blamed her for the mishap.

"Well!" cried Frankie to herself, hands on hips. "Well, of all the abominable coxcombs!" Of the several incidents he had instigated, this surely was the one least to be comprehended. She had been nowhere near him, she thought. His *faux pas* certainly had not been the fault of her proximity; she had been clear across the room when he had begun stumbling about. Little did she realize that the very sight of her had driven Sterling into headlong flight and such careless speed on his part had precipitated the accident.


Tolland wanted to annihilate the woman. The most satisfying thing he could think of doing was to dash those hideous spectacles to the ground, stare the woman straight in the eye, and give her the sharpest edge of his tongue he had ever loosed on anyone. The moment he spotted the tall, bespectacled, dark-haired woman in Lady Wynchcombe's dining room, he had decided to remove himself forthwith, fearing the most dire consequences should he remain in her vicinity. He had only spied the distinctive eyeglasses and hair style without noting the modish gown beneath. Unfortunately, his very haste had caused him to blunder into someone yet again! Why should the presence of that dowd have such a disastrous effect on him? Who was she, anyway, that she was always about at *ton* functions? he wondered.

He stormed and he raged on his way home, running his fingers through his hair again and again. Revenge! He would have revenge! . . . But nothing suitable seemed to occur to him. To exact his revenge he would have to seek out the accursed woman. The very thought made him shudder with distaste. He hoped she would fade into a benign obscurity without delay. He had no desire even to learn her name.

He rubbed his chin as he morosely concluded that the damage to his reputation would be beyond repair now. Never again would he be known as the impeccable M'lord

Perfection in a social setting. At least his reputation as a Corinthian was intact, he consoled himself.

Lady Amelia Reynard had been trying in vain to push her way through the crowd at Lady Wynchcombe's, fanning her face furiously the while and demanding, "Air, air." She was desperate to continue the search for her quarry. She was sure he was about; her nose almost twitched with his scent. If only she could spot him . . . She had been craning her neck and looking about the large, crowded room during the performance, without success.

Just as she gained the doorway to the outer rooms, she was stopped in her tracks by a most unwelcome sight. She spied the lank form of Sir Montagu Addlecumber blocking her path. He had somehow got wind of her whereabouts, she fumed. He had a foolish smile on his sallow face as he made her an elaborate bow and extended his yellow satin embroidered sleeve.

"Happy to be of servitude, Lady A. Was you wishful of a glass of negus? Devilish stuff, don't y'know."

Amelia snapped her fan to, and only an acute awareness of her surroundings prevented her from giving the harebrained Addlecumber a waspish setdown.

"Sir Montagu." She inclined her head a fraction of an inch and ignored his bent arm. She decided to make use of him instead. "Is your cousin André about? I most particularly wish to speak to him." She smiled her most insincere smile at the poor lovelorn knight.

"M'cousin André? Ain't got a Frenchie cousin." He scratched his head, puzzled.

"You must know I mean Viscount Sterling."

"Eh? Tol? Stap me if I know where he is, m'lady. Always slap up to the mark, m'coz, y'know. If he ain't here, ten to one this party ain't at all the thing . . . *Can't* be the thing, though, y'know," he said after deep cogitation. "The caterwaulin' in here's almost enough to rattle m'bone box. Tell you what, allow me to cart you to some other 'do.'"

Amelia almost screamed with vexation at Addle-cumber's witless chatter. Then she caught sight of Sterling's tall form down the long hallway just as he was being handed his hat and cloak at the front door. She made a lunge to go after him, but instead found herself caught up in Sir Montagu's arms.

"Here, I say, Lady A. No need to brew a scene, m'girl. Be glad to shake the rust from this place. Take you someplace else, by gad."

"Unhand me, you nodcock, you rag-mannered buffoon." Amelia slapped at Monty's arms with her fan. Addlecumber released her without more ado and scratched his head in puzzlement as she flounced away from him, wondering what he had done wrong now in his courting of the tempestuous, fiery-haired beauty.

The morning following the musicale the ladies of the Whittgrove household spent a leisurely two hours attending to their correspondence. Frankie could make neither head nor tail of her latest communication from her trusted groom, Trotmore. However excellent a groom he was, he was not a well-lettered man, that was sure, she thought as she dashed off an urgent missive to him, demanding exact details about each of the horses at the Meadows.

Daphne alternately smiled and sighed as she read over her dearest Alfie's latest letter and tried to put pen to paper and tell her spouse the hundred and one things she had stored up in her head for his erudition. At six and thirty Daphne had been extremely surprised and puzzled to find herself with child once again; she had only a vague

148

idea that age had not much to do with the conception of children.

The eldest of the Verdant children, she had been a mere seventeen when she had married Baron Whittgrove, her dearest Alfie. Laurel had arrived ten months later. She had presented her loving mate with five children over regular intervals in nineteen years of marriage, though George (her last child as she had assumed at the time) had arrived more than six years previously. She sighed and leaned her cheek upon her hand, wondering how the years had sped by so quickly, then smiled and began to tell Alfie all about how she was finally succeeding in changing Frankie's appearance.

Laurel mooned about, thinking fondly of her several meetings with Lord Harry, wondering how she was going to comply with her mother's request that she see less of him, as she tried to pen thank-you notes to her recent hostesses. Mama was a dear, but it would be hard to be obedient in this instance. 'Twas enough to cast one into the glooms.

By afternoon, after being cooped up in the house since early that morning, Frankie was ready for another ride, but Laurel persuaded her to have the barouche called out instead so that they could go for a drive in the park.

The possibility of an encounter with her dear Markham brought a glow to Laurel's eyes. And Frankie was more than ready to go outdoors after sitting still for what had seemed like hours before luncheon while the coiffeur had cropped and curled and combed her hair into the latest style. It had been tedious in the extreme; though Daphne was in alt and said it was a famous notion of hers to have Frankie's hair cut. Frankie was obliged to own that the new style did make her look quite different, and every time she glanced in the looking glass, she wondered who it was peering back at her.

Much to her sorrow, Laurel, feeling herself obliged to comply with her mama's wishes, had turned down Lord Harry's very flattering offer to escort her to a forthcoming ball at the home of Lord and Lady Sefton, an event that promised to be one of the most glittering affairs of the new season.

She had conveyed these unhappy tidings to Lord Harry with a tear in her eye at last evening's musicale, and he had immediately understood. Lady Daphne was after bigger game. He hadn't realized that the Whittgroves were so ambitious for Laurel. He sighed, but was not surprised. Anxious mamas had been hinting their daughters away from him for several years now because of his papa's circumstances and his own lack of means. But he had not found it painful until now. He decided he must find a way to secure gainful employment, though he knew in his set a working man was sometimes scorned even more than one who maintained a leisurely life as a gentleman despite a lack of funds. He would just have to find a way to make himself independent if he were ever to have a chance to make Laurel his.


Frankie had again ridden in the park that morning, this time clad in her new habit from Madame Eugénie. She had once more dared to gallop Demon through the open space and, again, had not drawn the attention of any other early risers. Now she hoped to persuade Daph that she should be allowed to take the ribbons of the barouche herself, feeling that it would be too tame to just sit and let herself be driven. But, alas, her hope fell afoul of Daphne's notions of decorum.

"Frankie, dear," Daph had said, "'tis not at all the thing. Try to remember that you're not at Verdant Meadows now. You must exhibit conduct more befitting a lady. I thought you wished to learn how to go on among the fashionable set. Well, then, sit quietly and let Woods drive you. Show off your new hair style under that smart hat. Smile and flirt to your heart's content."

"Flirt? Good lord! Do you take me for a widgeon, Daph?" Frankie laughed at her sister. Only dear Daph would think to offer her such idiotic advice. Why, she wouldn't know how to flirt to save her life, even if she didn't think it an exceedingly silly pastime.

Accordingly, aunt and niece joined the fashionable promenade thronging Hyde Park between the hours of five and six in the afternoon.

After shaking her head over Daphne's earlier admonitions as she saw several ladies tooling their own vehicles, Frankie remarked with a gleam in her eye, "Well, Laurel, I do wish your mama was a little less stringent in her notions of propriety. There are several ladies here who drive their own carriages. And I see that some of them have taken the ribbons of these new high-perch phaetons, too." Laurel was not paying any attention. She was scanning every passing carriage and rider for a certain gentleman.

"And I wish she would put dinner forward a trifle for I see not how you can all wait until eight o'clock to eat. I am in a fair way to being famished," Frankie remarked. She was still not used to the late hours Daphne kept and was longing to dine.

"Oh, Aunt Frankie, a lady is *never* famished—maybe a trifle peckish, now and again, Mama would say, but never famished." Laurel giggled.

At that moment Lord Harry Markham rode up to the barouche and tipped his hat to the two ladies. Laurel immediately bade Woods pull up so that she could converse with him.

"Why, Miss Verdant, that's a most becoming hair style!" Harry bowed to Frankie with a smile and a compliment. "You and Miss Whittgrove quite take the

151

shine out of all the other ladies taking the air this afternoon."

Frankie smiled at what she took to be his nonsense as he turned to her niece.

In the course of their three-minute conversation, Lord Harry requested the pleasure of two dances with Laurel at the Seftons' ball, as well as the privilege of leading her into supper. Since he was not allowed to be in her company for the entire evening, he was determined to reserve as much of her time as he could without flouting the conventions.

Laurel glowingly accepted. He rode on, feeling gratified but mildly guilty. Lady Whittgrove would be displeased by his continued marked attention to her daughter and by Laurel's acceptance of his partnership for supper. He was sorry, but he could not comply with her mother's wishes. It could not be helped, however, for he was in love with Laurel and his feelings took precedence over her mother's reproofs.

Frankie paid them not much heed, used to their billing and cooing by now and not realizing that Daph objected rather strongly to Lord Harry's showing Laurel so much attention. She peered myopically out at passing carriages and equestrians. Suddenly she beheld a sight that caused her to sit up and take note.

She clamped the lorgnette to her eyes and feasted on the sight of Sterling astride a magnificent white-stockinged chestnut that she had no trouble categorizing as "Slap up to the mark. A strong-muscled, big-boned creature with tons of heart. A high-blooded animal if ever I saw one!"

"What, Aunt Frankie?" Laurel turned her pretty head to see what Frankie was exclaiming over as Markham tipped his hat to her and rode away. "Oh, that's Viscount Sterling . . . You see, I told you he was a Corinthian. You cannot continue to think of him as a starched-up dandy, for all the world knows him for a nonesuch."

"I must say, I am impressed with his mount. Such a smooth gait; full of frisk, but not an ounce of vice. He must have a silken mouth to match his glossy coat. A high-spirited stallion, too. I wonder how he performs at stud?"

Laurel squealed. "Oh, Aunt Frankie! You must not mention such things!" She put her gloved hand to her mouth and giggled.

Frankie took no notice—she was too busy watching Tolland. "There! See how that little dog got away from its mistress and nipped at the chestnut's heels. Sterling controlled the animal perfectly. Another man would have dropped his hands and the horse would have bolted," Frankie marvelled.

"He has an iron hand, but a care for the animal's mouth, too. He stopped the stallion's fidgeting and sidling in an instant and is now walking sedately along. Extraordinary . . . extraordinary! I have never seen such elegance of manner combined with such a sure touch. How wonderful!" Frankie, used to the rough and ready, though extremely competent, manners of the local Fox Hunt Club, knew instinctively after watching Sterling that riding could be as elegant an endeavor as it was an exercise requiring skill and control.

"There. He's given the stallion a good hard pat and whispered in his ear to calm him. He knows just how to go on," Frankie said. "See how the chestnut whinnies and cocks his ear!"

"You sound surprised, Aunt Frankie."

"Somehow I did not expect it. I thought he would be all show and no heart."

"What, that beautiful horse, Aunt?"

"No, as I believe you very well know, I was referring to the rider, my girl." Frankie laughed, then mused, "Look at those wide shoulders, and the way he narrows through

153

the hips, and those long, powerful legs . . . such perfect proportions."

"Why, Aunt Frankie! Do you refer to Lord Sterling?"

"No, you goose! To that beautiful chestnut." Frankie continued to gaze at horse and rider while Laurel giggled at her aunt's infatuation with a horse. "Like most of his species, Laurel, he is a proud, self-satisfied beast," she said. It was a description that could equally well be applied to his master, she added to herself. My Lord Perfection, indeed.

# Chapter Ten

"I declare, you and Laurel will put all the other ladies quite in the shade tonight, dearest," Daphne exclaimed as she came into Frankie's room for the third time in ten minutes on the night of the Sefton ball. She was eagerly anticipating the sight of Frankie in her new white silk ball gown. Daphne thought Madame Eugénie had excelled herself in the cut and design of the garment that now lay carefully draped across the bed. She couldn't wait for Frankie to put it on.

Daphne was in hopes that both Laurel and Frankie would make a good impression. They must do so, if they were to stand a chance of receiving cards for Almack's, for Clara Chatterington had informed her that several of Lady Sefton's sister patronesses of the "Marriage Mart" were expected to be in attendance. She hurried back and forth between the two rooms with high energy, fussing over details such as which shawl, fan, jewelry, hair ribbon, gloves, and reticule was just right for each of them, chatting excitedly the while and loving every moment of it.

"Good lord, Daph, are you sure all this running about is good for you? Will it not harm the babe?" Frankie asked, sitting impatiently in her dressing room while she waited for Tizzy to finish arranging her hair. It had been cut into soft curls round her face as Lady Chatterington's abigail had suggested, but left long in back by Daphne's coiffeur. Tizzy had dressed it in the Greek style tonight, winding through the curls a velvet ribbon that matched the violet-blue decoration on her dress. "I know I try to keep my mares calm when they are heavy with foal."

"As I am not one of your mares, Frankie dear, I'll thank you to remember that I've done this five times before and come through with flying colors."

"So you have. A good breeder, are you?"

"I vow, all the Verdants are, from what Mama has said. Don't you wish to try it for yourself one day?" Daphne questioned archly, fishing for a response.

"Perhaps I shall."

"Oh, Frankie," Daphne laughed and clapped her hands, "do you have a special flirt? a *tendre* for someone? Pray tell, do."

"No, no. I spoke on a whim . . . Come in," Frankie responded to Fennel's knock on her door.

"Lady Chatterin'ton's 'ere, m'lady. She's awaitin' below," Fennel informed her mistress.

"Please ask Hedge to serve her a glass of wine, and tell her the girls will be with her directly," Daphne instructed. "Thank you, Fennel."

"I declare, Frankie dear, you should feel relieved that Clara has agreed to take you up tonight," Daphne said as she watched Tizzy put the finishing touches to Frankie's hair. Really, she thought, the girl was a wonder; Tizzy had followed the coiffeur's instructions to the letter. The little maid was a rare find. She had such a way for arranging hair, for all she seemed a bit daft at times.

"Ah, yes. She has decided I'm much too countrified a person to chaperon *your* daughter," Frankie remarked dryly.

"Pooh. It is because you are so young and in need of a

duenna yourself that she has volunteered to watch over the two of you as well as her own Sally."

"Me young! She forgets that I am well on the shelf at four and twenty. However, I have no objection to the arrangement. Your friend Clara is a very good sort of woman, I believe, and Laurel does enjoy Sally's company a great deal." Frankie was resigned to the arrangement.

That good lady had indeed decided that a chaperon would well serve Daphne's strong-willed but inexperienced younger sister, for Clara had been present when Frankie had tried on her new gowns and emerged altered beyond recognition.

"Daphne, dear, your sister has no idea what a sensation she will create when she appears at the Sefton ball. She will be all the rage with the gentlemen," Clara said as she and Daphne enjoyed a comfortable coze over a pot of tea on the previous day. "But she is not quite used to our *ton*ish ways, just yet."

"Oh, dear, Clara, I fear you are right; she is quite lacking in town bronze. It is too bad that she must act as a chaperon when it is clear that she should be making her own debut. I own, I had some such stratagem in mind when I invited her to go about with Laurel," Daphne confided.

"My dear, I dislike to distress you, but Francesca is no more suited to be a duenna than my Sally. Why, she's less experienced than our two girls. If you should not dislike it, I would be most happy to take both Laurel and your sister about with me."

"Oh, Clara, you are a love! I cannot imagine a better scheme."

Young Sally's debut into society was progressing satisfactorily in her mother's considered opinion, with the requisite number of young men requesting her hand at dancing parties, a small but interesting number of eligible morning callers, no *faux pas* of significance laid

157

at her door, and no tantrums or megrims to try a mother's patience. Clara, though, was puzzled by Sally's unnatural penchant for the company of Sir Montagu Addlecumber, a foppish, foolish sort of fellow for her sensible daughter to favor.

So Lady Chatterington was well disposed to take the other two young women about with her. "I shall be glad to have them both under my umbrella" was how she had expressed it to Daphne.

"Your sister's ignorance of *ton* ways could land her and dearest Laurel in a fine bubble broth," she had declared, unless they were both under the aegis of a more mature and experienced person such as her own good self. Yes, she was the very one to guide and advise dear Daphne's two charges—and it did not hurt that Sally met many more young men by being the intimate friend of the captivating Laurel.


Laurel was a breathtaking sight indeed on the much anticipated evening. Glittering spangles were sewn into the spider-gauze half-slip which covered her lovely ball gown of palest fawn silk. Her fond, and easily swayed, mama had again allowed her to deviate from the rule that all debs were to wear muslins. Some of the spangles were woven into the elaborate coiffure Tizzy had concocted for the occasion, too, and Laurel sparkled as she moved. Her soft green eyes rivaled her attire for brightness, and her mother was in alt over her beautiful girl-child.

"Yes indeed, Mama. I will be glad to go with Lady Chatterington and Sally," Laurel agreed meekly, and smiled to herself. She looked forward to the Sefton ball with excited expectation. She would see Lord Harry there, even if she could not go under his escort, and she had promised him those two dances and to partner him at supper as well.

She was to waltz for the first time that evening, and she had determined that her dearest Harry would have the privilege of leading her out for those two dances. She could not bear to think of being in anyone else's arms or of seeing him with his arms around another.

Laurel knew that she had formed a lasting passion, her soft heart told her so. First to bring the gentleman up to the mark, she thought, then she would deal with her parents according to the dictates of her hard head.

"Behold me transformed." Frankie laughed at the expression on Daphne's face as she finally slipped on her gown.

"Oh, Frankie! Oh! . . . Is it you indeed? I knew you would look beautiful, but I did not know you would look so . . . so . . . Why, you're enough to take a man's breath away!" Daphne was in transports of delight, and could not conceal her rapture as she saw her sister in the beautiful white silk gown.

And Frankie was stunning. Daphne felt like an artist who had created a masterpiece, as though her sibling's looks were all her own doing.

"Oh, it was pure inspiration for Madame Eugénie to make up these vandykes in this deep violet-blue and to edge the dress in a matching velvet ribbon. The color quite matches your eyes, my dear," Daphne said approvingly. Frankie's silk gown was cut along more sophisticated lines than Laurel's, with fewer frills and not so full in the skirt.

"The dress does cling rather tightly, though," Frankie said pensively, as she looked at herself in the tall pier glass in the corner of the room. She was a bit disconcerted to see how low the gown was cut over her full bosom.

"Oh, no. Décolletage is the fashion. And your waist is

159

so small, my dear. How lucky you are!" Daphne sighed gustily, bemoaning her own increasing girth.

"So I will do, will I?" Frankie grinned.

"I vow . . . you look just the thing tonight," Daphne assured her. She had not known that her "little" sister was such a glamorous creature. Frankie's lovely complexion and the darkness of her brows and lashes were emphasized by the shimmering lightness of the gown, and her figure was tantalizing revealed as the lustrous material clung to her and softly swished around her long legs as she moved. Her small waist automatically accentuated the curves of her figure, and her height gave her a graceful and elegant look.

"In fact . . ." On the tip of Daphne's tongue was a warning that some of the gentlemen would not be able to resist her and to be on her guard, but she reconsidered. Let the evening unfold as it may. Frankie is due some excitement. I'm sure she will quell any gentleman who tries to go beyond the line, Daphne thought.

"Mayhap 'tis still not too late," she whispered to herself as she beheld her sister metamorphosed like Galatea. "There are men aplenty who will find her magnificent, and Papa did arrange for an adequate dowry. 'Tis a pity she's so tall, but at least she has abandoned those ugly eyeglasses."

Frankie, determined to rely on the lorgnette tonight, had decided not to even take her spectacles. If they were handy she might forget and clamp them on her nose as she had at the musicale. She supposed she would just have to blindly find her way about if necessary. For this night she had decided to act the empty-headed, vain, society miss in the expectation of having some fun with the pompous *ton*. And really, she thought as she glanced at herself again, she didn't look half bad at that.

He—that is, no one will recognize me as the same woman who took a tumble in the Chatterington

# 4 FREE BOOKS

## TO GET YOUR 4 FREE BOOKS WORTH $18.00 — MAIL IN THE FREE BOOK CERTIFICATE T O D A Y

Fill in the Free Book Certificate below, and we'll send your FREE BOOKS to you as soon as we receive it.

If the certificate is missing below, write to: Zebra Home Subscription Service, Inc., P.O. Box 5214, 120 Brighton Road, Clifton, New Jersey 07015-5214.

---

## FREE BOOK CERTIFICATE

## 4 FREE BOOKS

### ZEBRA HOME SUBSCRIPTION SERVICE, INC.

**YES!** Please start my subscription to Zebra Historical Romances and send me my first 4 books absolutely FREE. I understand that each month I may preview four new Zebra Historical Romances free for 10 days. If I'm not satisfied with them, I may return the four books within 10 days and owe nothing. Otherwise, I will pay the low preferred subscriber's price of just $3.75 each; a total of $15.00, *a savings off the publisher's price of $3.00.* I may return any shipment and I may cancel this subscription at any time. There is no obligation to buy any shipment and there are no shipping, handling or other hidden charges. Regardless of what I decide, the four free books are mine to keep.

NAME

ADDRESS _____ APT _____

CITY _____ STATE _____ ZIP _____

TELEPHONE
(       )

SIGNATURE _____ (if under 18, parent or guardian must sign)

Terms, offer and prices subject to change without notice. Subscription subject to acceptance by Zebra Books. Zebra Books reserves the right to reject any order or cancel any subscription.

ZB0493

GET
FOUR
FREE
BOOKS
(AN $18.00 VALUE)

ZEBRA HOME SUBSCRIPTION
SERVICE, INC.
120 BRIGHTON ROAD
P.O. Box 5214
CLIFTON, NEW JERSEY 07015-5214

AFFIX
STAMP
HERE

refreshment room, she told herself laughingly.

As Daphne fastened a thin necklet of diamonds at her sister's nape, she gave her a squeeze and enthused, "We shall have multitudes of suitors on the doorstep tomorrow for both you *and* my darling Laurel . . . Umm! What is that wonderful scent in your hair?"

"It's one of my famous concoctions, Daph," Frankie teased. "Actually, 'tis a hair rinse made from several kinds of floral oils and crushed petals and leaves—a recipe I found in one of my 'horrid books,' you know." Frankie laughed at the look of amazement on her sister's face.

"Why, I declare! 'Tis as good as the French scent Alfie procured for me before the war, the one I have been saving up so carefully. I can see that reading all those silly, dusty old books is of some use, after all. Will you make me some?"

"Help yourself. It's in the green bottle on the dressing table," Frankie directed Daphne.

"Just remember to walk at a ladylike pace, my dear, instead of striding ahead in that masculine way you have . . . and if you could manage to speak more lightly and raise your voice a register; it's so low and hoarse, not feminine at all," Daphne advised.

"Dear Daph, what a goose you are! You can change the way I dress and do my hair, but there's no changing the way I walk or talk, you know." Frankie grinned at her.

"You think me overbearing, but—"

"No, indeed, Daph. 'Tis impossible to be overbearing when you are a good deal shorter than I am."

"Yes, and not half so headstrong either!"

No, Frankie thought to herself, Daph was not an overbearing woman, only occasionally a bit of peagoose, but a lovable one.

\*　　　\*　　　\*

161

On this unexpectedly balmy evening in the normally chill English spring, there was an air of expectation to the carriage's four occupants. Laurel and Sally giggled together, and the good-humored Lady Chatterington was bubbling over with laughter in anticipation of a delightful evening of gossip with her cronies while watching the triumph of "her Three Graces," as she dubbed them.

Her own Sally was in looks tonight, Lady Clara thought fondly, dressed as she was in pale turquoise muslin, a color that flattered her soft red hair. And it would be as good as a play to see how the gentlemen reacted to Francesca. "Lord save us," she muttered under her breath. The girl was sure to cause a few masculine heads to swivel this night.

The ladies disembarked in front of Lord Sefton's mansion and followed the press of people up the winding, candle-lit staircase. Frankie was infected with the general air of excitement as she short-sightedly peered about. She wondered what she would do if she came face to face with Sterling. Would he recognize her? She would give him an almighty set-down, and make him sorry for his past treatment of her, if he dared glance her way. Caught up by the idea of gulling the high society nobs, she expected some pleasure in that business as well. She pasted her widest smile on her face and entered the ballroom.

A heady feeling of triumph surged through her when their party was announced and she could sense rather than see several males turn admiring glances her way. She felt different tonight somehow, softer and more feminine. Gone was her somewhat managing, hard-headed, business and country personage, and for the first time in her life Frankie enjoyed feeling the power of her womanhood.

There was a general stampede of males in their

162

direction as she, Laurel, and Sally were immediately surrounded and solicited for dances by men both young and old. Lady Chatterington stood aside, talking nineteen to the dozen with one of her cronies. The gilt-edged card dangling from Laurel's wrist was soon full and Sally's contained a gratifying number of names. Frankie was not quite as popular with the younger gentlemen as the two girls; the youths were shy of her, not daring to approach such a statuesque creature who looked much too sophisticated for their more juvenile tastes.

However, she was claimed for the first set by a famous bachelor duke, and a cabinet minister led her into the second. As she was going down the third set with a rather antiquated dandy, a gentleman who had just entered the room was unhurriedly surveying the crowd through his quizzing glass. He stepped back just as Frankie's partner was bowing over her hand and felt himself pitch into someone who uttered a low-pitched exclamation—a definitely feminine exclamation. He turned quickly, his glass still to his eye, and stopped in his tracks. For a fraction of a second he was afraid that he had encountered his dowd again.

But the creature before him caused him to draw in his breath sharply. A tall, shapely woman with dark hair and striking eyes stood not a foot away. It was surely his dark angel who appeared miraculously before him again, Tolland thought, in a daze.

A strange sensation overcame him as he gazed at the beautiful apparition he had just stumbled against. He felt as though all the air had been knocked from his lungs; but he didn't think that portion of his anatomy had been involved when his lean hips had been intimately pressed against a soft, shapely derriere. It was several seconds before he could catch his breath.

"Angel!" he breathed, stunned. "Is it really you?" he wondered in a whisper. Was it? His recollection of their

163

meeting was foggy, consisting of half-remembered and half-imagined pictures of her. *I must be dreaming*, he told himself, *but if such be a dream, then lead on, bright angel!*

"Your pardon, ma'am. I beg you will forgive my clumsiness," he said more calmly when he was able to make a recovery.

Frankie stifled a gasp of laughter. It was Viscount Sterling—and they had managed to collide yet again! She took in the exquisitely cut evening jacket of black superfine that was hugging his broad shoulders and the pristine whiteness of the carefully arranged cravat resting against the strong column of his neck. A strong sense of his vital masculinity assailed her. She swallowed uneasily.

With a frisson of excitement, she wondered if he would recognize her.

"I trust you are not hurt?" he inquired in accents far removed from his usual cool, haughty tones—certainly different from the tone he had used with her after their previous skirmishes.

"No, I am quite unharmed," Frankie responded to his solicitous inquiry. Then she quickly took several steps backward. She was surprised to find herself unwilling to administer the cool set-down she had planned now that she was in the presence of the gentleman. This was one fence she could not take in her usual neck-or-nothing style, she found.

Before either could react further, they were interrupted. Freddy Drake bowed over her hand, changing the tenor of the scene. And Sir Montagu Addlecumber was determinedly making his way to her other side.

"'Evening, Miss Verdant . . . Hello, Tol," Freddy spared barely a glance for his friend as he bowed over Frankie's hand in a fervent salute.

"Well, good evening, Mr. Drake. 'Tis good to see a

friend here, though I thought you might be tempted elsewhere. I heard there is to be a horse fair in Barnet tomorrow."

"Yes, I heard that, too, and I admit I was tempted, but I am trying to negotiate for a splendid pair of grays here in town"—he looked with raised brows at the viscount—"and decided to give it a miss. I must say, Miss Verdant, you look slap up to the mark, tonight, ma'am!" Freddy complimented her as he still held onto her hand.

Tolland was astounded to see Drake, a man more noted for his Corinthian exploits than doing the pretty with the ladies, bowing and even kissing the lady's hand! So . . . Freddy was already acquainted with his angel. Verdant, he had called her, Miss Verdant. Good! At least he had learned her name, Tolland thought.

And was she not the woman he had seen from a distance riding in the park with Freddy last week? But how had Freddy met her anyway? And stolen a march on him. Tolland's jaw clamped shut. He intended to find out!

". . . If you would so honor me, Miss Verdant, my evening would be complete, for you are the loveliest lady here!" Freddy was saying.

Was he asking a lady to dance? Tolland wondered in disbelief. Could this be his friend? Freddy usually spent his time at affairs such as this in the card room, if he could tear himself away from some sporting pursuit or other to grace them with his presence, and his interest in females had hitherto been confined to those of the equine variety. An accountable feeling of disquiet rose in Tolland's breast.

He was somewhat mollified by the lady's answer to Freddy's request.

"Oh, Mr. Drake, you know not what you ask!" Frankie replied jokingly. "Truly, I'm an indifferent dancer at best, and the movements of that particular set of steps quite defeat me. I would disgrace you most

165

dreadfully, you know. I don't think the powers that be have extended their approval for me to waltz. Most wise of them."

This was uttered in that same low, musical voice that Tolland remembered had affected him so strongly in Chatterington's dressing room. With thoughts rushing in jumbled confusion through his head, he stood mute as his cousin Monty also came up to Miss Verdant and made her his typical flourishing bow. Freddy still had not relinquished his place at her other side, and Tolland found it was next to impossible to get at her, sandwiched as she was between his two friends.

It was with a haste totally contrary to his usual languid movements that Tolland stepped forward and edged his cousin out of the way so that he could stand within a hair's breadth of the lady. Deciding to reclaim the initiative, the viscount turned to his friend, a determined smile on his handsome face. "Freddy, will you do the honors and introduce me to this beautiful lady?"

And turning to Frankie, Tolland looked her full in the face from only inches away, with not a flicker of recognition of her as the woman he had ripped up at and ridiculed after his recent accidents. It seemed he did not in the least recognize her as his calamitous lady in any shape, manner, or form. But the soft look on his countenance and the anticipatory gleam in his eyes told Frankie he remembered their *other* encounter well enough!

"Eh, Tol, you here?" Monty asked, breaking the spell. "Thought you was still tied by the leg; didn't know you was able to caper about yet, hee-hee. And tryin' to cut me out even before I can lay m'preposition before the lady, by gad. A despisable thing to do, don't y'know," complained Addlecumber, shaking his head as he straightened up from his bow and wagged a finger at his relative.

166

"Complete to a shade, m'coz, here," Monty remarked to Frankie. "Beats the rest of us all to flanders. Such a devilish indelible gent, always get so the most beautified ladies first. Finds favor with 'em, too," he nodded his head wisely from just beyond Tolland's broad shoulder.

"Does he, indeed?" Frankie asked, arching a brow at Monty.

"Quiet, you nodcock," Tolland admonished his garrulous cousin in an undertone.

Frankie's lips quirked upward slightly, and Tolland thought her eyes widened. He was completely mesmerized as he gazed into those extraordinary blue-violet eyes, so well remembered. Even dreamed about, he realized with a jolt. But dreams paled by comparison with reality. His whole face softened as he looked at her. There was a look of bemusement on his countenance, an expression quite different from his usual cool indifference.

Freddy, looking put out to have his dance proposal interrupted, did as requested and performed a brief introduction. "Miss Verdant, Andrew Tolland Hansohm . . . the *famous* Viscount Sterling."

Tolland smiled widely at Frankie, not even annoyed by Freddy's disparagement.

"Miss Francesca Verdant, Tol, sister of Lady Whittgrove . . . And here's Sir Montagu Addlecumber, too, Miss Verdant. Can't miss Addle the Rattle at a party—he's the exquisite with the loud waistcoats."

Monty flashed his friend a wounded look.

"Miss Verdant, I am truly enchanted to meet you *formally*." Tolland, recovering his aplomb, took Frankie's gloved hand in a smooth movement and raised it to his lips. "Do I mistake? Surely we have met somewhere before, in a more, ah, informal setting," he added wickedly.

"Have we indeed, my lord? I cannot seem to recall any

167

such, er, informal, occasion," Frankie answered mendaciously.

"Ah, in that case I shall attempt to refresh your memory, Miss Verdant . . . As I cannot at all imagine how you have endured so sweetly the chatter of Freddy here, I shall offer *my* hand as a substitute for the ensuing waltz. I promise you, I'm a patient teacher, if you really are in need of instruction, which I find difficult to believe. An angelic lady such as yourself would grace any endeavor. But I would be honored beyond my just deserts if you would just accept my hand."

"You honor me, Lord Sterling"—Frankie was determined to resist him—"but I could not possibly. I have not been granted permission to waltz, you see, as I have explained to Mr. Drake." She smiled at Freddy. If it came to a battle of wills she was ready to match hers against the viscount's any day.

"Afraid of wounding Freddy's feelings, are you?" an equally determined and even stronger-willed Tolland asked. "He can easily be palmed off with a country dance later, eh, Freddy?" The viscount's lifted eyebrow bespoke a command to his crony.

"I say, Tol, coming it much too strong!" Freddy protested aggrieved.

"You will remember a certain matter we discussed last week, Freddy." Tolland was not above using bribery to have this particular dance with this particular lady. He was determined to cut out his friends and have his angel all to himself. "Well, if you come round tomorrow you may find me more amenable to your offer."

This mysterious conversation referred to the pair of grays that Freddy was longing to buy from the viscount. So far, his quite generous offer had been repulsed. Now Sterling seemed to be coming round—all for a dance with Miss Verdant. Incredible! Freddy almost whistled through his teeth.

168

"Miss Verdant, I would be honored if you would accept my hand for a country dance after supper." Freddy reluctantly capitulated, forgetting that he was promised to Laurel Whittgrove for that identical set.

"Of course, I will save that dance for you, Mr. Drake, if that is what you would prefer," Frankie replied. She looked challengingly at Sterling while Freddy signed the small card that dangled from her wrist.

The orchestra began to play the compelling strains of the waltz.

"And now I believe this is my dance, Miss Verdant." Tolland held his hand out to her.

"I do not believe I have agreed to dance with you, Lord Sterling." Frankie was indignant at the high-handed treatment meted out to Freddy. Her eyes glittered behind her polite smile.

"Come, Miss Verdant . . . I have something *most* particular I wish to say to you," Tolland insisted. "Or, are you afraid?"

Frankie raised her chin and stared at him challengingly.

". . . Afraid that you will not be granted permission to waltz, that is," Tolland continued smoothly. "But that is easily remedied, my dear Miss Verdant. I am acquainted with Lady Sefton, you know, and I believe that she would not deny my request, if I were to ask her permission."

No one could get away with accusing Frankie Verdant of cowardice. She had never been afraid of anything in her life! She put her hand on his arm and let him lead her away as she recollected her plan. Things were falling out nicely, after all. She smiled to herself, thinking how heady it was to have him seeking her favor rather than berating her, and allowed him to lead her to Lady Sefton who stood holding court nearby.

Freddy stood, open-mouthed, as he watched them leave. He was too dumbfounded by Tolland's unprecedented behavior to protest. "If that don't beat all!" he finally managed to utter.

"M'cousin, don't y'know." Monty, standing beside him, gave him a poke in the ribs with his elbow. "Has so much redress the ladies can't desist him. . . . Ain't seen Lady Amelia about, have you?"

Freddy shook his head. Addlecumber was off, his loose-limbed lank form garbed in a garish green and gold brocade jacket more suited to the last century. "Sure to be here, don't y'know. 'M off to nose her out."

Instead of nosing out Lady Amelia, Monty's long, thin olfactory organ led him straight to Sally Chatterington, who stood tall and slim at the edge of the dance floor, smilingly watching her brother Philip lead a rather pert little brunette onto the floor. She was relieved that he seemed to have recovered from his infatuation for Laurel, for she knew that her friend's interest was turned in quite another direction.

To Sir Monty's eyes Sally looked most attractive in her turquoise gown with her soft red hair plaited in a new style. The hopeful look in the young lady's eyes as she spied him pulled him up short, and his quest for the Fox was abandoned as he trotted up to her.

"'Must say, Miss Chatterin'tongue," he exclaimed with a bow and an appreciative look in his eye, "look radishin' tonight, by gad."

"Why, thank you, Sir Montagu. This compliment coming from an epicure such as yourself is high praise, indeed." She laughed and her smile lit up her whole face.

Monty beamed down at her as he took her hand and carried it to his lips in an uncharacteristically graceful gesture. Those friends who subsequently saw them romping through the waltz with much gay laughter lifted their eyebrows in quizzical surprise and began to whisper about this latest tidbit of gossip.

With polished ease, Tolland secured permission for Frankie to waltz from their high-in-the-instep hostess, Maria Sefton. The lady was no more immune to his practiced charm than her sister patronesses of Almack's, Sally Jersey and Countess Lieven.

Tolland immediately led Frankie to the dance floor, for the music had already started. Now, she thought as he took her gloved hand in his, she would give him a piece of her mind. It was time to take her revenge, one part of her mind told her, while her body told her something else, something unfamiliar that she did not yet understand. As a result when it came to the point her indignation faded and she hesitated to give him the rare trimming she had planned, her desire to embarrass him no longer so pressing.

As he led her into the dance, Tolland noticed that although her head came well up past his chin, Miss Verdant carried herself very gracefully. Her soft dark curls tickled his chin as he bent toward her in a tight turn, and he noted some indefinable light floral fragrance drifting to him from her curls to tantalize his senses. In addition, her voice, so low and seductive—that angel's voice—sent a warm glow through him whenever she spoke: The effect was relaxing yet strangely exciting. He must have been too foxed to appreciate her when they met before, he thought with a rueful twist of his lips.

The man was elegant, no doubt about it, Frankie decided. No one could have looked more perfectly correct, dressed as he was in the subdued black evening coat with white lace edging his stock and cuffs, and he held her so tightly about the waist that she was in no danger of making a misstep. She had no choice but to follow his lead. He was effortlessly directing her steps, bending her body to his will, while she was enjoying the sensation of being held in his arms too much to speak. All her earlier plans of revenge were completely forgotten as she gazed into blue eyes alight with a warm glow—only inches from her own.

She was unprepared for the effect his splendid masculine form had on her. Her senses, unawakened until now, were stirred as she gazed up into his strong, male face and felt the tight muscles of his broad shoulder beneath her hand. Her mind told her one thing, her woman's instincts another, as she absorbed his physical presence. Frankie the unflappable became Frankie the flustered.

She had caught the rhythm of the dance from him, and the unaccustomed feeling in her midsection abated somewhat. She decided the best way to get over that odd feeling was to confront him. She had always found it best to jump right back in the saddle again after one had been thrown, no matter how shaky one felt. It did no good whatsoever to let the horse think, even for a moment, that he had the upper hand.

She silently laughed at herself as she compared her partner to a sleek thoroughbred, then said, "What was it you wished so urgently to say to me, my lord?"

"So . . . Miss Francesca Verdant." He looked at her consideringly and finally said, "You say you don't remember our previous encounter." His smile glinted down at her. "Perhaps it was all a dream, after all."

"What encounter was that, my lord?" Frankie breathed throatily, allowing herself to play along.

"Were you not at the Chatterington ball, Miss Verdant?"

"Yes, indeed, I was. I accompanied my niece, Laurel Whittgrove, on that occasion."

"Miss Whittgrove?" Tolland was momentarily distracted by the name, remembering that this was the name of Harry's new love; a little girl, all dewy-eyed and with glowing blond curls.

"Yes. I am come to town to act as her chaperon, you know." Frankie knew she was babbling—so unlike herself—but at least she had succeeded in changing the subject for the moment.

"You do remember attending the Chatterington ball, then. And on that occasion were you not looking for someone called Higgins?"

"Higgins? . . . Higgins? Hmm . . . Ah, you must mean Lady Chatterington's abigail."

"Abigail! I thought it was a man you were looking for!"

"You were strangely misinformed, my lord." Frankie was thinking that she hadn't been looking for a man, but she had certainly found one.

"Then what were you doing in Philip Chatterington's dressing room? I hope you don't make a habit of barging into men's private rooms, Miss Verdant."

"You dare to question my behavior? That's rich coming from you, my Lord Sterling!" Frankie was indignant, but she was having a hard time controlling her breathing as the viscount twirled her so expertly around the ballroom. It didn't help, either, that his thighs occasionally brushed against hers and her breasts grazed his chest when he spun her through a turn. Before she could open her mouth to set him down as she wished to do, he took the wind out of her sails.

"I'm sorry, Miss Verdant. My temper got the better of me. Allow me to extend my abject apologies for my ill manners now and for my ungentlemanly behavior on that other occasion," Tolland said sincerely, wondering what in the world had possessed him to subject her to such an inquisition when his whole purpose was to inveigle himself into her good graces, not to upbraid her

173

for her previous conduct or to force her to admit that she, too, remembered their embrace.

"I was not quite, ah, myself on that occasion. I think it would be best for us both if we were to forget the incident."

"I quite agree." Frankie smiled triumphantly; she had gotten an apology out of him, after all.

Seeing her good humor restored, he adroitly changed the subject.

"Why have I not heard your name before tonight, Miss Francesca Verdant? . . . Surely you've been to town before? Though I don't recollect having the pleasure of running into you until this season. I'm certain I would have been knocked quite off my feet the first time I saw you," he added. There was an air about her that enchanted him, it was not just her beauty. He felt the need to know more about her and began to question her lightly.

At his words, the spell that had gripped them was broken, and they both relaxed into a more friendly conversation. Frankie felt her mood change. She became the old calm and collected Frankie once again. The man she danced with did not seem in the least like the perfectly enraged or empassioned Viscount Sterling she had encountered on previous occasions with such unfortunate consequences.

Frankie explained her relationship to the Whittgroves and told him that she usually lived in Cambridgeshire and had been to London before only on brief visits to her sister.

"The Verdant Meadows Stables?" He was astonished by her answer to his question of what she found to do with herself in the country. "But, my dear girl, that's a breeding farm!"

"That's right, my lord." She grinned at him. "But I assure you, I do run the Meadows Stables."

"But you can't possibly oversee the, er, services rendered there."

"No? Why ever not?" She arched a brow at him.

After his initial shock, he began to laugh, and Frankie joined in. He looked at her with dawning respect.

"You must miss your horses," he commented.

"Yes, immensely. But since I am here to chaperon my niece—there she is waltzing with Lord Harry"—she glanced at the couple dancing quite nearby just then—"I am kept quite busy so I have no time to brood. And Trot, my groom, keeps me informed."

"No! You a duenna? Doing it much too brown. I can't believe you have enough years in your dish to qualify. You mustn't try to make a May game of me, Miss Verdant, for I am more than one and twenty, you know."

"Indeed, my lord, so am I . . . A great deal more. In fact, I can assure you that I am quite, quite on the shelf."

Tolland laughed, a deep rumbling sound that Frankie felt down to her toes, and asked her why, if that were the case, she had not had a season at the proper time.

"Oh, my family were never fond of coming to town. It was no sacrifice on my part, believe me, to stay at home."

"But surely if your mother was unwilling to perform the task, your sister, Lady Whittgrove, would have sponsored your come-out?"

"But you see, the *task*, my lord, was so great an undertaking that even one as intrepid as dear Daph was daunted." She laughed at him, her eye sparkling.

He smiled back as he looked at her inquiringly.

"Well . . . with my unfashionable inches and my short sight—ah, ahem, the shortness of time I could spend away from the horses, it was impossible."

"You must have been disappointed." He continued to smile down at her. "Indeed, I believe it is not yet too late." This last was uttered so softly that Frankie was not sure if she heard him correctly.

"No. I find all this society business rather silly. And, you see, I preferred to stay at Verdant Meadows. They could not manage without me once my brother James went off to the continent with Wellington's staff. I do enjoy my work with our cattle above all things, you know."

"Indeed, so you've given me to understand, ma'am." His lips twitched as he looked down at her. "So, you are a lady of parts . . . But I find it difficult to believe that you can manage a breeding stables with no masculine relative to assist you."

"You think me incapable then, my lord?"

"What I think you, my dear, is . . . delightful." The sincere note in his voice and the warm gleam in his eyes left Frankie speechless. Delightful? she thought unbelieving. Her family and friends generally found her strong, capable, reliable—if a wee bit overmanaging at times—with an odd sense of humor about her now and again . . . but never delightful. What a novel idea!

She was indeed delightful, more than delightful, delectable, Tolland thought as he gazed at her wide lips. He was utterly bewitched. She must be a veritable Circe to cast a spell over him so easily and so completely.

"So . . . now you can waltz almost as if you were born to it, Miss Verdant," Tolland said as the music came to an end. "But perhaps you need just a little more of my expert tuition." So saying, he lifted her slim wrist and put his name down on her dance card for the next waltz.

And then he stood on the sidelines, watching Frankie go off to dance first with a rather short, sandy-haired young man—certainly *much* too young for her—and then with that blasted rake, Lord Roger Reynard, Amelia's ne'er-do-well brother. Tolland fumed. As soon as the dance with Reynard ended, he was at Frankie's side, possessively picking up her hand and resting it on

176

his sleeve. He covered it lightly with his other hand as he turned to her.

"You must be in need of some refreshment, my dear. Allow me to escort you to the dining room."

Frankie was astonished at his familiarity. He was not her escort for the night, yet he was acting as if he had a claim on her. He took her to the dining room, where he procured them each a glass of champagne.

As he made his way to her side again, Frankie began to object, "Really, Lord Sterling, it is not necessary for you to . . ." but the orchestra started to play again before she could complete her scold.

Tolland looked at her and said, "It's our waltz, Miss Verdant."

Frankie hesitated.

He noticed her wavering and said, "Please," favoring her with a rather crooked, boyish smile that she had not seen before now. Her resistance melted as she looked into his blue eyes, and she demurred no longer.

She put her hand lightly upon the one the viscount held out to her saying, "Well, if you're brave enough to try it again."

All the time she had danced with her two other partners, between waltzes with Sterling, she had been thinking of him and of how she had felt when he held her in his arms—and now he wanted to hold her again!

What in the world was causing that strange fluttering feeling in her midsection that had begun the moment he took her hand and placed it on his arm? she wondered dazedly. He was certainly having a most peculiar effect on her! She just couldn't seem to think straight when he touched her! Frankie the light-hearted became Frankie the light-headed.

Really, Tolland thought as they danced, his hand trembling slightly under hers, no woman had *ever* had such an effect on him as this tall, dark-haired lady with

177

her musical voice and mesmerizing eyes. He wished she would speak again. "Only angels have voices like yours," he mused in a low voice. His words echoed his thoughts so that he was surprised he had spoken aloud.

Frankie laughed. "Daph says I speak in too low a register for a woman. She's threatened to hire a voice teacher to teach me to speak in a higher range—but I'm no simpering girl, my lord."

"Indeed you're not! Don't even *think* of trying to change your voice. I absolutely forbid it!"

She laughed again. "No need to resort to violent prohibitions, my lord. 'Twould be an impossible task to alter my voice."

"Good!" He pulled her more tightly against himself and spun her down the room.

He was very aware of the warmth of their physical contact wherever they touched, of how her long, delicate fingers felt through the glove on the hand he held in his, and of his hand resting lightly on her trim waist, hers just touching his shoulder.

He swallowed and said, "You waltz wonderfully well, *mon an*—my dear, Miss Verdant. How came you to say that you would disgrace a partner? Yours is the most graceful body I have ever held!" With this outburst Tolland surprised himself and was aware of an unaccustomed heat flushing his neck and face. "I do apologize, Miss Verdant. My immoderate thoughts keep finding their way to my tongue despite my efforts to curb them."

"Oh, let us have no modesty on your part, my lord. It is your expert tuition that has gotten us through this dance without any missteps." Her eyes laughed at him, and Tolland felt a distinct jolt at hearing her glorious voice while he was treated to the sight of her generous mouth curved up in the wide, warm smile that lit up those laughing eyes. He was almost knocked back on his

178

heels as he gazed at her. He was thunderstruck . . . in awe . . . in love!

No! What was he thinking! He was admiring a certain physical beauty, that was all; lustrous hair, a flawless complexion, a generous mouth—and those exquisite eyes so gloriously colored and thickly lashed . . . not to mention her shapely figure. His eyes rested on the smooth skin above the décolletage of her gown for a moment. His cravat suddenly seemed too tight and he felt himself flushing again, something he hadn't done since he was a schoolboy.

Why, he felt as awkward as one, he admitted. Where was the cool composure he was famous for now? he wondered. Could he be experiencing his first *tendre?* A passing fancy was all it was, he told himself. He felt sure by tomorrow he would have regained his senses and would have recovered from such a ridiculous infatuation for a too-tall, too-old spinster engaged in the unladylike occupation of breeding horses!

She stumbled against him slightly and trod on his toe.

"Forgive me, Miss Verdant."

"Forgive you for having your toe trodden on? No, no. 'Twas my fault entirely, my lord. But you would insist on dancing with me. I did warn you, you know." She grinned lopsidedly as she apologized. "At least we are well matched for height. Indeed, one of my partners was quite short, and I believe he was not quite so ready to take the blame when I trod on his toe!"

Tolland tightened his hold on her once more and drank in her beauty. Really, he had never been so attracted to a woman before. His leg brushed against hers in a turn of the dance and her full breasts pressed slightly against his waistcoat causing him to want to press her fully against himself.

Perhaps old Sam Coleridge had been right when he'd complained that the waltz was immodest for "the Man and

179

his Partner embrace each other, arms and waists, and knees almost touching, and then whirl round and round . . . to lascivious music." But he had waltzed countless times, Tolland mused, and had never been affected like this before!

And just who was Francesca Verdant, anyway? . . . In the course of two dances he had learned that she was new to society, and a chaperon to her niece. She was dark and fairly tall, when the fashion was for petite blond beauties. Her voice was almost masculine in its register, when the fashion was for girlish giggles and simpering. She was past the age when females first made their come-outs, when the fashion was for seventeen and eighteen-year-old debutantes, and, indeed, she was acting as chaperon to just such a young girl.

She was womanly, when the fashion was for child-like females. She liked to be active and useful, not delicately decorative. She admitted to a liking for athletic activities, hunting, hacking, walking, when the fashion was for the more usual feminine activities of sewing, music, sketching, dancing, gossip, managing a house full of people . . . not a stable full of horses.

Was she the perfect woman sent to captivate him at last? he wondered.

Frankie was utterly bemused. It was a moment out of time. She felt as though she were in the midst of a dream, for though she tried hard to hold her mind aloof, her body was responding to new sensations and her plan to bring this man to his knees was taking on a whole new connotation!

Tomorrow she would rethink her plan. Tomorrow. Tonight . . . well, tonight she would just let herself enjoy the dance.

180

# *Chapter Eleven*

As the music died and the couples in their vicinity stopped whirling around, Tolland realized that the dance had ended and reluctantly released his hold on Frankie. He wanted nothing more than to remain by her side.

They little realized it but they had set tongues to wagging and were the talk of the hour. So lost in his new world was Tolland that he hadn't noticed they were under close observation, and Frankie couldn't see others looking at them anyway without her spectacles. The sensational news spread from one interested observer to another.

"Imagine," said one gossip to her crony, "Sterling actually claimed the hand of that long Meg *twice*—and both times for *waltzes!* Why, it's unheard of!"

"Yes, I saw," snickered a second tattlemonger behind her fan. "But, my dear, who in the world *is* she, I want to know?"

"The chaperon of one of this year's crop of debutantes, I've heard. Too old to be making a come-out herself," said a third snidely. "Came up to town from the *country*, you know." And they all laughed maliciously behind their fans.

*    *    *

Tolland was walking aimlessly to the edge of the floor with Frankie on his arm, chatting abstractedly, when he was suddenly accosted.

"Ah, André." The strident female voice broke in upon them. Frenchifying the viscount's first name as was her wont, Lady Amelia stepped to Tolland's other side and linked her arm through his, taking a possessive grip on his limb.

The viscount started. He had been unaware of his surroundings, so Amelia seemed to appear from nowhere, creeping up on his left flank to take him by surprise and spoil the moment. It took him a moment or two to recover.

"I was in hopes of finding you here tonight, *mon cher.* What a *très chic* affair, would you not agree? I have missed you these last two weeks, but I understand you were indisposed, *n'est-ce pas?*" Lady Amelia Reynard tittered affectedly. She, along with everyone else, had seen him waltz twice with this unknown woman.

Frankie took in Lady Amelia Reynard in all her glory, auburn hair arranged à la Sappho and burnished gold satin gown cut low over her bosom and obviously damped so that it clung to her abundantly ripe figure as though it had been painted on. It was evident that she had dispensed with the modest undercovering of a petticoat. A gold necklace emblazoned with emeralds decorated her neck and matching earrings dangled from her lobes.

Remembering this previous encounter in the park, Frankie looked critically at the woman's outfit. Had she thought her own gown daring? Why, it was quite modest by comparison with the one Lady Amelia wore—the hussy!

"Ah, Amelia. What a pleasant affair this is. You look to be in high color tonight—I'm sure your partners have

182

appreciated your efforts," the viscount said coolly.

"Miss Verdant and I were just about to adjourn to the supper room for a bit of sustenance. We shall undoubtedly see you there. Had you better not go in search of your own partner?" Such a dismissal would have sent most woman away defeated, shivering from the man's icy glare, but the Fox was made of sterner stuff.

Tolland tried to shake his arm free of her hold, but he didn't count on the lady's limpetlike clinging and determination to have him to herself.

"Ah, *mon cher,* I don't believe that I have been introduced to Miss, ah, Verdure, here."

"This is Miss Francesca Ver*dant*, Amelia . . . Miss Verdant, may I present Lady Amelia Reynard, only daughter of the Earl of Foxwell."

Frankie looked at the woman who was glaring at her with sparkling green eyes. A challenging look came into her own eyes, and her lips quirked upward slightly at the thought of crossing swords with her new acquaintance.

If he knew the Fox, and Tolland was much afraid that he did, she was sure to say something rude or outrageous to Francesca, as he called Frankie.

"Miss Ver*dure*," Amelia said with deliberate obtuseness, right on cue. "What a very odd name. I do not believe I am familiar with it. Are you new in town?" she uttered in a falsely sweet tone.

"Yes, quite *new* to all this society business," answered Frankie.

Ha! Amelia thought to herself, the woman's as green as her name.

"I take it from your manner you are an *old* hand at such affairs as this," Frankie continued.

"You have someone *well connected* to sponsor you, of course." Amelia raised her brows, hoping to set down the interloper.

"I am staying with my sister, Lady Daphne Whitt-

183

grove." Frankie, scenting the attack, was ready to parry it.

"Oh, Lady Whittgrove . . . the woman who is always presenting her spouse with pledges of her affection. She is not a familiar figure in society. I believe her figure is always too circular for her to circulate much in my circles," Amelia tittered.

"Ah, no. It's not surprising you haven't encountered her. Running in circles is not dear Daph's style. She lives in Grosvenor *Square*, you see." Tolland bit back a grin at Frankie's retort. "As long as you've been on the town, I'm sure you will be familiar with the location."

"Indeed." Amelia decided on another tack. She looked Frankie up and down, and remarked, "Your gown, Miss Verdure . . . if I may say so, is so . . . ah, so jejune, shall we say." Her expression conveyed clearly enough that she found Frankie's attire not quite à la mode. "As you choose to wear white, one assumes you occupy a debutante's station . . . yet . . . yet not."

Frankie would have reared if she had been a horse. As it was, her nostrils flared and she fired back, "And, if I may say so, brass suits you, Lady Amelia—perfectly. It is obvious what guides you in your selection of hunting attire, er, evening frock."

Amelia's eyes nearly bulged from her head at this unprecedented counterattack. She positively bristled from her red mane to her painted toenails.

Tolland held himself aloof from the fray, his lips twitching once or twice as he listened to Frankie pulling caps with the Fox. He almost whistled through his teeth when Frankie landed a good flush hit in the gown department, disparaging Amelia's taste.

"I am here this evening with Lady Chatterington, you know," Frankie continued. "Her *ton*, or so I am given to understand, is of the highest. Perhaps that doesn't qualify her to run in your, ah, circles."

184

Tolland was ready to swear that the Fox had just suffered a stinging uppercut, if the jerk on his arm when she jumped back as if bitten was any indication.

"Oh, André, *mon chéri*, I fear that name has unpleasant associations for you." Amelia, sparring for wind, deviously changed the subject. "So thoughtless of Miss Verdure to bring it up . . . Were you in attendance the evening André was assaulted at the Chatterington ball, Miss Verdure?"

Amelia's barb went home, hitting more deeply than she knew. Frankie's eyes flashed angrily, but it was too dangerous to reply. Amelia's counterpunch left her slightly off balance for a moment.

Frankie felt Sterling's arm muscles clench under the hand that lay on his sleeve. He gallantly took up the cudgels. "I know not where you had your information, Amelia, but I assure you that I look back to the Chatterington Ball with some pleasure, for it was there that I first encountered Miss Verdant." Amelia dropped her hold on his arm and stepped back with ill-concealed annoyance.

Why, she looked as if he had just thrown cold water on her! Frankie stifled her laughter at the look on Lady Amelia's face—and at the viscount's words. Poor Lord Sterling didn't know that he was defending the very woman who had supposedly "assaulted" him.

Her niece and Lord Harry approached them at this instant, and Frankie would have pulled free of the viscount's arm and joined them but Sterling held tight to her at feeling her slight movement.

Laurel had a prounounced look of surprise on her face to see her aunt with Viscount Sterling. "Do you wish to join us for supper, Aunt?" she asked. She was *very* curious about how this circumstance had come about. Had the viscount yet recognized her aunt as the woman he had knocked down on that previous social occasion?

185

she wondered in some trepidation.

"We were just about to go in," Tolland declared, feeling harried.

"Oh, do let us all go together," Amelia cried, as she took a firm grip on the viscount's arm once again. She leaned across him, generously displaying her charms right under his nose, Frankie saw with displeasure.

Tolland had all he could do not to shake her off and create a shocking scene.

Amelia's smile was brittle as she kept her hold on him. She was not about to stand by and let some little—well, not so little, she amended—provincial spinster get her claws into Sterling when she had been plotting and planning to make him her own for these three years now. She had even turned down two perfectly decent offers, as well as several ineligible ones, because she preferred to be Lady Sterling, and enjoy all such a union entailed.

They were about to proceed when Monty Addlecumber spied his adored one on Tolland's arm and rushed over. He had just reluctantly relinquished one fair lady to another partner. Sally was being taken in to supper by Lucius Pendergast, a boon companion of her brother Philip.

"By gad, Tol, see you have two beauties—one on each wing. Unfair . . . Unfair. Be glad to gallivant one of 'em, don't y'know." He politely offered his green and gold brocade-clad arm to Lady Amelia, who pretended she didn't see it.

Frankie moved to take Monty's arm, but Tolland would not release her. An unseemly scuffle ensued as the four wrestled about at the door to the supper room effectively blocking the entrance to the couples who had come up behind them. Finally the two ladies preceded the gentlemen into the room. Tolland forgot to be embarrassed, despite the eyes of the curious upon his party, so intent was he on watching Frankie.

186

Supper was an uncomfortable farrago. Somehow several other single gentlemen had joined them, including Freddy Drake and Lord Roger Reynard, Amelia's brother. The various occupants of the table engaged in tangled maneuvering to the satisfaction of almost no one. Laurel and Markham were the only couple not to notice the strain. They talked quietly and exclusively to one another as they sat side by side and remained oblivious to the comic scene being enacted round about them.

In the general confusion of finding seats Tolland was separated from Frankie and found himself sitting opposite her and next to Amelia, the worst of all possible arrangements in his estimation. Frankie had Drake seated to her left and Reynard to her right.

They were both making sheep's eyes at her, Tolland thought, clenching his jaw angrily. The two men were monopolizing her to such an extent that he had no chance for continued conversation with her. He could only watch in simmering frustration as his friends flirted with her and he imagined them as captivated by her siren's voice as he was.

To his considerable consternation, two other gentlemen stopped by the table and signed Frankie's dance card. Tolland wanted to be the one she was smiling at, the one she responded to in her low, husky voice. He wanted to gaze at her eyes and her mouth and to occasionally touch her hand. Damn! This was a ridiculous situation.

Amelia looked on with growing concern as she saw the viscount's eyes fixed on her rival. She was furious. "Damn and blast the woman!" she muttered under her breath. The Verdure creature was flirting with others to make André jealous—and it was working, she saw to her utter disbelief. Sterling looked as lovesick as a newborn calf, and over a provincial antidote who was well on the shelf, too!

What to do? . . . Ah, she would have a word with her

brother. Roger sat next to the Verdure woman and seemed to be trying to make up to her. Though what he saw in such a tall, gawky, countrified old maid, Amelia was sure she could not begin to imagine. She would tell him to get the hussy out of the way; he would cooperate or she would reveal his latest peccadillo to their father, and Amelia knew she could count on the earl to curtail her brother's funds forthwith. Roger would not care for *that* in the least! And anyway, Roger was sure to be willing, she thought as she watched him. Why, he was flirting his head off with the countrified creature!

Frankie left the table on Drake's arm. She knew that she had been rude to Freddy earlier in leaving him and going off to waltz with the viscount. Besides, she could not bear to sit any longer constantly aware of that bold Reynard woman casting out lures to Sterling, and flaunting her considerable cleavage at him in the most vulgar way as she blatantly leaned toward him.

In an effort to see where Frankie was going, Tolland turned sharply . . . and knocked over a glass of wine that spilled all down the front of Amelia's golden dress and splashed onto his own knee-breeches in the process.

Amelia let out a screen of dismay, jumped up, and fled to the ladies' withdrawing room as the red stain quickly soaked through her gown. In all likelihood the garment had been irreparably ruined.

Tolland sat dabbing at his breeches with a cloth brought by a footman, furious with himself. Damnation! he thought, if that dratted Fox hadn't been pressing herself against his arm, he never would have knocked over the glass! And now he would have to take the distasteful step of appeasing Amelia over the ruin of her gown!

Guests seated at nearby tables concealed their grins

behind their hands or smiled openly to see My Lord Perfection come to grief yet again.

Two besotted occupants of the table remained unaware of the incident as Lord Harry escorted Laurel back to the ballroom.

"My dearest Miss Whittgrove, it is of all things most unfair that I cannot have more than two dances with you."

"Yes," breathed Laurel, gazing into his eyes in total agreement, "very unfair, my lord. But we dare not risk breaking the rules, I'm afraid."

"Do you think we would offend propriety if we were to sit out this set together?" begged an infatuated Lord Harry, his habitual light bantering manner abandoned for once.

"I would like it of all things, my lord," Laurel said artlessly, making no effort to conceal her desire to remain in his company. "But I'm afraid I'm already promised to your friend, Mr. Drake for this set."

Markham looked up and saw Freddy leading Laurel's aunt out onto the floor. He smiled. "I don't know how it is possible that anyone would miss the chance of being in the company of the divine Miss Whittgrove for even a *moment*, much less for a whole set of dances, but I fear your partner has forgotten to claim you." He indicated to her the couple taking their place in the country dance.

Laurel smiled up at him happily, and the two strayed to the conservatory where they sat among the potted palms and concealing plants for half an hour, talking nonsense and enjoying one another's company. And if Lord Harry was able to steal a kiss, or was granted one quite freely, who was there to see and tell?

\* \* \*

Frankie danced and danced, going from one partner to another, wishing she dared a peep through her lorgnette to see what the viscount was up to. Much as she squinted, it was not often that she could make out his tall form above others in the room. Occasionally she could distinguish him at a distance by his height and his plain black garb, though of course the expression on his face was lost to her unfocused eyes. One of her partners finally brought her attention back to the dance by inquiring, "Do you have something in your eye, Miss Verdant?"

At first Tolland danced, too, with a slightly damp and unmollified Lady Amelia and then with Laurel when she finally emerged, smiling and flushed, from her tête-á-tête with Lord Harry. Later, he walked about, speaking with acquaintances; then he just leaned negligently against the wall, watching the dancers. Watching her! Frankie realized it as she danced quite near to him. But his expression seemed cold and haughty. Had he found out who she was then? Frankie wondered, and stumbled slightly in her steps.

"Are you feeling as warm as I am after our exertions, Miss Verdant?" Lord Roger Reynard, her present partner, asked as the set ended. "Would you care to stroll out on the balcony for a breath of air?"

"Yes, a breath of air would be most welcome, thank you," Frankie said gratefully, beginning to think that at last Lord Roger began to show some sign of sense after all the nonsense he had just been spouting in her ear over supper and during their dance. However, she hadn't attended to his chatter above half, distracted as she was by a certain *other* gentleman.

Lord Roger led her through a curtained entrance to the balcony, and they were suddenly in the cool darkness— quite alone.

\*      \*      \*

Ah, the cool breeze felt good against her warm face, Frankie thought, immediately refreshed. Lord Roger was a sensible chap, after all, she decided, despite all those outrageous things he had said at supper and while they were dancing. When she caught the drift of his comments, she hadn't been able to resist making jokes of his silly compliments. He hadn't much appreciated her attempts to deflate his fulsome speeches, if the frustrated look on his face had been anything to go by.

Frankie felt a soothing hand at the nape of her neck, caressing her curls. She relaxed for a fraction of a second, then froze. What was the man about?

She turned sharply toward Lord Roger. He gripped one of her arms and tightened his hold on the back of her neck forcing her head toward his.

"What do you think you are doing, sirrah!" she uttered sharply and struggled to break free. "Unhand me at once!" She trod down heavily on his toe to emphasize her demand, but with no noticeable effect.

"What, my beauty, changed your mind, have you? You *did* agree to step out here with me, you know," said Reynard. He was a tall man and there was a strength in his grip that even Frankie, fit as she was, couldn't break.

"I came out here for a breath of air, not to be mauled about by you!" she uttered hoarsely as his mouth descended toward hers. She pushed against his chest but to no avail. Though she did manage to land a kick on one of his shins, his mouth covered hers in a hard, wet kiss.

Suddenly he was yanked away and a fist crashed into his face with a bone-crunching sound.

"Don't you ever touch her again!" Frankie heard the unmistakable accents of Viscount Sterling. He had certainly wasted no time in coming to the rescue, she reflected thankfully.

Tolland had been watching Frankie's every move since supper and when she stepped through the curtain with

Reynard, he knew that he couldn't stand it a minute longer. He had followed them out posthaste.

Reynard picked himself up from where he had fallen and disappeared around the corner of the building as Frankie turned to face a furious Tolland.

She was taken aback by the murderous look in his eyes as she began to say, "Why, thank you, Lord Ster—"

"What did you mean by coming out here with that rake, madam?" he questioned with teeth-clenching ferocity.

"Rake? How was I to know he was a rake?" Frankie fired back.

He took her shoulders in a hard grip. "Never, never leave a ball without your chaperon."

Frankie began to laugh. It was ludicrous—*she* was the chaperon. "You mean like the last time . . ."

Tolland shook her.

She stopped laughing and saw the fierce glow in his eyes.

The next moment she was crushed in his arms, his hard mouth hot and demanding on hers. Frankie was furiously angry . . . then she found herself enjoying the sensation of being kissed by this particular gentleman . . . and soon she was as lost to all sense of propriety as was Tolland. The tension between them had been building to this all evening.

His kiss became softer. Her arms went up to encircle his neck as he pulled her closer. She felt a tremor move through his body as he tightened his hold and pulled her fully against himself. She caressed the back of his neck and the side of his jaw with her hands, delighting in the feel of his skin under her palms. His shaven cheeks were rough against her soft face. She moved her hands to entangle them in his thick hair and was surprised by its silky smoothness. She could get to like kissing him, she thought hazily.

The tempo changed. His arms were laced round her so tightly that she could feel his heart beating as his mouth moved hotly over hers, deepening the kiss.

He had released her lips and was saying something. What was it? Frankie couldn't breathe, let alone hear what he was saying above the rushing in her ears.

"I think that I'm . . . I must tell you . . . I can't . . ." He stopped and then said urgently, "Come with me." He held her arm in a tight clasp and began to drag her deeper into the garden.

Frankie stumbled on the flagstone path due to the viscount's insistent pulling on her arm. All at once her senses righted themselves and reality returned. "Let me go, my lord!" she demanded, forcefully if not calmly. "Stop at once and let me go. *Now,* Sterling. You're hurting me."

Tolland stopped and looked at her uncomprehendingly, not realizing what an iron grip he had on her arm.

"Let go, please," she said again, more quietly. "I must return inside now, my lord. I am grateful that you rescued me from that rake Reynard, but I cannot remain with you now."

Tolland released her, a look of puzzlement and hurt in his eyes at her rejection. Did she not feel as he did, then? "Please Francesca . . ." he whispered, one hand held out to her. But Frankie did not see it. She had already turned and was walking quickly back to the balcony door.


Tolland was thrown completely off his stride. He walked out of the garden and made his way back to Bruton Place, shaken and upset not only by what had just happened but by his behavior from the moment he had first run into Francesca Verdant in the Seftons' ballroom. To cut out his friend, Freddy, to waltz with her not just once but twice! And then not to let go of her hand until forced to do so at the supper table! To be aware of her every action and listen to her every word from across that table, then to prop up the wall and jealously watch her as she moved from partner to partner! What an utter *cake* he had made of himself!

He had been knocked off his pins when he had seen her again tonight and had somehow allowed himself to get completely carried away physically. But to actually embrace and kiss a respectable woman with complete abandon and then try to take her deeper into the garden for God-only-knew what further acts of passion amid a house full of people was an act of madness that was totally incomprehensible! It was a thing so uncharacteristic as to cause him to wonder if his mind had been disordered by that first collision with the unknown at the Chatterington ball.


An hour later, safely ensconced in his study, Tolland loosened his cravat and ran his fingers through his hair as he tried to understand his recent actions. His life had been turned upside down in the past few weeks by these women who kept suddenly appearing in his path. He, with his reputation for perfection, who never put a foot wrong, had been completely overset—though in a quite, quite different way this time.

He would have had to marry Francesca Verdant if his rash act had met with no resistance! he thought wildly. If she insisted, he supposed he really had compromised her already, and if one of her relatives summoned him on the morrow, demanding the ultimate restitution, he would not be surprised. He would have to marry his angel . . .

Good God! Was he actually hoping for such a thing! He, who had never planned to marry, who had sworn off marriage as if it were the plague! He *marry?* He had successfully evaded all entanglements with females in his

194

long career ere now. He looked bleary-eyed at the half-empty brandy bottle on the table beside him. What was the matter with him? he wondered, rubbing his chin. Must be castaway, he decided. It was the fault of all these blasted women who were driving him to imbibe more deeply than was his habit.

There was nothing else for it. He would give up entertainments where the sexes mixed and devote himself to his club and his favorite outdoor activities for the time being, at least until he could regain his sang-froid and shake off this foolish attraciton to the tall, dark-haired woman. At least he was still accounted a nonpareil in his sporting pursuits, thank God!

If a sneaking suspicion that he was deceiving himself flitted through the alcoholic fumes clouding his brain, it was banished by the thought that all these women plaguing his life—the unknown dowd in the spectacles, the Fox, the lovely Francesca—were a confounded nuisance. Discretion was clearly the better part of valor in this instance, and an orderly retreat was better than a rout! He would banish thoughts of the violet-eyed enchantress with the angelic voice in sleep.

Frankie went about in somewhat of a daze for a day or two until her own common sense reasserted itself and the viscount's absence from society reinforced her belief that the evening she had spent with him at the Sefton ball could not have been all as she remembered it. She half thought she had dreamed many of the things that had happened—or maybe she had had too much champagne at supper. She laughed at herself.

But she couldn't help remembering how Sterling had looked at her, with such a soft, fond expression on his face, several times and how warm and pleasant his voice had been when he'd spoken. His whole manner had seemed less stiff and formidable than it had been at Lady Chatterington's—before they had met under the table there, anyway! She grinned.

And he had kissed her passionately—again! She didn't think he could have been foxed this time. What an unprecedented thing to happen to her! Was it possible that a man found *her*—countrified, unfashionable Frankie Verdant—that attractive? Well, her lips were still swollen the next day, so something must have occurred. Daph had noticed and, to her considerable embarrassment, had asked, "What in the world has happened to your lips, Frankie dear. You look as if you have been thoroughly kissed!"

Sterling's name had come up when Laurel had come out of the clouds of her own preoccupation with Lord Harry long enough to ask, "How did you like waltzing with Viscount Sterling, Aunt Frankie? Everyone was commenting on it."

Daphne's ears had perked up. "What! Oh, Frankie, dear, you are certain to be all the rage now if Sterling deigned to dance with you!"

"Is he not a bit of a rake, though, Daph?"

"Oh, no! Not Viscount Sterling. He has quite a spotless reputation, always 'correct' in his dealings with the *ton*," Daph had assured her. "And he's been on the town forever. Everyone admires him. He's accounted a great Corinthian, you know, quite a manly man."

His attraction to her seemed to have been quite temporary, however, a thing of the moment only, for he had not sought her out again as she had half expected him to do. Handsome is as Hansohm does, I suppose, she thought, shrugging her shoulders. Daph did not think him a rake. Perhaps his behavior had not been his typical way of carrying on, as hers certainly hadn't. She had never reacted to a man in such a way before!

Well, if his manner of carrying on in the Seftons'

garden had not been typical, then it was just as uncharacteristic of his reputed way of behaving as on those other occasions when the supposedly "perfect" gentleman had turned clumsy in her presence and showed a deplorable lack of manners in ripping up at her so rudely. Something about her, in whatever guise, seemed to have a strange effect on him.

Still, she did not repine; hadn't she achieved her purpose in tricking him? She savored the thought that she had scored a minor victory over the man in gaining his interest and hoaxing him into believing he had never met her before.


Frankie put aside thoughts of the puzzling viscount and began to enjoy a certain popularity. To her surprise and Daphne's delight, quite a few gentlemen had been calling on her as well as on Laurel since the night of the Sefton ball, and she had gone riding several times. The gentlemen invariably asked her out riding when they found it was her favorite pastime. All the better for her to judge the way they handled their cattle, she reasoned.

She discouraged all but the most persistent of her admirers, or those few whom she liked or whose mounts found favor in her eyes. Freddy Drake qualified on both counts. Her favorite destination was, of course, the park whether he called with his curricle or on horseback.

Although she continued to accompany Laurel to various functions with the added chaperonage of Lady Chatterington, and though she tried not to raise her lorgnette and look about at the assembled crowd, she couldn't help but notice that the viscount had not been present once. On none of her outings was Sterling so much as glimpsed, though his doggedly daft cousin Addlecumber was frequently seen attempting to ride beside Lady Amelia Reynard at the fashionable hour in the park.

On several occasions Frankie had seen the lady try in vain to guide her horse away from the vicinity of the garishly costumed Sir Montagu, but her skills in horsemanship were so lacking that she frequently brought other riders or carriages to a stand, causing a great deal of disturbance and annoyance. The sight of one of these entanglements never failed to bring a wide smile to Frankie's lips as she put her spectacles up to her eyes for a moment and gazed in the direction of the commotion.

She was amused more than flattered by Drake's constant attentions. In her opinion, Freddy had taken a fancy to her horse. "A prime goer, ma'am. A real bang-up piece of blood and bone!" he had exclaimed on first viewing the big, black gelding. He had not yet dared ask permission to ride him, but Frankie felt that it was just a matter of time before he got up his courage to do so. Perhaps he was even trying to think of a way to convince her to sell the animal to him. His covetous glances were certainly not for her person.

Freddy had escorted Frankie and Laurel on afternoon rides in the park twice in the past week, during which Lord Harry had just "happened" upon them and, as a matter of course, had been invited to join their party.

Daphne was not happy with the evident attraction between Lord Harry and her daughter. Bowing to her mother's wishes, Laurel had refused Markham's offer of escort three times now, but had indulged in a fit of the dismals each time, whereas she was in distinctly high spirits when she returned from engagements where she had "unexpectedly" encountered him. She seemed to be making no effort to encourage any of the other gentlemen, to Daphne's vexation.

"I haven't the least notion of forbidding Laurel to

198

speak to Lord Harry, Frankie dear, but as Laurel's chaperon you must not allow her to be so much alone in his company whenever they meet. Could you not draw Lord Harry's attention more to yourself when you are out with Mr. Drake and put Freddy more in Laurel's way?

"Freddy is certainly the more eligible *parti*. I would be glad if he would pay more attention to Laurel and less to you. Not that I do not wish you to contract an eligible alliance, Frankie dear, I certainly do, but something must be done to cool the ardor that Lord Harry shows toward my darling girl. I am much afraid that my dearest Alfie would not approve of such an improvident alliance. He would sigh and frown and call me a 'peagoose,' which I'm sure I'm not," Daphne said worriedly, pressing her dainty lace handkerchief to her lips and shaking her head unhappily, for she was in a quandary.

"I assure you, Daph, Mr. Drake is not the least interested in my person. He has designs on my Demon. He would go to any lengths to get him away from me." Frankie laughed. "I suppose he would even go so far as to propose to me if it meant that that was the only way he could get his hands on Black Demon.

"Do not be alarmed, however. I have no intention of giving up my horse, any more than I do my person, to Mr. Drake . . . Now if you could only persuade Laurel to ride an animal more worthy of his notice, perhaps his eyes would turn toward her."

"Mayhap Lord Harry is interested in your horse, too," Daphne said hopefully.

"Alas, Daph, Lord Harry is much more interested in your daughter."

"But you must prevent him from showing so much attention to Laurel. I rely on you in this matter, my dear, for what I am to say to dear Alfie I haven't the least notion."

But Frankie had no idea how to draw Lord Harry's

199

attention to herself and push Freddy at Laurel. She soon saw that the task was impossible. Lord Harry and her niece were totally absorbed in one another's company. Laurel appeared to glow in Markham's presence, and she always seemed more relaxed and happy when conversing with him. As for Harry he doted on her; her wishes and comfort were always his first concern.

Frankie did not like to report this to Daphne, for her sister would then either worry all the more or have to take stronger steps to separate them, and, in Frankie's opinion, this would be most unkind to the feelings of both. Besides, she approved of Markham. His mount was well chosen, sleek, and compact with just a trace of playfulness in its manner but always well under control. No, she could find no flaw in his horsemanship. Her niece would have no cause for complaint if she chose to run in tandem with that gent.

As for Freddy, his only interest was in talking, endlessly talking, about horses and hunting, riding and driving. He repeatedly bemoaned the fact that her Demon had been gelded, for he had several mares he wished could have been matched with the big black horse. Frankie took pleasure from their conversation, but sometimes even *she* wished that they might talk of something else for a change, especially when Freddy described in excruciating detail every hunt of his long career. Frankie was ready to throw up her hands in exasperation when, for the twentieth time, he began a conversation, "Did I tell you about the run I had with the Quorn when . . ."

Freddy was rarely seen at *ton* functions, though. Frankie knew that he was busy with other pursuits: cockfights, curricle races, mills, turf racing at Newmarket and elsewhere, anything of a sporting nature quickly drew his attention. Still, he was a pleasant young man and Frankie enjoyed his company. She doubted that

Laurel had exchanged more than ten words with the gentleman in the past two weeks and did not think they would suit, despite Daph's optimistic hopes.

When he learned of Frankie's ability to handle a team as well as she sat a horse, Freddy turned the reins of his curricle over to her during an afternoon's drive in the park. She amazed all passers-by with her skill in controlling his recently acquired, highly spirited team of grays and with the way she could maneuver through the heavy park traffic. Freddy smugly refused to tell her just where he had acquired the matched pair, despite her persistent questioning.

They were a trifle squeezed when Drake brought his curricle round early one afternoon, for Laurel had accompanied them on this excursion. Inevitably they met Markham who was on horseback, and just as inevitably he dismounted and helped Laurel down from the carriage so that they could walk along one of the less frequented lanes, he leading his horse as Frankie drove away with a beaming Freddy sitting up beside her.

The sun glinted through the overhanging branches, forming patterns of light and shade as Laurel and Harry walked down the long, leafy avenue. Laurel spoke first.

"I'm afraid that my Mama has her heart set on me making a match with Mr. Drake," she commented sadly.

"No! How could any parent be so unnatural as to wish such a fate on one's daughter," Harry replied, a laughing light in his eye.

"Well, she seems to think he calls so frequently to see *me*. When it's really Aunt Frankie he wants to prose on to about some boring sporting activity or other . . . I don't see how she stands it."

"Ah, I see what it is. I have a rival for your affections," Harry said with his hand over his heart.

"No! How can you say so!" Laurel, quite shocked, turned to look at him. "I could never admire Mr. Drake."

Markham grinned. "Well, you exclaimed so petulantly that Freddy would rather talk to your aunt than to you . . . so I naturally assumed that you were jealous."

"Oh, Lord Harry, you're teasing me again," Laurel protested, lightly pounding his arm with her daintily gloved fist.

"I would be pleased if you would drop the 'Lord' when you address me, my dear," he said, suddenly serious, his gaze fixed on her mouth.

Laurel blushed as she looked up at him with wide green eyes. "I couldn't do that, my lord. Why then I would be calling you just 'Harry.'"

"Precisely so, my dearest Miss Whittgrove—just Harry."

"It wouldn't be right for you to continue calling me Miss Whittgrove, then," she replied in a whisper.

"No, Laurel, my dearest, it wouldn't." He looked at her intently.

"Oh," she murmured as he took her chin in his hand and claimed her lips in a light, tender kiss. He released her immediately and glanced quickly round to note that they were unobserved by any but his horse.

Laurel still looked at him with wide eyes, but their expression had changed from one of surprise to one of wonder.

"Harry? Do you love me?"

"No, I hate you—very, very much."

"Ohh . . . will you be serious for once."

"Indeed, my dearest Laurel, I have never been more so. Of course, I love you, my darling. I've loved you since I first laid eyes on you, and it would be beyond my just deserts if you were to return even half of my affection."

"Oh Harry, how can you doubt that I am near to dying with love for you, my dear, dear boy . . ."

He put a gentle finger to her lips and said, "Shh, my love. Not now." He offered her his arm, and they continued their walk as two gentlemen and a lady approached them along a lane that wound through the trees.

They settled it between them that they would continue to see one another frequently, and when Lady Whittgrove saw that her daughter's interest was truly fixed and quite immovable, they felt that perhaps she would look on the match more favorably.

"We shall come about, my dearest, never fear," Harry assured his beloved, a twinkle in his eye.

"Oh, Harry, you have a scheme!" Laurel exclaimed brightly. "I *knew* you would manage to secure a position, not that you need to with my dowry. Tell me what it is," she demanded as she clung with both hands to his arm.

Harry just smiled at her and warmly covered both her small hands with his larger one. "I shan't tell you just yet, dearest, but my plan should please your father."

He had prevailed upon his own sire, the Duke of Ampleforth, to use whatever influence he might command to secure a government position for him. However much the duke might deplore the idea of a son of his working for a living, Lord Harry had convinced his father that the life of a wastrel was not for him and that his heart was set on marriage with Miss Laurel Whittgrove.

Lord Harry resolved to write to Laurel's father and set out his prospects as soon as he had received notification that the post in the diplomatic corps he pinned his hopes on was indeed to be his. He trusted that this course of action would appeal to Laurel as much as it appealed to him, and if his efforts met with success, he was sure that Sir Alfred would be more amenable to the match.

# Chapter Twelve

Tolland had been true to his scheme, absenting himself from the social whirl for the last few weeks. It was all very well, he supposed, to give up every chance of seeing Miss Verdant—Francesca—as he thought of her now, but to dream about her every night was intolerable! And such dreams they were, too! Why, he woke up in a heat, reaching for insubstantial air, *again* last night. He had not seen her since the Sefton ball.

The dreams were vivid and graphic. He was holding her, kissing her . . . and more . . . Then she would disappear, frequently just at the climactic moment, and he would be left hot and uncomfortable and more than a little frustrated. He shifted uncomfortably in his saddle at the very thought.

What was he to do? These many nights of tossing and turning had left him haggard and unrested. His peace was quite cut up.

He could not go on like this, he thought, as he slid the leather reins back and forth through his fingers. Finally he wheeled his chestnut stallion, Orion, around for an early morning ride in the park. No one was about. Good, he could set hid mount to a fast pace and perhaps outrun some of his blue devils.

His attention was distracted from his disquieting thoughts by the sight of a woman in a jade habit thundering along somewhere to his left. "My God," he thought, "her horse has bolted! Where is her groom?"

He wheeled quickly and was off, Orion's heels tearing up the turf as they gained on the woman who was clinging low over the neck of a large, well-set-up black gelding.

As Tolland approached he realized that the horse was not bolting with the woman, but that she was actually in control. And galloping hell for leather over the sward. "By God, can that woman ride!" he muttered unbelievingly. There, she jumped a small stream with perfect control, her horse's feet flying out behind as she landed on the other side. "What a clipping rider she is!" he exclaimed.

With a whoop of joy, Tolland decided to join in the madcap gallop. He urged Orion on, and the great-hearted chestnut responded. His hat flew off. Damn! No time to retrieve it now. The chase was on. Ah, it felt good to go this fast, breathing in the frosty morning air, enjoying the sight of another good rider on a magnificent horse.

Now! He was almost even with the female rider.

She turned and looked at him out of her unmistakable eyes.

His mouth fell open as shock flooded him. He felt as though he were dreaming again, and he promptly lost control of his mount. He soon found himself on the ground, outridden by a woman and thrown from a horse for the first time in his life! His head was swimming, and his still-weak left ankle had twisted under him.

Frankie was as surprised to see Sterling as the viscount was to see her, but she managed to slow her own horse and brought Demon quickly back to where he had fallen. His chestnut had stopped and stood grazing nearby, looking as shamefaced as it was possible for a horse to look. Thank God, the stallion seemed to be unharmed, at

206

least! she thought as she dismounted. She quickly threw Demon's reins over a bush, caught the stallion's loose reins, and tied him up near where the viscount had fallen.

She was bending over the hapless rider, gingerly feeling the back of his head for any injury when he opened his blue eyes widely, smiled up at her, and said, "Do I dream, or is it you, Francesca? . . . You won't disappear *this* time, will you?"

"No, I won't," she answered, soothingly.

Tolland was still woozy as he watched Frankie's movements. With some difficulty, she tried as best she could to examine his foot and ankle through his leather riding boot. She fully expected that he had broken a bone or two. She let out a sigh of relief when she couldn't detect any obvious sign of a break, though she couldn't be sure until the boot was cut off. The foot was swelling fast and she knew that, at the very least, it was bound to be badly sprained.

She took her spectacles from a buttoned pocket of her habit and put them on to further inspect the man lying dazed, his head now in her lap. She was afraid she might have missed something, for she had relied mainly on her experienced, probing fingers to tell her of any injury. Detecting no further damage, she hoped that Sterling would be able to sit his horse for the ride home. There was a chance he was concussed. Lying on the cold, damp ground, as he was, surely had to be extremely uncomfortable, yet he made no move to rise.

Frankie was looking round for a source of water to bathe his head or another rider to call to their assistance when she heard him shout, "You!" in accents of loathing.

As the wooziness faded and Tolland realized where he was, he looked up and beheld a woman in spectacles. The very woman who had been the cause of all his recent mishaps, he thought in shock. "You again! Get away from me! I thought you were Francesca! Oh, my God! You *are* Francesca! It's a nightmare!" He closed his eyes in utter disbelief.

"Lord Sterling, if you can possibly make the effort, I think we should try to get you home now so your injury can be attended to," Frankie said calmly, disregarding the ravings of the injured man.

His eyes flew open. "No. Not with you, madam," he insisted heatedly.

"All right, then," she said in her best no-nonsense manner. "How do you propose to make the trip? I shall have to leave you here while I ride for help otherwise."

"No," he said without thinking.

"Well, what do you expect me to do?" she asked, in growing exasperation. "I cannot just go away, you know."

"I will get up and mount my horse."

"Oh, you will, will you, my lord? I would like to see you do it!"

"Madam, I am not an invalid!"

"Your head must have taken a more severe blow than you know if you think you can walk without assistance at the moment, Sterling."

"I can and I will!"

"All right, if you wish to be stubborn. Do it!"

"Leave me."

"I can't do that in all good conscience."

Tolland growled deep in his throat. He attempted to heave himself up, but no amount of clamping his jaws shut against the pain was of any use. His injured ankle just would not bear his weight. After sitting for several moments, clearing his head and considering his awful dilemma, he realized that he had very little choice.

"All right, madam, you win. If you would assist me to rise, I shall try to limp to my horse." He became a little less angry. Clearly he must rely on her assistance to get out of the latest devilishly awkward situation.

He knelt and placed his right foot on the ground. Frankie came around and put her arm under his right shoulder. He stifled a groan as she helped him rise, bidding him keep his weight on her and off the left foot.

"I don't think the ankle is broken, Sterling. It was probably weak from the previous injury and now is in much worse case." Frankie chattered on as he lifted his head and grittily limped on. "I will make up some of my special ointment for you. I always have my groom, Trot, use it when there is an injury in the stables at home. Takes the swelling down almost immediately."

"Madam, I am *not* a *horse!*" he ground out.

"No, no, of course you are not," she soothed, pleased that his color was better anyway. "If you were a horse, we should have to shoot you!"

He flashed her a look, making it abundantly clear that he did not appreciate her humor.

"But remember, Sterling, we, too, have ligaments and muscles in our legs that swell from injury and respond to the same treatment. If it makes you feel any better, Johnnie, the Smithy's son, used my ointment with great efficacy when he wrenched his shoulder."

Tolland muttered curses. At the moment he had no breath to spare for arguing with the perfidious Miss Francesca Verdant.

They were moving slowly to where his horse stood. Frankie tried to distract Tolland from his injury by prattling on about various equine ailments. "Why, I remember when Red Devil, our prize stud, you know, hit the top of the South Farm gate so hard he splintered it in two. Thought I would have to put him down and could not bear the thought of that, as you can imagine. I was vastly relieved when I saw that there were no broken bones, only the laceration and sprained hock. Trot and I applied the poultice hourly for about six and thirty hours

209

and he was right as rain in about a month or two."

"So you think I will be 'right as rain' in a month or two," Tolland growled between heavy breaths.

"Why, certainly. You'll be able to caper about with the best of 'em. Though I expect you will be a bear to live with for the next fortnight."

"I shall *not* be a bear, madam! Not a bear, a horse, or any other kind of four-legged beast!" he shouted.

Frankie clucked her tongue against her teeth. "Your staff will have much to put up with in the next few days."

Tolland only grimaced, too out of breath to shout her down. He was very pale, with sweat running down his face as he gritted his teeth determinedly. She didn't think she could manage to get him on his horse by herself. She would have to jolt him into making the effort himself.

She administered the necessary impetus. "I cannot carry you, you know, Sterling." He squared his shoulders at her words and moved a bit faster.

She managed to lug him the last ten yards to his horse. He leaned against the side of his mount while she grabbed the reins. "You look as if you have shot the cat, my lord." A spurt of energy went through him at her words. He gritted his teeth and heaved himself up into the saddle.

"That's the ticket! Why, you're plucky as a Trojan for guttiness and determination, Sterling. We'll have you home directly."

Frankie held the chestnut's head and stroked his silky nose as she murmured soothingly to the stallion while Tolland settled himself in the saddle. She sneaked a quick glimpse at the chestnut's mouth and could see from his soft, firm lips that he had suffered no cow-handed treatment from his rider. She nodded with satisfaction and smiled to herself while whispering to the stallion, "I knew your master was a right 'un, my beauty."

Tolland was disgusted to see his nervous stallion respond to her. Orion, the treacherous beast, actually dipped his head for her to scratch his nose! Why, the animal was famous for his lack of sociability and had never allowed anyone other than Tolland or his groom to come near him before.

Frankie did not leave at the front door of the viscount's townhouse, as he might have expected. Instead she sailed blithely in, without regard to the impropriety of her presence in a single gentleman's establishment, without a thought in her head, in fact, except to supervise the nursing of a recalcitrant patient and see him made comfortable.

Once she had summoned his valet and butler to carry him inside and deposit him on the drawing room settee, she followed and supervised the men as they cut off the boot and raised his foot onto a cushion. Much to his mortification, she expertly ran her hand over his bare ankle and pronounced it not broken, but badly sprained. She also recommended to Tolland's housekeeper that his cook be instructed to prepare a nourishing broth for him.

Tolland responded to this last example of her interference by objecting, "I am not *ill*, you know, Miss Verdant. All I need right now is a drink."

"You may have been concussed, Sterling. Alcohol will only increase the headache you are bound to have, you know. I shall just check on your chestnut to see that he has taken no injury," she said as she took herself out to his mews without so much as a by-your-leave.

Later Tolland could not explain to himself why he had not immediately ordered her from his house. But at the time he was in no hurry for her to leave. Her commanding presence was soothing to him somehow; he enjoyed seeing her lording it over his household staff—until she turned her commands on him, that was. His mind went blank when he tried to reconcile the fact that

Francesca Verdant was both his lovely vision *and* the unknown, short-sighted quiz of a woman whose presence had precipitated his recent mishaps, culminating in today's tumble in the park.

Alas, he concluded sadly, visions are seldom what they seem.

As Frankie expertly ran her hands over Orion, she found that he had a sore foreleg. It wasn't a dangerous injury, but she knew that the stallion would benefit from her ointment as much as his master would. She grinned when she thought of how Sterling would rip up at her when he found he was sharing the same treatment as his horse.

She went back into the townhouse and disappeared into the nether regions of the kitchen, and when she reemerged some time later she was carrying a bowl of ointment and a towel over her arm. The ointment was a special mixture of her own specially for sprains, made from the flowers and leaves of the marjoram plant combined with olive oil, these ingredients heated together, then filtered and cooled. She had sent one of the servants out to the mews with a bowl of the mixture and instructions to Sterling's groom to apply it to Orion's foreleg every four hours or so. Now she would see to the viscount.

Sterling was dozing, stretched out on the long rolled-armed settee with an empty brandy glass by his side when Frankie returned to the room. She proceeded to lift his foot carefully onto the towel and inspect his swollen ankle. She still wore her spectacles. It had not occurred to her to remove them since she had put them on in the park. There would have been little point anyway, now that he had recognized her.

"How lucky that your cook had on hand the in-

212

gredients I needed to make up my poultice!" she said bracingly.

He jumped at the sound of her voice. "I have no intention of letting you put that horse liniment on me!" he roused woozily to exclaim when he saw what she was about.

"Come, come, Sterling, do not fall into a fit of the vapors," she said, her lips quirking up in a wide smile. She hoped to tease him into a better humor.

"Vapors . . ." he sputtered faintly, feeling mildly hysterical.

"You do not enjoy being hamstrung, do you? . . . The poultice will help take down the swelling and that will ease the ache, you know. But if you are determined to lounge here in pain for twice as long as necessary, then I will leave you to it!" she said, setting her pot on the floor; a sprinkling of the mixture splashed out onto the precious red and green flowered Aubusson carpet as she did so.

Tolland audibly ground his teeth. "You may go to the devil, ma'am."

"Is the pain so bad then? . . . Shall I make you a tissane for your headache?" she sympathized.

"I do *not* have the headache—I have *never* had the headache in my life! What I have is an *uninvited, managing* female *nagging* at me," he enunciated each word with great deliberation. "Why are you still here, Miss Verdant? I don't need an angel of mercy at this or any other time!" What I want is my other angel back, he thought; the one I kissed in the Seftons' garden. She would soothe me and sympathize with me and kiss my brow, not argue with me while my head pounds so.

"Don't try to make an angel out of me, my lord. I'm too much flesh and blood for canonization."

"No, you're a most devilish lady to plague me so!"

"I have a certain experience in easing injuries of the

213

kind you have sustained, is all. And it would be churlish of me not to offer my help since it is on my account that you are in such a case, though I deny that it was my *fault.* 'Twas your own doing entirely.''

"What can I say to make you understand that I want none of your solicitation, no matter how much experience you have?"

"I see that your spirits are sadly out of order, Sterling, for your manners to desert you so." Frankie cocked a brow at him as though he were a recalcitrant child. "Perhaps these spirits are responsible," she said as she picked up the brandy bottle from the table beside the settee.

"Put down that bottle!" he ordered as she continued to stand and look at him out of those damned laughing eyes. Even if they were partially hidden by her spectacles, he could see their expression well enough—and their beauty. What a fool he had been not to have recognized her earlier, he thought.

"Must we brangle every time we meet, my lord? Let us resolve to try for a little more conduct with one another, shall we? Perhaps we can put our unfortunate contretemps behind us with a good grace and start anew." She walked over to an elegantly carved mahogany sideboard where she put the bottle down, well out of his reach.

They hadn't "brangled" the last time they'd met, he thought with a pang—far from it!

He gritted his teeth and ground out, "Put the damned stuff on, if you must, and then go away."

Frankie, trying to hide her triumphant smile, proceeded to quickly smooth the mixture on his ankle and bind it up in the towel. She tried not to think about the intimate feel of his skin under her fingertips, to concentrate only on the task at hand.

He watched her dark head bent over his foot as she worked, swiftly and competently but with a gentle touch.

"I'm sorry I ripped up at you," he said in a softened tone as he ran a hand through his disordered locks, "today . . . and in the past. The circumstances were unfortunate and my temper got the better of me . . . I apologize."

She looked up briefly with a smile. "Of course. I understand . . . I have a temper, too."

He smiled back, but her head had bent to her work again. As he lay back and relaxed, Tolland decided he rather liked having a female stroke his ankle so tenderly—especially this particular female. His thoughts drifted back over their several meetings . . . Could this possibly be the fright of a woman he had tripped over at that accursed ball? The angel of a woman he had danced with and kissed so passionately in Lady Sefton's garden? The enchanting woman he had dreamed about night after night! No! He ruthlessly cut off that line of thought before it could fully develop and lead who-knew-where . . . But it was as sure as the devil was always up to mischief that she was the woman who had been the unwitting cause of all his accidents and uncharacteristic behavior in the past few weeks.

He knew her at last for what she was—his nemesis!

morning, Sterling." Why wasn't he down on his knees begging her longer, man? "Is your stubbornness such that, then?"

# Chapter Thirteen

Tolland was in a foul temper. After a wretched night of tossing and turning on the hard settee, he still lay there the next morning, immobile and uncomfortable. He had not been able to get upstairs to bed. He was just that bit too large to make it practical for his staff to carry him up, and besides he couldn't have borne the indignity of being carried to bed. He still couldn't put any weight on his ankle.

Today there was a white plaster decorating his chin and covering a deep scratch, the result of poor Worthy's attempts to shave him.

"Sorry, m'lord. Your lordship would seem to be in a bad skin this morning," Worthy had remarked disparagingly as he accidentally nicked his master with the razor. Tolland had immediately sat as still as a statue, but the damage had already been done.

With some leftover irritation, Tolland remembered that his nemesis had departed, eventually, yesterday, but not before leaving strict instructions with him and his staff, not only about the application of the ointment to his ankle but also about a restricted diet he was to follow during the evening to insure that he would overcome, without any unnecessary digestive complications, the effects of the shock and concussion he had suffered.

She had informed him about the injury to Orion before she'd left, and he was grateful for her attentions to his horse at least, if not to himself, he thought grumpily.

Frankie had left a recipe with his cook for some foul-tasting broth. When it was duly served up to him that evening, Tolland had indignantly refused to eat it, calling for some roast chicken instead. And the minute she had left the room yesterday, he had ordered the brandy bottle she had had the audacity to remove brought back to the table near the settee where he could reach it. He had made considerable inroads into it during the course of the evening and night.

So it was no wonder that he was feeling restless and a bit the worse for wear now, ready to quarrel with anyone who crossed his path. He wished desperately for some diversion. The members of his staff who had business outside the room where he lay took care to tiptoe by, lest by any sudden noise they call down his curses on their sorely tried heads. Those who had no occupation to take them near the drawing room took care to stay well away. They all hoped that their dignified employer would recover his customary even temper soon.

At eleven o'clock precisely, Jenks entered the room to announce, "You have a visitor, my lord."

The viscount's staff had been impressed by Miss Verdant's medical knowledge and competence in dealing with their high-in-the-instep master yesterday, and while it was somewhat irregular for a single lady to wait on a gentleman in his rooms, Tolland's correct butler felt that an exception was warranted in this case. The lady, who had been in the house alone for upwards of two hours the previous day, was today chaperoned by her maid. She had already been out to the mews to look at his lordship's prize horse and, in Jenks's view, it was quite above board for her now to stop in for a brief chat with his master.

Before Tolland could inquire who it was, Frankie walked into the room. He immediately reached up to remove the sticking plaster from his chin as he saw her.

She was wearing a dark mauve spencer over a walking dress of pale cream trimmed in blue, looking complete to a shade and very lovely in Tolland's eyes. His observation irritated him further for reasons he couldn't fathom. A little maid accompanied her to play propriety, he saw. The timid girl followed her mistress into the room and curtsied to him several times in a distracting fashion.

"To what do I owe the pleasure, ma'am? I don't recall Jenks inquiring whether or not I wished to receive you," he said stiffly. "Indeed, I do not believe I am up to it."

Frankie lifted her lorgnette briefly and saw the viscount reclining where she had left him the day before. She was glad to note that he kept the injured foot elevated on the pillow she had placed under it.

"And a good morning to you, too, Lord Sterling." She ignored his outburst as she greeted him cheerfully. "I thought you would like a report on Orion. I have seen him this morning and I can assure you that his injury is healing satisfactorily. You need have no fears on that head."

Despite the elegance of his dishabille—Tolland wore a heavy brocaded dressing gown embroidered with gold threads in place of a jacket over his shirt and trousers—Frankie thought the viscount looked thoroughly out of sorts. Judging from the mess he was making with the morning paper—it was strewn over all the nearby furniture, the floor, and himself, with one piece still dangling from his hand when she entered—she concluded that the poor man was in a sad state, which was not to be wondered at. It had been a good idea to stop by

219

the house. He badly needed some amusement, she could see.

"Feeling a bit liverish today, are you Sterling?" Frankie cocked a brow at him as she lowered the lorgnette and put it away in her reticule.

"*Liverish!*" he exploded, "'Od's bones, madam—" Tolland bit off the curse that rose readily to his tongue. He realized he was being baited and clamped his teeth shut, determined not to give her the rise she so clearly intended to provoke. His sportive lady would not make a game of him again today, he vowed. He had thought of little else since she left yesterday but her, and how beautiful she had looked on some occasions and how dowdy on others, how graceful she was on a horse and how awkward she had seemed to him at the Chatterington residence—and of his own disastrous behavior every time she came near him.

"I trust you are feeling better than when I left you yesterday. Have you been diligent in applying the poultice? And has it brought the swelling down?" She came forward, with the intention of unwrapping his ankle and inspecting his injured limb for herself, he saw.

Tolland drew his foot sharply away from her touch and groaned at the sudden movement. She wasn't deterred in the least.

"I see that the ointment has been freshly applied. Do keep it up. You can be assured that it will help."

"You should not be here, you know."

"What! An elderly spinster accompanied by her maid visiting a middle-aged gentleman tied by the leg?" She laughed. "Besides, I don't regard society's dictums, you know."

"Don't you? You should."

Frankie waved her hand airily in dismissal of such silly rules. "And did my broth serve its purpose?"

"I had cook throw it out," Tolland stated with a martial gleam in his eye.

"No. How silly of you," Frankie said. Tizzy gawked at her mistress insulting a great lord so.

"Off your feed, were you? I'm not surprised . . . such a blow as you took to the head would naturally cause you to feel queasy for some time, Sterling. However, I have brought a fresh batch with me today. I'm sure you will be able to manage some." She turned to her maid, missing the astonished look Tolland gave her, and said, "Tizzy, take the covered dish in the hall down to the kitchens, please.

"It's an infusion of parsnip, asparagus, holly, and gentian roots, with a few bramble leaves and some thyme, boiled up in water. Truly, it will help relieve the swelling in your ankle—and the pain, too. It's actually a recipe for gout, you know." She smiled dazzlingly at him.

"Gout!" Tolland burst out. "Damnation, madam! You're not my mother or my nurse. I wish you would go to the devil and take that confounded brew with you!"

"Yes, you mentioned the 'devil' yesterday. Do you often invoke his presence, Sterling? I had not thought you would be particularly fond of his company, fastidious as you are in your choice of friends." She looked at him with an expression of merriment in her eyes.

At this sally, Tolland had a hard time keeping his countenance. He tried to glower but failed miserably and would have been sputtering with laughter if they had not been interrupted at that moment by Jenks, who came to announce, "Lord Harry Markham and Sir Montagu Addlecumber to see your lordship."

"Ah, visitors. Good morning, one and all. Have you come to see the latest marvel? I've decided to set a new fashion, you see. A sprained ankle makes one so much more interesting, don't you think?" Tolland raised an eyebrow by way of greeting as his friends came into the room. He supposed he would have to resign himself to the fact that news of his latest fall had spread quickly through the *ton*; his seemingly never-ending series of accidents was no doubt providing not just a savory tidbit but a positive *meal* for the prattlemongers.

"Good morning, Miss Verdant," Harry greeted Frankie before turning to his friend. He was surprised and intrigued to see her there.

"Well, Tol, what a poor spirited greeting to your guests who've come to cheer you up," Markham said as he lifted his tail coat and sat down, crossing one shiny Hessian boot over the other as he did so. "Just because you're tied to your bed and blue deviled because you can't ride or get about for a few days is no reason to be out of temper with us." Harry was prepared to be amused, for his friend had been acting strangely of late. Tol's much vaunted air of superiority seemed to have completely deserted him, along with his perfect manners.

"Ah, Harry, you do well to remind me of my shortcomings. I might have known I could count on you for soothing words and cheerful conversation." Markham's twitting gibe had brought forth a cutting reply from his host.

"By gad, ain't you glad to see us, coz?" Monty piped up, coming forward to have a closer look at his relative. "Thought we'd give a look in and see how you was goin' on in your invalidated state. Didn't expect you'd be so out of frame." He cocked his head on one side. "'Must say, look as though you could do with a bit of squarin' up, don't y'know."

Tolland groaned by way of reply and turned to stare at Frankie as though he had her to blame for these unwanted guests and their various jibes and uncomfortable offers of comfort. She took no notice as she settled herself in a chair near the end of the settee where his foot was propped up.

"You see, my lord," she said soothingly, "you have much better company than that gentleman you were expressing a wish for just now."

Tolland chewed on a grin and managed a strangled "Humph." He was having a hard time controlling the spasm of mirth that threatened to overtake him at these words. Why had he not realized at the Seftons' ball that his angel had such a humorous bent to her nature? He caught himself up; it wouldn't do to start admiring yet another aspect of the woman. He must keep reminding himself that she was a managing, pest of a spinster . . . As far as being an "angel," ha! Devilish minx more likely!

Noting the interesting byplay between his friend and Laurel's aunt, Harry moved to fill the conversational hiatus in the room. "Let me interpret your refusal to vouchsafe a few words to us poor mortals, Tol. I shall answer our polite queries about your health without putting you to the trouble: 'Yes, you are going on as well as can be expected. No, you didn't have a very restful night. Yes, you do plan to offer refreshments to your visitors, who were so kind as to stop by to see how you go on. No, you can't reach the bell pull. Yes, you would be grateful if I rang for you.'" Lord Harry rose from his seat and suited action to words.

"'No, you don't desire us to plump up your pillows. Yes, you are really quite comfortable at the moment, thank you, and, no, there's nothing we can get you for the nonce.'" A satisfied smile crossed Markham's boyish visage at this sally. Everyone laughed and the atmosphere lightened.

"Now, Lord Harry, your quips are provoking my patient." Frankie laughed. "One can see that the poor man is suffering agonies. If he would only drink my herbal broth and allow me to reapply the ointment to his ankle, he would go on so much better. But I think he is

223

one of those people who enjoy suffering and having friends rally round, you know."

"Yep, m' cousin is a machinist in such matters," Monty commented while sagely nodding his head. "He'd rather suffer antigones than admit to being dismembered by pain." Monty's comments only served to increase the general atmosphere of hilarity that the gathering had taken on as they all laughed again at his disjointed pronouncement.

"You discombobulate me, cousin. My only claim to masochism is in the fact that I continue to suffer *your* presence," Tolland commented, trying not to let mirth get the better of him.

"I believe Tolland would prefer Madame Cognac as the best medicine for his 'antigones,' " Markham interjected, with a huge wink to the group at large as he continued to rag his friend.

"Who's she?" asked a puzzled Addlecumber. "Ain't acquitted with her, m'self. Bound to be a looker if she's a friend of Tol's, though."

Harry and Tolland laughed as Frankie explained to Addlecumber that Lord Harry was playfully referring to alcoholic spirits.

After a servant entered with a tea tray and cakes for the guests, Tolland distinguished himself by spilling hot tea on the sleeve of his dressing gown. "Ouch!" he yelped, biting back the curse that came to his lips just in time.

"Ah, I can see that you are determined to entertain us this morning, Tol. Do you have any more tricks up your, ah, sleeve?" Harry quipped as Frankie handed the viscount a cloth so that he could wipe off the scalding liquid that was dripping onto his left hand.

Tolland grinned sheepishly into Frankie's eyes as she bent toward him. Being in her presence just seemed to make him graceless, he thought with resignation.

"Another visitor has *insisted* on seeing you, my lord,

and demanded to be admitted when she heard that there were others with you." Once again Jenks's words left Tolland wishing to deny a visitor admittance. Just when he was reestablishing a pleasant rapport with Francesca, who should come in to cut up his peace but the Fox, followed closely by her hatchet-faced companion, Mademoiselle Menaçant. This morning the auburn-haired beauty had chosen to wear a costume of iridescent green and gold that outlined her excellent figure outrageously but did little to recommend her taste. The warm atmosphere in the room evaporated, and the jovial party was quite effectively dampened by the entrance of the two women.

Markham glanced to his friend with one brow raised. Tolland remembered that Harry had once observed to him that "the Menaçant" was enough to put one in mind of the grim reaper.

"Well, André, *mon cher*, I was terribly distressed this morning to hear that you had suffered a most unfortunate injury," Amelia remarked to Tolland in a simpering tone. "I knew that you would be quite restive in your loneliness—so boring to have to put off one's activities for a day or two and not see one's *particular* friends. So I've come to bear you company." She glanced around at the assembled company. "I see you are not quite as abandoned as I had imagined." She tittered. The unbidden thought that she was the abandoned one crossed the viscount's mind.

Amelia moved purposefully to the settee and stood looking down at Tolland as she presented him with her hand to be kissed. Indignant at her forward manner, he kissed the air above her glove with an ill grace and almost flung her hand away afterward. However, she had gained her objective and she sat down gracefully in a chair near the head of the settee, almost purring, it seemed to Frankie.

Mademoiselle Menaçant took a chair, holding up her high nose disdainfully at the others in the room, while Frankie was busy presenting Lady Amelia with a cup of tea and a challenging look.

Amelia was extremely vexed to find a teacup thrust into her gloved hand by "that Verdure woman." What was she doing here, and why had she taken it upon herself to act as hostess? she wondered, scowling angrily.

A crackle of electricity vibrated through the room. Harry and Tolland grinned as they glanced at one another and exchanged knowing looks, then leaned back to enjoy the fun.

"Remind me to visit you more often, Tol. Coming to your house is as good as going to a farce," Harry remarked *sotto voce* to Tolland. "And it saves the price of a ticket, as well."

Hostilities commenced forthwith.

"Why, thank you for the tea, Miss Verdure. Fancy seeing you here." Amelia fired the first volley. "I'm glad to see that you know how to make yourself useful. But"—she laughed artificially—"that's what companions are for, is it not? And you *are* serving as chaperon to Miss Witless this season, are you not? So convenient for one's *younger* female relations to have an elderly aunt to companion them, *n'est-ce pas?*"

It didn't seem to occur to Amelia that she was offending her own companion, the frowning Mademoiselle Menaçant, who stiffened at this tactless remark.

"Quite right, my lady. I know how to make myself useful in any number of ways." Frankie laughed outright at the lady's attempt not so much to set her down as to set her firmly on the shelf, out of Sterling's reach. "I'm here more in the capacity of medical adviser. I've come to deliver an herbal mixture that Sterling is using to take the swelling down in his sprained ankle. And how do you plan to make *yourself* of any use?"

"Why, André and I are the *best* of friends," Amelia reached over the settee to catch up his hand in hers, but Tolland pulled away in time and she patted him on the arm instead. "Is that not so, *mon cher?*" Tolland knew better than to answer her rhetorical question.

"Ah, that accounts for it, then," Frankie said.

"What?" Amelia rose to Frankie's bait.

"Why, if you're only a *common* friend that accounts for your overly familiar behavior."

Amelia pokered up, then turned to Tolland, determined to take no more notice of the interloper. "André, *s'il vous plaît*, will you be well enough to accompany me to Lucy Berringer's picnic on Thursday?" she asked with a saccharin smile pasted on her painted face.

"I doubt very much, Amelia, that I will be able to hobble forth to that particular treat," he replied sardonically. As the picnic was only two days away, Tolland knew he was safe. His injury was proving to have a hidden benefit, after all.

Amelia made a moue of disappointment, disfiguring her rose red mouth, its perfect color owing more to art than nature.

"Would be devilish honored if you'd allow me to gallivant you to Lucy's picnic, m'dearest Lady Amelia," Monty declared. He had been gazing raptly at his lady love since she'd come in. "Only say the syllabub and m' elbow's yours. Always glad to be at your servitude, y'know," he said, executing an exaggerated bow.

"*Mon frère* Roger will escort me if André is not up to it," answered a frowning Amelia, impolitely.

Addlecumber looked miserable at these words. He had never heard of this Manfred Rojee; perhaps Amelia had a new "gallivant," he thought unhappily.

Frankie took up the cudgels on Addlecumber's behalf. "I think you are a very gallant gentleman, Sir Monty. Lady Amelia is more fortunate than she deserves to be, to

227

have your devotion."

Monty looked quite cheered by Frankie's comment. She was nice, he thought, smiling fatuously at her, just like Miss Chatterin'tongue. P'rhaps he should call round to see Miss Sally and pour out his troubles; she was always ready to listen to him and accept his escort.

Markham turned to Frankie and asked, "Did you take your mount—Black Demon, isn't it?—to the park this morning, Miss Verdant?"

"Oh, yes, indeed, Lord Harry. He and I enjoyed a good hour's exercise before the rest of the world was up," Frankie admitted smilingly.

Tolland rather envied her this exercise.

"He is a superb animal, Miss Verdant, and I believe there is not another woman alive who could handle him as you do."

As Harry complimented her, the viscount silently concurred, for he remembered her riding hell for leather through the park yesterday before he so unwisely gave chase.

"Rides like a regular trapazon, Miss Verdurant does," Monty said, beaming at Frankie.

"Amazon, Monty, Amazon," Markham corrected. "A trapezoid is a shape."

"Heh?" Sir Monty scratched his pate. "Oh, aye, a shape."

"Indeed, a most admirable one. The shape of a warrior queen . . . er, Amazons were creatures out of Greek myth, you know. They were female warriors. And certainly Miss Verdant would have been welcome in their company. She's the best *female* rider I've ever seen." Not quite meaning to compliment Frankie so fulsomely, Tolland found himself doing so anyway.

"Heh, told you she's a right 'un, coz." Monty beamed. Tolland, miffed with himself, frowned at his cousin's words.

228

Amelia spoke up, tired of having all the attention focused on her rival. "Ah, those of us who are much in demand in society must recuperate in our beds in the mornings. 'Tis most unfashionable to arise before noon, *n'est-ce pas?*"

"Those who can't make the running should stay out of the race, I always say. With advancing age one must have more rest, or so I have been given to understand by elderly persons of my acquaintance," Frankie replied with deceptive geniality.

"So unladylike to urge one's horse to speed, is it not, Mademoiselle Menaçant?" Amelia, her fur thoroughly ruffled, turned to her companion for support. "One's hair and clothes may become disordered, and there is a danger that one might lose one's hat. Then, too, for those who don't see particularly well, it could be dangerous. There is no telling what sort of accident you might have. Your horse might stumble in a rabbit hole, or you might run down some unsuspecting pedestrian or another horseman."

Harry spewed his tea back into his cup at these words and Tolland choked.

"If one cannot handle one's horse under any circumstances, one has no business riding at all." Frankie looked daggers at Amelia.

"In the highest society, you know, Miss Verdure, it is considered impolite to contradict one's superiors." Amelia spat out the words.

"As you say, it's considered extremely ill mannered to criticize where one lacks superior knowledge," Frankie retorted, while the light from her eyes glinted at her opponent.

Sterling and Harry grinned at one another. "Piqued and repiqued," Tolland commented in an aside to Harry. He watched Frankie, admiring her flashing eyes and the way a smile played about her lips, thinking that she was

229

pluck to the backbone to counter every one of Amelia's thrusts without batting an eyelash.

Addlecumber looked befuddled. He had been desperately trying to capture Lady Amelia's attention with a series of grimaces and smirks directed her way. Finally he cleared his throat and said loudly, "M'dearest Lady A., won't you accept m'escort to wherever 'tis you're headin'? Don't want to shag-out m'cousin here, y'know. Best leave him in peace—even though he ain't all in one piece, hee-hee. Dare say he'll recover momentously."

Amelia, battered and reeling, but not put to rout, was determined not to budge. "So kind, Sir Montagu. But I have my own carriage waiting. I think I shall stay to cheer André for a while longer."

"Oh, no, do not consider me. Think of your horses. I think it most unwise to keep them waiting longer, Amelia," was the harried viscount's pointed remark.

The combatants seemed to have reached an impasse.

"I must go, Lord Sterling, I have an appointment to drive out with Freddy Drake. I wish you a speedy recovery, and I hope you enjoy your *soup* course this evening," Frankie teased as she rose from her chair. As she did so, a small volume fell from her skirt pocket.

"Well, Tol, I believe we've 'cheered' you enough for one morning," Harry joked as he got up. "We shall leave you to recuperate in peace." He winked at his friend as he neatly forced Amelia and the sternly mute Madame Menaçant to make ready to leave as well.

A devil prompted Tolland to a bit of mischief. "Would you be so kind as to stop in tomorrow, Miss Verdant? I'm sure you wouldn't want your patient to suffer a setback—all your work for nothing. I would be most grateful if you would supervise the application of your healing ointment and check on the progress of my recovery," he said to heap more coals on the Fox's head.

"Why, certainly I shall come and see you, Lord

Sterling," she answered his mocking request.

"I believe you've dropped something, Miss Verdant."

Frankie stooped to pick up the book. "Ah, yes. Perhaps you would care to glance through this." She handed it to Tolland. "It's a volume of herbal remedies."

Reluctantly, Tolland accepted the small red book, looking down at it with distaste.

"You will find the ointment for sprains and the soothing broth set out in there. Perhaps you will want to copy out the recipes," she said with a twinkle in her eye. "You never know when you might need them again."

"Ah, so kind, Miss Verdant," said Tolland as he held the book gingerly with his fingertips. She was making sport of him again, he knew. There was a look in her eyes he could only describe as mischievous. "As always your *thoughtfulness* in such matters overcomes my manners. I am sure you will understand if I don't thank you properly," he continued, regretting the loss of their happy accord of moments before. Just when he had been in such charity with her, too, for the effective way she had silenced Amelia. He regretted the devilment that had prompted him to invite her to visit him.

And, perversely, he was furious with her for going off to drive with Drake while she left him to the tender mercies of Amelia Reynard, who outstayed the others that she might have the last word. The Fox took a prolonged farewell of him, alternately casting out lures at one moment and making disparaging comments about "that Verdure woman" the next, before she finally left him in peace.

attention to herself; and particularly as Lionel Verrinder saw that the task was impossible. Lord Roughcast's two nieces were totally absorbed in one another's company

# Chapter Fourteen

Tolland had nothing to do after his visitors left but brood on how Miss Francesca Verdant always left him feeling agitated to an uncomfortable degree.

He was determined that the perfection of his existence would not be affected by a managing country spinster, no matter how beautiful she was or what a beguiling voice she had! He tried not to think of how her friendly teasing, of a likeness to that doled out by his cronies like Harry, had improved his spirits a hundredfold. No, he didn't want to dwell on her many attributes . . . her humor, her horsemanship, her eyes, her voice, her shapely fig—

"Damnation, my lad, you've got to stop this!" he said aloud, refusing to ask himself *why* Francesca's presence always left him in physical or emotional turmoil.

How he would like to give that disturbing female her just deserts for all he had suffered at her hands: his reputation as a Corinthian sadly dented, his dignity in tatters, his foot likely maimed for life, not to mention that he responded to her like an overheated schoolboy.

He glanced at the little book he was bouncing up down in his right hand. He idly flipped through the pages as his thoughts took him first in one direction, then another as a plot took shape in his mind. A wicked smile came to his face, and there was a decided gleam in his eye.

When the lady herself called the next afternoon Tolland was ready for her. Joss sticks were burning in the darkened room, giving off a sweet, musky, exotic scent. He reclined on the settee, pretending to be asleep as Frankie was announced. He peeped through closed eyelids, relieved to see that the bobbing wench wasn't with her.

Frankie intended to stay only a moment to look in on Orion and Sterling before proceeding to Hookham's Library to exchange her book on the care and treatment of horses for one on estate management. She knew she should not have come alone, but she had wanted an excuse to see him—to assure herself that her patient was progressing satisfactorily, of course, she told herself. Why else? Daph would be horrified if she found out, but Tizzy had been required to go with Laurel to the modiste's for a final fitting of the gown she was to wear for her presentation at the Queen's Drawing Room, and Frankie didn't rub along all that well with Daph's abigail, Fennel.

She was puzzled to find the drawing room in semidarkness when she entered, the drapes drawn and the lighting low, only a few candles burning.

"Ah, Miss Verdant, good afternoon. I have been expecting you. I know you will understand if I don't get up. Please be seated." Tolland waved a languid hand at her as she entered.

"Good afternoon, my lord. Allow me to open the draperies for you, Sterling. It's almost pitch black in here. How can you stand the gloom?"

"Ah, no, no. Please do not . . . I'm afraid I've strained my eyes from poring over the book you so kindly left for my, ah, entertainment. I find they are quite sensitive to the light today."

"That sounds like a faradiddle if ever I've heard one."

"Nevertheless, please humor a poor invalid. I've prepared a surprise for you, and I wouldn't want the ah, atmosphere, spoiled."

Frankie was skeptical, but she obediently sat down, reaching for her spectacles in her reticule as she did so, so that she could see through the murk. Smoke from the dozen sticks of incense set in front of some sort of Chinese idol filled the hazy room with a heavy exotic scent. The drug-like smoke stung her eyes, and they teared behind her glasses. Something about the atmosphere of the room made her heart beat just a little erratically.

She saw that the Sterling lay on the settee in a considerable state of dishabille. He wore an elaborate dressing gown of varicolored silk, while slippers covered his bare feet. A portion of his darkly matted chest was visible above the vee of his gown. Why, he had dispensed with his shirt! Frankie realized with a start.

"Ah, pardon me, Sterling, but I really don't think I should stay." She rose from her chair on the words.

"Oh, please don't go just yet. Stay for cup of tea, at least. I have had my cook make up a special tea for you to try. It's an interesting brew that my Uncle Fortesque was very fond of, and, most remarkably, it bears an uncanny similarity to a recipe I found in your very own book—the one you so kindly lent me yesterday," he said in a relaxed voice. "Will you not stay and have a cup? I shall be most hurt if you do not even taste it . . . Stay with me for a bare five minutes . . . please." Tolland smiled mischievously at her, little devils dancing in the depths of his eyes.

Frankie sat again, in a chair across the room from the viscount, wondering if she were wise to give in to his request.

"You see how I have brought out Uncle Fortesque's chinoiserie. He was quite a traveller and brought back many souvenirs from his journeys. I find it amusing to sit here and contemplate these curiosities from another culture. Do you not think it a diverting occupation for an invalid?" he asked.

Frankie tried to look closely at Sterling through the gloom. He did not seem foxed, precisely, but he certainly seemed to be in a strange mood. Her eyes fell to that disturbing gap in his dressing gown again. She cleared her throat uneasily.

"Will you pour for me?" Tolland asked, indicating the tea tray that was already set out on a nearby claw-footed table.

Frankie arose to pour the tea as he requested, stripping off the lavender kid gloves that matched the spencer she wore over her new green- and lavender-figured walking dress as she did so. Tolland watched her every move, and noticed how well the modish velvet hat tilted to an angle over her dark curls suited her with its dashing feather curling close to one cheek, drawing attention to those eyes of hers. He swallowed with a little difficulty.

Frankie took a cup to him, then collected her own and sat back to sip at the strange-smelling brew. It was certainly not regular tea. "This isn't China tea, then?"

"Ah, of a kind, but not, I daresay, what you are used to drinking. Is it not to your liking? I had it prepared especially to go with the mood of the room. It was one of Uncle's favorites, and I thought it would interest you as it is said to have many healing properties, among other things." With his brow furrowed in feigned anxiety, Tolland made as if to get up and order something else for his guest, but acting as though the effort were too great, he sank back against the cushions of the sofa, resting his arm across his brow as he did so in a rather melodramatic

236

fashion. He peered from beneath lowered lashes to see her reaction.

"The tea is not unpleasant actually, but I mustn't stay longer."

"Mustn't you?" he inquired sadly. "Have just one more cup at least, and then I *would* be grateful if you would anoint my ankle."

"I think you can do that for yourself now, Sterling," Frankie replied, becoming impatient. "I will have half a cup and then go."

She arose to refill her cup. "Shall I pour another for you?"

"Yes, please, if you would be so kind."

As Frankie handed him his cup, Tolland's long fingers deliberately brushed hers, causing a frisson of excitement to tingle down her spine. A smile played about Tolland's mouth as he watched her.

"What *is* in the tea, Lord Sterling?"

"Ah, I *knew* it would interest you. It's made with a plant from the Orient that's said to have medicinal qualities. My uncle brought back these Eastern accouterments, as well as many unusual food-stuffs, when he returned from China about ten years ago. He was particularly fond of a drink made with ginseng, and used to have his cook prepare it whenever I visited him as a boy," he remarked conversationally.

"Ginseng. Umm, I believe I have heard of it. Efficacious in a number of ways if I remember rightly. Especially good for cases of stress, heart palpitations; promotes healing in cases where there is an inflammation of the lungs . . ." Frankie remained standing next to the settee as she tried to remember what else she had heard about this Eastern root.

"And nutmeg," Tolland added, as he watched her carefully over the rim of his cup, his blue eyes dancing and wide open for once. Her low, sultry voice was playing

237

havoc with his pulses, but he was enjoying his game.

"Oh. Nutmeg. Yes, good for rheumatism and digestive upsets." Her cheeks were slightly heated as she remembered that nutmeg was used in certain women's complaints and . . . something else that eluded her. The answer was there at the edge of her thoughts, but she couldn't quite concentrate at the moment.

Frankie was oddly off balance. She had been in the room a good ten minutes and had not questioned Sterling about how his ankle was going on and whether or not he had been stringent in the application of her ointment. She realized that it had been a mistake to come. She should leave . . . but something held her in place.

Everything was rather odd. She felt peculiar. The feather in her hat had wilted and was tickling her cheek uncomfortably. Sterling was behaving strangely. There was a warm sluggishness invading her limbs. The warmth and smokey odor in the room together with the herbal tea, made her feel hot and sleepy. She could not bring herself to move.

Tolland was now smiling at her in an openly seductive manner.

Frankie felt herself smiling back.

"Francesca . . . may I call you Francesca?" Tolland asked in a low voice.

"Why?" she got out. "Everyone else calls me 'Frankie.'"

"But *I* am not 'everyone else,' my dear girl. Your name *is* Francesca, is it not? Has no one told you before that you are *much* more a Francesca than a Frankie? Frankie is *much* too masculine a name for you."

Frankie shook her head, too listless to speak. Tolland was almost whispering as he extended his hand to her and spoke again. "It is something about your eyes, I think. Come, sit by me so that I may see them at closer range and better explain why I think of you as Francesca."

238

Languidly Frankie sat down beside him, placing her cup down on the table next to his.

"That's better," he said as she turned toward him. He removed her spectacles and laid them aside. "And you must call me Drew; it's a name reserved for only my most *intimate* friends."

"Drew," she murmured, as he took the pin out of her hat, lifted it off, and set it down beside them, causing a few unruly curls to tumble down round her face. He turned to her and raised a hand to her cheek. His thumb caressed the side of her face as he gazed at her.

My God, Tolland thought, she really does have the most beautiful eyes in the world. I could drown in them. This was not his plain and homely nemesis, not the high-handed Frankie Verdant, but his lovely Angel, an enchantress sent to tempt him. Suddenly the game he was playing to teach her that he would not brook her interference in his smooth existence was abandoned and pure desire took over.

He felt heat rising in his body. "Francesca . . ."

As his gaze shifted from her eyes to her lips, his long, slender fingers framed her face, and he slowly inclined his head until his lips met hers. He kissed her softly for a moment, until Frankie's lips returned the pressure of his. Her enthusiasm matched his ardor. She unconsciously raised one of her hands and softly touched the hair on his chest where it was visible above the edge of his dressing gown.

Her slight touch on his skin ignited a fire in Tolland. He increased the pressure of the kiss, and his mouth opened over hers as his arms came tightly round her. Soon she allowed his tongue to invade her yielding mouth, and put her other hand round the back of his neck to caress the skin there and then entwine it in his thick, silky hair. She was very aware of her breasts crushed against his chest and of her other hand caught

239

between them where her fingers were entangled in the soft mat of hair on his chest. As she unconsciously twisted it with her fingers, his dressing gown fell open to the waist. He gave little sighs of pleasure while he teased at her lips.

Tolland was in the midst of his dream again, kissing his angel tenderly on the lips and she was responding. He increasd the pressure, allowing his tongue to take her mouth deeply . . . This was better than his dream—this was real. He could feel her heart beating against his hand as he murmured endearments against her face, her hair, her mouth. His angel wouldn't disappear this time!

Frankie wanted to touch him as he was touching her. She pushed his dressing gown off his shoulders and ran her hands over his chest, delighting in the rough feel of his skin, in his hard, muscular frame.

He had pushed her spencer aside and was kissing the soft skin along her shoulder and neck, savoring the subtle perfume that lingered there.

Frankie could taste the flavor of the herbs they had drunk in their tea on his tongue, the flavor lingering as he moved his mouth elsewhere. Ginseng—unfamiliar. Nutmeg, well known, and cautioned against because of— its *aphrodisiac* properties!

That was it—the thought that had escaped her. These herbs were reputed to be *aphrodisiacs* if used in sufficient quantities. What was she doing!

"What are you doing?" Frankie uttered hoarsely, as she pushed him away and sat up.

"Wha—? What's the matter?" Tolland asked in a ragged voice.

"Oh, you monster, you tricked me! That tea was a love potion!"

Consciousness seemed to return as his eyes registered understanding. "Oh God, Francesca, I'm sorry," he ground out hoarsely.

She jumped up and made for the door, not hearing his plea: "Wait, Francesca, please . . ." But she was gone.

With hands that still shook, Tolland pounded a cushion on the settee, cursing himself, "God, I'm a prize fool! Damn, oh damn." He lay back, with an arm across his eyes, until his heartbeats slowed and a kind of numbness set in.

Rousing himself from his stupor, Tolland looked down and realized his state of dishabille. He shrugged his dressing gown back over his shoulders, pulling the material tightly across his bare chest. Monty would have said that he had been dished by that "ole dizzy bee" again, he reflected dejectedly. His slow-witted relative would certainly have been in the right of it this time!

He had planned the afternoon in order to show his nemesis a lesson, concocting the exotic setting where he would pretend to seduce her. All because of his petulance at her daring to turn his household upside down in a day, so that his staff were all doing *her* bidding—and because of the number of times she had humiliated him in public, causing him to make a cake of himself over her at the Sefton ball, dosing him with that unpalatable broth. Even causing him to fall off his horse, for God's sake! He had thought he would give her a taste of her own medicine. He would be in charge for a change, and she would be the one to feel foolish.

Ha! His brain must have been as addled as that of his cousin Monty to have come up with such a scheme!

He had been amused when he'd seen several recipes listed for aphrodisiacs on thumbing through her book yesterday. That was when the glimmer of an idea had come to him. He had had his cook make up an herbal tea with ginseng and nutmeg per the instructions in Francesca's own book. He had never dreamed of the tangled, compromising situation he would land them in.

Had he thought he had been disgraced before? Surely

241

now he had taken his worst tumble yet—right into a leg shackle, and all through his own fault. He had set the trap and then jumped in with both eyes open.

He picked up her feathered hat, unknowingly crushed beneath them on the settee, and fingered the soft material. How could he forget how she had affected him at the Sefton ball? how every time he was near her his emotions were in a turmoil of anger or passion? Did he disregard his physical reaction to the lovely "Angel" just because he wanted revenge on the unattractive Miss Verdant?

He leaned his head into his hands. He had been completely unable to resist her and had made a besotted idiot of himself. No, not that . . . worse . . . he had compromised an innocent, well-born lady.

There was nothing else for it. He would have to make it up to his topsy-turvy lady—the managing Miss Verdant and the infinitely desirable Francesca. She *must* accept the protection of his name so that he could recover some credibility in his own mind, some right to the name of gentleman.

Tomorrow. It must be done tomorrow, he thought, if he were ambulatory by then. Damn! He would arrange for his servants to carry him in a litter if he had to, and would get to the Whittgrove residence at the crack of dawn.

Yes, he would offer her his hand. His honor demanded it . . . but never his heart.

# Chapter Fifteen

Tolland convinced himself during a sleepless night that, even if marriage itself was not a state to be desired, perhaps marriage to *Francesca* would not be so bad. He wanted her, and much as he had always hated the very thought of tying himself up for life, marriage was the only way he could have his angelic nemesis. Anyway, she needed someone to take care of her. Look at what had happened at the Sefton ball when she'd gone outside with that snake of a Reynard!

He dressed hastily, thankful he was able to get a soft evening pump over his swollen foot, and tried to eat a breakfast that tasted of sawdust. He managed only one scalding cup of coffee before he called for his carriage to be brought round at a ridulously early hour. He desired to get the deed over with before he should lose his resolve.

He hobbled to his carriage with the aid of Jenks on one side and Worthy on the other, his arms over their shoulders, while he grasped Frankie's forgotten hat in one hand and a dozen red roses in the other. He would have to return her hat along with her reticule, her spectacles tucked inside it, which he carried in his pocket. Francesca had departed in such haste yesterday that she had left behind all her belongings. The flowers were mangled somewhat as he stepped awkwardly through the door of his carriage to seat himself, and he managed to pierce his hand on the thorns on the blasted stems in the process.

An astonished Hedge opened the door of Whittgrove House to Viscount Sterling's insistent knocking at the unheard hour of half past nine in the morning. Tolland's servants supported him inside, where he handed the bedraggled bouquet to the butler. Hedge asked one of the footmen to summon Lady Whittgrove as he showed the little band into the morning room where Worthy and Jenks left their master leaning heavily upon his cane.

A flustered Daphne received the viscount, wondering if it were correct to do so. Ordinarily she appeared before none but the family when she was increasing. However, Viscount Sterling had been most insistent that he speak with her, and she supposed that she could make an exception this once.

"Ah, Lady Whittgrove, good morning. I fear that I am inconveniencing you, but the circumstances are exceptional, as I'm sure you will agree when I've . . . when I've explained." Tolland, laboring under a great strain, spoke in cold, formal terms.

"It is most unfortunate, and I'm sorry for it, but your sister, ah, Miss Verdant that is, was unchaperoned in my presence for much of the afternoon yesterday." Though extremely ill at ease, he went on quickly. "I feel that her honor has been compromised and I . . . I have come to offer for her hand."

"Do you mean marriage?" Daphne stared at him with openmouthed astonishment.

"Yes, I'm afraid that I do."

"To Frankie?" she squeaked.

"To Francesca, yes."

"Cer-certainly, my lord," Daphne was flabbergasted. "I shall summon her to you." And with as much haste as her condition permitted, she took herself off to tell Frankie the astounding news.

Tolland was left to run a finger round his too-tight collar and to muse on how beautiful Lady Whittgrove looked in her present state. This woman's natural charms were enhanced by her pregnancy and lent her an ethereal air. She positively glowed with health and happiness.

He had always averted his eyes when confronted by a woman with child, considering it a necessary state but one to be concealed from view. Yet again a woman—and a Verdant woman, too!—was upsetting the certainties of his world, causing him to reevaluate his opinions. Whereas in the past he had gone to great lengths to avoid even thinking of marriage and children, they no longer seemed encumbrances to be avoided. He surprised himself exceedingly when he realized he was actually looking forward to this new existence with some pleasure. He was changing in spite of himself, even though he couldn't understand what accounted for his changing attitudes.

"H'it's that dreadful fallin'-down man, Miss," an untidy Tizzy announced to Frankie as she bobbed a curtsey and handed her the mangled roses. "'E's come callin' with flow'rs."

"What! Not Viscount Sterling?" Frankie exclaimed in surprise.

"Aye, h'it's 'im, ma'am."

Daphne waddled into Frankie's room hard on Tizzy's heels, came up to her sister, hugged her—further crushing the much abused roses—and kissed her on the cheek.

"I can't quite believe it, Frankie," she said, bubbling over with excitement, "but Viscount Sterling is waiting for you below, barely able to walk, poor man. Imagine! He had to be assisted into the house by his servants.

"'Tis famous, his coming here like this with these beauti—ah, *nice* roses for you," she amended after a glance at the bedraggled flowers. "He means to propose to you, you know, Frankie dear! Oh, make haste and go down to him. How wonderful for you. I didn't dare dream of him for Laurel, but he will suit *you* right down to the ground. Why, I believe he likes horses as much as you do," Daphne chattered as she bustled about the room. She was fussing through the wardrobe, looking for just the right shawl to complement the gown Frankie was wearing.

"Sterling come to propose to me? There must be some mistake. Why would he propose to *me*?" Frankie exclaimed, looking doubtfully at the drooping flowers in her arms.

"Well, dear, he tells me you and he were alone in his rooms yesterday," Daphne replied, trying to look stern but too full of glee to bring it off. "Here"—she handed Frankie her reticule—"he tells me you left this behind. Your spectacles are inside. Now, make haste. It is all so exciting!"

Frankie had spent a fitful night tossing and turning in her bed, remembering the way she had responded to Drew. She, who had never had any physical dealings with a man before she met the viscount, had never dreamed a man's embrace would excite her so. And Drew had seemed as attracted to her as she was to him. But then, their tea had been laced with those potent herbs, so perhaps that accounted for their reactions. Why would he do such a thing, anyway? Why would he want to seduce *her*?

Maybe it had been the tea yesterday, but today she had

246

to admit she wouldn't mind kissing him again in such a way. It had been a tingling experience. Goodness, if they married, they could engage in such activities whenever they wished. Why, it was as much fun as a fast gallop on her favorite mount. Better, even! she grinned.

Imagine, hoaxing her in such a way, though. He certainly *did* owe her an apology. Well, she would see what Drew had to say for himself.


Frankie came down the stairs determined to be dignified and magnanimous in forgiving her suitor. As to his suit itself, well, she would see. Marriage had never been part of her plans, but then she hadn't met Drew and found out how she would feel in his arms. Her eyes glowed and her mouth quirked up in a smile as she whisked herself into the morning room. She tripped on the carpet as she did so and sent a silver urn crashing to the floor. "The devil," she cursed at the now-dented urn, then picked it up and replaced it on its stand.

Tolland saw her scowl as he turned, thinking she spoke to him. He knew she had cause to be angry with him, but was taken aback by such a greeting. It didn't make his task any easier.

Frankie stood the length of the room from Sterling, and since she had neglected to remove her spectacles from the reticule, her eyes were a bit unfocused as she looked at him. On his tense countenance was what looked like a decidedly haughty sneer to her.

Tolland spoke stiffly, "Good morning, Miss Verdant." Somehow she didn't appear to be the same woman he had kissed yesterday. "I trust you are in fine fettle this morning. It looks to be a fine day." To himself he sounded nervous, to her, aloof.

Back to Miss Verdant then, Frankie thought impatiently. This didn't sound like a proposal. "Good morning, Sterling." Why wasn't he down on his knees, begging her forgiveness? "Is your ankle much improved, then?"

"I can manage," he replied in a clipped tone, clenching his teeth as he leaned more heavily upon his cane. He was endeavoring to forget the discomfort this morning's activity had cost him and could do without any reminder of the injury.

Blast and damn! this wasn't going at all well, Tolland thought. What was the matter with him that when confronted with her all rational thought flew out of his head? It was his much-sought-after hand that he was offering, not his heart; no emotions to worry about here. He was doing the woman a favor. It should be easy. Why was he so agitated?

He plunged headlong into his proposal. "I'm afraid my honor demands that I offer you my hand after yesterday's incident," he said quickly and quite undiplomatically, a cold look upon his face.

"Where was your 'honor' yesterday when you tricked me?" Frankie took fire at his unexpected and arrogant words. "What possible reason could you have for doing such a thing?" she asked bluntly.

"Dev—deuce take it! I wanted to make you see that I was not to be trifled with, dosed, and ordered about . . . but . . . ." He ground to a halt as he heard his own damning words. Hell and the devil. He was making matters worse! He ran a finger under his too-tight cravat again.

"So that's why you kissed me, is it? That seems a strange reason. You didn't want to be dosed and ordered about, so you decided to 'dose' me?" Frankie fired back, her anger growing. "Is it a pastime among town bucks like you to perpetrate such hoaxes on unsuspecting females?"

Tolland drew himself up to his full height, despite the

248

effort it cost him to put his weight on his injured foot. "I'm here to make amends for my uncalled-for behavior," he responded stiffly, trying to damp down his ire at her sarcasm. "If I've compromised you, Miss Verdant, then I must suffer for it. I'm now offering to do the gentlemanly thing. My honor demands it."

"Ah, your 'honor' demands it, does it? I would have thought your 'honor' would prompt you to a more 'gentlemanly' way of phrasing your proposal than telling me you would 'suffer' being married to me."

"Well, you don't expect me to offer my heart, do you?" Tolland could feel himself losing control of his emotions again.

"Do you have one?"

"Of course I do!"

"It must be made of stone, then. What does My Lord Perfection's heart look like? A stone sundial? It must be perfectly correct. Keeps time to the second does it?"

"Let us cease this bickering. I am asking you to wed me for your own good. It doesn't have to be a *real* marriage. We don't need to see much of one another, or even live together. We could maintain separate establishments, if you wish. You could continue to breed your horses . . ." God, what am I saying! Tolland couldn't believe his own ears. The only compensation for him in the proposed marriage was the fact that he would get her in his bed.

"Oh, is this a trick to get your hands on the Verdant Meadows Stud, then?" Frankie glowered.

"No, no. You misunderstand. I think you need someone to take care of you—"

"You think I need someone to take care of me, do you? someone to order me about? Someone to be my lord and master, perhaps?"

"Yes. Just look what happened to you at Lady Sefton's when you went out on the balcony with that blasted rake Reynard." This incident had never ceased to worry him.

249

"What! This from you? After yesterday? You must be mad! If I were married to you, you wouldn't be my *master*, I assure you!"

"You think to manage me once we're married, do you? You mistake, madam. *I*, not you, will be the master of our household. Our children will look to *me* as the head—"

"Our *children?*" Frankie uttered in failing accents. She would laugh hysterically if only she weren't so angry. He didn't want to live with her, but he wanted to take care of her, to be the master of their household, and to have children! His brain must have been sprained as well as his ankle in that fall. "You presume too much, Sterling."

He cleared his throat again. Damn it! He couldn't think! His brain felt as though it were cloaked in cotton wool. He looked down at his shoes, leaning heavily upon his cane; he hadn't a clue in his benumbed brain of how to persuade her to accept him.

"Well, when do you wish to wed?" he demanded, though he had just decided that the best course would be to cajole her, even plead with her.

"Oh, Sterling, don't be silly. We would never suit. You've said that you were forced to this offer. Now you can be thankful that you've had a lucky escape. No one need know about yesterday. I'll consider your offer today as an apology for your 'ungentlemanly' behavior and will accept it. We're quits now."

He was staggered. "But you *must* marry me!"

"No, I think not."

"Give me one good reason why not."

"I don't want my life turned upside down! You don't want a wife, Sterling, you want a horse, a nice placid one, who will respond to your every whim. Well, I'm not a horse to have a man's controlling hand on my bridle and his spur digging into my side, always obedient to his slightest touch. I've trotted along happily enough for many years now on my own . . . and I don't like the

250

future you propose. I never thought to marry, but I suppose if I ever do, it will be to someone I can love and who loves me. It's clear you don't really wish to marry me, any more than I do you."

"But Francesca . . ."

"And speaking of horses, I haven't ridden yet this morning. You will have to excuse me, Sterling." So she left him, not seeing the pleading look in his eyes, or the hand, clutching her ruined velvet hat, outstretched to her.

As he watched her go, Tolland felt the need to go home and nurse his wounds. I've made a dashed mull of it, he thought. Typical. Everything I do in her presence is muddled.

As he limped to the door he looked down and noticed Francesca's forgotten hat, a talisman of his troubles, still in his hand. He flung the poor, disheveled object into the damaged urn on his way out. "You've had a run-in with Francesca Verdant, too"—he addressed the inanimate object—"and just like me, you've come away dented."

His life seemed to be in just such a shambles. What had happened to his calm, ordered existence? Gone was Tolland Hansohm, the perfect viscount, and in his place stood an ordinary man. His perfect manners and famous address had disappeared. Even his prowess in the sporting field was now open to question after the tumble he had taken. He couldn't go anywhere without tripping over himself or someone else, his whole philosophy about women and marriage was in chaos, there was a perceptible dent in his *amour-propre*, and his foot hurt like the very devil.

"Damnation!" he muttered darkly to himself. "Should have saved myself the trouble . . . What should I have expected from such a headstrong, shortsighted, green

251

female!" He had done her the inexpressible honor of offering her his hand in marriage, something he had *never* intended to do with any woman. And what had she done? Flung that offer back in his face! Any other single woman below the age of thirty would *kill* for an offer from him.

Tolland clapped his curly-brimmed beaver hat on his head, leaned on his cane, and made his way to the door of the Whittgrove townhouse with what speed he could muster, only to collide in the doorway with someone entering in a rush. There was a momentary scuffle as both parties tried to disentangle their arms and legs.

"Why, Tol, my dear fellow, are you hurt? No . . . Yes, of course you are. All right, then? . . . Here's your cane . . . Well, fancy you being up and about so early. Is the foot better? Not calling on Laur—Miss Whittgrove, were you?" asked a worried Lord Harry, whose own errand bore a similarity to that of his friend.

With Markham's help Tolland righted himself. "Miss Laurel Whittgrove is a child and a widgeon to boot. You are welcome to make a cake of yourself over her if that is your wish, Harry."

"What has cast you into such a black mood?" Harry inquired, astonished at his friend's words.

"Marriage is an institution for cork-brained fools!" Tolland barked sourly, leaving Lord Harry mystified as to his presence in the Whittgrove house. The viscount quickly summoned his own servants, who aided him to his carriage as his friend stared after him in bewilderment.

Frankie stood looking blindly out the window of her room, wondering if she'd done the right thing, and wishing Sterling hadn't made her so mad. She refused to admit any regret for her rejection of his ill-delivered proposal, however. Although they had seemed to be finding a way to be friends after his accident in the park, yesterday's performance and this morning's revelation that it had been a hoax to teach her some kind of lesson had put an end to their promising relationship. It seemed that her attractive "Drew" had disappeared entirely, and only the cold, haughty shell of Tolland Hansohm remained. She stared ironically at the crushed roses as though they represented her crushed hopes.

Her response of the day before did not mean that she was in love with the man. Heavens, no! It was the atmosphere in the room and the aphrodisiac herbs in the tea, of course, that had caused her to kiss him with such warmth and reckless abandon.

Why, she should have accepted him, by Jupiter! Even if it were the fault of the herbs, he had pretty well compromised her, hadn't he? That would have shown him! . . . But she would not marry a man who regarded her as someone who would be at the periphery of his life, living apart from him—a man who, nonetheless, demanded that she submit to him as her lord and master. It was clear after this morning's explanation that he really felt nothing at all for her as a woman.

Of course he wouldn't want to live with her, she thought to herself. Her presence in his life had been nothing but an embarrassment and an unending series of disasters. He came a cropper every time he was near her. It didn't occur to her that this very day, while trying to make his proposal, was one of those times.

Let the episode teach him to tamper with aphrodisiacs, though! Those herbal recipes had been tested and used for generations. They had worked on Lord Sterling—and herself—when he considered them only a gimmick. They certainly had stirred up his physical desires, anyway, she thought on a half-smile.

No, a man who put his own honor above her feelings,

253

and who would offer such an insulting proposal, couldn't hope to tempt her to marriage. She was glad she hadn't entertained his suit—wasn't she? Let him rejoice at his lucky escape! If she had a suspicion of a soreness at heart, she imagined it was just indigestion from gulping down hot tea too fast at breakfast.

She would avoid him in future. It certainly hadn't been her intention to make up to men when she came to town. Indeed not! Her duty was as Laurel's chaperon and to advertise the Verdant Meadows Stables among likely clients, such as Freddy Drake. Now there was a nice man. Such a worthy Corinthian. So interested in horses. Alas, why did she find him so dull?

"Frankie, my love, may I come in?" Daphne called, as she swished in and stood sideways to bestow a scented embrace on her sister.

"I'm so excited. My little sister a viscountess! I vow, I can't believe it! Imagine you taking precedence over me at social functions." Daphne giggled girlishly.

"Well, you do not have to strain your imagination. I am not going to be a viscountess," Frankie replied flippantly.

"Wha—? You're not to be Lady Sterling?" Daphne stared openmouthed.

"No, I am not."

"Why, Viscount Sterling was here to propose to you! I'm sure he said so." Daphne put a finger beside her bow-shaped mouth, wondering if she had somehow got it muddled again.

"Yes, well, he did say that honor demanded he offer me the protection of his name, just because I was alone in his presence for a brief time. I am too old for these silly conventions . . . You do see, don't you, that I could not possibly accept him for that reason?"

"Oh, Frankie, my dear. Did he say that indeed? Well, of all the clodpoles! And yes, I can understand your

254

refusal. We Verdants *always* marry for love. 'Tis a good thing you snubbed him, my dear . . . But," Daphne continued after a few moments of trying to bring her jumbled thoughts into focus, "he *is* a viscount, you know. Quite the Corinthian. And such a tall and handsome man! Much sought after by the *ton*. You would have been greatly envied. And he loves horses as much as you do. Are you sure you would not have suited? . . . You're not afraid of him, are you?"

"Afraid of a stiff-necked *ton* dandy! Of course not," Frankie insisted.

"Beggin' your pardon, m'lady, but you's wanted below," Tizzy interrupted them, curtseying several times to Daphne. "Mr. 'Edge said there's another swell, er, gent'lman come to call."

"I'm not receiving. Oh, Tizzy, you know that, and surely *Hedge* didn't send you up to summon me?"

"H'indeed, 'e did, m'lady. 'E said to tell you Lord 'Arry Mark'am desires h'urgent speech with you, m'lady," Tizzy insisted, curtseying yet again.

With an exasperated sigh, Daphne resigned herself to again appear before a morning visitor. Why she didn't just dispense with her custom of not receiving while she was in her 'expanded state' she really did not know. The house seemed to be at sixes and sevens these days was her thought as she made her way slowly downstairs.


Daphne peeped through the door of the morning room to see an elegantly turned-out gentleman pacing a hole in her Aubusson carpet. The light coming in through the long windows glinted off his pale locks, and the dark brown of his well-fitting superfine jacket contrasted nicely with his snug biscuit-colored pantaloons.

"Oh dear, he's come about Laurel, I suppose," Daphne whispered worriedly to herself before bravely stepping

255

forward. She opened the door wider and entered the room.

"Good morning, Lord Harry. I declare, 'tis not at all the thing for me to receive visitors while I am . . . umm . . . in my state." She gestured vaguely toward her flowing draperies as little wisps of hair flew about her face, gleaming in the morning light flooding the room.

"Lady Whittgrove, forgive me for disturbing you so early. I know that you are not receiving at present, but I most urgently wanted—*had*—to see you," began Lord Harry earnestly. He was clearly nervous.

"You say the matter is urgent?"

"Yes. To me, it is most pressing. Lady Whittgrove, I know I should more properly see your husband, Sir Alfred, but as he is not here . . . In short, dear lady, I would like your leave to send a letter to him requesting his permission to address Lau—ah, your daughter."

At the slight negative shake of her glowing head and the look of distress on her lovely features, Lord Harry hurried into speech. "I know my prospects are limited and you have the right to expect a much better match for Miss Whittgrove. But, dear lady, I have now secured promise of government employment—in a diplomatic secretariat, actually. It is an area that interests me greatly and . . . I thought . . . I thought this would find favor with Sir Alfred. Indeed, I would not have been so presumptuous as to ask to pay my addresses to Miss Whittgrove if I had not made some push to better my fortunes, and I hope—indeed I know—that I will be able to adequately provide for a wife and family.

"Do not deny me the chance to put my case to your husband. Please, Lady Whittgrove. You can have no conception of how ardently I admire and love your daughter. I would not press my suit if I thought I would have inadequate means to support her or . . . or if a match with me would bring her harm in any way." So saying, Lord Harry smiled crookedly and extended a hand in supplication to Daphne, who was as little proof against his charm as her daughter.

Putting her hand in his, she said, "Oh, Lord Harry, I have known that Laurel . . . that she has a *tendre* for you. Yes, I have guessed it. You are a well-favored young man, but I cannot know if it would be the best life for my daughter. You do see, do you not? . . . Oh, indeed, you have disconcerted me . . . Of course I give you my permission to write to Sir Alfred, but I cannot promise anything more . . ."

Lord Harry lifted her delicate hand to his lips and saluted it fervently. He looked down at the small woman before him, gazing into eyes so like his Laurel's. "That is enough, dear lady," he said ardently. "I ask for nothing more. I cannot expect you to plead my case for me." He gave her hand a further squeeze before letting it go, then took his leave with a final grateful smile lighting his face.

"The shocks of this day are too much for me," Daphne sighed over the distracting events of the morning. While she would have gladly welcomed a match between Viscount Sterling and her sister, it seemed it was not to be. And a less attractive match between her daughter and Lord Harry seemed to be in the making. He was a most charming young man, but she had hoped Laurel would have married more comfortably. And then a smile brightened her delicate features. La, if she had been in Laurel's place she would certainly have preferred Lord Harry to all the other dull dogs about this season.

It all depended on Sir Alfred, however, and although she had said she would not interfere, she could not help gathering her skirts and rushing off as fast as her condition permitted to fetch her writing things. As she took up her pen to plead the case of the young people to her husband, a smile of delight dimpled her cheeks. Dearest Alfie had never refused her anything; young love would triumph through her benevolent efforts.

If only there were some way to play Cupid for Frankie, too . . . She sighed.

Several hours later Daphne was surprised when Laurel rushed into her arms to give her a hug and enthused, "You have seen Harry and you have not turned him off. Indeed, Mama, I knew you could not! He is everything a young man should be, is he not? I don't know how I can live without him," she intoned dramatically as she released her mother.

"It is by no means certain that your father . . ." Daphne could get no further before Laurel's smiles turned to tears.

"Indeed, Mama, Papa must give his permission. I shall die an old maid else! I could not possibly marry *another!*" Pathos reigned.

"There's no saying what may be in your dear papa's head, no saying at all, my love."

"You *will* persuade Papa. Promise me you will, Mama!"

All attempts to restore calm and reason were beyond Daphne, who had been just such a passionate beauty in her own youth.

"My dear, I have hopes . . . but we must wait and see," she cautioned her budding Thespian of a daughter.

# *Chapter Sixteen*

Tolland sat home during the next few days indulging his anger, not daring to risk making a fool of himself in public again. His ankle was giving him little trouble, except for an occasional twinge. He hated to admit it, even to himself, but Francesca's ointment had worked wonderfully well. Nonetheless, he continued to nurse the foot and always elevated it when visitors were present. Unwilling to forgo his favorite form of exercise, he rode out almost stealthily in the very early morning. Often he would go to the Green Park or even down to Richmond to avoid meeting his friends who might be riding in the more popular Hyde Park. Why he didn't just take himself off to his country seat and indulge his fit of the megrims was something he tried not to think about.

Despite the vigilance of Jenks, who had strict orders to forbid her the house, the crafty Lady Amelia got past that eagle-eyed sentinel by appearing on the arm of Monty Addlecumber one morning a week after the botched proposal.

Sir Monty's tenacious pursuit of the lady had finally been rewarded when she had agreed to drive out with him. Her purpose was nefarious—to get inside his relative's door, heretofore barred to her.

To say that Tolland was irritated to see the Fox in his drawing room again was an understatement. She swept over his portal in swirls of dusty red satin, a satisfied smirk on her face. She looked round carefully, wrinkling her nose and trying to detect any evidence that would proclaim the recent presence of the uncouth Miss "Verdure."

Tolland fixed his unfortunate cousin with a piercing look that promised later revenge. The unsuspecting Monty was unaware of the danger he stood in and greeted his cousin with a sweet smile pasted over his long, sallow face. His flaccid locks drooped against the bright satin of his yellow morning coat, while a number of chains and fobs hung from his garishly flowered waistcoat.

"How do, Tol. Ain't it a fine day? Thought we'd have a look in and see how you go on. Still gamey legged are you?" Monty asked, as he gazed across at his disheveled relative who sat stiffly with his foot resting on a stool in front of him. Tolland's subdued dress—a rather worn buff-colored riding coat, brown trousers, and carpet slippers—was not at all what Monty was used to seeing on the sartorially correct cousin he so much admired but didn't emulate. Monty shook his shaggy locks, not believing that Tol, usually such a high-stickler, could look so countrified in his fine London townhouse.

"Ah, André, *mon chéri*," Amelia gushed, as she came up to Tolland and bent forward to press her powdered cheek to his. "I knew you could not be feeling at all the thing when your man would not let me in the last several times I called with Mademoiselle Menaçant. Sir Montagu has been so kind as to escort me here so that we can both cheer you up." An openly seductive smile crossed her painted features, making Tolland feel distinctly hunted. He had seen that same look on her brother's face when Roger had ogled an innocent young beauty. A shiver of revulsion ran through his tall frame.

260

"Eh, coz, ain't she a beauty. Just castin' your peepers over 'er should send you into alt," Monty enthused. Amelia smirked at them both and preened herself, settling her colorful plumage about her as she settled herself on the chair nearest to where Tolland sat on the rolled-armed settee.

"So, you two are paying morning calls together. What a treat for all your acquaintance," Tolland remarked sardonically.

Amelia smiled coquettishly. "Ah, André, do not be odiously sarcastic. You know that you are the main object of our solicitation," she cooed unctuously.

All too well did he know it—and shuddered at the thought.

"What, pray, is *that?*" said Amelia as she pointed to the settee on which Tolland sat. She got up and retrieved the object from behind a cushion. It proved to be the remains of a giddily colored feather, rather the worse for wear. "Hmm, a purple feather. How garish! How did such an unsavory article come to be residing in your settee, André, *mon cher?*"

Tolland positively glowered at his cousin and tried to avoid Amelia's eyes. Oh, he was going to murder Monty for bringing her here!

Amelia immediately scented the purple-eyed "Verdure" hussy and put her scheme into action sooner than she had planned.

"Sir Montagu, dear, I think you promised me something earlier, did you not?" she asked, batting her lashes at the besotted Addlecumber. She looked both beguiling and determined.

"Eh?" Monty goggled, unable to follow her meaning.

"You did say that you would place a wager for me on this afternoon's meeting at Epsom. Why don't you hurry down to your club and have them open the betting book? Put the wager in your own name, mind. Not a word as to

261

my identity." She gave him a large wink. "Why, you could do it for me now! While I keep André company." Amelia smiled up at Monty, peeping through her lashes. The gesture was one suited to a jejune miss and looked quite ludicrous upon the countenance of a creature as sophisticated as the daughter of the Earl of Foxwell.

Addlecumber scratched his yellow pate in his habitual thinking pose and tried to recollect such a promise. He failed, but nothing loath, promised to see the thing done in the "turnin' of an ankle, by gad."

"You nodcock, Monty," Tolland hissed in a furious aside. "Don't you dare leave now!" But Monty was deaf and blind to all but his glorious Lady A.

"Your wish is m'commendment, m'lady," he declared, as he departed with a fatuous smile fastened upon his long countenance.

Amelia wasted not a second of the time that Addlecumber's absence gave her. She immediately stood up and went to sit next to the viscount, saying as she did so, "Your absurd relative seems not to know when he is *de trop*, does he, *mon cher?*"

Tolland, unprepared for the swiftness of her attack, just shrugged his shoulders. He moved forward to ease himself away from the settee. Her close proximity and cloying perfume made him exceedingly uncomfortable. Unfortunately, he put his weight on the much-abused ankle, which gave way.

Amelia scented her opportunity and jumped up to put her arms round her ill-fated quarry, ostensibly to steady him, but she did not let go once he had regained his balance. The lady was of a goodly height, and strong, and as the viscount's lips were on a level with her own, she immediately tried to press hers to them. After an unseemly struggle, Tolland managed to push her away. He limped quite swiftly to the bell pull and gave it a vigorous yank. His butler was in on them in the three seconds it took that worthy man to straighten himself up, rise from his seat in the hallway outside the drawing room, and walk the two steps to the door.

"André, really, no need to observe the proprieties with me, *mon amour . . .*" poor Lady Amelia tried to protest.

"Yes, m'lord?" intoned the unperturbed Jenks.

Swinging his eyes in the direction of the lady, Tolland said, "Lady Amelia is ready to leave, Jenks. Be so kind as to show her the door." The viscount's honeyed tones indicated his extreme annoyance, alerting Jenks to the fact that his employer was ready to turf the lady out if she wouldn't go willingly.

Amelia's red lips formed themselves into an unattractive pout as she fumed over the failure of her carefully laid plans. Her brother was due to arrive in another ten minutes to see her compromised and to demand that the viscount make proper restitution by offering for her.

"Lady Amelia requires her wrap." Tolland leaned on a chair by the open door and indicated that he waited for her exit. "Now, Jenks."

"André," she protested vigorously, "you know Papa awaits your visit at Foxwell House. The Earl can be quite fierce, but he will welcome *you,* I promise. You may call at any time."

"Amelia, you do me too much honor. Really you do. I find that I cannot avail myself of the opportunity you offer, unworthy as I am of your notice."

The lady drew herself up to her not inconsiderable height and looked down the length of her not unnoteworthy nose and said in tones one would have had difficulty calling dulcet, "Well! I see that what everyone is whispering about you is true! You've become a recluse, a rude, rustic sort of person.

"They say that fall in the park knocked you senseless, and now I can affirm that it has indeed impaired the man of impeccable manners we all hailed as a Corinthian and leader of the *ton*. I knew you had lost your much vaunted taste when I found you entertaining that 'Verdure' woman. Such a perverse, squinting, shabby creature can only lessen your consequence, you know. Your abominable manners toward *me* shall not go unreported."

And on that Parthian shot she swept past him without further adieu, proving once again that hell hath no fury like a woman spurned in her matrimonial objective.

True to his vow, Tolland absented himself from social affairs during the next fortnight, but he continued to suffer the frequent visits of his cousin, sans the Fox. Poor Monty was taken severely to task over the folly of bringing Lady Amelia to Tolland's abode in the first place, then having so little sense as to leave her alone there. However, Monty was unconvinced that his dear Lady A. could be a danger to anyone.

"Would've been just the ticket—you caught alone with 'er, Tol. Would've shackled 'er to me!" Monty beamed. Tolland hadn't the heart to berate his relative for this buffleheaded idea. It was utterly impossible that Monty would have been acceptable as a substitute groom. And Tolland thought it would be an equally impossible task to convince him of it without sounding unbearably conceited while inflicting a hard truth upon his foolish but genial relative.

Tolland sat back instead to listen with an appreciative grin on his face as his cousin recounted the recent behavior of the fashionable fribbles of the *ton*, tales made more amusing by Monty's idiosyncratic way of speaking. Though Monty frequently got his words and facts topsy-turvy, some semblance of the true state of affairs could be gleaned by a careful listener. Having exhausted his store of gossip, Monty finally remembered why he had come to visit the viscount.

"I say, coz, ain't you gonna get up and go to the mill tonight in Barnet? 'Tis the Belcher fightin', y'know." Even Monty, obtuse as he customarily was, realized that a sprained ankle didn't take weeks to heal.

"It's all the same to me whether I go or stay at home," Tolland replied with a sigh.

"Eh! Never say you're tired of the fancy!" Monty's eyebrows flew up in amazement. "Can see why you ain't fond of balls and drawin' rooms and doin' the pretty. Don't savory it much m'self. Only go to see Lady A., don't y'know. But, a mill, Tol! Surely you ain't plannin' to miss that!" He goggled at his cousin, his eyes protruding alarmingly as he digested this possibility.

"Gettin' to be just as bad as Harry. He don't want to do anythin' but trail after that little Miss Whittgroove."

"Oh, the Belcher's to fight, is he? Well, I guess I may as well attend if you will take me up in your carriage," Tolland said with a noticeable lack of enthusiasm.

"Go with me! Not drive your own team? Can see you ain't feelin' at all the thing, Tol." Monty hadn't been informed that the magnificent grays no longer made their home in his cousin's stables. "Indulgin' in a fit of the dismissals." Addlecumber nodded wisely.

"I am *not* having a 'fit of the dismals,'" Tolland protested sharply. "Only females indulge in such fanciful maladies," he grumbled.

"Heh? fancy melodies? Ain't got a handle on what you're on about at all, coz." Monty peered at him. "That ole bee been pesterin' you again?"

"Are you ready to leave, Monty?" Tolland inquired with deceptive sweetness. "Because if you are, I shall be delighted to have Jenks show you the door."

"Seen your door, Tol. Made of wood shanks. Same as any other . . . ain't it?"

Tolland sat back, shaking his head and muttering,

"Sometimes I think it's really quite deliberate, you know."

"Heh?"

"You can't possibly be such a bacon-brained idiot, can you?" Tolland put his hand up to cover his face and now peered between his fingers at his cousin.

"Related to *you*, don't y'know."

"Are you saying that I'm! . . ." Tolland nearly exploded.

"You're such a knowin' 'un. Proud to be your coz, y'know."

"All right, all right, peace! Why don't you tell me what you've heard at the club recently."

Monty began to relate a few remaining tidbits of gossip in an effort to divert his cousin. Tolland wasn't really attending as he jabbered on, not until a famliar name caught his ear.

"Looks like Harry has a *tendre* for Miss Whittgroove. Forever sittin' in her pocket, don't y'know . . . And that Miss Verdurant, Miss Whittgroove's aunt, y'know, goin' about everywhere with Freddy Drake. Ain't never seen Freddy so smitten. Must be a match in the cards, Harry says."

"What!" Tolland exclaimed, snapping to attention. "Not Drake and Fran—Miss Verdant?" His worst fears seemed to be coming true.

"Must say, can see why you're surprised. Mean to say, *Freddy!* Always been on the fidgets round women. Wouldn't have anything to do with 'em. Wouldn't be surprised if he's afraid to ask his mama if he can get leg-shackled, though. Lady Drake . . . a hairy-dame, y'know." Monty shook his head sadly.

This information served to dispel Tolland's ennui. "Why does Harry think there's a match in the air between Freddy and Miss Verdant?" Tolland asked, not caring what kind of harridan Lady Drake was.

"Well, mean to say, Miss Verdurant's devilish fond of horses, and y'know Freddy's fatuation for the beasts. Ride every day in the park, they do, with Harry and young Miss Whittgroove. Been seen toolin' Freddy's curricle, Miss Verdurant has. Stap me if he's ever let a female touch the ribbons in his life before!"

"But, Miss Verdant . . . she's a barb-tongued female . . . well on the shelf, too," Tolland pressed. "And has a devilish managing way about her, too. Why would Freddy want her when he might have had any of the dewy-eyed females who've come to market the past eight years?"

"Guess he ain't scared of 'er. She don't put on airs and braces. Ain't missionish, y'know. Can be cozy with 'er. Likes horses. Fine seat. Hunts, too. Don't think he cares if she sits on a deuced shelf." Monty scratched his head. "Can't say I've ever seen 'er managin' anything but horses, m'self. Don't she have quite mistmertizin' eyes? Purple, ain't they? That accounts for it." He nodded wisely.

"I daresay," Tolland muttered, suddenly consumed with jealousy. Addlecumber's chatter had put him in a black mood. How dare that shortsighted, headstrong woman, who had had the gall to turn him down, now be casting out lures to Drake, a most unlikely ladies' man! Drake was a worthy Corinthian who, though he wasn't all that comfortable in a ballroom or drawing room, shone on horseback, in the hunting field, driving his curricle or high-perch phaeton, or going a few rounds in the ring with Gentleman Jackson. An ideal match, in fact, for the no-nonsense Miss Francesca Verdant.

"Are we to expect an announcement, then?" Tolland couldn't stop himself from asking.

Monty looked puzzled as he said, "Curst if I know. Ain't officious, but Harry thinks it's as sure as a three-legged dog has fleas. Ask him yourself . . . if you can pry

267

him away from Miss Whittgroove's skirts long enough. Pretty little chit—but small."

"Young, I would have said," Tolland countered.

"Was competing 'er with Lady A., don't y'know."

"There *is* no comparison. Though she's young, Miss Whittgrove *is* a lady," Tolland retorted through compressed lips.

"Eh? What the deuce! You sayin' Lady A. ain't a lady, Tol?" Monty was offended.

"Oh, the Fox is a 'Lady,' all right, and she don't let others forget it."

"How could they deuced forget it? She's Lady Amelia Reynard."

"Vixen," Tolland muttered under his breath.

The information Monty had let fall about Francesca and Freddy finally roused Tolland from the stupor he had been in since she had rejected him, and set him to thinking furiously. He had a burning need to see how the land lay for himself. He cancelled his engagement with Monty and decided to go out on the town for the evening.

"I don't think I shall go with you to this mill after all. I find I am not up to it."

"Eh! Not go to the mill! Why, it's unheard of! Thought you was a top-sawyer Corinthian. You ain't gonna let a little thing like a gamey foot stop you? Might see Freddy there, y'know. He won't sit around and miss a chance to see the Belcher. That'll strip him away from Miss Verdurant's skirts, see if it don't!" Monty took himself off, shaking his head in disbelief at his cousin's disinterest in a boxing match.

Time suddenly seemed of the essence as Monty's words crystalized what Tolland had known subconsciously for weeks. He wanted to marry Francesca for reasons far removed from those of honor and obligation.

268

He was wildly, head over heels, in love with her. He *must* make her see him in a different light, and now that he had admitted his feelings, he was impatient to see her again and find some way to make her love him back. He had to go out and try to find her tonight. He sorted through his invitations, trying to decide where to begin his search.

Freddy was going to Barnet. Francesca would have to accompany her niece, with Markham their probable escort. Where would Harry take them? Tolland chose one or two likely evening parties he had cards for and thought he would call in and see if he could stumble across her. He scanned the morning's paper to see what evening entertainments were offered for the general public. Ah, there was a play on at Drury Lane and an opera at Covent Garden. Ladies generally liked the theatre. Well, he did himself and so did Harry. Tolland decided if he had no luck at the parties, he would try the theatre. He had hired a box there for the season, as usual, even though he had yet to use it this year.

After an unsuccessful evening spent trying to find Francesca at what surely were the two most boring parties he had ever attended, Tolland went on to Drury Lane, though without much anticipation of success there either.

He had had to shake off a clinging Amelia, who had greeted him rapturously, at the second house he had visited. It had been an ordeal. He had assumed that after their last meeting, she would snub him, but instead she saw his appearance at a *ton* event as evidence that he intended to rejoin society and took it as a compliment to herself. She had been most persistent, and he had escaped her clutches with difficulty.

He was weary and frustrated when he had finally managed to extricate himself and take his leave. There was a decided ache in his ankle; it wasn't used to the hard workout it was getting that night. If Harry and the ladies weren't at Drury Lane, Tolland decided that he would just sit and watch the play. He was too tired to hunt further that evening.

The ride to the theatre in his coach had seemed unusually jolting. He arrived shortly before the interval, then took his seat in his box, cursing as he finally lifted the weight off his sore foot. He sat back in weariness. His smart evening clothes were sadly crushed after all his rushing about. The care he had taken in dressing, for the first time in a long while, seemed all for nought. After a few moments of repose his tired brain began to clear and he survyed his surroundings. He looked about without much hope. But there, across and to the right of him, was Harry with Laurel Whittgrove and Francesca! Tolland's spirits lifted with triumph. His quest was rewarded.

Frankie must have felt Tolland's stare, for she glanced in his direction through her lorgnette and saw him smiling at her, and a warm, friendly smile it was, too. Her heart did a flip-flop in her breast to see him again and looking so elegant as he did tonight.

He rose and moved to his right to bow to her. In the midst of his bow, he leaned sideways and knocked his head slightly against an overhanging lamp at the edge of the box. "Damnation, not again!" he muttered, as he fell back heavily into his seat and put a hand up to his brow.

"Of all the ill luck!" Frankie exclaimed. He would no doubt blame *her* for his accident. She glanced at him again through the lorgnette, trying to see if he needed assistance. But she recollected that he would only say that her solicitation was uncalled for if she were to go to him, and would dub her a managing female.

Well, at least he seems comparatively unhurt this time, she thought as she watched him get up and disappear through the curtained entrance to his box. She wondered where he was going for perhaps half a minute. Then she could sit still no longer and got up to follow him.


Tolland decided he needed a drink after this latest *faux pas*. Hell and the devil, he raged, he had looked foolish yet again. Then he sighed. He was becoming almost resigned to the inevitable. All it took was the sight of her to make him lose control of his limbs.

As the interval arrived, people poured out into the lobby beyond the private boxes to seek refreshment and to exchange news and gossip with their friends. Tolland had gone down one flight of stairs in his search for a liquid potation and now wanted to make his way quickly back to the relative privacy of his box. He didn't wish to be caught up in conversation with anyone. He was walking hastily toward the stairs when he looked up and saw Francesca, not five feet away, lose her balance and trip down the last two steps.

He caught her.

She would have fallen indeed if Tolland hadn't shown great presence of mind in taking her in his arms and holding her tightly to his chest. Unfortunately, the drink he still carried spilled over both of them. She looked at him with a slightly abashed twinkle in her eye, but a twinkle nonetheless. He began to laugh, his blue eyes crinkled in merriment as he reluctantly released her. He heard Francesca utter a low-pitched gurgle, and soon she, too, was laughing outright.

"Well, we are determined to outdo one another in gracelessness tonight, aren't we, Angel?" Tolland said when he got his breath back.

Frankie's eyes were sparkling as she answered in the voice that never failed to melt his bones, "Yes, it seems we are a matched pair, Drew."

She heard his sharp intake of breath and saw an intense expression come into his eyes as he looked at her. His grin had vanished. "Do you mean that, Francesca?"

They were jostled as they stood at the edge of the stairs by a couple coming down. "I do beg your pardon, Sterling," Frankie replied. "Thank you for acting with such agility in saving me from a very nasty tumble just now. I should never have doubted your sportsmanship. Only a born athlete could have done the trick, catching me like that and steadying us both. And only a true gentleman would have risked looking foolish to make the attempt." Then with a dazzling smile she was gone.

Tolland was left standing there, wondering if he could believe his ears. Hadn't she just praised him to the skies? Perhaps he was making some headway after all. A smile played about his lips as he watched her retreating back. "You're a coward to run away, Angel," he murmured softly. "But you can't run from me forever!"

## Chapter Seventeen

Some hours after her encounter with Sterling at Drury Lane, Frankie took Black Demon out to the park. It was very early on a raw, drizzly morning, and the dampness seemed to penetrate the thick, warm velvet of her habit. Even the feather in her hat drooped in the moist air. The heavy mist made it impossible for her to see through her spectacles, as moisture continually dripped down the lenses, making it necessary to wipe them every few minutes. She put them away.

She had taken the precaution of having one of Sir Alfred's grooms accompany her, but the man was huddled miserably under an inadequate oilskin cape and followed her with great reluctance on a grey cob.

There were patches of mist drifting over the green expanses of the park and floating just above the surface of the Serpentine. In the quiet and dimness of the scene she was tempted to have a good hard gallop to shake the fidgets out of the Demon who was restively sidling and tossing his head, chafing, no doubt, at the slow pace she had set thus far this morning. She also wanted to shake off her own confused reactions upon seeing the viscount at Drury Lane.

She had taken one look at Drew across the theatre,

smiling that heartstopping smile of his, looking the way he had when they had waltzed at the Sefton ball, and now she could no longer hope to deny the attraction she felt for him. Attraction, ha! she thought ruefully. Thrown her cap over the windmill, more like!

Frankie Verdant, independent spinster that she was, had fallen in love, just as Daph had always wanted her to do. And she had to admit to herself that it was a painful state of affairs. Because she could never accept him under the terms he had laid out. And anyway, a match with Drew might be disastrous for them both. She grinned. She could just imagine the catastrophes they would experience in one another's company. Undoubtedly, one, or both, of them would be permanently maimed within a year!

Frankie shook off her blue devils and put on her spectacles for a moment to have a look round. Good, it was as she hoped. No one about, only her groom in attendance. She would be sure to grease his fist when they returned to the Whittgrove Mews after her ride so that he wouldn't report her to his mistress.

Demon snorted and shook his head, sending a shower of droplets over her glasses again. She could see the cloud made by her warm breath in the heavy morning air and breathed in the strong scent of wet leather and the pungent aroma of damp horse that hung in the air. The smells evoked nothing but pleasant memories for her.

She had just put her spectacles away again and decided that she could risk an all-out gallop when she heard hoofbeats. She could tell that they were coming in her direction before she saw the horse and rider through the swirls of mist and drizzle. Botheration! she muttered. Another rider to spoil her plans. The man was on a well-set-up bay. As he got closer she saw that it was Freddy on his mount Charity. "What good luck!" she exclaimed.

"'Morning, Miss Verdant. Surprised to see a lady out

so early and in such weather, too."

"Good morning to you, Mr. Drake. I hope you shan't tell if I have violated yet another stricture laid down by the powers that be."

"Ha-ha. No such thing. Only thought you ladies needed the morning to recuperate. Don't tell me you weren't out raking last night. That would be pitching it much too rum."

"I am not such a poor creature. Indeed, I did accompany my niece to the theatre last evening, but such a paltry thing wouldn't keep me from a morning ride. At home, as you know, I am frequently up and in the saddle exercising one of the horses before breakfast."

"Knew you was a right 'un. What say you we shake the fidgets out of our mounts?"

"Gallop, you mean?" Frankie asked. Her eyes gleamed and her face lit up with a smile. "Well, Mr. Drake, I will race you to that stand of trees and back." She squinted and pointed with her riding crop to some purple beeches in the distance.

"And would you care to wager on the outcome, Miss Verdant?"

"A wager?" Frankie paused to consider. "What do you suggest, sir?"

"Well, I know that your Red Devil is descended from the Godolphin Arabian. I would breed him to my Charity, here." Freddy pointed to his bay mare, a magnificent creature with great sloping shoulders and as smooth an action as Frankie had ever seen. "And you would forgo the fee, if I win—an outcome of which there can be no doubt."

Frankie raised an eyebrow. "And if I *do* somehow manage to overcome all your obvious advantages and reach the finish line first?"

"Not likely, but you would keep the foal."

"Hmm. Interesting. Are you sure, sir?"

Freddy nodded.

"You're on," she said as she extended her hand to seal the bargain.

And they were off, their horses' hooves throwing up bits of wet turf as they charged through the grey puffs of fog swirling around them. Frankie rode swiftly, the wind pulling wisps of hair about her face and the drops of rain in the air stinging her eyes as they hit her at speed. Black Demon snorted heavily, leaving great clouds of steam in his wake. Her own breath was coming in gasps. Frankie was exhilarated! The strangeness of the scene made her feel that she was riding through a cloud above the ground, only the familiar smoothness of Demon's action beneath her. Her whole mind was concentrated on the task before her. She was aware of Drake just to her left. They were neck and neck as they flew along.

Another rider was approaching the stand of trees as the two horses bore down on him. He heard the thundering hooves and his keen blue eyes were able to pierce the fog and distinguish the riders. He recognized the lady immediately, and the bay mare of the gentleman was as well known to him as his own mount. Orion's ears were pricked to attention, but the chestnut stallion stood calmly under Tolland's firm control. For the connoisseur of racing the two riders made quite a striking picture as they flew along side by side, both horses running full out. But the viscount was in no mood to appreciate the scene.

He had decided to ride here in the park, then to call on Francesca and ask her to drive out with him that afternoon so they could talk. But there she was, as though he had conjured her up. There she was—in danger!

"Oh, my God!" Tolland exclaimed, his heart in his throat. His lips tightened grimly as his fear turned to anger. The anger progressed from simmering to boiling as the riders neared with their heads low over their horses' necks.

276

"Stop," bellowed Tolland, but his voice could not penetrate to the riders' ears above the hoofbeats of their galloping horses and the animals' snorting breaths. He quickly wheeled his stallion about and charged across the path of the racers, signalling them to stop with a raised hand.

It spoke well for the skills of each that Frankie and Freddy were able to slow their galloping mounts in a relatively small space of time from full speed to an easy canter, then to a walk. Freddy rode up to the viscount, panting from the exercise. "I say, Tol, why did you ride across our path like that? We were enjoying capital sport."

"Were you, indeed?" Tolland asked stiffly, trying to still his pounding heart. "And did you stop to consider what would have happened to Miss Verdant's reputation, Freddy, and that of the young lady she is chaperoning about this season, if some other early morning rider had observed you galloping hell for leather through the park and was intent on bearing the tale through the *ton?*"

Freddy looked a little shamefaced. "Who was there to see us at this hour?"

"You will observe that *I* am here."

"But, Tol, you wouldn't spoil sport, would you?" Freddy asked, not believing his ears.

"I believe Lord Sterling is just jealous of our gallop," Frankie said huskily as she came up to the two men. Demon was snorting heavily, and great clouds of steam rose from his wet flanks. "What do you gentlemen say to all three of us having a good run while no one's about?"

"How can you think of such a thing on a morning like this?" Tolland grew more upset as he turned to her and broached the heart of the matter. "What if you had lost control! The ground is slick and vision impaired this morning, and you don't see well, anyway! You could be lying here even now with a broken neck!"

277

"You make too much of nothing, Sterling," Frankie said, unrepentant. "I have galloped over wet ground hundreds of times at home, and I am not *blind* you know! I can see well enough to guide Demon over any obstacle you care to name!"

"Yes, and you've spoiled the bet, too," Freddy interrupted unwisely.

"Bet?" Tolland asked, lowering his brows. "You had a bet with a lady over a horse race, Drake? May I ask the stakes?"

Freddy began to tell him but was cut off by Frankie. "It is of no consequence now."

Tolland brought his own chestnut next to Black Demon, reached over and grabbed Frankie's bridle. "Don't you realize the harm this could do you?"

"What the *ton* thinks is of no interest to me," Frankie declared, glaring at him as Demon sidled and fidgeted at all the standing about.

"Listen to me, Miss Hot-at-Hand! Your sister's credit will suffer and so will your niece's. If you don't care for yourself, at least have a care for the good names of your relatives."

"Your concern is misplaced, Sterling. Why do you take it upon yourself to lecture me and interfere in my affairs?" Frankie's temper was up, and she couldn't see that Tolland was speaking out of his care for her. It seemed to her that he was as insulting now as he had been the first time she had encountered him.

"Ah, the boot's on the other foot now, and you don't like it! When you saw fit to interfere in my affairs I was told not to be so childish. When I am telling you to do something for your own good, you resent it!" Tolland said hotly. All sense of the resolution he had made to soothe his lovely Francesca's wounded feelings and bring her round to view him in a more favorable light evaporated in the heat of his anger.

And Frankie, for the first time in her life, felt angry tears start to her eyes. She dashed them away with an impatient hand. A lump came to Tolland's throat when he saw he had made his angel cry. He dropped her bridle and put out his hand to smooth away the teardrops on her cheek, whispering, "I'm sorry, love." But other riders could now be heard approaching them, and Frankie drew sharply on Demon's reins and turned away from him.

"Allow me to escort you home, Miss Verdant," Freddy interrupted to break the tension of the awkward moment. Until then, he had been sitting quietly watching the scene between the two. "I apologize for leading you into this muddle. It was my suggestion, and I see that I was wrong."

He turned to Tolland. "Do not be taking the lady to task, Tol. She succumbed to my persuasion. I was at fault, and I accept the blame." Freddy reached over to pat Frankie's hand where it rested against Black Demon's neck. She smiled halfheartedly at him.

Tolland watched the gesture and his Francesca's response with a sinking heart. So much for his resolve to edge his way into her good graces and woo her in earnest. His blasted temper had put paid to any such plans. She would surely hate him now. He looked at them with sadness in his eyes, touched his hat, and rode away.


Sally Chatterington sat up beside Sir Montagu Addlecumber, looking pleased as punch to be there, as he tooled her about the park in his modest carriage. His chariot was decorated in an uncharacteristically subdued style, too, she noted with interest. But then she listened doubtfully as he told her that he was convinced he would soon be able to realize his fondest dream and make Lady Amelia Reynard his.

Sally hoped that he was wrong, for such a marriage

would leave both parties unhappy in her admittedly biased estimation. She had conceived a very warm spot in her heart for the sunny-natured knight. She thought he was an amazingly comfortable companion, so uncritical, so easygoing . . . and so entertaining.

"Had a visitation last night," he told her with a furtive air.

"Did you?" she asked, eying him in fascination.

He nodded. "Prodigious great bird . . . ten-feet high . . . parked on the end of m'bedpost. Plaguey thing sat there like a munument," he said in hushed tones. "A romen, don't y'know," he added dramatically.

"I suspect you mean an omen, Sir Montagu. I should think it was just a nightmare, you know," the practical Sally tried to reassure him as she reached over and patted his arm.

"Had a shiny gold omelet round its neck—brought a message redressed to me." He nodded importantly. Sally giggled behind her gloved hand and sputtered, "You mean a golden amulet, Sir Montagu."

He nodded again. "Lady A., been givin' me a receptacle lately, y'know. Think it agues well for m'preposition?"

"Oh, she's letting you in the front door, at last, is she? A great boon, I'm sure," responded Sally drily.

"Can have no deception of how arduously I adore 'er, Miss Chatterin'tongue. Tol ain't deposed to cast any disperions on 'er, y'know. Says she's 'the most sedimented of women.' A bang-up depiction, don't y'think? He don't want 'er himself, though." Why this should be so defied Monty's powers of reasoning.

"In truth, I can't conceive how *you* have come to admire her, either," Sally murmured.

Monty pursued his own line of thought. "Yep, was one of those Greek coves last night. Fate, ain't it? . . . Very suspicious."

"Are you sure you don't mean an auspicious Roman,"

Sally said laughingly.

"One of them hysterical chaps, at any odds . . . Wonder if it's the same cove as is chasin' Tol about? . . . Weren't a bee, though. Was a bird with a great long beak . . . always mutilatin' their shapes, though, those Greek coves. Told me I'd be a tenant for life soon. Must mean Lady A. will accept m'heart if I lay it before 'er."

Sally thought the Fox was more likely to tread on his heart than cherish it. "A fate greatly *not* to be desired, I should think, Sir Montagu, no matter what shape it takes," she declared energetically.

"Ain't it though!" Monty turned to her and smiled. "Think I'll pop the question tomorrow."

A discouraged Sally could hardly restrain herself from lifting her rolled umbrella and bringing it down on poor Sir Montagu's head. She was saved from such an immodest and violent act by her own good manners and the knowledge that Lady Amelia Reynard was not in the least likely to accept Sir Montagu's proposal of marriage. Sir Montagu might cast himself into Amelia's arms, but Sally would lay odds that the lady would be unwilling in the extreme to receive him. Sally smiled ruefully as she pictured poor Sir Montagu dropping to the floor with a thud.


The attention of the *ton* had been riveted for some time on the gala opening for an exhibition of paintings at the Royal Academy in the Great Exhibition Hall at Somerset House. There was much excitement when the doors finally opened and the *beau monde* flocked to the event like so many lemmings to the sea.

Two days after the unhappy meeting with Francesca in the park, Tolland decided to attend the exhibition and see for himself what all the fuss was about. He had decided that it was time for him to quit hiding and resume his normal existence.

"The blue superfine, m'lord?" Worthy assisted the viscount as he dressed. "Mr. Weston did a superb job in fitting this jacket to your lordship's shoulders."

"Did he? Good," Tolland commented absently as Worthy laid out his clothes.

"And the buff inexpressibles, m'lord?" At Tolland's nod Worthy remarked, "Only a man with your lordship's build should wear this form of garment. I don't approve of those gentlemen who have to use buckram wadding to pad out their calves."

"No, you wouldn't." Tolland gave a half-smile, remembering Worthy's disparaging remarks about that form of affectation.

He allowed Worthy to arrange his neckcloth, even bowing to his valet's insistence that a single gold stickpin among its carefully arranged folds would add just the right touch. After much pleading, Worthy had finally been allowed to call in a barber, too. He had told his master bluntly, "M'lord, you've allowed your hair to grow long and untidy during your convalescence." Thus Tolland's dark hair was newly trimmed into its customary neat style, Worthy's care and attention to detail helping to renew his feeilngs of unruffled superiority.

Tolland hoped that by re-creating the old Viscount Sterling he could resume his former existence and put Francesca from his every waking thought—and night-time dream. Just maybe he could get rid of the feeling in his chest, uncommonly like a pain, that seemed to plague him whenever he thought of her.

Tolland had been strolling about the exhibition rooms

for some time, greeting his friends and admiring particularly an exhibition of Stubbs's paintings. Many of the pictures displayed were of rather static racehorses, probably commissioned by their proud owners. According to his catalogue, some of Stubbs's more recent canvases "represented a new way of painting animals, showing all the romantic nobility and violence of nature." And indeed the horses portrayed in these works seemed to exude power and explosive motion to Tolland's thinking. He studied Stubbs's paintings with interest, admiring the way the artist had captured the musculature and movement of the animals.

Everyone he chatted with seemed genuinely pleased to see him up and about. He breathed a sigh of relief when he realized that Amelia's poisonous tongue hadn't turned the tide of his popularity. He even dusted off his infamous quizzing glass and enjoyed using it to advantage on more than one young miss who blushed when seeing herself observed by such a tall, elegant gentleman. His old power and confidence were returning.

Just when he was feeling rather smug, he glanced up and saw Markham enter with Laurel Whittgrove on one arm and Francesca on the other. He faltered in his step. Oh, God, there she was, looking more beautiful than ever, he thought. His determination to remain unperturbed flew out the window. He turned away briefly, trying to calm his breathing. So much for his efforts to banish all feeling for her!

He realized that trying to put her from his mind and heart was a hopeless task. He could not go back to his previous existence. He *had* changed; he was in love and pretending otherwise was only to fool himself.

He couldn't help but turn back almost immediately and watch her as she studied her catalogue through her lorgnette. Harry had moved away, his head bent to catch what his companion was saying, and Francesca was moving slowly after them as she read. None of Markham's party had spotted him yet. Before Tolland knew he had moved, his steps took him to her side.

"Good afternoon, Francesca," he said as he took up her fingers and bowed over her gloved hand. "I trust you are enjoying the exhibit. Have you seen Stubbs's work yet?"

"Sterling!" Frankie was greatly surprised to see him there before her, taking her hand and tucking it snugly through his arm, after he had ripped up at her so angrily in the park only two days before. He was looking at her with a warmth in his blue gaze that sent her pulses racing.

"I'm glad to see your ankle has finally recovered so that you can get about more on foot. Is there any discomfort still?" Take it light and easy, she told herself, hoping he could not feel the nerves jumping in her fingertips where they touched his arm.

"Alas, you won't find me entering any footraces in the foreseeable future," he replied in a melodramatic way, placing his free hand over his heart. "I'm afraid I will never be quite the same fleet-footed lad I once was."

She laughed at his light-hearted tone. "Ah, but Father Time has a lot to do with that you know."

"Francesca! Are you saying that I'm *old?*" he asked in mock displeasure.

"Not at all. You've reached a 'golden' maturity. 'Maturity' is the word we want when referring to ourselves, Drew."

Tolland felt himself drawn toward her by the laughter in her eyes as she bantered with him in such playful high spirits.

"'Beautiful' is the word I want when referring to you, Angel," he said, as he moved a step closer and caught her slipper under his boot. She grabbed his shoulders and he her waist as they tottered briefly, then regained their balance. They looked at one another for a surprised

284

moment. Then, unable to restrain their mirth, they collapsed in unselfconscious laughter.

They sobered immediately as they gazed at one another. The air between them was charged with unspoken feelings.

"Francesca, please forgive me for ripping up at you the other day," Tolland said urgently. "It was only that I was so concerned for your safety."

"Ah, who's the 'mother hen' now?" Her lips parted in a slightly lopsided smile.

Tolland leaned forward. He didn't believe he could resist the urge to kiss her then and there. But several other couples had wandered close to them and he stopped himself. He kept his hold on her and continued to look at her intently.

Frankie, aware now of other people milling about nearby, broke eye contact with him. She looked down, releasing her hold on his shoulders as she did so, and stepped back. Tolland was torn. He wanted to secure her to himself, yet all his lifelong resistance to marriage reared up and he hesitated. He had had a lucky escape when she had turned him down before, hadn't he? Shouldn't he flee now before he committed himself irrevocably? Oh, hell, he thought, I'm going to make a damned fool of myself again.

"Miss Verdant. Oh, there you are, dear girl. I've been looking everywhere for you. Sorry I was delayed. There's a devil of a lot of traffic hereabouts today. Some heavy-handed whipster has overturned his tilbury in the middle of the Strand," Freddy remarked, as he came upon them in this quiet corner of the exhibition rooms.

Tolland felt completely deflated as Francesca looked up with a wide smile on her face to greet Freddy Drake.

"You here, Tol? Didn't know you was getting about on foot yet. Thought you was only able to go out hacking." Freddy looked round the room. "Don't know what all the

285

fuss is about. Nothing here but a lot of fusty old art works."

"Beauty is always worth admiring," Tolland said quietly, looking at Frankie.

"Oh, ho, you've been admiring the Stubbs's, have you, Tol? Can't keep you away from horseflesh. Even if it's only paint." Drake quizzed his friend, pleased with himself for this observation.

"Really, Freddy, you're becoming as bad as Monty," Tolland admonished.

Frankie had taken the arm Freddy extended to her, and he was patting her fingers possessively with his other hand. "Congratulate me, Tol. Miss Verdant's done me a great favor. I've finally won her over. She's agreed to my proposal. Still can't believe my good fortune."

Tolland looked thunderstruck. A flush mounted to his cheeks and that familiar painful feeling in his stomach hit him again hard and low. It hurt to breathe for a moment.

Frankie was smiling at Freddy in a friendly manner, but Tolland thought she looked as smitten as Drake did. Freddy was positively glowing.

"I can guess," Tolland said dispiritedly. His hopes, running so high only a few moments ago, were dashed. He felt his heart plummet to his shoes.

"You can?" Freddy looked surprised. "No, Tol, how could you?"

"It's written all over your face. Well," Tolland said briskly, wanting desperately to leave before he made an even greater cake of himself, "your mutual interest in horses should stand you in good stead. I congratulate you both. I hope you will be very happy." And with a travesty of a smile on his face, he bowed to them, turned on his heel, and rapidly left the building.

Freddy scratched his head in Addlecumber-like fashion. "How could Tol know you've agreed to sell me two of Red Devil's colts? I ain't told anyone yet. Had you been discussing it with him before I found you?"

"Why no, Freddy. I believe Lord Sterling is laboring under a misapprehension," Frankie said, her smile widening. Unaccountably, her spirits rose as she guessed at Drew's thoughts.

Monty arrived at Tolland's townhouse around midnight that evening. He staggered into the study where he found the viscount sitting in shirt sleeves, his hair in wild disarray, downing a bottle of brandy.

"She won't have me, coz. M'deportment don't suit 'er farcical ideas," Monty moaned dramatically. He lurched into the room with neckcloth askew, looking sadly the worse for wear. "Threw me out like an old shoe. Think m'heart is broken." He paused and seemed to listen for a moment. "It don't seem to be tickin' no more."

Tolland looked up owlishly from the armchair where he sprawled, his booted feet propped up on the edge of his desk. "Who won't have you, Monty? You don't mean Francesca?"

"Franchestica? Who in Hades is Franchestica? . . . No, I mean Lady A.—Amelia, don't y'know. Popped the question. Went on m'knees, too—most damagin' to m'new tailorin'. Told me I looked silly. Said she wouldn't have me if I was served up to 'er on a platter," Monty concluded sadly. He poured himself a generous measure of the brandy and flopped into Tolland's desk chair, which creaked dangerously under such rough treatment.

"That Amelia. She's the very devil," Tolland said, only slightly slurring his words. Monty nodded morosely. "All women are the very devil," Tolland added.

"But beauteous, Tol, devilish women are the most beautemous," Monty decided, as he threw his head on the desk in agony. The memory of the beautiful Lady Amelia laughing in his face as he recited his much-

rehearsed proposal was too much for him. He began to
sing in an off-key, falsetto:

> "But when I came—alas!—to wive,
> By swaggering could I never thrive . . .
> Hey, 'Tol,' jolly 'Tol,'
> Tell me how thy lady does."

The effect of the brandy, compounded with the
quantity of champagne he had downed earlier in the
evening to give himself courage, quickly rendered Monty
well-nigh incoherent.

"To beautiful women, Monty. To my beautiful
Angel." Tolland raised his drink in a toast, slightly
sloshing the brandy over the rim due to his unsteady
hand.

"You shot the cat, coz?" Monty inquired in a muzzy
voice.

"No, no. Only a trifle disguised. 'Temporarily
banished care,' is all," Tolland assured him with a wave
of his hand.

Monty raised his head and his glass so that he could
toast angels, too.

"To her beautiful voice—like an angel's." Tolland
lifted his glass again.

Monty raised his, then lowered it and squinted over at
his dishevelled cousin. "You love Amelia, too, coz?"

"No, no, not her . . . Angel. Angel call'd Fran-
chessca's the woman I love," Tolland declared.

Monty repeated, "Tol loves Franchestica," and raised
his glass. "You love an angel, Tol? That deuced visitation
get to you, too?"

"But she don't love me."

Monty lowered his glass. "Don't love you, Tol?
Heh? . . . You sure? Thought all women loved you . . .
Amelia loves you. You sure Franchestica's a woman,

Tol?" the addled Monty asked. "Outlandish sort of name—never heard a woman called Franchestica before . . . Well, an angel, after all . . . just goes to show."

"No, Amelia don't love me. She only loves . . . Amelia. She ain't worth it, coz."

"No." Monty nodded wisely and after a moment said, "Your angel ain't worth it, either, Tol."

The viscount got unsteadily to his feet and came toward Addlecumber's slumped form, saying, "Don't you say that, Monty. Haf to call you out." Tolland gestured at Monty and dropped his empty glass. "Damnation," he swore, as he knelt down to pick up the pieces.

"You on your knees, Tol? Won't do you any good. She ain't here," Monty uttered in deep distress for his cousin.

"No, not here," Tolland agreed. "Gonna marry Freddy."

"Freddy gettin' leg-shackled? Who'd have *him?*"

"Fran—Miss Verdan's gonna marry Freddy," Tolland said, as he decided to stretch out on the carpet for a brief rest from his troubles.

"Ain't so, Tol. Saw Freddy tonight . . . in alt 'cause Miss Verdurant's trading him some nags for a bit of the ready. Y'know, Freddy and horseflesh, well . . . as dicked in the nob as you, coz. Gonna be a horse-coper, is Freddy. Breeding 'em like, y'know. Said he was glad he met 'er. Said she was a good fellow. Not going to marry 'er, ole boy," Monty assured him.

"Tol, Tol, you all right?" Monty squinted down owlishly, finally noticing his cousin on the floor.

"Bless m'soul! You ain't snivelling, Tol?" Monty asked, horrified at such an unprecedented possibility. But as a snore issued from his recumbent relative's lips at that moment, Monty's mind was relieved. "Tha's the thicket, then," he decided, as he proceeded to sink into a state of oblivion as profound as that of the viscount.

# Chapter Eighteen

"Mama! Tizzy told me you have just received an express from Papa!" Laurel shouted as she burst into the morning room and rushed toward her parent.

"Tsk. How did that girl find out so quickly? I vow and declare, the servants always seem to be the first to know any news in this house." Daphne had been reposing decorously on the sofa in the sunny room, holding a sheet of paper in her hand and smiling to herself. Dear Alfie, she thought fondly, you are always so good. It was as she had expected.

"What does Papa say?" Laurel clutched the material of her frivolous pink and cream morning dress nervously and looked at her mother anxiously.

"My dear child!" Daphne reached a hand out to her. "Your papa is entirely too good! It is as we hoped."

Laurel hugged herself with happiness as her mother continued, "Lord Harry has written to Papa and satisfied him with regard to your future comfort. All is well. You may consider yourself formally betrothed . . . And Papa has been given leave to come home. With any luck, he will be here when his child is born. Is not that good news!"

Laurel's face was wreathed in a wide smile as she lifted

her eyes to the ceiling in thankful joy. When she turned to Daphne they were filled with tears.

"Oh, Mama. I am so happy! May I send for Harry?"

"You are as impulsive as I was in my youth." Daphne laughed girlishly, remembering her own excitement on her betrothal to Alfie. "Indeed, send for your Harry, my dear. You may ask Hedge to dispatch one of the footmen with a message, if you wish."

With that, Laurel left the room, as full of energy as when she had entered it only moments before, her errand giving wings to her feet and her joy generating unladylike haste.

Sir Montagu Addlecumber arrived at the Chatterington residence to take tea with Sally at the same moment Laurel was running to find a footman in Grosvenor Square. Sally welcomed him with a beaming smile. She poured out a cup of the warm brew, while Monty began pouring out his heart.

"M'hopes are quite butchered, Miss Chatterin'tongue! Spoked m'wheel, she did. Lady A. looked at me with indigestion as I laid m'heart before 'er, then shook 'er head and . . . laughed. Quite discomposing it was . . . The short of it is—she won't have me." Since Sally had been the recipient of his hopes concerning Lady Amelia from the inception of their acquaintance and had heard all his woes during that ill-fated courtship, she was at no loss to understand him.

"No!" Almost as shocked as she was relieved, Sally set the teapot down rather too abruptly and caused the tea things to rattle on their silver tray.

"Been danglin' at 'er shoelaces forever, don't y'know." Monty nodded sadly, his flaxen locks hardly moved as he shook his head. He had had them specially trimmed, cut quite tightly to his head in the modern style, for his proposal; and his tailoring had undergone a transformation as well.

He had seen himself in his "visitation" clad thus, so he now more nearly resembled a gentleman of the early nineteenth century in his olive green frock coat and yellow pantaloons. He had dispensed with his fobs and chains and other jewelry as well, fearing that the gigantic bird that had sat on his bedpost in his dream might be attracted to the shiny objects and would come back to haunt him. The only remaining concession to his former dandyism could be seen in his elaborately tied white cravat.

Though Sir Montagu's tidings brought joy to her ears, Sally's ready compassion was fully aroused nonetheless at his disappointment, and she reached across the table to pat his hand. "The woman must have bats in the belfry to turn down an offer from you, my dear sir, not to mention a heart as cold as stone." Montagu was *much* too good for Amelia Reynard, she thought.

Monty felt immediately cheered. He had known he would find a sympathetic listener in 'Miss Chatterin'-tongue' . . . and her soft red hair looked so pretty done up in a coronet, he noticed.

"Most beckonin', Miss Sally," he complimented, glancing at her hair.

"What? . . . Oh." She smiled as she noted the direction of his gaze. "You mean my hair, I suppose. Why, thank you for the compliment, sir. You are always so amazingly fulsome. May I say that you look extremely fashionable in your new togs, as well, Sir Montagu."

Monty sat for a moment with a pleased smile on his face as he gazed at Sally, then almost dropped his cup and saucer as a most original thought popped into his head. "By gad, Miss Chatterin'tongue . . . just hit upon the most famous notion, don't y'know."

"Oh, you may call me Sally, Sir Montagu," Sally said, smiling brightly.

"Sally. It's a deal easier to get m'tongue around than Chatterin'tongue," he nodded happily. "M'handle's Monty, y'know. Be pleased if you'd use it—all m'friends do."

"What was your notion, Monty?"

"Tell you what, m'dear . . . think you'd suit me to a turnip."

"Do you, Monty?"

"Yep—know it for a factor. What's more, have another notion."

"Do you? I thought you might."

"Fancy gettin' leg-shackled, Miss Chatter—er, Sally, m'dear? It's what I'd like. Be pleased if you'd accept m'hand—glad to lay m'fortune in your lap, don't y'know."

"Oh, Monty dear, I should like it above all things! How clever of you to have such a splendid notion!"

Monty beamed. Sally glowed. Her arrantly frivolous knight kissed her hand over the tea tray and sealed their bargain.


In the Whittgrove residence Laurel and Harry were ensconced on the very sofa earlier occupied by Daphne. Her head lay on his shoulder and their faces were wreathed in smiles.

"Do you really not mind the life you will lead as a diplomat's wife, my dearest? Should you not take more time to consider? I'm afraid we cannot expect to be settled for some years. I dislike thinking of you not being comfortably situated."

"Oh, Harry. How can you be so foolish. To be with you is all I need to be 'comfortably situated.'" Laurel regarded him fondly. They exchanged a satisfying fervent kiss, then Laurel again settled her head comfortably against his shoulder and proceeded to wheedle

294

him into doing her will.

"Now that that is all settled, my love, we must consider your present duties as my betrothed. I think it encumbent upon you, dearest, to escort Aunt Frankie and me to Lady Makepeace's masquerade on Friday next."

"What! You can't mean to go to that rubbishy affair. Why, every rake and rattle in the kingdom will be in attendance!" Harry remonstrated.

"Ah, but I shall have you to protect me," she whispered, batting her eyelashes at him playfully while winding one arm more tightly round his neck. "But seriously, my darling, it's not for myself that I beg your escort. I think Aunt Frankie desires to go."

"Your aunt? But why would she want to go to a masquerade ball except as your chaperon? Thought her main interest was in horses . . . and plaguing Tol." A smile played about Harry's mouth as memories of his friend's encounters with the lady danced through his head.

"Well, Aunt Frankie has actually bought a costume for the affair, so she must be interested in going. It's usually so difficult to get her to take any notice of her clothes. She's gone around the house with a most peculiar smile on her face for the last week, too. She's got something mysterious in mind, I just know it . . . Perhaps Mr. Drake?"

"Perhaps the foal that will result when she breeds Freddy's mare to the Verdant meadow's Red Devil," Harry said with intended irony.

"Oh, you," his beloved protested, hitting him softly with her dainty fist to emphasize her displeasure at his teasing.


Lady Makepeace was a thoroughly respectable matron

295

of mature years whose ripe charms were now distinctly withered on the vine. However, her masquerade ball was an occasion gleefully anticipated by the *beau monde*, despite Harry's disparagement of the affair to Laurel. A ball at which the participants were costumed and masked was of itself a rather daring occasion—just what the *ton* favored for divertissement. It could give rise to all manner of less than proper behavior. The choice of costume gave proper young ladies scope to be a bit naughty, and being unable to resist temptation, most of them, save those who were too prim or too shy, took full advantage of it.

Themes with an Eastern bent were popular, having caught the romantic imagination of many poets, painters, and furniture makers of the day, not to mention the Prince Regent himself with his fantastical Pavilion at Brighton. And so the ladies' clothiers' shops were full of dress reflecting this style. A costume featuring trousers had caught Frankie's eye. She bought it without examining it too closely or trying it on. She just asked Madame Eugénie to make one up in her size and send it along to Grosvenor Square. She didn't realize that it was a costume for a Turkish dancing girl.

Daphne was horrified when Frankie unwrapped the package containing the costume. Frankie looked amused as she held up a pair of flowing gauze trousers, a shimmering white blouse that would leave the tops of her shoulders uncovered, and a long, bright gold and purple scarf to tie round her waist. Daphne thought the costume too immodest by half.

"Why, Frankie, you will look like a member of the demimonde with your legs exposed like that!" Daphne declared as vehemently as her gentle nature would allow. "'Tis much too risqué. I cannot like it."

"But I often wear trousers at Verdant Meadows. I cannot stride about in the confines of a skirt. My legs tend to get themselves tangled up, you know. This is the perfect costume for me."

"Oh, yes, we know your habits and manner of dress at home all too well." Daphne had a martyred expression on her face. "But these are not regular trousers, Frankie dear. Why, they are almost *sheer!* I fear they may be too daring. You will shock the *ton.*"

"Oh, Daph, I feel daring. What is one more small peccadillo to the scandal-ridden *ton,* in any case? They all seem to carry on as though they are concubines half the time, as it is. I don't doubt there will be a whole harem of ladies dressed as I am."

"Well, you were always daring, little sister, ever since you were a child and climbed to the top of the tallest tree in the garden and insisted on riding the most untamed of the horses and assisted at all the foalings and all those other nasty things you were bent on doing." Daphne shivered delicately.

"You mean like helping to set James's leg when he broke it in that nasty fall he took at the North Farm gate and going to help at Mrs. Grimes' lying-in?" Frankie grinned.

Frankie decided to wear the costume despite Daphne's objections. Since she *was* accustomed to wearing trousers at Verdant Meadows, any costume that freed her limbs so that she might stretch out her lithe, long legs in full stride had immediate appeal. However, she agreed to wear heavy cotton stockings rather than silk ones under the gauze trousers at Daphne's suggestion.

An ingenious method of fitting her aunt's spectacles into the half-mask was proposed by the inventive Laurel. With the mask fashioned not only to hide her eyes but to incorporate her glasses as well, Frankie felt she would be free to look about easily.

The ever-faithful Freddy Drake had offered to escort Frankie to the ball, but the prospect of collecting the two colts out of Red Devil from Verdant Meadows had proved too much of a temptation to withstand any delay. She released him from the engagement with good will. Accordingly, he set out for Cambridgeshire after accompanying Frankie home from the Exhibition. There was regret in his eyes as he left her—he had never known a lady to be such a good fellow—but his fear of his mama and his overriding interest in horseflesh prevented him from developing any serious feelings for Frankie. Any contemplation of a matrimonial plunge was easily discarded. Pity, though, he thought as he left her, Miss Verdant would have been a devilishly bang-up companion to hunt with.

"Well, I vow and declare, I had no notion that the costume would suit you so extremely," Daphne exclaimed as she assisted Frankie to dress on the night of the ball. "These heavy stockings will lend you some propriety, and the blouse is less décolleté than your ball gowns. La, Frankie, dear, I do not think it immodest, after all. 'Tis really quite famous."

"Well, Daph, I think I will do," Frankie said as she tied on her mask. "I had no notion that I should grow to like the idea of disguising myself and playing at being something I'm not. It's almost as good as a full-out run on Demon."

"I wish I could hide in Lady Makepeace's gallery and watch you." Daphne giggled, then grasped her side for a moment as a sudden stitch left her short of breath.

Harry pretended that he did not recognize Frankie when he called for the ladies in his carriage. "Laurel, my love, you did not tell me we would be accompanied by *two* ladies. Who is this apparition? And where is your aunt?"

Frankie grinned behind her mask at his jest. Harry was a knowing gent. In her opinion, he would make an excellent spouse for her sometimes headstrong niece.

Markham gave a low whistle of true appreciation. He had never noticed that Miss Verdant was such a dasher before. Although her face was hidden, the costume revealed the lady's figure in all its glory: creamy shoulders, well-curved bust, narrow waist and hips, and long, slender legs. Tol was in for a shock. He grinned, for he knew his friend had been strangely affected by Laurel's aunt. Harry promised himself that he would keep an eye out for any meeting between the two at the masquerade in expectation of being able to twit his friend about it later.

Laurel, somewhat sheepishly, had decided to go as a rural country lass with Harry as her rustic swain. She was dressed as a rather lavish shepherdess in layers and layers of tulle, and Harry was heard to complain that he couldn't get near her for the width of her skirt. Indeed her betrothed teasingly addressed her as "Miss Bo Peep."

"You are the 'Beau,' sir," Laurel retorted.

"Mind if I have a peep, then?" Harry requested, waggling his eyebrows up and down suggestively. Laurel slapped him on the arm with her ivory-stick fan before turning her shoulder and marching to the door.


Harry and the ladies arrived at the Makepeace home to find the place lit up like Vauxhall Gardens. There were a goodly quantity of flambeaux lining the drive and scattered about the grounds around the house. "Enough to burn down Whitehall," Harry remarked to Laurel as they alit from the carriage.

Many couples were already strolling about outside on this rather muggy night. Several days of rainy weather had thoroughly soaked the ground, and the air was heavy with the unseasonably warm temperatures. The sounds of stringed instruments and a pianoforte came through the two-tiered ballroom windows as the musicians tuned up between sets. Merry laughter in several registers—high-pitched, deep, trilling—resonated all around them. Masquerades were notoriously boisterous as the ladies as well as the gentlemen enjoyed a certain lack of restraint and gave vent to their high spirits in rather rowdy ways.

Numerous candles lit up the ballroom, their light reflected ten-fold in crystal chandeliers and large, gold-framed mirrors. There were banks of flowers and swirls of color everywhere. Standing on the minstrel's gallery above the ballroom with her niece and Markham, Frankie looked down at the tumultuous scene below her. Why, it was as exciting as a horse auction, almost, she thought on a grin.

Everyone was masked; many wore wigs and dominoes. There was a heavy scent of perfume in the air as Frankie descended the stairs to the dancing floor below. The occasion seemed to have called forth excess from both sexes, in the matter of fragrance as in all other matters pertinent to a masquerade—costume, paint, elaborate coiffures. She noted a general flamboyance in dress, gesture, and action everywhere she looked.

Markham had a lady on each arm as he made his way to the ballroom floor. Monty Addlecumber, dressed as Falstaff, with an enormous ruff round his neck and his waistcoat stuffed with what appeared to be a whole set of bed linen, waddled up to the group. He recognized Markham, whose disguise was transparent even to the slow-witted knight, and requested the pleasure of a dance with one of Harry's companions.

"Must say, Harry, unfair. You have two chicks—one on each wing—and I have none. Much obliged to reprieve you of one of 'em, don't y'know . . . Leastways till Sally arrives with 'er mama," the affianced gentleman added conscientiously.

"I don't know how you'll manage to dance with that

300

hideous belly protruding two feet in front of you, Sir John," Harry twitted him.

"Eh, it's me—Monty—don't y'know," Addlecumber whispered in an audible aside to Harry. "Ain't acquitted with any 'Sir John.'"

"And I don't suppose you're dressed up as Sir John Falstaff, either?" Harry replied in a patient tone.

"Heh? Oh, the cove was Sir *John Falstaff,* was he? . . . Thought his handle was Wagstaff—leastways that's what Tol told me. Must've been funnin' again. Y'know Tol, always funnin' one."

"Tell you what, Monty, he was having a game with you. Always so witty, that cousin of yours."

"Not witty lately. Been mopin'. On account of some female—or was it an angel? Been havin' visions, Tol has, and dippin' too deep in the brandy bottle. Always goin' on about 'er. Who is she? You know?"

Harry was stumped. He couldn't tell who Monty meant. It might have been anyone—or no one.

Frankie was not in such a quandary. Drew had mentioned her to his cousin, then. But in what way? He may have been bemoaning his unfortunate acquaintance with her. No, Frankie could not believe that. He only called her "Angel" when he was feeling that undeniable tug of attraction between them.

Markham relinquished Frankie's hand to Monty who promptly led her to the floor for a country dance. Lord Harry watched the comical Addlecumber leaping about, his overstuffed midriff threatening to spill its contents at any moment, until the pressure of Laurel's hand on his arm reminded him that his lady love demanded his undivided attention.

# *Chapter Nineteen*

Leaning his folded arms on the balustrade railing, Tolland stood on the gallery, staring at the dancers below much as Frankie had done half an hour earlier. He was dressed rather casually as a Gypsy with a sheathed dagger stuffed down the side of one shiny boot. He scanned the room until he spotted the lady he had come to see. She was going through some awkward gyrations with his cousin Monty. Well, Francesca was dancing quite gracefully at least, but his bacon-brained relative seemed to be hopping about holding onto his monstrous stomach.

He had been waiting for this night since he had learned from Monty that Frankie was not to marry Freddy Drake after all. That nugget of information had penetrated his soggy brain and given him cause for hope. Tonight he would do everything in his power to claim Francesca for his own and not tamely take no for an answer as he had done before.

Tolland gazed at her again, letting his eyes take in all the delights of her costume. Stirred by the long, shapely legs outlined through the thin gauze of her trousers when she moved so that the light shone behind her, he straightened abruptly as her blouse seemed to slip fur-

ther off her shoulders. That costume was altogether too
revealing! He saw that the dance had ended, and although
Monty stood beside her trying to rearrange his padding,
Lord Roger Reynard, in seventeenth-century cavalier
fashion, had approached Francesca and was raising her
hand to his lips. That ugly customer could only mean
mischief. Tolland rushed down the stairs, rudely pushing
aside those in his path.

A tall Gypsy materialized suddenly at Frankie's side. "I
believe this is my dance, *mademoiselle*," he said with a
rough French accent, smoothly taking her hand and
laying it on his arm while glaring belligerently at
Reynard. Lord Roger recognized Sterling immediately
and unconsciously fingered his chin, remembering the
punch that had landed there at the Sefton ball. He
stepped back, bowed, and turned away.

Frankie knew Sterling instantly and answered in an
assumed accent of her own. "Ah, you are so chivalrous,
*monsieur*."

"Is *mademoiselle* thirsty?" Tolland inquired, his eyes
glittering behind his concealing black half-mask.

"*Oui, monsieur*."

Tolland took two fluted glasses of champagne from a
tray carried by a passing servant and presented one to
Frankie. He lifted his glass in a toast to her. "To your
beautiful eyes, *mademoiselle*. I drown in them," he
murmured as he drank deeply.

"*Vous êtes galant, monsieur*," she replied. The game
was heady, and Frankie reveled in the excitement as she
gazed at the masked Gypsy before her. A red kerchief was
knotted negligently round his neck, and he had
mysteriously fastened a gold earring to one ear. His tight
black trousers did nothing to disguise his muscular
thighs, while his open-necked shirt stretched over

impossibly wide shoulders and left the dark hair on his chest just visible below the kerchief. Frankie could hardly restrain her desire to reach out and touch him there.

The handsome Gypsy was himself finding it almost impossible not to lean forward and claim a quick kiss from the wide, smiling lips of his Turkish dancing lady.

So absorbed in gazing at one another were they, they did not hear the strains of a waltz being played by the orchestra. As they became aware of the music, Tolland put their empty glasses aside, extended his hand. "Shall we dance, *mon ange?*"

Frankie was conscious of his warm hand tightening on her waist as she came into his outstretched arms. She had no thought of resisting him this time. He drew her very close, so close she became aware of the heat of his body and a faint but pleasant scent emanating from his bare chest—it held not a hint of starch, she noted giddily. The toplofty Tolland Hansohm had completely vanished sometime ago, she realized dimly, and here now was only her own dear Drew.

As they twirled through the dance, his muscular thighs occasionally touched hers as he spun her around the floor. His long fingers felt surprisingly slender in hers as he clasped her ungloved right hand in a strong, warm grip.

Frankie sensed a vulnerability in this tall, athletic man. Consciously she cherished this reminder of his human fragility even as her body was responding to the hard contours of his masculine physique.

"So Francesca, you've decided to play the roguish lady tonight, have you? Well," he whispered against her ear, "I like it. You can be as devilish as you wish, *mon ange*— as long as it's only with *me* you act so, my dear *managing* Miss Verdant."

"Me, I do not understand you, *monsieur.*" Frankie

305

laughed, trying to gauge his mood and hoping they weren't in for another argument. "Who is this 'managing' Miss Verdant?"

"Oh, I believe you know well enough of whom I speak. It is no good trying to disguise yourself behind a pair of unattractive spectacles and gowns that conceal your figure. The *real* Francesca will out."

Frankie did not answer, and after dancing for several minutes without further speech between them, Tolland spoke. "I would like to speak with you privately, if you will permit."

"If you wish. I have no objection."

"Shall we take a turn in the garden, then?" he asked as he steered her through the open doors of the wide veranda. In a moment they were outdoors. The garden was festooned with colorful Chinese lanterns hung here and there amongst the shrubbery. Several masked couples drifted by as Tolland led Frankie down the steps.

They could hear the music coming from the house and the setting, together with their masked state, added to the unreality of the occasion. Tolland continued to twirl her in the steps of the waltz when they reached the path. He gazed intently into her eyes the while. It seemed to Frankie that almost every part of her body was pressed to his, and she could not quite steady her breath. She could not tell if it was her heart that was beating so erratically, or his. Was it her breathing that sounded so unsteady in her ears, or his? Were those her hands that were trembling, or his?

She longed for him to kiss her as he had on several other occasions, and when he led her down the pathway and deeper into the garden, passing many other couples—talking, laughing, or sometimes embracing—she went eagerly.

Tolland found an unoccupied bench and seated her on it, keeping his hold of her hand as he did so. He had gone weak at the knees with love for this woman. His hand went out to caress her face. Her cheek was soft, so soft to his gentle touch. Frankie was by now quite pleasantly giddy from the champagne, the unfamiliar clothes, and from seeing Drew look at her with such tenderness in his eyes.

"What was it you wanted to speak to me about, Drew?" she breathed huskily.

"Tell me, *mon ange*, is this the *real* Francesca I behold tonight?" he questioned in a low voice, stroking her soft cheek again with a gentle thumb. She could feel the slightly roughened skin of his palm as he stroked along the edge of her jaw.

"As 'real' as I can be, disguised as something I am decidedly not." Frankie laughed in her musical voice, then turned her head into his caressing hand. She was fascinated by the whirl of dark hair she could see on the inside of his wrist where the cuff of his shirt fell away. She knew an overpowering desire to press her lips to that spot. She bent forward and kissed the downy skin there.

Tolland groaned softly and lifted Frankie's face to his. He tugged off her mask impatiently. "Will you kiss me on the lips as well?" he whispered hoarsely, but when she didn't respond immediately he said roughly, "If you will not kiss me, then I shall kiss you. I don't believe I can resist, you know." And he bent his head and softly kissed her lips, pulling away his own mask as he did so.

Frankie's arms came up immediately to grasp him around the neck, and Tolland's tender kiss gave way under the turmoil of his emotions. He opened his mouth over hers and began kissing her with passionate intensity. Frankie matched his passion with an ardent urgency of her own. His hands were moving over her body now. He pushed the thin blouse down over her shoulders and caressed her, tasting her skin with soft

307

kisses and murmuring endearments against her face, her neck, her breasts.

Her hands were wound tightly in Tolland's hair. She kissed the hollow at the base of his neck and ran her hands over the hard muscles of his chest before his mouth claimed hers again in a hard, possessive kiss. She could taste the champagne they had drunk earlier in his mouth and on his tongue. The excitement was becoming almost unbearable.

He shifted to bring her body into even closer contact with his own . . . and miscalculated the distance to the edge of the bench. They both tumbled to the ground, where they fell under an exceedingly damp bush, his muscular legs entangling with her slender ones. After an "Ummph," from Frankie as she hit the ground, Tolland leaned up on one elbow to inquire anxiously, "Francesca, are you hurt?"

"No, Drew. What about you?" Frankie asked, then began to laugh; it was inevitable that yet another "accident" befall them.

"We're doomed, Drew!" she declared as mirth overtook her again. And Tolland, seeing the humor in the situation at last, gave a great shout of laughter. Soon they collapsed in one another's arms along the length of the ground, laughing as if they would never stop. Tolland was effectively pinning Frankie to the earth as he had fallen virtually on top of her. The slight movement of their bodies against one another as they laughed soon provoked sensations both pleasurable and exciting, but even more dangerous than their earlier movements on the bench when they had both had two feet on the ground. Frankie could feel the excitement swell through Tolland's body. She lifted her lips away from his and spoke reluctantly.

"Drew? Drew, the ground is really very wet. I believe my back is soaked through," she told him. There was a part of her that didn't want to move, but she knew she must.

Tolland looked regretful but, realizing that he was drenched as well, kissed her on the nose and said, "Let me get you inside where you can recover your dignity and get dry and warm again, my love." He pulled her blouse up to respectably cover her shoulders once again and wished desperately for his long cloak to conceal and warm her.

As they began to get up, they heard a familiar voice addressing them.

"Oh goodness, gracious me! What are you doing down there, my dear Lord Sterling?" Lady Clara Chatterington inquired worriedly, as she peered down at them. Who was the bedraggled lady with the viscount? she wondered. Oh heavens above—it couldn't be—but, oh dear yes, it must be—dear Lady Whittgrove's sister! "And my dear Miss Verdant! You must be wet through!"

"I say, old man, what happened here? Lots of wet grass about. Did you try to take advantage of the lady, or did she slip?" Harry arrived on the scene with Laurel on his arm as Tolland pulled Frankie to her feet.

"Oh, Aunt, what happened? Are you hurt?" Laurel asked. "Oh, come away, Aunt Frankie, do."

But Frankie had no intention of being bundled away and took no notice of the crowd of persons who had suddenly descended on them. She was smiling widely. Drew's "my love" had sent delicious sensations surging through her veins.

Tolland and Frankie continued to smile softly at one another. They may as well have been the only two persons present for all the notice they took of the others milling about them.

"Listen, Aunt Frankie, do." Laurel shook Frankie's arm to get her attention and whispered, "Mama has sent a footman to fetch us home. Her baby is on the way and she wants you. We must leave now."

Tolland overheard Laurel's communication. "I shall escort your aunt to the coach, Miss Whittgrove," he said promptly. "If Harry will take you on ahead to summon your coachman, we shall follow."

Harry grinned at his friend and gallantly offered his free arm to Lady Chatterington. The poor woman had been so shocked by the proceedings that she was bereft of speech for once in her life.

The party of three moved off, and Tolland turned to Frankie again.

"Don't want to put a damper on the evenin', but you're wet as a goose, coz." Monty appeared in their path with Sally Chatterington on his arm. Sally laughed merrily at his comment.

"Why don't you take yourself off, Monty?" Tolland recommended, as he retied Frankie's mask for her.

"That curst insect landed you in the basket again, coz?" questioned the ever-solicitous Monty. "Could've been one of those Greek coves . . . always manglin' their shapes, don't y'know . . . Leastways you ain't undressed this time," he noticed, peering fixedly at his cousin.

The viscount pursed his lips, valiantly resisting the urge to strangle his ridiculous relative. "Miss Chatterington is cold. I suggest you sally forth and find her some warmth, coz."

But Monty was right, Tolland thought. Fate had landed square on his broad shoulders this time. And, if he were in the basket for sure, he could think of only one cozier place he'd rather be, provided his partner in the enterprise was the same lady who stood beside him now.

"Those two seem to have paired off to their mutual satisfaction," Tolland remarked to Frankie as Monty followed his suggestion and proceeded up the path to the house with Sally. "I'm happy to see that Monty has some sense in that yellow cockloft of his."

"Yes, Sally will appreciate his, ah, humor."

"Undoubtedly . . . and his absolute devotion. Let us hope that all his 'sallies' will be directed toward her in future. It's a relief that he has abandoned 'Fox' hunting, too."

"Yes. He did make a habit of coming a cropper, did he not?"

"Fell at the fence every time," Tolland added, and they both laughed.

"You must get home and change into dry clothes now," Tolland said as he turned to Frankie and offered his arm. "But I shall call on you tomorrow, shall I, my love?" He reached with his free hand to warmly squeeze hers where it rested on his sleeve.

"Yes, Drew, I will certainly be happy to entertain you tomorrow." Frankie's lips curved up in a smile—too delicious for Tolland to resist. He bent forward and kissed her quite hard on the mouth but with his own lips firmly closed.

"Francesca . . . ." he began, but they were interrupted by other couples coming out to recover from their efforts on the dance floor and catch their breaths, or to engage in even more strenuous exertions among the ornamental hedge rows that would effectively exhaust their revitalized air passages. Tolland moved away from Frankie, but kept his hold of her hand, playing gently with her fingers.

"Until tomorrow—at eleven, then." He was reluctant to let her go. Should he not just blurt out his proposal now? But no, the coach awaited her. She should go to her sister.


Frankie got no sleep that night. She had been with Daphne until her third son made his extremely boisterous entrance into the world at four in the morning. Excitement and anticipation made sleep quite

311

impossible after that. She began to count the hours until she could expect to see Drew again. She knew he was coming to ask her to marry him, and there could be no doubt of her acceptance this time.

Frankie had learned a lot about herself since she had first met him. Her reactions to the viscount had been extreme from the first. Inexperienced as she was in romantic dealings, it had taken her some time before she realized that he affected her so strongly because she was so attracted to him. She had foolishly tried to deny that attraction—as had he, she realized, reflecting back over their several arguments . . . and several heated embraces. She had fallen ever more deeply in love, though, despite their misunderstandings, and now she hoped they would reach a mutually satisfying agreement about their future.

She could not keep still as she waited for Drew. She put her spectacles on, then removed them again. She walked upstairs, and she walked downstairs, going in to check on a sleeping Daphne and baby Charles several times in her perambulations.

Tolland was in even worse case as he had had no distracting event to occupy his thoughts. He had paced about all night, running his fingers through his hair and practicing his proposal. The temptation to seek solace from the brandy bottle in his study had been successfully resisted. He wanted no alcoholic fumes marring his meeting with Francesca on the morrow. Why he had not just asked her if she would marry him there in the garden and saved himself all this agonizing, he didn't know. Events had overtaken them before he got round to it, he supposed, for it had certainly been his intention to have her promise to wed him with all possible haste before he let her go last night. Now he would have to go to

Whittgrove House and formally propose marriage to her for the second time.

But this time he would gather his courage and tell her his feelings and not pretend that he was offering her his hand only to avoid a scandal or out of pity, as though he were doing her some great favor. What a coward he had been! He who prided himself on his fearlessness in sporting activities, his social polish, his famous address, had been afraid to admit the truth to himself—and to her. No more timorous shirking. He would confess his love and desire for her—even get down on his knees and beg her to marry him, if necessary.

He thought of taking her flowers again . . . but, no, that gesture would be a reminder of his badly mangled first proposal, as badly mangled as the flowers had been, he remembered, abashed. There would be no hint of that infelicitous morning!

And then he knew—this time it must be Rundell and Bridge's for a ring. He would have her promise and his ring would be on her finger before the day was out. There was no way he would let her refuse him now!

When eleven o'clock came and went, Frankie could bear the suspense no longer. She rushed upstairs and threw on her habit, then stomped out to the stables and had her mount saddled. She went tearing out of the mews at the rear of the house on Demon's back and nearly ran down an elegantly dressed gentleman as he crossed the street to the Whittgrove house. Demon actually reared up a bit as she pulled tightly on the reins to halt her horse before he reached the man whom she was finally near enough to see clearly. It was Drew! He had come!

Tolland looked a bit nonplused to see his Francesca departing on horseback as he quickly scrambled out of

313

her way. He had intended to humbly beg pardon for the lateness of his arrival. The jewelers had not had a ring made up that would meet his specifications, and he had insisted that a particular diamond be mounted in a particular setting before he left the shop. He had had to wait half an hour longer than he had anticipated and here he was, late.

However, he had certainly not expected to see Francesca mounted on her horse and charging out of the stables as though determined to get away from him as fast as possible. But he quickly realized that it was too much to expect his spirited Francesca to wait demurely for his arrival like some timid ninnyhammer.

"May I escort you somewhere, Miss Verdant?" he inquired politely, as he lifted his hat to her.

"No . . . Yes . . ." Frankie came to an exasperated stop.

He lifted his brow in question, "Yes . . . no . . . Which is it to be?"

"Oh, I suppose I may as well postpone my ride. I thought you weren't coming," she blurted out.

"Not coming!" Tolland exclaimed as he grasped her waist to help her dismount. "Why would you think such a thing?" They gazed eagerly into one another's eyes as he lifted her down . . . then she stepped heavily on his foot.

"Ouch!" he shouted. "Francesca, this must stop! We are two well-coordinated adults. We both excel on horseback and on the dance floor. There is nothing the matter with us that would doom us to be forever behaving like clumsy idiots when we are in one another's vicinity." His eyes were teasing her. "I have an idea I want to put to you about how we can cure one another of this unaccountable behavior. Will you accompany me into the house?" he asked as he extended his arm to her.

"Well, we could agree to avoid each other completely

314

in future," she told him, as she relinquished the reins of her horse to a stable boy and took Tolland's arm. "I am going home soon to Verdant Meadows. You need never cross my path again, Sterling, after you stand up with Lord Harry at my niece's wedding ceremony."

"Yes, I hope to 'cross your path' soon at a wedding ceremony," he murmured. "And you're to call me Drew, remember?"

"So you see, Lord Sterling, if you will have a little patience, you will be free of my bumbling presence forever!" Frankie was prattling. She thought she was giving him the perfect way to end their catastrophe-strewn acquaintance.

Tolland shook his head at her saying, "Tsk, tsk. You do take delight in making ridiculous statements, do you not, Francesca?"

"Why do you persist in calling me Francesca? I've always been known as Frankie."

"But you're not a 'Frankie' to me, as I've told you before. Francesca—I like the sound of it rolling off my tongue, a lovely name for a beautiful woman. I think of you that way; not as that nonsensical masculine appellation."

Frankie turned away at this flattering speech and led Tolland to the unoccupied morning room where the sun streamed in through the bright yellow and white drapes.

She tossed her green-feathered riding hat onto a table, then took her spectacles out of the pocket of her habit and placed them on her nose with great deliberation. She addressed him gruffly, "State your business, Lord Sterling."

Tolland grinned sheepishly and rubbed his chin, finding it difficult to get to the point when an angry woman was staring at him from across the room. "*Now* what have I done to offend you, Francesca? You knew I was coming today, did you not? I am sorry that I am a little late, but I had a very important errand to run before I came here. On your behalf, too." He smiled warmly and patted the pocket where the engagement ring lay.

"Oh?" she gave him an opening, but Tolland, troubled by a sudden attack of nerves, cleared his throat uncertainly. His legs suddenly felt as if they wouldn't hold him up much longer. He indicated that she be seated on the small settee facing the long windows.

Frankie flounced to the seat and flopped down quite ungracefully. Truth to tell, she was feeling none too calm herself.

Tolland followed more slowly, lifted the tail of his morning coat, then sat down abruptly—so abruptly and so near to her that he knocked his chin on the top of her head. There was a mighty crack. "Ouch! Oh dear," Frankie exclaimed, while Tolland cursed under his breath as he wiped blood from his mouth where his teeth had cut his lip.

"I am sorry, Angel."

"Humph!"

He took Frankie by the shoulders and said urgently, "I am sorry, you know. I believe we are awkward with each other because we feel unsettled in one another's presence . . . And why is that? I ask myself.

"Because something in me turns to jelly when I look at you, when I am with you, when I touch you. And something in you does the same when you're near me. Our bodies are responding, and as much as our minds try to deny the attraction, it is there. I think I collide with you so often because my body so much wants to be next to yours that I will do anything to accomplish that intimate physical contact. Even the most absurd and painful things," he concluded with a boyish grin. Frankie did not look at him, so didn't realize how much he was roasting her.

"What should we do about it, do you think?" he asked,

as he raised her chin gently with his fingertips and looked into her eyes, smiling lopsidedly.

"I told you, I am going away. You need never see me again."

"I don't think I would like that, Francesca. I don't think I would like that at all," he whispered, shaking his head at her as he held her gaze. "I think I would be very unhappy if you went out of my life, Francesca. Would you be unhappy if you were to never see me again?"

"Yes, I would, Drew," Frankie admitted with an open, honest look.

Tolland gently removed Frankie's spectacles. Then he leaned forward, took her face between his hands, and kissed her very gently on the lips. "You see. If we are careful, I think we can manage without hurting one another. Do you think it's worth a try, my love?"

"If you're willing to risk it, Drew," she answered, sorry that he had removed his lips from hers so soon, "and not blame me if you suffer any adverse effects from the experiment. We can always resort to my book of herbal remedies to sort us out, I suppose, if you really think we are wise to try it."

"I'm willing to take that risk, my love." He leaned forward and kissed her again, then drew back to say, "Francesca, do you think if we are *very* careful we might manage a lifetime of trying?"

"We can try, Drew," she answered, even more huskily than usual.

"You know I love you beyond rational thought—or you ought to know it, after all the absurd things I've done in your presence . . . Do you love me, too? Will you marry me, my darling girl? Please."

"Yes, Drew. I do love you." Frankie smiled her generous smile and spoke in the voice that always sent a warmth coursing through his veins. "I think I've always loved you—from the moment I saw you lying on the floor at Lady Chatterington's ball, looking so utterly discomposed with your hair falling into your eyes and flowers on your head. And I would be deliriously happy to be your wife and be with you always—if you really want me to."

"Oh, Francesca! If I really want you to? Oh, love!" Tolland could restrain himself no longer. He pulled his love into his arms and proceeded to kiss and caress her until her lips swelled and her body tingled. If they got a little carried away in their embrace, it was not to be wondered at. At least this time they had no meandering couples to interrupt them and a soft, dry floor instead of the wet ground to land on as they tumbled into love.

So Andrew Tolland Hansohm and Francesca Viola Verdant were married in her parish church three weeks later and not a moment too soon for the viscount's peace of mind. The groom, in addition to being head over ears in love with his beautiful, managing, long-legged, shortsighted bride and anxious to have her all to himself, was relieved when the wedding ceremony was completed without incident. He and the new viscountess were unscarred and unembarrassed by any disconcerting little incidents of a likeness to those that had plagued their courtship. There was not even a suggestion of a mishap. Everything had gone perfectly. Now he could relax.

Never again was Viscount Sterling clumsy or awkward in public or in private, with strangers or friends, with his growing family or his darling wife. He regained his reputation for perfectly correct behavior on all occasions, not that the *ton* saw much of Lord and Lady Sterling. They were busy in the country breeding horses—and children.

The same could not quite be said of the viscountess. At

her husband's insistence, Lady Sterling wore her spectacles at all times, except in bed, but an occasional lack of attention to her surroundings sometimes caused her to blunder into things. When she noticed, she was always most apologetic, but her loving husband just smiled indulgently and blessed his lucky stars for his nemesis.

# A Memorable Collection of Regency Romances

## BY ANTHEA MALCOLM AND VALERIE KING

**THE COUNTERFEIT HEART**                    (3425, $3.95/$4.95)
by Anthea Malcolm
Nicola Crawford was hardly surprised when her cousin's betrothed disappeared on some mysterious quest. Anyone engaged to such an unromantic, but handsome man was bound to run off sooner or later. Nicola could never entrust her heart to such a conventional, but so deucedly handsome man. . . .

**THE COURTING OF PHILIPPA**                 (2714, $3.95/$4.95)
by Anthea Malcolm
Miss Philippa was a very successful author of romantic novels. Thus she was chagrined to be snubbed by the handsome writer Henry Ashton whose own books she admired. And when she learned he considered love stories completely beneath his notice, she vowed to teach him a thing or two about the subject of love. . . .

**THE WIDOW'S GAMBIT**                        (2357, $3.50/$4.50)
by Anthea Malcolm
The eldest of the orphaned Neville sisters needed a chaperone for a London season. So the ever-resourceful Livia added several years to her age, invented a deceased husband, and became the respectable Widow Royce. She was certain she'd never regret abandoning her girlhood until she met dashing Nicholas Warwick. . . .

**A DARING WAGER**                            (2558, $3.95/$4.95)
by Valerie King
Ellie Dearborne's penchant for gaming had finally led her to ruin. It seemed like such a lark, wagering her devious cousin George that she would obtain the snuffboxes of three of society's most dashing peers in one month's time. She could easily succeed, too, were it not for that exasperating Lord Ravenworth. . . .

**THE WILLFUL WIDOW**                         (3323, $3.95/$4.95)
by Valerie King
The lovely young widow, Mrs. Henrietta Harte, was not all inclined to pursue the sort of romantic folly the persistent King Brandish had in mind. She had to concentrate on marrying off her penniless sisters and managing her spendthrift mama. Surely Mr. Brandish could fit in with her plans somehow . . .

*Available wherever paperbacks are sold, or order direct from the Publisher. Send cover price plus 50¢ per copy for mailing and handling to Zebra Books, Dept. 4140, 475 Park Avenue South, New York, N.Y. 10016. Residents of New York and Tennessee must include sales tax. DO NOT SEND CASH. For a free Zebra/ Pinnacle catalog please write to the above address.*